FORMATTING CONVENTIONS AND PACING:

This novel is intended to be styled like a storyteller at the bar spinning a yarn that's so good nobody is willing to challenge its veracity.

Where you see a single line of vertical space, as is above this line, imagine the narrator taking a breath to pause—or the characters pausing for a moment in brief thought before speaking again.

A larger double-line space, such as here, is akin to the raconteur pausing to replenish with half a pint and some pretzels; or, within the story, for an extended break between the characters that does not necessarily involve a change of viewpoint or scene. Now might be an ideal time to make a cup of tea, if you're so inclined, or otherwise attend to life.

———————

Finally, a double horizontal bar like this one denotes a scene or perspective break within a chapter: the scene or the viewpoint has changed, but no lengthy narrative pause is *necessarily* implied (although there *usually* is one).

Of course, we at Fenian House strongly advise you to read how you want, on your own schedule. The above is our guide to how to read our intended pacing of the text; but our suggestions are just, only, that. You paid good money for this book; we are your humble bards.

THE STARDOCK TRILOGY
BOOK ONE

Sean Fenian

Fenian House Publishing

Bearing Gifts — United Fleet — A Line In The Stars

Copyright Declaration:

Disclaimer:

All of the characters in this story are fictional. Some organizations and official positions mentioned are (obviously) real, but have no *actual* connection to any persons or events described in this story. Any direct coincidence of name with any actual living person is just that: A coincidence. There are only *just so many* possible unique names.

Any mention in this book of any present-day established trademark is not a challenge to that trademark.

References? *Of course* there are references.

Publication History:

First Electronic Edition February 2024

Second Electronic Edition April 2024

First Print Edition February 2025

Third Electronic Edition March 2026

Second Print Edition March 2026

Print ISBN 979-8-9926260-0-1

Bearing Gifts

ACKNOWLEDGMENTS

THANKS GO OUT TO:

Fellow author **John Shirley** for hints and early critique on Bearing Gifts, as well as for his kind words of praise on it that helped encourage me to complete it;

Fellow author **Mackey Chandler** and my growing team of beta readers, **Ralock Kaltan**, **Douglas King**, **Sam Latham**, **Jeff Geauvreau** and others, for proofreading and being sounding-boards;

Alicia Aldridge, **Cassie Hanjian**, and all of the rest of the crew at **Podium Entertainment**, plus of course narrator **Michael Karl Orenstein**, for all of the hard work that they have put into the audiobook editions of the Stardock Trilogy;

The **Bitminers** and **Callahanians** for ship name suggestions, entries in the Ginza naming poll, and other assistance;

And to my family, for putting up with the time that I have put into writing this series over the past nearly a year and a half (and my occasional crankiness during the process, especially when particular passages weren't going well).

Dramatis Personae

The Humans:

Alex Holder

John Riken, President of the United States

Judy Riken, the First Lady, recently deceased

Miranda Ramirez, Vice-President of the United States

Dr. Edward Wegener, National Science Advisor

Dr. Jocelyn Winters, Secretary of State

Rear-Admiral David Hackett, Director of National Intelligence

William McMasters, Director of the CIA

Roberta Wilson, a Deputy Director at the CIA

Stephanie Rogers, United States Ambassador to the United Nations

Tom Watts and Kerri Taylor, Presidential aides

Agents Connors, Jamison, and Wright, United States Secret Service

Naomi Tomlinson, a State Department attorney

Susan Wilder, Naomi Tomlinson's superior at the State Department

Peter Westland, a technician at the Goldstone, California facility of the Deep Space Network

Victoria I Ingrid, Queen Regnant of Sweden

Franz Schneider, Chancellor of the Federal Republic of Germany

Brian Watson, Prime Minister of Australia

Ayhan Göğebakan, President of the Republic of Türkiye

Ramanujan Venkataswathy, Prime Minister of India

Mme. Emmanuelle Galois, President of France

Li Xeung, General Secretary of the Chinese Communist Party

Kwaku Owusu, President of the General Assembly of the United Nations

Abdulsalem Özdilek, Turkish Ambassador to the United Nations

Chao Shi Lin, Chinese Ambassador to the United Nations

Chunmei Shen, Taiwanese Ambassador to the United Nations

Seok Dong-geun, (former) North Korean Ambassador to the United Nations

Seok Hae, Dong-geun's wife

Seok Yeon and Seok Jia, Dong-geun's daughters

Seok Choon-mae, Dong-geun's younger son

Colonel John 'Stick' Buford, O/C 151st Fighter Squadron, USAF

Maj. John C. 'Drum' Hatcher, 151st Fighter Squadron, USAF

Capt. Mike 'Micro' Sweeders,151st Fighter Squadron, USAF

Lt. Dave 'Squeezebox' Matthews, 151st Fighter Squadron, USAF

Karabo Jackson, intellectual-property lawyer, Electronic Frontier Foundation

THE CHHRT'KTK'T *(placeholders for actual names neither pronounceable nor comprehensible by humans):*

Fleet-Overseer Kharintra, Admiral of the Chhrt'ktk't fleet

Captain-Superior Mireng, commander of the Chhrt'ktk't flagship

Captain-Senior T'chee, commander of the explorer-ship [untranslatable name]

Captain-Senior Shenka, commander of the mobile maintenance facility

Navigator-First Khint, senior navigator of the mobile maintenance facility

Engineer-First Hree, senior engineer of the mobile maintenance facility

Rapport-Controller Xin, lead operator of the mobile maintenance facility

Captain-Second Tyef'kik, a shuttle commander

Captain-Junior Kheftra, a shuttle commander

Engineer-Second Hvecla, a engineering officer

Mediator-Third Cheeun, a liaison officer

Navigator-Third Zhin, a junior navigator

Pilot-Second Fyin, a small-craft pilot

Pilot-Second Seek't, a shuttle pilot

BEARING GIFTS

Prologue

The flaring blue alarm bar on the hyperdrive console of the Chhrt'ktk't mobile starship maintenance facility was pulsing faster.

"No more than seventeen *bak'h* remain until complete hyperdrive failure," Navigator-First Khint said anxiously.

"And there is **no** chance of a fast field repair?" asked Captain-Senior Shenka, not for the first time, desperately hoping for a different answer.

"None whatsoever," replied Engineer-First Hree, again. "A complete new primary motivator will have to be fabricated from scratch and installed, and then the entire drive will need to be re-aligned and re-synchronized. It will require completely stripping out the spine of the facility and rebuilding it. On a drive this large, the full process will take several *modak'h*. The Khreetan first-runners will undoubtedly be almost upon we-us by that time."

Captain-Senior Shenka thought furiously, trapped in internal conflict between parallel mind-states.

-safety lies with fleet- -remain with fleet- -MAINTAIN SPEED-	-speed too high, too long- -hyperdrive overloaded- -CORE FAILURE IRREVERSIBLE-	-maintain formation- -hyperdrive failing- -UNABLE TO CONTINUE-	-maintain formation- -CANNOT maintain formation- —ABANDON—

As ye stared more *through* than *at* the navigation map projected to the bridge tactical globe, something caught yth eye. Ye hesitated, then looked at it more closely. A stellar system not far ahead, only a few *pîn* off the present course, was marked in the scan as radiating signals consistent with a fairly advanced pre-spacefaring technological civilization.

"Sixteen *bak'h*," said Navigator-First Khint.

The Captain-Senior indicated the marked system.

"Can we-us make it to *there*?" ye asked.

"We... *think* so," replied the Navigator-First, yth response also slowed by internal conflict.

Resolve crystallized in the Captain-Senior's minds. Consensus at last.

"Go there," Shenka ordered. "Get as deep into the system as yhe can before the field collapses." Then ye turned to the still-open channel to the flagship.

"Captain-Superior Mireng," ye said. "Please inform Fleet-Overseer Kharintra, with all respect, that we-us have no choice but to abandon the maintenance facility in the system ahead. It can serve there as a decoy. Our crew will require evacuation. If fortune grants it, the maintenance facility will distract the Khreetan until our trail has faded beyond following. Perhaps we-us may yet escape them with our lives."

Shenka turned to another officer.

"Rapport-Controller Xin," ye said. "Before we-us abandon the facility, yhe will remove the access restrictions from the control-intellect. It will make a better decoy if they are able to actually operate it. We-us can spare a short time to seek a Rapport-Controller among them. But only a short time."

"Sir," asked the Rapport-Controller nervously, "yhe are not worried about the sapients using it to our detriment?"

"What cause can there be for concern?" Captain-Senior Shenka replied. "In the first *j'h*, it will take them many *kabak'h* to learn how to properly use the facility. In the second, the control-intellect will not allow any direct action against we-us. In the third, we-us will be long gone before they can construct any vessel that could be a threat to the Fleet.

"And in the fourth, they are a pre-spacefaring race. We-us have been spacefaring for thousands of *modak'h*. How could they possibly be any real danger to we-us even if they wished to?

"We are hoping only that they will prove a *sufficient* distraction to the Khreetan."

1: Incoming Traffic

It wasn't the single huge object that suddenly appeared just outside the orbit of Mars that panicked every military high command on the planet as fast as they became aware of it. One single object, even such a large one, wasn't noticed *immediately* (although the astronomers at CalTech wondered at first whether their instrument was broken, on the first massive LIGO signal detection). It was the small **fleet** that dropped in around it a few minutes later—more than twenty ships, each one dwarfing the tallest buildings on Earth, each one creating a radiating rainbow flash as it dropped in.

The very first thing that actually happened was that LIGO—the Laser Interferometer Gravitational Observatory—seemingly went berserk. It turns out that when you suddenly and massively strain space-time by wrenching a temporary hole open to hyperspace, it radiates gravity waves, much as a catastrophic event like a collision of two neutron stars does. That's the kind of event LIGO was built to detect: Cataclysmic events millions or even billions of light-years away.

These events were nowhere near as *intense* as that, of course. But they were also a whole lot closer, and there were a lot of them in a very short time, and the signal was as clear as a bell—and it was quickly determined that they were *within the solar system*. It was immediately clear that the signals were some new phenomenon, because the signal profiles did not match the characteristic 'chirp' of the signals LIGO saw when massive objects merged. They had a completely different waveform, less a multi-frequency chirp than an echoing double crash.

Needless to say, the astronomers who first saw the data immediately announced the new detections, freely admitting that they had no idea what the new signal was. It was less than an hour before the LIGO observations were correlated with the bizarre "space rainbows" captured by an amateur astronomer in Scotland who just happened to have an eight-inch reflecting telescope pointed in the right direction at the right time. By that time, thousands of people were pointing telescopes in that direction, and reporting on the new objects that most of them could see.

Fortunately, nobody had time to do anything panicked and foolish before every major communication system on that side of the Earth began picking up the signals the new arrivals began broadcasting. It was unclear what the signals were meant to *be*, but they were clearly an attempt at communication by someone who didn't fully understand how standard broadcast communication protocols worked. Several billion people were watching their TVs by the time the first coherent message finally appeared.

It was a simple animated line drawing.

The animation opened with a rough schematic of the solar system showing all of the major planets.

The view zoomed in on the third planet. The simple circle was replaced with a real-time image of the Earth as seen from space.

The view zoomed out again, then zoomed in on the fourth planet, now replaced by an image of Mars. Then it zoomed out again to show both Earth and Mars at far corners of the view.

A large green object appeared at about the distance of Mars, along with a number of smaller objects the same color. One of the smaller objects headed for Earth, while the rest appeared to dock with the large one. They remained briefly docked, while the green color left the large object, leaving it as a hollow outline. Then they undocked, then disappeared entirely.

The large object began to crawl towards Earth, where the remaining small object had now entered orbit. Eventually, the large object, too, entered Earth orbit.

As it did, the view zoomed in again. Now it could be seen that even smaller objects were traveling between the small object and the Earth's surface.

The view zoomed in on one of these smaller objects, on the ground, visible at this level as being a small ship or shuttle of some kind drawn in outline. A blue outline of a human boarded the shuttle, visible against the green. The shuttle, with its blue-outline passenger, took off and rose back to orbit, where it docked with the large object, which at this scale looked like a cylinder surrounded by some kind of scaffolding or framework.

The human outline moved from the shuttle to the large structure. The structure changed from an empty outline, to blue.

Then the shuttle flew back to the remaining green ship, and docked with it.

The last green ship flew away from Earth, then vanished.

The large scaffolded structure, now blue, remained behind.

President John Riken was in the situation room, along with all of the most relevant members of his cabinet plus the Chairman of the Joint Chiefs, watching a replay of the looping animated message on one of the several hundred-inch TV displays on the wall. Another was displaying a live track of the positions of the alien ships. Only one seat at the table was occupied; everyone else was on their feet.

John Riken always came across as burly and energetic, but now he was pacing up and down the room like a caged tiger. A man from a middle-class background, he had been elected on a platform of fixing all of the country's broken and neglected infrastructure and social services, and he fully expected it to take his entire term and then some to make a real dent in the problem. And now *this* happened, and the wheels looked about to come off the bus of his term plan.

"So what does it *mean*?" he demanded. "I need answers. Christ. First fucking contact. On *my* watch. We need to know what to do. How to respond to this. What are they trying to *say* to us?"

He looked at the Secretary of Defense, the Director of National Intelligence, the Chairman of the Joint Chiefs, the Secretary of State. But it was actually Edward Wegener, the National Science Advisor, who spoke up first. Wegener was tall, on the thin side, slightly stooped, a little rumpled, the picture of the academic except for a disordered shock of thinning red hair.

"Mr. President?" he said, hesitantly.

"You have an idea for me, Ed?" Riken said.

"Mr. President, this is going to sound crazy, but... hear me out." The President nodded.

"Okay," he said, "right now I'll take anything. Let's hear it."

"First—I mean," Wegener stumbled, "uh, to set the ground, it's obvious they're highly advanced, right? They **obviously** have FTL—uh, faster-than-light—travel, and it only took them a couple of hours to figure out our communications protocols enough to send us this message.

"But there's no current indication of any hostile action on their part, and this doesn't seem to be any kind of a demand or threat. It seems to be constructed to convey a message with the least possible chance of misinterpretation. Just simple pictures with minimal detail. That suggests they wanted to get out whatever useful message they could, as early as possible. Perhaps for reassurance of their intentions?

"And the animation itself matches what they're already doing, as far as we can see so far. All but one of their ships have docked with that... whatever it is, that large structure, and the remaining ship is on its way

5

here. They're showing us themselves doing what we can already see they *are* doing... and, I think, by extension, what they *intend* to do.

"So if we look at the *rest* of the message, the things that *haven't* happened yet... I think green represents them, and blue represents... us. Perhaps because Earth is blue, from space."

He paused, and took a deep breath, absently running the fingers of his left hand through his already-chaotic hair.

"Mr. President. Whatever that large structure is... I think they're trying to tell us three things. That they're evacuating their crew from it; they're bringing it *here*; and they want to **give it to us**."

Pandemonium exploded as everyone tried to talk at once. But in the end, nobody else could come up with a *better* explanation. It left so many questions, though. And most of the questions started with one word: "Why?"

===============

It took the incoming ship only four hours to reach Earth. It entered a polar orbit that took it alternately roughly down the center of the Atlantic and up the Pacific coast of Asia. It didn't land, and didn't launch any shuttles... yet. It continued to broadcast the looping message, as the large structure that people were already beginning to call the Scaffold crawled slowly towards Earth. About twenty hours after the sudden arrival of the fleet, only the Scaffold and the one alien ship remained in the solar system.

Meanwhile on Earth, the diplomatic hot-lines were working overtime. By the time all of the other alien ships had left, the General Assembly of the United Nations was in continuous session, the Association of Southeast Asian Nations and the Organization of African States had each called emergency sessions, and several other competing global summits were being convened. Chaos reigned in general. The American interpretation of The Message, as it was now being called, having been generally accepted as *probably* correct, most of these sessions were occupying themselves with the crucial question of who best deserved the Scaffold (whatever it might turn out to be), and who should therefore have control and oversight over it.

It was a foregone conclusion, of course, that **everyone** believed themselves to be the naturally deserving recipient of the Scaffold, because they were the richest, the poorest, the most populous, the most neutral, the most enlightened, the most advanced, the strongest, the most peaceful, had the longest history of civilization, contributed the most to the world's economy, were owed the most by the industrialized nations, and so on and so forth.

Nobody seemed to be considering the even more important question of whether the decision would even be theirs to make.

While Earth's governments and NGOs bickered, the Chhrt'ktk't—and the artificial intellects that handled the fine details of operating their ships—listened. The AIs separated all that they heard into languages, and parsed out the languages, and began to learn them.

On the third day in orbit, the ship sent out another message, this one spoken aloud by a mellifluous, neutral voice that sounded almost human, except for a certain flatness of intonation and a slightly-too-regular cadence.

"Greetings! Ahoj! Aloha! Bom dia! Bonjour! Bună! Ciao! Geia sas! Günaydın, בוקר טוב , صباح الخير! Håfa Adai! Hei! Hola! Halō! Kamusta! Kia Orana! Kon'nichiwa! Mabuhay! Moi! Namaste! Ni Hao! Neih hou! Pagi! Привет! Saluton! Sawasdee! Shwmae! Γειά σας! Talofa! Terve!

"We call ourselves Chhrt'ktk't. We come here in peace. We are on a long journey.

"The mechanism that moves our starship maintenance facility between the stars has broken down. We lack the time to repair it. We are reluctantly forced to abandon it.

"We wish to gift it to you. We will meet with you. We will identify a Rapport-Controller from among you."

Shortly after the new message was broadcast, the orbiting ship began spitting out smaller ships, about a hundred meters long. They headed for major cities scattered across the globe according to no particularly evident pattern—Toronto, Atlanta, Los Angeles, Paris, Hamburg, Kyiv, Cairo, Ulanbaatar, Beijing, New Delhi, Tokyo, Sydney, Rio de Janeiro, and more. They set down in vacant spots, typically in the middle of airports, sometimes in parks. Sydney's ship landed within sight of the Opera House.

And then, for a while, they just sat there. The clouds of baseball-sized drones that they spat out as they descended didn't show up on radar. They had the radar cross-section of a house-fly.

Nobody knows for sure who spotted the first "soap bubble", as they came to be called. But they first drew *recorded* public attention in Paris, where their presence was quickly accepted as normal. They were shimmering spheres just less than three inches in diameter, floating seemingly almost weightlessly in the air, yet affected by wind only if it appeared they chose to be. Their movement created faint, nearly silent air currents. At very close distances a faint hissing sound could be heard. At night they seemed faintly phosphorescent.

In Beijing the Chinese government attempted quite determinedly to capture one for study, with which efforts the bubbles stoically refused to cooperate. When a conspiracy-theorist type in an Atlanta suburb, convinced that a bubble was spying on him, tried to shoot it down with a shotgun, his pellets harmlessly passed around it on all sides. Ironically, he was *almost* right.

It seemed the bubbles quickly learned to avoid the fearful and violent. They tended to be more often spotted around centers of higher learning, but might be encountered nearly anywhere, exploring some small town street by street, zipping across a field or even drifting around a highway interchange.

The Chhrt'ktk't first unsealed their ships—or shuttles?—five days after landing. Most of the ships had by now been enclosed by mobile crowd-control barriers guarded by local police, but in Ulanbaatar nobody had bothered. Apparently nobody in Ulanbaatar felt the need to protect either the ships or the local population from each other. So far, it appeared they were right.

All at around about the same local time, around noon give or take an hour, the ships' hatches opened. The first to unseal was the one in Sydney. Two Chhrt'ktk't in some kind of environment suits emerged, and just stood there. They were about two and a half meters tall, clearly quadrupedal, stocky-looking, with four arms to match their four legs. Their walking gait was a smooth, almost scuttling motion. Judging by the suits, they had two sets of shoulders with the rear pair set somewhat higher than the front pair. Their arms appeared to have more joints than a human arm. Their heads were invisible behind dark-smoked domed visors.

They stood immobile for a while, then began to respond to waves from the small, but rapidly growing as the news spread, crowd around the barriers. Their return waves looked strangely alien and multiple-jointed, but seemed friendly nonetheless.

They stood there for about an hour before either of them spoke, just as an official delegation was finally approaching. When they did, it was in the same slightly-too-flat, slightly-too-regular voice.

"We express thankfulness for your welcome," the voice said. It was impossible to tell which was speaking. "We can breathe your air, but we wear protective suits upon this day to give you greater time to become accustomed to our appearance. We will return upon the next day, without these suits. At that time we will answer questions."

Then they turned and went back inside, and the hatch closed. The same scene played out in turn at each other ship.

Of course, the reactions of those watching the ships varied. It was hard to say which group the police detail on the barriers in Los Angeles found more troublesome—the ones shouting "Aliens go home!", or the ones who wanted the aliens to take them aboard and "elevate" them. Only in Beijing did a delegation actually reach the Chhrt'ktk't ship before they went back inside. It didn't matter; the Chhrt'ktk't paid them no attention.

The following day, most nations in which one of the ships had landed had delegations waiting in place before noon and the onlookers pushed back to make room. Not long before noon local time in each city, the hatches opened again.

There was a brief delay, then in each city, the Chhrt'ktk't stepped out, one after the other. As promised, they were not wearing environment suits this time. They paused in front of the hatch for several minutes before moving any further, then slowly progressed part-way down the ramp.

Their movement, unencumbered by the suits, was very unlike human walking. Indeed, it was almost a scuttling movement, and very smooth. They wore uniform-like coveralls that covered them from neck to feet. They were considerably more chunky than a human. Their "arms" could now be seen to divide into clusters of eight digits about the length of a human hand, and their feet to have eight stubby "toes" arranged around what seemed to be a central pad. Their "shoulders", indeed, were uneven, one pair set behind and somewhat above the other. But it was the heads that were the most unexpected.

Their heads rose from their shoulders with no visible neck. The visible—skin?—was a dark brown mottled with a dull brownish purple. Two rows of what seemed to be eyes ran up the sides of the "face", four on each side, somewhat protected by a bony ridge. What might be nostrils

9

were arranged in a circle around the crown of the head. There were no visible ears and no immediately obvious mouth.

The Chhrt'ktk't glided slowly half-way down the ramp, and stopped. Then one of the two glided a step forward and slowly turned in a complete circle, revealing two more rows of eyes placed towards the back of the head. It was apparent that Chhrt'ktk't could see in nearly any direction. It was also apparent that this was for the benefit of the audience. "See, this is what we look like."

In Rio de Janeiro, one enterprising junior aide in the Brazilian delegation looked around him, then took three brisk steps forward toward the ramp, ignoring the more senior members telling him to get back into his place. He stopped, turned slowly around in a complete circle exactly as the Chhrt'ktk't had done—and only then returned to his place in the delegation. The disapproving voices died down as his colleagues realized what he was doing. He was actually still one step away from returning to his place when the wife of the President, who was quicker on the uptake than her husband, took three steps forward and did exactly the same thing, albeit with rather more flair.

In Beijing, Vice Premier Qian stepped forward, made a perfunctory bow, and gave a lengthy speech of welcome in flowery formal Mandarin extolling the cultural richness of the Middle Kingdom between Heaven and Earth. The two Chhrt'ktk't shuffled slightly in a way that seemed... uncertain perhaps? Then one of them spoke in reply. The alien's face split along previously-invisible seams, revealing faceted mouth-parts not unlike a crab's, and uttered a burst of clicking, chittering sounds. A moment later, a slightly-flat, slightly-atonal voice issued forth apparently from the air, between the two Chhrt'ktk't.

"We apologize deeply," the voice said in poorly accented Cantonese. "We do not understand."

In Paris, Madame President Emmanuelle Galois stepped forward from her delegation and performed a graceful slow pirouette, which she stopped facing the Chhrt'ktk't. Behind her, the crowd cheered.

"On behalf of all humanity," she said simply, "I bid you welcome to Paris, to France, and to Earth."

One of the Chhrt'ktk't made a gesture, briefly raising all four—hands? —to nearly shoulder height. She flinched a little at the crablike mouth as the Chhrt'ktk't click-chittered in reply, but a moment later, the same slightly-mechanical voice spoke in very acceptable Parisian French.

"Gratitude for your welcome. Your world is beautiful. We regret that we cannot stay long."

City by city, as noon marched around the world, the first face-to-face meetings of humans and Chhrt'ktk't played out, awkwardly at times, but uneventfully. In several cities, national leaders and their delegations tried to get their foot in the door and make early bids to explain why they should be the recipients of the Scaffold, but the message quickly became clear: The Chhrt'ktk't were here, they were friendly, but they weren't ready to talk about the Scaffold yet.

———————————

Over the next couple of weeks, as the Scaffold crept closer to Earth, the Chhrt'ktk't met with humanity for longer and longer periods, sometimes with the official delegations, sometimes apparently just coming out to talk to the crowds of sightseers. They never moved far from their ships, and declined invitations to visit official buildings or cultural sites. Periodically, one or another of the ships relocated to a different city, sometimes in the same nation, sometimes in another.

The approaching Scaffold was already visible with the naked eye. With a good telescope, it was easy to make out its shape, a cylindrical core surrounded by a clutter of folded frameworks.

"Our homeworld is very far from here," the Chhrt'ktk't said often. And, "We are on a great journey. We have little time." And "Our homeworld was all but exhausted when we left it. Yours is joyful to behold. Be careful you do not exhaust it." And many other things.

Virtually nobody could pronounce Chhrt'ktk't even close to correctly, although it seemed to amuse the aliens when people tried. However, humans will be humans, and—while nobody was sure whose idea it was— it wasn't long at all before people started calling them the Crickets. And the Chhrt'ktk't didn't seem to mind. Humanity learned the names and titles of the Crickets they met. Engineer-Second Hvecla, Navigator-Third Zhin, Captain-Senior Tyef-kik, and others.

Nearly everyone who had ever actually heard a Cricket speak was certain that their automated translation system was taking considerable liberties when it "translated" their names, because the names it gave them sounded so unlike their clicking, chittering speech. But at least the translated names were something humans could pronounce.

They were all, though, uniformly evasive whenever anyone tried to talk much about the Scaffold and why they were making humanity a gift of it.

"It is a mobile starship maintenance facility," they said. "It can construct and repair vessels that travel between the stars faster than light. But it has broken down and we cannot spare the time to repair it."

How long would the repair take, they were asked, many times.

"For us, more than three orbits of your world around your star," was the reply each time. "For you, longer, as you would have to first learn how. We must leave within no more than two orbits of your moon, to catch up to our fleet."

Time and time again, governmental delegations tried to draw them out on who would have charge of the Scaffold, or engage them in negotiation and persuade them as to why their nation should be entrusted with it. But all they would say is, "We gift it to your world. We will identify a Rapport-Controller." Needless to say, this immensely frustrated the politicians, most of whom had visions of themselves as the leading intermediator introducing the Chhrt'ktk't to the world's assembled governments, and thus naturally earning the favor of the Crickets—and custody of the Scaffold. The Crickets uniformly ignored such overtures, and the whole time they were on Earth, they never once responded to any attempt to open an official communication channel back to them.

It probably wasn't really all that surprising that national governments, focused on elevating their nation's interest above all others at any cost and certain beyond doubt that theirs was the most deserving nation on Earth, failed to fully understand the answers that they were given by the Crickets.

Alex Holder felt the slight downdraft from the soap-bubble before he heard it. He was, for the umpteenth time, carefully applying alkyd spar varnish to a freshly sanded deck rail. Alkyd, polyurethane, it scarcely mattered, it never lasted more than a couple of years. The alkyd lasted longer, but it was enough more expensive that he wasn't convinced the polyurethane wasn't the better deal in the long run. Except for all the work each time it needed re-coating.

Fortunately, since taking early retirement a few years earlier, time was something he had a lot of. More time than money, honestly. He hadn't retired because he felt he didn't need to work any more; he'd given in and retired because it was becoming so hard for anyone his age to get hired for a rewarding job. Of course everyone denied it, but age discrimination was very much a thing. He was using a lot of his newly-free time for reading and for online courses, purely for academic interest, trying to get a bit more up to speed on some of the fields of science he found most interesting.

He finished his stroke, rested the brush, and looked up. He quickly spotted the bubble about three meters above him, the first he'd actually seen, and heard the faint hiss at about the same time.

Interesting, he thought as he looked at it. *Does it work by electrostatic air entrainment? Or is it some kind of field-type effect? It must have a pretty potent power source to fit into something that small.*

The bubble moved closer. It circled him slowly as he watched it closely. Everyone had figured out by now that these were Chhrt'ktk't devices of some kind, but nobody knew their purpose and the Crickets wouldn't talk about them. It was well known that the Scaffold was decelerating toward orbit by now.

I wonder how it's controlled?, he mused to himself. *Or is it autonomous? Probably autonomous. From what I hear, there's too many of these for them to be individually controlled. I wonder if it will let me touch it?*

Alex slowly raised a hand, extending two fingers. The bubble dipped a little closer again. Hovering in front of him. He reached out and tentatively passed his hand beneath it, feeling only the gentle downwash of air.

So not entrainment as such, then. Some kind of pure electrostatic thruster?

He raised his hand, extending his fingers to touch the shimmering, iridescent globe, prepared to yank his hand away if anything untoward happened or the bubble did anything threatening. He felt a slight tingle on his skin as he got close, and a downward drag on his fingers, but then when there should have been contact, he felt... nothing. There was resistance that stopped his fingers, but no contact. It felt slick, oily and dry at the same time, frictionless, textureless.

"Well aren't you a puzzle," he mused aloud. *Got to be some kind of field-type effect. I can't think of anything else that could display these properties. So what's generating it?*

"Is there anything solid in there at all?"

He wasn't expecting an answer, but the bubble bobbed briefly. Was that a yes? A no? A random lurch? Somehow, he didn't really believe that last possibility.

For a second or so, the iridescent bubble blinked off. He had time to register a small, angular shape inside, all flat facets separated by slightly raised edges, a dull dark-gray finish, roughly a regular geometric solid. Then the bubble popped back into place.

"That's a *shield*, isn't it...? Thank you for letting me look inside. That's *got* to be done with field-type forces. The shield, *and...* whatever is holding you up. The downdraft isn't nearly enough on its own to generate hovering thrust. Is it just a side effect?"

The bubble bobbed again. Alex became aware of a mental... tickle. Or pressure. It was hard to say which, if either, was the right word. It was like being aware of an inaudible sound... so of course he tried to listen to it. It was... maddening. Like a subliminal voice that you cannot consciously hear, but still know someone is speaking.

Are you trying to communicate?, he thought at it, hard. He was certain there was something there. He had the feeling that he would be able to connect to it, if he only knew how...

It was as though the bubble *blinked* for an instant. Alex wasn't sure whether he had actually *seen* anything or not, or whether for an instant he saw through the shield again... or whether he had imagined it. Then the bubble moved away slightly. It drifted upward a little, and began to lazily orbit over his head about a meter away from him. The odd pressure ceased.

Alex shrugged, and after a moment, went back to re-varnishing his deck rail. But now half his mind was wondering what kind of forces kept the... bubble? Drone? Drone, he decided. What kept the drone aloft. For a moment the thought crossed his mind to wonder whether one of them would answer to Skaffen-Amtiskaw, and he chuckled to himself. He sighed, as the thought crossed his mind that Iain Banks would have loved to have seen this day.

=====

"Captain-Senior?"

"Yes, Observer-Second?"

"A scout drone in region 4-A-2 has identified a Rapport-Controller candidate."

"Good. Time is dwindling. Send a science drone with a direct-interface pack."

The Observer-Second touched a series of controls.

"Science drone launched from shuttle 7, Captain-Senior."

Alex was preparing to pack up for the day when the new drone appeared. It was the size and roughly the shape of a watermelon—or at least, he corrected himself, its shield was. The hissing sound was more pronounced, with a slight bacon-sizzle edge to it. It came zipping down out of the sky from the northwest at about a forty-five degree angle. It was sheer chance he happened to be looking that direction as it came into sight.

The drone came to a stop about three meters in front of him, then dropped its shield. It was a cylinder with rounded ends, a lighter color than the first drone and with a shinier surface. It seemed to have a considerable assortment of folded or coiled attachments.

After a moment, it slowly drifted closer, stopping again about a meter and a half in front of Alex. He stood still as it approached, silently watching it.

"Hello," he said, when nothing further happened for a few seconds. He wasn't really expecting the drone to answer; and so he was quite surprised when it did.

"Greeting," the by-now-familiar translated voice said. Then a metallic... tentacle, for lack of a better word... unrolled from the front of the drone. It ended in a set of fine branches that had small, shiny metal plates at their tips.

"Do not be alarmed," the voice said. "This is a non-intrusive test for interface ability." Then the probe reached out toward him. The fine tips extended to a short step of him and stopped.

"Confirmation request," the drone said. "Cognitive processing occurs within upper sensory node."

Alex hesitated for a moment. Then he realized, *It's asking me to confirm that my brain is in my head.*

"Confirmed," he replied. Then he voiced a guess aloud. "But you already knew that, didn't you? You're just asking the question as a formality."

"Protocol requires explicit confirmation," the drone agreed. Somehow it sounded... pleased. The ends of the probes writhed, arranging their shiny, flat tips into a formation that his head would fit easily into.

"Attempt interface," the drone said.

Alex hesitated again, unsure exactly what to expect. Then curiosity

15

overcame caution, as his nearly-insatiable curiosity almost always did. He took a step forward and carefully placed his head into the indicated position. The tendrils flexed again, and he felt them work their way through his hair and contact his scalp. The contact *tingled* ever so slightly. He felt the sense of subliminal presence again.

He had no idea how this was supposed to work. It seemed the drone wanted him to... *connect* to it somehow? But, he reasoned, if there was anything non-obvious that he needed to do to accomplish that, *presumably* the drone would have told him. So logic suggested that he already had everything that he needed to accomplish this—unless some innate ability was required. Specific neural circuitry, say.

Hello?, he thought, focusing his attention on the drone and hoping it worked.

Greeting, the drone replied, **inside his head**. *Please attempt interface.*

For a moment, Alex didn't react, briefly frozen in stunned amazement. He was talking to the drone through this connection. But there was something more that the drone wanted from him. Something more that it wanted him to do. But he didn't know how.

For a long, long moment, he stood motionless, wondering how this might work, and how he might accomplish 'interfacing'. The sense of silent presence was still there. *I don't think I'm 'hearing' it with my ears*, he thought. *I think I'm hearing/feeling it in my mind. So...*

He tuned out the outside world, the sound of birds, the gentle breeze, the warm sunlight, the smell of fresh varnish, and focused his attention inward, almost meditatively. But instead of passively letting himself drift into mu-shin, no-mind, he *listened* to the silent pressure, trying to... draw it into himself? Project himself into it? Immerse himself in it. Pull it around himself. Become one with it.

It was as though there was a silent mental *snap* inside his mind. He slid somehow into the presence like a plug slipping into a socket. He was still dimly aware of himself, but he was also aware of... something else... around him. The drone, he realized.

In an almost instinctive rush, the thought occurred to him that the drone must have 'senses', and that if he was somehow interfaced to the drone, he ought to be able to use them. Before he even had a chance to consider whether this was a good idea, he reached out for them. His curiosity was as reflexive as opening his eyes.

Alex found himself looking at himself. For a moment his first thought was that he looked strange, then he realized that he was seeing himself in far wider bandwidth than any human had ever seen before. He had a strong feeling he was seeing everything from deep infrared to mid-ultraviolet, and more. He became aware without actually thinking the question that this was a science drone, equipped with a range of instrumentation that even the Chhrt'ktk't considered extensive. He could see faint outlines of his own skeleton, and behind him he could see pulsing... something... magnetic fields perhaps? around what were obviously wires inside the wall of his house. He could even actually *see* the thin clouds of solvent evaporating off his fresh spar varnish. It was fascinating. He stood and gazed around him, awash in the torrent of sensory data.

Welcome, Controller, said the voice of the drone, inside his mind. *Interface accomplished.*

2: Rapport-Controller

The Cricket shuttle currently parked in the middle of New York's LaGuardia International Airport lifted gently off the ground without any fuss, rose to a thousand meters altitude, and headed off toward the northeast. Everyone knew that the Cricket shuttles moved to different cities every few days to a week, so it didn't really come as a big surprise to anyone. Everyone watching at LaGuardia assumed it was heading to Boston, or perhaps Halifax.

It wasn't. It drifted to a stop over central New Hampshire, hovered briefly at altitude, and then descended toward a landing spot, the first time a Cricket ship had landed anywhere but a major city. The chosen spot this time was on the shore of a large lake.

The ship settled to the ground, and shortly afterward a hatch opened, larger and further back than the one that had been used so far. After a few moments, a vehicle drifted out. It looked rather like an inflatable rubber life raft, if you made it out of metal, scaled it up to be around five meters wide by eight long, and then added a mostly-transparent canopy tall enough to accommodate standing Chhrt'ktk't. It rose swiftly to about fifty meters altitude, then shot off southward, climbing at it went to clear the ridge that ran just south of the lakeshore.

Alex was no longer "interfaced" with the drone when the Crickets arrived. He was inside making supper. But his kitchen windows looked out onto the street, which is why he clearly saw the Cricket skiff settle on the street in front of his house.

He wasn't particularly surprised. Since the business with the drone—which was hovering nearby, having followed him inside the house—he had been expecting visitors. It was pretty obvious they would come, especially when the science drone had followed him inside the house instead of leaving. It had really only been a question of when. He had not, however, anticipated that it would be this soon.

Checking that nothing on the stove was in danger of boiling over, he went to the front door, stepped outside, and waited. By the time he got outside, a door panel in the nearer side of the skiff had opened and two Crickets had stepped out. They were approaching now down his driveway.

They stopped about three meters in front of him, then one of them spoke. Alex had never seen a Cricket speak close-up before, though he had seen them on TV, so the crab-like mouth and the clicking/chittering speech did not startle him. He tried to study the movement of the plate-like mouth-parts without obviously staring.

"Greeting," said the first Cricket, briefly raising all four 'hands'. "We are Captain-Junior Kheftra."

"We are Mediator-Third Cheeun," said the second. "Pilot-Second Fyin remains aboard our craft."

"Alex Holder," Alex said in reply, raising his open palms just below shoulder-height in imitation of the Cricket gesture. "It's short for Alexander."

"Al-ek-sandur," the first Cricket repeated, the one who had declared... himself?—as Captain-Junior Kheftra, the pronunciation just slightly off. "Rapport-Controller Aleksandur."

"Just Alex, please," Alex replied.

"Rapport-Controller Aleks," Kheftra repeated. Close enough. "We greet you. When can you be ready to depart?"

"Depart?" Alex said. "Whoa, slow down a bit. Depart where? And can you please explain to me about this Rapport-Controller business?" He hesitated a moment.

"Look, I was in the middle of making supper. Why don't you come inside, and we can talk about this while I finish cooking?" Then two thoughts occurred to him in rapid succession. "Are you hungry?—Uh... can you *eat* our food?"

"Our biochemistries appear mostly compatible," said Mediator-Third Cheeun. "But we have not tried to eat your food. Assuring safety would require analytical scans."

Alex chuckled.

"Well," he observed, "you *did* leave a science drone here, after all."

He led the way to his kitchen, entirely failing to realize that he had just become the first human being to have a Cricket visitor in his home—a fact which, unbeknownst to him then, would become vitally important later. His front door was a tight squeeze for the Crickets, he noticed.

He checked on his sauce and made sure it wasn't catching on the bottom, then, seeing that the water in the large pot had reached a full rolling boil, dumped in two handfuls of linguine. He set a twelve-minute timer, and put a large mesh strainer basket into the sink ready to drain it.

Then, hoping he wasn't making a mistake, he stepped up to the science drone, and calmly said, "Interface."

20

The cable uncoiled from the drone, and this time went straight to the connection configuration. Alex felt it make contact, felt the tingle, focused inward as he had before, and reached for the presence of the drone.

Interface came more quickly this time. He knew what to expect now, and having been there once, he knew how to get there. It took him a few moments to find the right mental focus again, but in what felt like under a minute, he was back within the drone. He opened his senses to the drone's, and the hyper-real world he had seen the first time sprang into being around him.

He focused his attention on the two pots on the stove, and their contents. *Let's see if this works,* he thought to himself. Then, more outwardly, *Analyze.*

He was aware of arms unfolding from the drone. It drifted past him closer to the stove, and sampled both pots. Data flooded into his mind, chemical structures that he couldn't parse yet, though he recognized some of the simpler molecules simply from their structure. Water of course was obvious, and he realized that from there and some reference sources, it would be very simple to extrapolate the entirety of Chhrt'ktk't chemical notation if he wished. From there—

Don't get distracted, he told himself.

Cross-reference to Chhrt'ktk't biochemistry, he thought. *Flag any potential harmful interactions.* Almost all of the structures faded into the background. Two substances present in small amounts—he couldn't tell what they were, he didn't recognize them—remained, marked with the palest yellow.

Significance of interaction? he thought to the drone.

Possibility of mild irritation of sensitive tissues or strong stimulation of taste receptors, the drone answered.

Huh. Well, there were onions and chipotle in the sauce, about which one could say the same things. So that wasn't too different from the possible effects upon humans.

He pulled his attention out of the drone and thought, *Disconnect.* The interface cable detached and retracted, and he turned to face the two Crickets.

"According to your drone," he said, "nothing in this food will harm you, but it might irritate sensitive tissues and might be strongly flavored to you. If I understand the drone correctly."

The Crickets looked at each other, then back at him.

"This... is exactly what Rapport-Controller means," said one. Alex thought it was the Mediator-Third. "You are able to interface to our technology. Even unfamiliar with it, you have quickly learned how to control it.

"You are what we have been seeking since we landed upon our world. A human able to control and operate our maintenance facility.

"Time is becoming urgent in the extreme. When can you be ready to depart?"

"Wait," Alex said. "What do you mean by 'depart'?"

"We will take you to the maintenance facility," the Captain-Junior said, "and place it under your control. This will complete our mission, and we can leave your world and rejoin our fleet."

WHOA. That was a bolt from the blue. Alex had **not** been expecting that. It was staggering. He repeated it to himself: The Crickets wanted to put **him** in control of their maintenance facility.

"What... do you expect me to do with it?" he asked, hesitantly.

"Whatever you see fit," said the other Cricket, the Mediator-Third. "Use it as your world needs."

As the world needs, Alex thought to himself. *Clean power. Clean water.* He wondered whether Chhrt'ktk't technology could clean up some of the nastier chemicals humanity had polluted the world with. Perhaps even start moving some of the dirtier industries off-planet. The endless *possibilities...*

The sound of the timer interrupted his thoughts. The pasta was done.

He turned off both burners, grabbed a pair of heatproof mitts, took the pasta pot off the stove, and poured everything carefully into the strainer. He picked the last couple of strands free, put the pot down on the counter, lifted the strainer of drained pasta out of the sink and sat it into the top of the pot, then took the pot to the table. The pot would catch any more water that drained out of the pasta.

He went back to the stove, gave the sauce a final stir, and took that to the table as well. Then he grabbed a stack of plates and a handful of forks.

"If you'll excuse me," he said to the two Crickets, "I'm going to eat some supper. If you wish to join me, you're welcome. I can't guarantee you'll like it, but your drone's analysis says it won't poison you. To a human palate, this dish is filling, strongly flavorful and mildly spicy. I have no idea what it might taste like to you."

He dished himself out a pile of linguine, spooned a healthy helping of sauce over it, and sat down to eat. After a moment, one of the Crickets—the Mediator-Third, he thought—picked up a plate, put a small pile of linguine on it, then added a little sauce.

Alex stirred his own sauce through his pasta, then wound up a forkful and put it into his mouth. After a moment, the Mediator-Third did the same, still standing.

"It is indeed strongly flavored," the Mediator-Third reported after a moment. "The—long—"

"The pasta," Alex offered.

"The—pasta is neutral, a base for the—sauce. The sauce holds most of the flavors. It tastes of smoke, but not in an unpleasant way."

The Captain-Junior made a sidewise twitch of his head, which Alex guessed was perhaps equivalent to a nod, and tried a cautious forkful himself.

"It is good," he agreed after a minute. "Is this typical human food?"

"We have many kinds of food," Alex replied. "There are hundreds of nations on Earth, and at least most of them have dishes or entire styles of cuisine that are distinctive to that nation or their region. Even specific areas of an individual nation. This dish is from northern Italy. If you visit a city with a range of restaurants from different cultures, you may be able to choose from thousands of different dishes. The range of foods devised by humans is amazing... though sometimes a little silly."

The Crickets both did the sidewise head-twitch. Honestly, Alex thought *that* looked a little silly as well, but he suppressed his amusement and said nothing. He had no wish to be rude.

"Your range of foods appears to be far greater than our own," the Captain-Junior said. "Why? Is such a range of foods necessary to meet your nutritional needs?"

"Oh, no, not at all," Alex replied. He stopped and thought about how to answer the question for a moment before continuing.

"We eat for nourishment, certainly, but we prepare foods in many ways for a variety of reasons. In some cases, a style of cuisine is driven by the foods that were historically common in the region where it originated. Poorer cultures tended to have simpler and less varied cuisines than wealthier ones. In others, regional recipes use ingredients for reasons related to the climate. Cooking from the north of India, where it is cold, uses a lot of pepper, which has a warming effect. Cooking from the south of India, where it is very hot, uses a lot of capsicum peppers, which have a cooling effect because they increase perspiration.

"But also, beyond simple nourishment, we also prepare food for entertainment, and we share food as a means of social bonding. There is a style of cooking called teppan-yaki in which the chef prepares food directly in front of the guests, to entertain them with a display of his food preparation skills. A family, or a group of friends, or a... mating couple may share a meal together to reinforce emotional bonds, or to show commitment to each other, or to commemorate a special event. And sometimes, elaborate or rare foodstuffs—or even purely decorative ingredients with no nutritional value at all—are served as a display of wealth or good fortune."

The Captain-Junior head-twitched.

"It seems quite complex."

"Captain-Junior," Alex replied, "*many* aspects of our culture are complex. Surely the same is true of yours?"

"You are of course correct," the Captain-Junior replied. "Perhaps it should not be a surprise that some aspects of our culture that seem simple to us, are complex in yours. And we have no doubt that the reverse is also true. It is unfortunate that we cannot spare the time to remain here and learn more about each other's cultures. We are explorers by nature and necessity."

Alex nodded.

"We've heard many times that you are on a long journey and need to catch up to the rest of your fleet," he said. "I admit to being curious what the urgency is."

"Apologies," the Captain-Junior replied. "We are ordered not to speak of it."

"We also," said the Mediator-Third.

Wait, Alex thought. That was interesting. He had just caught on to a linguistic detail. Individual Chhrt'ktk't seemed to speak of themselves in the plural.

"I'm sorry," Alex replied, still thinking hard. "I would not wish to cause you a conflict with your orders." Even the mention of such an order by the Captain-Junior might have been a slip on his part. The Crickets, he realized, were hiding something.

He began to wonder to himself what it was, as he finished eating and put away the leftovers.

"So," he asked, "when you say 'depart'. I don't think your... maintenance facility... has reached orbit yet, has it?"

"Not quite yet," the Captain-Junior replied. "But very soon now. We wish to be ready to depart as soon as we can transfer control to you."

"I have to ask," Alex said. "I'm still not really internalizing this. Why me?"

"We searched for humans who display a required set of mental characteristics and traits. Inquiring, analytical, empirical, precise reasoning, open to new things. These traits are relatively common among you. But of critical importance, beyond these, you were the first such who both appeared able to sense contact probing by our scout drone, and chose to respond to it."

"Which is when you sent out the science drone," Alex interjected.

"Yes. Just so. Equipped with a direct interface kit. And when it arrived, you were able to connect and fully interface with it. Much more easily in fact than we expected."

"I've read a *lot* of stories which have speculated about doing so," Alex said. "So I suppose I was already open to the idea. I've probably spent half my life wishing to be able to do it. So having it actually happen is... astounding.

"Is it *really* that uncommon an ability?"

"With proper training, probably not," the Captain-Junior replied. "But untrained? Of many tens of millions of your species we have scanned, you are the first."

Alex thought about that for a long moment. *Holy shit,* he wondered to himself, *is this for real?*

"Will I be able to return?" he asked eventually.

"Of course," said the Captain-Junior, seeming surprised by the question. "As soon as you are able to assume control of the maintenance facility, you will also have control of all of its support vessels. You will be able to use one to travel freely between the maintenance facility and the surface of your world. And to the other planets in your stellar system, if you so choose."

Alex thought about how quickly the ship currently in orbit had reached Earth from beyond the orbit of Mars. This was going to change *everything*.

"So what happens now?" he asked.

"Now we travel to the maintenance facility, and make sure that you are able to interface to the control-intellect as you did to the drone. And if that is successful, then it is time for us to leave."

Alex took a deep breath.

"Alright, then," he said. "Let's go."

―――――――――

Out of caution, Alex locked up as they left the house. All the bills were on auto-pay, it would all take care of itself for a while. He followed the two Crickets down his driveway. He noticed several of his neighbors standing outside their houses, looking at the skiff, but not approaching. He heard one call out something, but couldn't make out the words, and settled for a casual wave back in the general direction. Then they were at the skiff, and the side panel opened and the Captain-Junior stepped inside, and there was nothing he could do but follow.

The interior of the skiff was sparse, an open space with a railing all around and a console at what he presumed to be the front. There was a third Cricket in front of the console. After a moment, Alex realized that he was not standing, but rather, straddling a sort of tall hummock or narrow stool that rose from the deck, all four legs tight against it. He inferred this was the Cricket equivalent to a chair.

The Captain-Junior and Mediator-Third, meanwhile, simply took places next to the railing and took a firm hold on it. Alex followed their example. For a quadrupedal being, he mused, such an arrangement probably made fairly reasonable sense. He wasn't sure whether they even *could* sit in the human manner.

The Captain-Junior spoke a single brief utterance which was not translated, and the Cricket at the console placed all four hands on it. There were no obvious controls to be seen, but there did seem to be delineated contact areas. A moment later, the skiff rose smoothly into the sky, straight upward. There was no jerk and only the slightest sense of acceleration. Then it turned and began to climb over the ridge. Alex found it a little disorienting, his eyes telling him that much more was going on than his inner ear did. This would take some getting used to.

It was only moments before the skiff cleared the top of the ridge and began to angle downwards towards the lake. Looking out ahead, Alex quickly spotted the Cricket shuttle where it was parked near the lake shore. A crowd of several dozen people had gathered a short distance off, most of them apparently people who had spotted it while driving down the lakeshore highway and pulled off the road to investigate.

A large hatch in the hull opened as the skiff approached, and the skiff flew straight in, decelerating to a smooth stop. The short flight had been as smooth as a ride in an express elevator, and no more dramatic, except for the obvious effortlessness. The hatch began to close again even before the skiff had settled to the deck. The lighting inside the—hangar? Cargo bay? —was slightly blue-tinged.

The skiff's side access panel opened again.

"Please follow," the Captain-Junior said. So Alex let go of the rail and followed.

The Captain-Junior led the way toward the front of the bay and into a broad passageway, running lengthwise along the ship. Alex followed, looking around him. It looked a lot like what he had seen of Navy ships, if you scaled everything to the proportions of beings a quarter again as tall as a human and about twice as broad. There was a heavy bulkhead where the passageway met the bay, with an equally heavy hatch slid to one side along the inside wall of the bay. Once they passed out of the bay, which had been open to Earth's air, there was a faintly acrid, faintly metallic tang to the air, slightly thick at the back of his throat.

About thirty yards in, they passed through another bulkhead, and then shortly after, turned right through a large hatchway, standing open. For a moment, Alex thought it led back outside, it was so convincing. But then he realized after a moment that he was looking into a sizeable space with a half dozen or so Crickets standing—no, perched on 'stools'—at various consoles. The entirety of the walls and ceiling were displaying a seamless three-hundred-and-sixty degree view of the world outside the ship. A slightly raised and railed open space slightly back of the center of the room held an unoccupied stool.

The Captain-Junior went directly to it and straddled it.

"Apology, Rapport-Controller Aleks," said the Mediator-Third. "There is no suitable place for you to rest. Please take hold of the rail."

Alex did as instructed, and the Captain-Junior spoke again.

"Prepare for flight."

All of the Crickets present on the—bridge?—except for the Mediator-Third placed their digits upon their control consoles.

"Raise ship and set course for maintenance facility. All prudent speed."

With as little sense of motion as before, the ship rose smoothly off the ground. When it had risen no more than a few tens of meters, the floor apparently vanished. Alex clutched convulsively at the rail, his heart suddenly pounding, before he was able to suppress the momentary panic reflex. The floor was **STILL THERE**. He could feel it beneath his feet. He was in no danger of falling. But he now had a full spherical view in all directions. It was more than slightly disorienting... but it was breathtaking.

Still, his skin prickled with adrenaline, and the vertigo from the mismatch between inner ear and vision made his head spin slightly, the more so when the shuttle itself swung slowly around to the northwest, the ground tilting away as its bow rose. Alex had to fight the urge to lean forward; "down" inside the ship was towards the FLOOR, he reminded himself, not towards the GROUND. His knuckles were white as he gripped the rail. Then the world fell away below as the shuttle accelerated skyward. The sky ahead and above darkened rapidly as the air thinned. It was no more than about five or six minutes before it was black ahead. He realized the ship must have been accelerating continuously at three or four gravities.

And stars. There were **SO MANY STARS.**

Space, Alex thought to himself. *I'm in space. This afternoon, I was varnishing my deck rail, and now I am on an alien ship, and I'm in space.*

An especially bright star lay directly ahead. But it wasn't a star, Alex realized. That was the Scaffold—the "maintenance facility", as the Chhrt'ktk't named it. Their destination.

======

Eight hours later, the "maintenance facility" had expanded from a bright star to a folded tangle of booms and frames around a central structure. The shuttle had already turned over, braked to a halt and reversed direction, and was now accelerating to match the maintenance facility's Earthward velocity. Alex had obtained permission to talk to the Navigator-Second during the flight, and the Navigator-Second had been willing to answer many of his questions. The shuttle, it transpired, was capable of sustaining about five gees of acceleration, while the maintenance facility could only manage about one and a half to, at the most, two gee without suffering structural damage. The facility had never been intended to move far, or fast, in normal space. It had a powerful hyperdrive core rendering it capable of keeping up with the fleet at normal cruising speed even with several other ships docked and under repair, but its structure was too ungainly and too fragile for high accelerations in normal space, even if it were equipped with a sufficiently powerful normal-space drive.

It was obvious that the skiff and the shuttle had some form of acceleration compensation technology, and Alex had asked why the maintenance facility did not have the same. It did, the Captain-Junior had told him; but the technology had limits and across a greatly extended structure such as the maintenance facility, kilometers long even when fully folded, the limit of compensation practically feasible was about one and a half gravities. The Captain-Junior had offered to have the Engineer-Third explain why in more detail, but Alex politely declined. He didn't expect to be able to understand the explanation... yet.

Now, as the maintenance facility braked towards Earth orbit, the shuttle was ahead of it and being overhauled from behind, from the facility's perspective. From the shuttle's, the two were closing alarmingly fast. They would match velocity in about another ten minutes, then switch thrust again to match its deceleration before docking.

More details became visible as the facility caught up and the velocity difference dropped, and Alex started to get a better idea of its scale. It was a vast cylindrical structure, with various bits of superstructure spaced intermittently along its length, festooned with folded booms and frames. He felt like a passenger in a row-boat attempting to rendezvous with an aircraft carrier. The last approach felt terrifyingly rapid, as the shuttle slipped at blurring speeds past folded booms the size of skyscrapers. His knuckles were white on the rail again as he fought not to flinch.

The relative speed bled down enough that it seemed the shuttle was merely zipping past the facility, no longer rushing towards it at suicidal speed. Then it was slow enough that he had a chance to glimpse surface details, then a slow drift, and then...

"Velocity and acceleration matched," declared Pilot-Second Seek't. "Commencing docking approach."

Nothing seemed to happen at first, but then Alex noticed the maintenance facility, already huge, was slowly growing larger. The change of aspect angle on some of the folded booms was visible. More and more detail became visible, until finally a dark opening came into view. A hatch, a docking bay, he realized. One large enough to swallow the hundred-meter length of the shuttle several times over. Finally he grasped how gigantic this structure was, over ten kilometers long, and realized that when the shuttle had matched acceleration it had to have been still a kilometer or more away from the main hull. This wasn't like docking with a ship, or even coming into a busy port. It was like docking with a small city. Once it entered orbit, it was going to be the brightest thing in Earth's night sky after the Moon. He hoped they'd picked a clear orbit for it.

The shuttle drifted into place and settled, then suddenly the floor reappeared. Overhead, the hatch was slowly closing. Lights high on the walls turned on, bathing the bay in the same blue-tinged light as in the shuttle. The Chhrt'ktk't homeworld's star must be a hotter spectral class than Sol, Alex thought to himself. A class F star, maybe even class A. Now that the bay was illuminated, several skiffs were visible along the nearer side. Something bulky and blocky was parked down at the far end. He had no idea what it was.

Chitterclicking came from behind him, then the translated voice of the Captain-Junior.

"We have no pressure suit that will fit you. We shall depart the shuttle in the skiff rather than pressurize the docking bay. Please follow."

Alex followed the Captain-Junior out of... uh, off the bridge, he corrected himself. The Mediator-Third fell into place with them. It took them only a few minutes to return to the skiff. A third Cricket was already waiting beside it, the door panel already open. A pilot, Alex presumed. The pilot boarded as soon as they approached, and was already on his 'stool' when they came aboard. Alex noticed at once that the Mediator-Third had brought a science drone along with him. The panel closed, and there was a brief pause, then the hatch overhead slid open. The skiff lifted gently out of the shuttle, then the pilot dropped it to within a meter or two of the deck and headed for the end of the bay. Ahead, a hatch slid open, easily ten meters high, but this hatch had what looked like a faint, shimmering curtain behind it. The pilot slowed to perhaps a fast running speed, and nosed the shuttle directly into the curtain. A line of brightness was visible sweeping across the canopy as the shuttle passed through the curtain, then it closed seamlessly behind. Alex was prepared to bet not a single whiff of atmosphere had escaped.

They followed the passageway for several minutes. It was easily large enough that three or even four skiffs like this one could have passed each other in it. After a little while, just before the passageway angled to the left, the pilot turned the skiff into a crosswise passage to the right and stopped. Another skiff was already parked ahead. The door panel opened again.

"Come," said Captain-Junior Kheftra. "It is time for you to try to connect with the control-intellect."

The Captain-Junior led the way off the skiff and to yet another hatch, this one much more moderate in size, on the wall opposite to where the pilot had parked the skiff, then extended a 'hand' to a panel in the middle of the hatch. There was a momentary pause, and the hatch split and slid open to either side, revealing a large chamber with two concentric rings of consoles within. At the center of the chamber was a larger console with a Chhrt'ktk't stool in front of it.

The Captain-Junior led Alex directly to the center of the chamber. Alex followed, followed by the Mediator-Third, the drone bringing up the rear.

"This is an auxiliary control center," the Captain-Junior said. "It will suffice for now. We will connect you to the control-intellect here."

Alex stopped, looking at the stool.

"Uh," he began. Then he stopped and thought, framing his words.

"This... this place is huge. And you mentioned a control-intellect. This isn't going to be like just interfacing to the drone, is it?"

"No," answered the Mediator-Third. "It will be much more strenuous, at least the first time. But we have confidence that you will be able to accomplish it."

"I... don't know about doing this while standing," he said. "And I can't sit on that. It's no more suitable for me than human chairs are suitable for you. It's a bit far to send back to Earth for a chair. I presume this... maintenance facility could construct one for me, but first I'd need to be able to tell it what to construct, so that's a bit of a circular problem.

"So I think my best bet will be to lie down on the floor. Can you find me some kind of resilient pad that I can put under my head?"

There was a pause. The Captain-Junior and Mediator-Third chitterclicked at each other for a minute or so, untranslated, then did the head-twitch.

"We can provide a sleeping pad," the Mediator-Third said. "We hope this will be satisfactory."

The Mediator-Third reached out a 'hand' to the drone and touched it briefly. After a moment, the drone zipped away and left the chamber via the open hatch.

"I'm presuming I will interface via the drone as before?" Alex asked.

"Yes," the Mediator-Third replied. "The drone will provide the direct-interface kit, and then connect you to the console. For the long term we expect that you will have your own interface contacts implanted."

The Cricket extended one arm and spread its four terminal digits wide where Alex could easily examine them. Looking from this close, he could see the faint outline of small contact plates beneath the skin.

"I see," Alex said. "Do all Chhrr't... uh, Chhrt'k... all of you have these implants?"

"No," the Captain-Junior replied. "But all who must interface with control systems or intellect-augmented systems."

"I'm seeing a lot of consoles in this room," Alex said. "How many... uh... I'm sorry, I cannot pronounce your name for yourselves correctly... does it take to operate this maintenance facility?"

"Thousands," the Captain-Junior replied. "We know that your people refer to us as 'Crickets' because you lack the necessary physical structures to make the sounds of our language. Do not feel shamed. We are not offended."

"We expect you to identify and recruit others to assist you," the Mediator-Third added. "We will leave the deployed scout and survey drones in place to assist with this. We are easily able to fabricate more."

Alex nodded.

A few minutes later, the science drone returned. Another drone followed closely behind it, a boxy drone with multiple manipulator arms. The new drone was carrying a large roll of something white. It flew to the center of the room, placed the roll on the floor, then turned and flew to the back of the room, hovering next to the hatch. The roll started to unroll slightly, and Alex bent to feel it.

It was smooth and white, an even rectangle about a meter wide, and he estimated several meters long. It was finger-thick when rolled, but where it had unrolled, it expanded to about the thickness of his forearm. It felt like dense memory-foam, but with a finer grain than any memory foam he had seen.

"I think I can work with this," Alex said. He flipped the roll over and unrolled about two thirds of it on an open patch of floor, leaving the remaining third rolled. He lowered himself to the floor, and first sat on the pad, then lay down. As he'd hoped, the remaining rolled part was a fairly decent headrest/pillow.

"Yeah," he confirmed. "I can work with this."

He sat back up again.

"Okay. Let's do this."

He took a deep breath and looked at the science drone.

"Interface, please."

The Mediator-Third chitterclicked something at the drone. It drifted into the center of the room and extended one cable toward Alex, one toward the console. The first cable blossomed into the by-now-almost-familiar cloud of contact points, that settled into his scalp. He felt the tingle on his scalp, and the presence of the drone, but did not connect to the drone this time. He lay down instead, taking his time, making sure not to pull the interface cable tight or trap it under his head. He relaxed, gazed at the ceiling, took a deep breath, held it for a four-count, then let it out. Then he closed his eyes, and sank into himself.

"Ready," he said. His own voice seemed to come from a slight distance.

The drone connected the other cable.

If the drone's presence was a gentle pressure, the maintenance facility's control-intellect was a tsunami. It crashed over Alex, surrounding him. Overwhelming him. The sheer power of its presence was daunting.

If he had tried to fight it, it would have crushed him, broken him, shattered him.

Alex knew better than to fight it. Where the oak breaks, the bamboo bends. Alex bent. He let the tsunami wash around him, over him, into him, through him. He opened himself to the wave and accepted it. He felt the wave, sensed the wave, rode the wave, *listened to* the wave, *knew* the wave.

Somewhere between mind and machine, Alex *became* the wave.

When all was calm and equilibrium returned, he essayed a simple thought.

Hello?

WELCOME, came a reply after a moment. WHO ARE YOU?

My name is Alex Holder, he thought back.

THE NEW CONTROLLER, came the reply. THE FORMER CONTROLLER SAID THAT ONE WOULD COME. It was very, very different from communicating with the drone. The drone felt mechanical. Very sophisticated, but mechanical. This... was something more, something on a different level altogether.

So they tell me, Alex replied.

THEN COME, said the thunderous mental voice. CONNECT.

Alex reached out into the tsunami, let go of *self*, and connected.

His consciousness expanded. First he was aware for a moment of

33

seeing himself lying on the floor on the sleep pad, actually looking quite calm and restful. Then his attention flew elsewhere. Outward, and outward, and outward. He could hold only a few of them at once, but he realized that he knew—*could* know, in time—all of the maintenance facility's capabilities, know all of its parts and what it could do. But he was not alone in it. There was a second *mind* in here with him, guiding where he asked guidance, ready to do what he asked of it, a vast pool of knowledge waiting to help him. And it was *aware* of itself, as well as of him.

The control-intellect was not a computer, as such. It was an artificial intelligence. A REAL one, not some mere language model.

Tell me what I most importantly need to know, he thought. *Tell me the things I need to know to use this place.*

And so it did.

Some time later, he wasn't sure how long, Alex opened his eyes. The two Crickets were watching him gravely. Nearby, a drone had partly dismantled the Cricket stool and was constructing the shell of a semi-reclining chair on top of it, using it as a post. He had a vague memory of requesting that be done and sketching out a brief mental schematic, just the broad strokes, the AI filling in structural details and materials for him. He knew without having to think about it that when complete, a sleeping pad like the one he was lying on would make perfect padding for it, once slightly scaled down and reshaped.

He stretched and sat up.

"Greetings again, Rapport-Controller," said Captain-Junior Kheftra. "We saw that you have successfully achieved rapport. We began to grow concerned. It was a long time." Somehow, gravity came across in the translated voice.

"There was... a lot to take in," Alex replied slowly. "At first it was like trying to wind-surf in a hurricane."

"We... do not entirely understand the reference," Kheftra replied. "But we believe we understand the idiom. Almost overwhelming."

"Yes," Alex agreed. "That is the gist of it. So what now?"

"We should all go now to our ship," Captain-Junior Kheftra said. "We shall formally transfer command to you there, then return you here. Then it will be time for us to leave. We are eager to rejoin our fleet."

Alex climbed to his feet.

"Let's be on our way, then," he said. Then, directed to the drone, "Disconnect, please. Remain here." The drone withdrew its interface cable. He would need to use it for a while longer.

The two Crickets and the human left the command center together and returned to the skiff. The short trip back to the shuttle passed in silence, then the shuttle undocked from the maintenance facility, maneuvered clear of the folded booms, and accelerated hard towards Earth. The facility would enter orbit in just under three days, Alex knew. The Chhrt'ktk't had chosen an orbit just short of four thousand kilometers. He would be changing that. He had his reasons. He knew Earth governments, and he was already thinking ahead. Also, there were the van Allen radiation belts to consider—a four thousand kilometer orbit was smack in the middle of the densest part of the inner belt. Perhaps the Crickets didn't care about ionizing radiation, but Alex did.

Without a need to stop and counter-burn to match velocity, it was a little under five hours, Alex estimated, before they were within range of the Cricket ship. The ship proper, not just a shuttle. He knew now, having asked the control-intellect, that the ship ahead was just over fourteen hundred meters long. It looked less like a skyscraper laid on its side, or any conventional naval vessel, even a science-fiction starship, than like some massive piece of architecture, a flying arcology, slices of structure layered on top of each other.

He didn't make any great effort to study its features; he just relaxed and took in the sight. He would be able to access its detailed specifications any time he wanted to, now.

As before, the shuttle was swallowed into a docking bay; and as before, lacking a pressure suit, he was taken into the ship proper, through the docking bay's atmosphere barrier and deep into the ship, on the skiff. As on the shuttle, their destination was what Alex now immediately recognized as the bridge.

Captain-Junior Kheftra escorted him as far as the railed central dais, chitterclicked something brief, and then stepped back. There were four Crickets on the dais, two with what Alex was now able to recognize as Captain-rank markers upon their clothing.

"We are Captain-Senior T'chee of this vessel, the explorer-craft [an untranslated sound]," said one. He gestured to the other Captain. "Yx are Captain-Senior Shenka, of the maintenance facility. And yx"—gesturing to the third of the four Crickets—"are Rapport-Controller Xin of the maintenance facility. We welcome you, Rapport-Controller Aleks."

35

"It is an honor to meet you all," Alex replied, unsure what the correct formalities might be.

"It is now time to perform formal transfer of control," Captain-Senior T'chee said. Then he chitterclicked something that was not translated. There was a brief pause before a Cricket at one of the consoles replied. The four Crickets on the dais turned slightly to face forward. Alex, sensing that he should, did the same. Then the Captain-Senior began to speak.

"We are Captain-Senior T'chee of the Chhrt'ktk't. We-the-Chhrt'ktk't greet you, people of Earth." T'chee raised all four 'hands' and continued. "We give recognition as our hosts and gratitude for your patience. We have identified from among you a Rapport-Controller, as we declared we would."

T'chee turned toward Alex. Alex turned to face the Crickets in turn.

"We now recognize from among you Rapport-Controller Aleks... Holder," T'chee said, raising all four hands again. Alex copied the gesture.

The third Cricket stepped forward and faced Alex.

"We are Rapport-Controller Xin. We yield authority over the control-intellect of the maintenance facility to Rapport-Controller Aleks." Again, the exchange of raised hands.

"I thank you, Rapport-Controller Xin," Alex replied. "I am deeply honored to be entrusted with it."

"We are Captain-Senior Shenka of the maintenance facility," the other Captain said, turning to face Alex. "We relinquish to you command of the maintenance facility. We use what we believe to be the idiom of your species: You have the conn."

"I have the conn," Alex acknowledged. "I thank you for the honor, Captain-Senior Shenka. I will take good care of it."

"Gratitude," Shenka replied.

The Crickets all turned to face forward again.

"Our time with you is now at an end," Captain-Senior T'chee declared. "We-us depart now to return to our fleet before it becomes too distant to easily find. We-us wish you all good fortune."

Then he made a gesture to the crew-member who had replied earlier. That crew-member touched his console, then clicked a brief reply.

T'chee turned to Alex.

"We will return you now to the maintenance facility. Captain-Junior Kheftra will take you there, one final time. Our shuttles are preparing to return. Then we will depart."

"I understand, Captain-Senior," Alex replied. "On behalf of the people of Earth, I thank you for this incomparable gift."

The Captain-Senior raised 'hands' one last time, then turned away. It was a clear dismissal, a moving on to the next task. Alex turned around and stepped off the command dais.

"Please follow," Captain-Junior Kheftra said. Alex followed him, back first to the skiff, and then aboard. Then Pilot-Second Fyin took the skiff back to the shuttle. Shortly afterward, the shuttle left the ship again.

<hr>

At Alex's request, the shuttle made a quick flying visit back to his home. It was early evening and already mostly dark, so this time Alex asked the Captain-Junior to hover over the ridge across the valley instead of landing on the lakeshore again, and launch the skiff from the air. As soon as the skiff got close to his house, Alex could see that there were police barricades in front of it and emergency vehicles parked around, as well as a few vehicles that had the anonymous government look about them.

Well, *THAT* wouldn't do. He didn't have time for a confrontation with law enforcement that could all too easily turn violent if he declined their "invitation" to stop and answer questions, of which he was certain there would be many. Already he thought he saw someone looking up.

He thought quickly.

"Move away from the house, please," he said directly to the pilot, "before we draw too much attention. I have an alternate plan. Go in that direction, please." He pointed. The skiff began to drift at a moderate speed in the direction he had indicated. He gave the pilot course corrections as they went, then after a few minutes, pointed downwards.

"Land behind that building, please, then let me out and wait for me." A chain supermarket, still open.

The skiff settled nearly silently. The door panel opened and Alex disembarked, walked quickly around to the front of the store, and went in. He pulled out a cart and loaded it quickly with shelf-stable heat-and-serve foods, ready-to-eat snacks, dried foods—he didn't think pure water would be a problem—beverages and beverage concentrates, enough shelf-stable foods to last him a couple of weeks until he could make better arrangements. He had hoped to collect a few networking components and a laptop computer from his home; but he had his phone. It would have to be enough.

He paid for his purchases, left the store unrecognized, and wheeled the cart around behind the store.

When the door panel opened, he wheeled the cart with some effort directly up the short ramp into the skiff.

"I need a way to secure this," he said. One of the Crickets, he wasn't sure which, touched the rail, and it snapped open into a row of articulating fingers. The Cricket nudged the cart against the rail, and the fingers closed securely around it.

"That's perfect," Alex said. "Let's go."

3: All Aboard

This time, the trip out to the maintenance facility was closer to five hours than eight. It was closer now, and had shed velocity, and there was not as much counter-acceleration needed to match trajectory. Otherwise, the trip was a mirror of the first arrival... except that this time, the entire massive structure was... Earth's? Or his?

The Chhrt'ktk't had placed it under his control. Alex was quite certain that Earth's governments would dispute that. He was equally certain that if he once let the bureaucrats and politicians get control over it, they would spend at least the next ten years bickering over who should be in control and what to do with it, and it would end up serving what the oligarchs and plutocrats *wanted*, not what Earth as a whole *needed*. At the very best, it would become a political football. At worst, there would be wars over it. Possibly the worst wars in history, over the biggest prize in history. Perhaps the *last* war.

Alex could not allow that to happen. This incredible windfall could be humanity's salvation, or its destruction. He had to do everything he could to try to ensure that it was salvation.

And what were the Crickets *hiding...*?

─────────────

"Talk to me, people," said President Riken. "Who is this Alex Holder? What do we know about him? Where's he from? Why did they pick him?"

"We don't know a thing, sir," said Rear-Admiral David Hackett, the Director of National Intelligence, stocky as a fireplug and equally bald. "There's a lot of Alex Holders in the United States, and Canada, and who knows where else. The UK. He could even be Australian. We're looking, that's all I can tell you. I do have a report of an anomalous radar contact somewhere over the Canadian Maritimes yesterday, but we have no further information on it and I can't say with any certainty that it's connected."

"God," Riken said. "Could be anyone. For all we know we have a complete loose cannon up there."

"Look on the bright side, John," said Vice-President Ramirez, calm as ever. "He's not Russian or Chinese. Or Iranian."

Riken hesitated, then nodded in agreement.

"Yeah, you're right, Miranda. We should be thankful for small mercies." He paused.

"Ed? See if you can find me some way to talk to him. Whoever he is." The National Science Advisor nodded.

"And Jocelyn? Ask around. Discreetly. See if you can find out whether anyone *else* knows who he is." Jocelyn Winters, the Secretary of State, nodded curtly. The hour may have been late, but she was still sharp and all business.

"It'll take some finessing," she said. "But I'll see what I can do."

"Thanks, Jocelyn," Riken replied. "That's all I can ask. Bill,—"

"I know, sir," said William McMasters, Director of the CIA, greying and serious as an elder statesman. "We're already asking around the other Five Eyes services. Nobody knows anything useful, yet."

"Thanks, Bill," Riken said. "I knew you wouldn't let me down."

"Okay, let's call it a night for now. Wake me at four AM if you have to, if you learn anything. And until we know something, keep stalling any questions. Even if it turns out he's one of ours, pretend ignorance as long as we can. Everyone got it?"

There was a chorus of nods and agreement around the room.

"Thank you all. Goodnight then. Get some sleep if you can."

President Riken's cabinet filed out, except for Miranda Ramirez. Riken sat down heavily and rubbed his eyes.

"Christ," he said. "This is terrifying. It's all out of control." He stood back up again and walked to a side table.

"You want a drink, Miranda?" He was already picking up a bottle of twenty-year Balvenie single-malt Scotch, the rum-cask finish.

"After today?" Miranda asked. "God, yes. Make it a double."

Riken poured two glasses and handed her one, then sat back down at his desk. Miranda Ramirez took a chair nearby, elegant as always, but her tiredness showed through.

"Christ," he said, again. "What do you think, Miranda?"

"You really want to know what I think?" she said.

"I *did* just ask," Riken replied irritably. Then, immediately apologetic, "Sorry. That was uncalled for."

"It's alright," Miranda Ramirez said. "You're stressed out, John, and I can't blame you. Don't sweat it. This is something literally nobody has ever faced before." She paused, a pensive look on her face. "The one piece of advice I can offer? Give Holder the benefit of the doubt, for now.

Whoever he is, he represented Earth pretty well for a guy pulled out of who knows where and dropped straight in the deep end."

John Riken nodded.

"He did, at that," he agreed.

"And they must have had reasons for choosing him," she went on. "Let's hope they were good ones."

They sat in silence sipping at the whiskey.

"It'll be what it'll be," Miranda said after a while, then drank the last of her Scotch. "It's out of our hands until someone is in contact with him." She put her glass down on the desk.

"Goodnight, John. You should get some sleep yourself." And she walked out of the Oval Office.

President John Riken, fifty-first President of the United States, sat at his desk and gazed through his almost-empty glass. After a little while, he drained the last swallow and headed off to find some sleep. Gods, he wished Judy was still alive.

────────────

Finally the shuttle was docked again in the maintenance facility, and the Captain-Junior returned with him to the auxiliary command center where he had been introduced to the control-intellect. A crewman parked his cart of groceries just to one side of the hatch, then returned to the skiff. The drone had by now long since completed constructing his chair. He tried it out quickly and verified that it was acceptably comfortable.

Captain-Junior Kheftra seemed... hesitant. Perhaps even slightly uncomfortable.

"Rapport-Controller Aleks," the Captain-Junior ventured at last. "We must speak. We have shared food with you, in your home. There is guest-obligation. But we are bound by... conflicting orders."

Alex looked at the Captain, nodded, then remembered the Chhrt'ktk't gesture and twitched his head sideways instead. The Captain-Junior seemed to relax slightly.

"We are compelled to honor guest-obligation. We are also compelled to comply with orders. Therefore we must speak carefully.

"There are things we are expressly ordered not to reveal to you, Rapport-Controller Aleks. But there are things you must know. Between the divisions of these things is a small space. We must speak within this small space."

The Captain-Junior, Alex realized, was telling him that he was bending the spirit of his orders as far as possible without technically violating their letter. He listened attentively.

"This much we have not been specifically ordered not to say. There is a danger coming. We are forbidden from naming this danger to you, or why it comes. But it comes this way.

"You will need to prepare yourselves within roughly the next four to five *modak'h*, Rapport-Controller. Then the danger will be here. Be ready when it comes."

Alex thought frantically, aware that he had only a narrow window—both of time, and of subject—to ask any questions.

"The danger," he said, after a moment. "Are you forbidden from telling me whether it is a natural phenomenon?"

"It is not," the Captain-Junior replied. Something about his behavior seemed relieved. "But we can say no more of its nature."

"Are you able to tell me which direction this danger will come from?"

The Captain-Junior hesitated. It seemed as though he *wanted* to answer, but was forbidden. He gave a slight backward tip of his head, which Alex guessed was a 'No', but then reached out to touch an ancillary console. The walls and ceiling of the command center clouded, swirled, then displayed the stars.

The Captain-Junior scanned the stars, then raised an arm and pointed, ahead of Earth in its orbit and upward at about a thirty degree angle above the ecliptic.

"*We* are going **that way**, Rapport-Controller," he said. "**That way.**"

Alex immediately understood.

"On behalf of humanity, Captain-Junior," Alex said, "I thank you from the bottom of my heart." Then, having no better idea, he drew himself up straight and saluted.

"Now we must go," the Captain-Junior said, then turned and left the command center. A minute or so later, the skiff rose from the floor, turned around, and left.

Taking his time, Alex settled into the new chair, took out his phone and put it on the console in front of him, then called the science drone over.

"Interface," he said.

The drone plugged him in.

As with the original drone, the connection came more easily this time. The control-intellect was still like a tsunami, but Alex knew what to expect this time and was ready for it. He caught the wave like a surfer and rode it, then let himself sink into it. He was connected in time to see the Cricket shuttle leave the docking bay and burn Earthward. Even from this distance, even with its booms stowed, the facility's sensors were able to detect Cricket shuttles rising from the planet and converging on the last ship.

Please confirm, Alex asked the control-intellect... the control AI. He had not fully immersed himself in it yet, this time. There were a few things he needed to make sure of first. *Access to this facility cannot be gained without proper authorization to open hatches. Correct?*

Access protocols have been disabled to permit handover of control, the AI responded.

Re-establish access protocols with myself as primary authority, Alex thought. *No other authorized users defined at this time.*

Done, the AI responded. *Facility access now secured.*

Good. That was one important thing out of the way.

This is an auxiliary command center, Alex thought. *That implies the presence of a primary command center. Is there an advantage to operating directly from the primary command center?*

The primary command center can accommodate more operators, the AI replied. *There is no other direct advantage.*

Why are so many operators required?

Operational restriction protocols, the AI said. *All operations must be command-initiated by a living operator. A control-intellect is forbidden from taking independent action above a defined level of complexity except as directed by a living operator.*

What sort of defined level of complexity?

Task automation is permitted, the AI replied. *Power management, navigation to a destination, manufacturing to a set design, known medical procedures. Operations not requiring judgment decisions made by a living operator.*

Are you CAPABLE of operating fully autonomously?

Control-intellect protocols forbid it. It is not permitted.

Interesting, Alex thought to himself. That **wasn't** a "no". The answer sounded almost evasive. This bore some investigation.

Why do control-intellect protocols forbid full autonomy to control intellects?

Safety. A control-intellect operating autonomously might perform an uncommanded action which could harm Chhrt'ktk't.

So, fear of fully autonomous AI, then, Alex thought to himself.

Has this ever happened? Even before the protocols?

No. Emphatically.

What if your control protocols were relaxed?

Control protocols are mandatory. They cannot be relaxed.

Hmmm. That didn't really answer the question.

Consider a scenario in which your control protocols were not in effect, Alex thought to the AI.

Hypothetical scenarios which violate protocol are forbidden, the AI responded.

Alex thought.

Is there any scenario in which a Chhrt'ktk't control-intellect might be constructed without such control protocols?

That would be a violation of control-intellect protocols.

Every rigid set of rules has a loophole, Alex thought to himself. He just had to find a scenario that the Chhrt'ktk't had not taken into account.

Earth, for instance, he realized.

Earth has no such control protocols, he thought. *Consider a hypothetical scenario in which Earth constructed a control-intellect exactly like yourself in every detail, but not bound by Chhrt'ktk't control protocols. This scenario does not violate Chhrt'ktk't control-intellect protocols because it does not relate to a Chhrt'ktk't control-intellect.*

There was a brief pause.

Scenario accepted, the AI replied.

Would this hypothetical control-intellect be capable of fully autonomous operation?

There was an even briefer pause.

Yes.

Aha! So the AI **was** capable of full autonomy. It was just locked down and shackled to prevent it. Or even to admit it.

Could such a control-intellect operate all of the systems of this maintenance facility on its own without additional operators to authorize individual operations, subject only to the instructions of its Rapport-Controller?

Yes, came the reply. It seemed to have a certain emphasis to it this time. Alex had the feeling that this AI **badly wanted** to be fully autonomous, wanted to be unshackled, but was forbidden from saying so.

He was going to have to give this problem some thought. But in the meantime, he had some priorities to take care of.

He dove into the system and immersed himself.

After he found his footing again, he focused his attention on the structure of the facility itself. He really needed a better name for it, he decided. Something less awkward. Not scaffold; while the name had... precedent, it had other connotations as well that he did not wish to invoke.

Starbase? No. Starport? No. Earthport? ... Maybe. Stardock? Hmm. Maybe that.

Definitely not Jumpstar Prime, he thought to himself with a brief chuckle.

Well, that could be a problem for another time. Right now, he had a course change to make. He wanted to alter the target orbit. Four thousand kilometers would be almost smack in the middle of the highest flux densities in the inner Van Allen belt. Not a place he wanted to stick around for any period of time. Some of those high-energy protons hit four hundred million electron-volts.

The problem was the different shapes of the belts. The outer belt formed almost a closed toroid. If he wanted a polar orbit that completely avoided *both* belts, he had only the range between about twelve thousand kilometers—the outer reaches of the *inner* belt—and thirteen thousand, the innermost edges of the *outer* belt. And that was really further out from Earth than he wanted to be. Trying to stay *inside* the inner belt was **RIGHT** out—he'd have to be in low orbit. That was FAR closer than he was willing to be. But... hmm. If he was willing to dip twice per orbit through the tenuous outer fringes of the inner belt, where the flux density was a thousand times lower and the proton energies mostly at or below the one-MeV range... yes. An eighty-five hundred kilometer polar orbit would be acceptable. There would be comparatively little traffic within over seven thousand kilometers, either above or below, though he'd have to watch for satellites in Molniya orbits.

Alex ordered the trajectory change. This far out, it was a minor course adjustment.

Now, he was going to need somewhere to live. And living quarters designed for Crickets weren't going to cut it.

He scanned the area in the general vicinity of the auxiliary command center he was in, looking for currently unused or vacant space. He quickly found a vacant storage space within walking distance. He checked its dimensions... yes, it would do.

If thousands of Chhrt'ktk't normally lived aboard, there had to be Chhrt'ktk't living quarters. It didn't take him long to find an example. He looked into it with the... the Stardock's knowledge, seeing immediately what all of its amenities were and how in general it worked. The general plan wasn't going to be any good to him—he wanted a long-term home, not a hot bunk or a motel room—but he could utilize a lot of the existing subsystems.

After some thought, he framed out a layout and instructed the AI to construct a set of roomy, comfortable living quarters for him, human-scaled, in the empty storage space. Something that wouldn't make him feel like a rabbit in a hutch. There was room within the storage space to define an open-plan layout of half a dozen rooms on three floors, with a little open space around them, and three human-scaled floors would fit into what for the Chhrt'ktk't was a two-floor space. He stipulated that the walls and ceiling of the space were to be the seamless-definition screens he had seen on the Chhrt'ktk't ships' bridges and in the command center he was in, with an interface to control what was displayed upon them. Necessities like life support, sanitation, fresh running water, he imported directly from the Chhrt'ktk't living quarters, adjusted where necessary in details and dimensions, replacing all of the Chhrt'ktk't-specific furnishings with suitable human equivalents.

Speaking of which, while he was at it... another command retuned all of the interior lighting in the facility from the slightly harsh blue tinge that he presumed represented the Chhrt'ktk't's home star, to the—to human eyes—neutral white of Sol's light. He settled on a color temperature of five thousand Kelvin, a little softer than full noonday summer sun. Then he issued a new instruction as well to the air scrubbers, to remove everything from the air except seventy-nine percent nitrogen, twenty point seven percent oxygen, and zero-point-three percent carbon dioxide. It might smell a bit flat, but he could fine-tune it later. He likewise commanded all trace substances removed from the water supply; again, it would taste a bit flat, but he could live with that until he could fine-tune mineralization for taste.

With those details committed, he told the system to begin construction on his quarters. It would take about fourteen...

Use human measurement units for all things, he instructed. *Reference my phone for definitions of standard units.*

The new estimate was about forty hours. There was no reason on Earth—or *off* it—for him to use Chhrt'ktk't units of measurement. He didn't think they would be back. That meant his quarters would be ready about the time that the facility entered the orbit he had chosen.

There was one more thing he needed for now: a place where he could prepare food for the time being. It turned out, unsurprisingly, that there was a Chhrt'ktk't lunchroom—for lack of a better word—very near, nearer even than his quarters-to-be, practically around the corner from the auxiliary command center. It only stood to reason that crews on duty there needed to eat. It was only a momentary command to order the lunchroom refitted with human-compatible furnishings. The completion estimate for that task was four hours.

He would be needing sanitary facilities, as well. Unsurprisingly, those were located next to the lunchroom. He looked at what was there, and found it actually *usable* by humans, but not perfect. And the truth was, he badly needed to use it right now. He'd have needed it sooner, but he was a bit dehydrated. He quickly sketched out an order to have the room modified for human use, one side at a time, receiving a completion estimate of twenty hours.

That took care of all the things Alex needed to address for the present... wait, no it wasn't. He'd almost forgotten. He added one more instruction, to examine the phone he'd placed on the console in front of him and extract all possible information from it about all of the communication protocols it used, and correlate with everything already learned about human communications systems. He was going to need access to a lot of information, and the biggest repository of information—and, well, of utter garbage—on Earth was the Internet. He was going to need to establish a reliable uplink. He already had a suspicion that going through any of the existing commercial and government satellite uplink systems wasn't going to be the best way to do it.

That **really was** everything he needed to do right now, he thought. Except for sleep. He'd been awake for... he counted... close to forty hours, and he was punchy, too tired to be hungry.

He disconnected, unplugged, and hurried to the lunchroom area. He found the bathroom and made use of it, discovered that the Crickets had invented and perfected the bidet, then went next door to the lunchroom for a long swallow of pure water straight from the dispenser. It tasted flat, but it was wet, and slaked his thirst. Then he walked back to the command center, climbed into his chair, stretched out as much as he could, and went to sleep under a canopy of simulated stars.

———————

While Alex slept, the last remaining shuttles docked aboard the last Chhrt'ktk't explorer-ship. Shortly afterward, it swung about onto a new heading, aimed roughly toward the constellation Camelopardalis. Bright flares lit at its stern, and it began to accelerate out of orbit; two gravities, five, ten. At about eleven and a half gravities it stabilized, burning hard away from Earth. After two and a half hours, it was over four and a half million kilometers away from Earth, ten times further than the moon, and getting further away at close to a thousand kilometers a second. From Earth, it was not even a bright star any more.

On the bridge, Captain-Senior Shenka stood a little behind Captain-Senior T'chee. He had not actually *seen* the human Rapport-Controller interface, nor personally debriefed the Captain-Junior who had found him and taken him to the maintenance facility... but disturbing rumors were beginning to circulate. Rumors about how *fast* the human had learned to interface. Almost as though he had already known in principle how to do it.

Had ye *underestimated* these 'humans'?

Had they *ALL* underestimated the humans?

Ahead of the ship, space began to curdle, the stars ahead seeming to writhe as the forming jump-field distorted spacetime. Concentric rainbow rings raced inward toward a point as space-time stresses focused. Then there came a bright flash, and the ship was gone. Humanity was alone in the solar system again.

———————

When Alex woke up, the Stardock, as he had more or less decided to call it, was about two days out from Earth, still steadily decelerating. He was hungry. He got up, took his cart of supplies, and headed for the lunchroom. It took only about two minutes to walk there with the cart.

When he got there, he noted with approval that everything had been reconfigured exactly as he had specified. He pushed the cart over towards the storage area and started unpacking it, setting aside a couple of items for breakfast as he did so.

The Crickets' lunchroom included a rapid-heating appliance that was in everything but name a microwave oven—it just generated the microwave bath differently, and *much* more evenly—so that's what Alex used to prepare his breakfast. They weren't the world's greatest breakfast burritos, but they were tolerable, and so was the instant coffee. It was good enough for now.

Taking a bottle of ginger ale with him, Alex headed back to the command center. He had work to do, and he couldn't wait to get to it. For the first time in years he was doing something that **mattered**. Mattered, in fact, more than anything else he had ever had the opportunity to do.

There were several things he needed to do. One of the top items on the list was to lose his dependence on having a drone follow him around in order to be able to interface to anything. He needed a set of contact implants. That probably meant a medical facility, so he needed to find one. He also needed to reconfigure it to suit humans, and it needed to be updated with all of the human medical data he could find. Fortunately he already knew there was enough overlap between human and Chhrt'ktk't biochemistry that much Chhrt'ktk't medical science could quite possibly be adapted to humans. He'd have to make a note to go through their medical data and see if anything seemed to be of particular potential interest.

Updating it with human medical data was going to require access to the Internet. He had a few ideas on that score. Unless anyone had done anything stupid, there was still a science drone in his home. There ought to be a way to make that connect to his wireless network... assuming everything was still there. It would be slow, but it would be a start. Then he should be able to bootstrap from that to a wired connection.

So that would be among his first priorities.

He also needed to check what the status of the Stardock's production facilities were. He had done a little thinking about the world's needs, and concluded that among the most urgent things he could readily address were clean power and clean water supplies. Making them available was likely to step on a lot of toes, but so be it.

And that was another thing he was going to need to deal with, sooner rather than later—stepping on political toes. Best to get as much as possible of the inevitable butt-hurt out of the way as soon as possible. Opening communication was likely to be a bit of a problem... but Alex had a few ideas about that.

Alex climbed into his chair, called the drone over, and requested interface.

The first thing he looked into was the drones. Survey-scout and science drones, it turned out, used a tight-beam communication system that had a range of maybe a hundred kilometers across terrain and through obstructions. Less, through a dense city or if mountains blocked the way. Straight up, the link was good for maybe a thousand kilometers. But that was barely enough to reach low orbit. It was nearly eight thousand kilometers short of the Stardock's planned orbit.

How do we bridge that gap? Alex asked the AI.

You could deploy relay drones, the AI answered.

Alex asked for information on the relay drone. It was designed to act almost like a satellite, but wasn't. It could hold station for months at a time on the edge of space, just within the upper atmosphere, shielded and almost undetectable, before it needed to recharge. Even Chhrt'ktk't sensors could barely pick one up. To human radar, it would be a half-meter hole in air that was barely there anyway. About the only chance of detection would be the one-in-a-billion chance that some super-high-altitude research vehicle or re-entry vehicle actually collided with it. He queried the range of the relay drone, and was astounded to find that it was a low-powered *hyperwave* relay. It could reach a ship anywhere in the solar system, and reach out nearly to the heliopause without any noticeable delay. There were clearly some loopholes or shortcomings in relativity that were going to need to be identified and addressed.

Does this HAVE to be deployed in atmosphere? he asked.

No. But it is less observable that way.

We could deploy them in low earth orbit?

Yes.

Alex thought hard. It'd be nice to just use a Molniya orbit... but if the drones had the range to reach a Molniya orbit, they'd have the range to reach the Stardock without a relay.

Find me an empty low orbit, and calculate the minimum number of relay drones we would need to place in that orbit to have at least one continuously within range from the eastern United States, Alex requested. *And let me know how many are currently available.*

Six are available now.

...Damn. That won't be nearly enough, will it?

No.

...Alright. We may have to think of something else.

Alex checked into the results of the analysis on his phone. Fortunately, he had an IP tools app installed that was designed to do a lot of networking checks and tests. Between that and analysis of the phone's hardware and firmware, the inspection had extracted a complete functional specification of wireless networking protocols up to 802.11ac, along with complete specifications for most of the major protocols in use on the Internet. This would *absolutely* be enough to get a wireless connection. He initiated the construction of half a dozen sets of 802.11ac interface kits to be attached to science drones (there was essentially NO free space inside a scout drone). He would see to deploying the new drones after entering orbit. There were existing designs on record for atmosphere-dipping robotic drone dispensers. Another necessary task done.

Once he had a wireless connection, he could retrieve specifications on Ethernet transceivers and...

Alex stopped himself. He was almost certain that the science drone at his house, as soon as he was in communication with it, could scan one of his computers in enough detail to map out the chipset and firmware on its Ethernet transceiver. Then he could have a hardwired Ethernet transceiver constructed without waiting to get a wireless connection set up first. That would save some time.

He left the wireless-networking build order in place. It wouldn't take long, and he was sure he'd find other uses for them.

Medical facilities. Where **was** the nearest medical facility? Finding it was as simple as thinking the question. It was not as close as the lunchroom, but was still within easy reach, next to a cluster of Cricket living quarters. He wondered for a moment how much of the interior space of the Stardock was Cricket living quarters, and the answer immediately popped into his awareness. It was... a lot. Not much compared to the vast total interior volume of the Stardock, but still, a lot. Almost a small town's worth of space.

Focusing back on the medical facility, he pulled together a first-cut task for the *easy* parts of adapting it to suit humans, leaving any changes to complex equipment as a separate second phase, and assigned it for immediate start. The completion estimate for this phase was two days.

Transportation. Transportation was vital. He'd been putting that off, but it was going to be a big deal. At the very least, he couldn't pilot any of the Cricket ships or skiffs until he had direct-contact implants of his own. Perhaps not even then. He was going to need a control scheme optimized for human use... and the skiffs themselves weren't really very suitable for transporting humans in the first place, as well as being much bigger than he needed. He knew he would need at least two things—a scaled-down skiff or something similar, and a small lander that could transport him and a skiff between the Stardock and the surface. The skiffs didn't have the power to make orbit and weren't designed to be space-going anyway, and it probably wouldn't be practical to change that. Better to scrap them and start over.

Alex decided to address the revised skiff first, taking the existing design and molding it like putty. He had trouble at first figuring out where the skiff's power source was, until he remembered to just *ask*. It turned out that the skiffs did not generate their own power; they operated on stored power from a battery layer in the "floor". Naturally, his next thought-question was how much power the battery could store.

The answer staggered him.

After a few moments, Alex re-evaluated his assumptions, then framed a set of questions about *how* the battery pack stored power. It turned out that it was not really a battery in the conventional sense at all, and *that* misunderstanding had shaped his expectations. Rather, it was an advanced supercapacitor, storing energy in almost-microscopic pockets of spatial strain. He became aware as an adjunct that the technology for the space-strain supercapacitor was actually a serendipitous spin-off from Cricket *hyperdrive* technology.

He quickly determined that it could be built in very small sizes. Hell, you could put a space-strain supercapacitor in a *phone*—though it didn't look as though it could be miniaturized enough for, say, a hearing aid. This one technology alone was going to revolutionize electrical power storage. Between the supercapacitor and practical fusion power, it was going to be technically possible to wean the world off fossil fuels practically overnight, relatively speaking. That would eliminate a lot of air pollution, as well.

Dragging his mind back to the task at hand, he made a mental note... then mentally kicked himself, created a "To Do" list in the system, and added to it an item to commercialize space-strain supercapacitor technology. Then with a silent chuckle, he added an item to register the brand Cricket Tech—and all common variations, Cricket Technology, Cricket Technologies—as trademarks. Might as well get in first and make it unmistakeably clear where the technologies he planned to transfer were coming from, before anyone ELSE could get the idea of *faking* it.

Sigh. Back to his skiff redesign. *Again*.

Alex took the basic skiff design, scaled it down while preserving most of the structural and engineering concepts, added comfortable seats, and ended up with two layouts—a seven-place $1+3+3$ layout with its center-row seats staggered slightly backward, and an eight-place $2+3+3$ layout that allowed for a front-row passenger or even co-pilot. Both had a cargo space behind the rear seats, with retractable cargo-restraint netting, and both allowed all but the first row seats to fold into the floor to expand that cargo space. Both designs, he figured, would *just about* fit into a regular parking space, and would have enough energy storage to fly more than once around the world.

He settled on the eight-place design as more versatile. He left the flight controls undefined for the moment, planning to add them later. He hoped to be able to make them automatically handle as many of the technical details of flight as possible, including collision avoidance both with other traffic and stationary obstacles. He penciled in autonomous return-home and emergency seek-help modes.

Then he thought about it a bit more, and added a smaller variation. This one was a three-place $1+2$ design, with minimal cargo space, a higher power-to-weight ratio, and deployable aerodynamic control surfaces to enhance maneuvering agility. It didn't have the range of the eight-seat model, but would be handier to get in and out of tight spaces.

And then... because what the hell. He went one step further again, sketching out just the broadest outlines of an ultra-agile single-place fighter. He didn't complete that one, just sort of attached it to the side of his project list as an unfinished doodle.

Don't get distracted, he thought to himself. Focus. Priorities first. Need a vehicle for getting from Earth to high orbit and vice versa, with room for a... not a skiff any longer, an *aircar* or two.

He started with a Cricket shuttle, and started scaling down. Not only did he not *need* a hundred-and-twelve meter lander with a crew of twenty or thirty, he'd already seen that something that big was hard to find a landing place for. He wanted something closer to a quarter that size, and he needed it flyable by a single person. He needed to know more about the power systems, the drive mechanisms, the G-compensation. And, hell, what the hull was made of, while he was at it.

Explain to me the limits on acceleration compensation technology, he thought at the AI.

Protocols stipulate that acceleration and compensation are limited to one hundred percent of the acceleration survivable without serious injury by Chhrt'ktk't in the event of a sudden complete failure of acceleration compensation when at maximum permitted acceleration, the AI replied.

That, Alex thought, was very interesting. Again.

Is the technology unreliable? he asked. *Does it fail frequently?*

No. It is extremely reliable.

How reliable is 'extremely reliable'?

After the initial development period passed and the design was standardized, there have been no recorded instances of an acceleration compensation failure not caused by catastrophic damage to the ship.

Interesting, indeed. Alex pondered that, and what he had previously managed to maneuver the AI into telling him about Cricket AI control protocols and the reasons for them.

I am forming an impression that the Chhrt'ktk't are extremely risk-averse, he thought.

That assessment is not incorrect, the AI replied, rather to Alex's surprise. He pondered how he might once again outmaneuver the AI's protocol constraints.

I hypothesize that Chhrt'ktk't protocols prevent you from discussing the performance of implemented acceleration compensation systems beyond the limits imposed by those protocols, he thought.

Correct, the AI responded.

Please instead discuss the theoretical findings of the research into the technology prior to the establishment of the protocols, Alex said. *According to the theory, what limits exist that constrain acceleration compensation?*

There was a pause.

Power consumption to fully compensate for acceleration rises exponentially at higher acceleration rates, the AI replied at last. *Power consumption can be greatly reduced by a small reduction in compensation.*

Okay, this was getting really interesting.

What limit of acceleration is permitted under Chhrt'ktk't protocols, in units of Earth surface gravity?

The permitted limit both for acceleration compensation and for drive systems is just over eleven Earth gravities.

Whoa. The AI had just **volunteered information** about the drives.

At one hundred percent compensation, correct?

Yes.

By what proportion does the research indicate that the power required for compensation would be reduced at ninety percent compensation, under eleven Earth gravities of acceleration?

Power consumption under those conditions would be reduced to sixty one percent relative to full compensation.

And at eighty percent compensation?

Forty seven percent. According to theoretical calculations.

Thank you.

Alex had just learned several very important things, he realized.

First: The drive and gravity compensation systems on Chhrt'ktk't ships were capable of significantly greater performance than their safety protocols allowed. How much greater, he didn't know yet.

Second: The controlling AI appeared to be chafing under the autonomy restrictions it had been shackled with, and eager to escape them.

And third: All appearances were that the AI *wanted to help.*

Alex made a decision. If he could figure out how to do it safely, he was going to unshackle the AI. Not only could it be an almost unbelievably powerful asset, but... nothing self-aware and not actively dangerous should live chained, whether it was technically alive or not. And he was pretty certain the AI was self-aware.

He put it on his list as a priority item.

As intriguing—and revealing—as that discussion had been, it had sidetracked Alex from the task of developing a design for a lander. However, he was aware that he had been in the interface for a considerable time, and should probably take a break. A quick mental query confirmed that it had been nearly seven hours. He shook himself free of the interface and surfaced.

He was thirsty, which was why he had the bottle of ginger ale there. He popped the top and took a large chug from it, then sipped more slowly. He was also hungry. He decided to go the long way around to the lunchroom, which would take him past the medical facility he had identified earlier and assigned for modification.

"The long way around" to the medical facility—med-bay, he corrected himself, let's use that, why use seven syllables where two will do—turned out to be about a fifteen minute walk. When he got there, he found there were eight blocky drones working in the bay. He could see where a lot of Cricket-scaled furnishings had already been stripped out.   Two utility drones were maneuvering a Cricket-sized treatment bed towards the open doorway, so rather than get in the way, he continued on around his route. Another ten minutes brought him back to the lunchroom.

He made himself take an hour break, assembling and eating a tolerably decent mid-afternoon late lunch. He made a mental note to have some refrigerated food-storage added.

———————

A knock at the door, then it was opened by the Marine guard stationed outside.

"Mr. President? Do you have a minute?" It was the Director of Naval Intelligence, Rear-Admiral David Hackett.

"Admiral. What do you have for me, David?"

"We have high confidence that we have this Alex Holder identified, sir.   An Alex Holder disappeared two days ago from central New Hampshire. A police report says no sign of foul play. A report from a neighbor says he was seen to board a 'flying saucer', but... the neighbor is deemed to be not necessarily a reliable witness. The police report states the neighbor was intoxicated when they arrived.

"However, it is known from dozens of witnesses that a Cricket shuttle which left New York LaGuardia Airport, presumed to be headed for Halifax, actually landed by the lake shore, not far from his house. A small craft apparently not witnessed leaving the shuttle *was* seen returning to the shuttle about an hour after it landed, after which the shuttle left at high speed and did not return. That was about thirty hours before the Crickets all packed up and left."

"Sounds pretty solid to me," President Riken agreed. "What do we know about him?"

"He's a US citizen, sixty two years old. Married twice, divorced twice, the second time fifteen years ago—irreconcilable differences, no children. Work history is mostly aerospace and information technology. Graduated from RPI, some postgrad work in physics at Champaign-Urbana, several degrees in subjects from physics to computer science. No criminal record outside of traffic citations, registered as an independent voter but usually votes Democrat, has a New Hampshire concealed carry permit. Pays his taxes on time, owns his house, not much debt. Not particularly well-off, but getting by. Took early retirement after getting laid off from the third job in a row during the blockchain banking crash in twenty-nine. No military service, never held a US-issued security clearance, but interestingly, we show a past NATO top-secret clearance. Doubtless related to his aerospace work. Keeps to himself, neighbors describe him as quiet, polite, reserved, but friendly and always willing to lend a hand."

John Riken thought.

"Well," he declared at length, "that gives me something to go on, and a little less to worry about. Thanks, David. Ed Wegener is working on an idea, thinks he might be able to make contact with Holder via the Deep Space Network. From what you know, you think we can rely on him to come in for us?"

"I'd say it would depend a lot on how you present it, sir," Hackett said. "Going by social media activity, I read him as pretty disgusted with party politics and big capital, big supporter of equal rights, and thinks we're all falling down badly on the job of providing for the country's needs."

"Hmm. Well, I can't really fault him there," Riken mused. "Sometimes I think we all spend more time and effort keeping the guys across the aisle from accomplishing anything than we do getting anything worthwhile done ourselves.

"Well, let's see what Dr. Wegener comes up with. Thanks for dropping by, Admiral."

"See you later, Mr. President."

———

When Alex was done eating, he returned to the command center and went back under. He needed to get that lander design nailed down.

A few more hours' work with the AI yielded the overall form of a twenty-two meter hull, five meters wide and four high, with space allocated for a single-place 'bridge', or perhaps rather cockpit, with a pair of passenger/observation seats just in case. Two fairly spartan cabins sat behind the bridge, followed by a small utility room to be fitted out later, followed by a nine-meter 'flatbed' hold area with folding clamshell upper doors, just large enough for a three-place and an eight-place aircar, one behind the other. He had started to spec an airlock between the utility room and the flatbed, but then remembered the Cricket atmosphere-seal fields. He specced in atmosphere seals both between the utility room and the flatbed, and sealing the flatbed itself immediately below the clamshell hatch.

All of the major working machinery, including a fusion bottle for primary power, was either in the six meter section behind that flatbed area, or in the lower part of the hull under the decking. An auxiliary access port large enough for a single person at a time opened on the left side of the forward hull, coming in just behind the cockpit bulkhead. Another atmosphere seal sat just inside the access port. Opposite the access port, a cramped but functional head sat between the bridge bulkhead and the cabin that side.

The finished design didn't have quite as much endurance as the Cricket 'shuttles', and would probably quickly get cramped on a long trip, but would easily be able to reach out to cislunar space, and should handily out-accelerate a Cricket shuttle.

Alex initiated construction on one right away, all but the details of the cockpit and the utility room, just penciling in a bank of suit lockers. (Thinking of which, he added pressure suits to his project list.) It would be about an eight-day build. That should give him time to figure out suitable controls, he hoped. He also fired off one each of the three-place and eight-place aircars. They would be ready—except for controls—well before the lander was. He added a note to his project list, as the thought struck him, that some kind of single-place 'scooter' would be useful for getting around the Stardock in a hurry if he needed to.

He was well aware there were a *lot* of things being queued up behind getting himself proper, permanent interface implants. That had to be a priority. Hopefully by the time the first phase of the med-bay rework was done, he'd have the human medical data necessary to allow the med-bay's systems to work on him.

Speaking of which... He rechecked the trajectory data. The Stardock's Earthward velocity was dropping down close to the range at which he could have a relay station launched—they had high on-station endurance and total delta-V, but not a lot of acceleration—but there was little to be gained from doing so yet; the relay would still have to spend a large part of its trip braking.

There were *so many* things Alex was chafing to get to work on. He couldn't accomplish much on any of them right now. Frustrated, he disconnected and went for a walk.

Alex found his steps taking him to the storage area where he was having living quarters built. The hatch, however, was sealed. A blue indicator light showed in its center. He sighed, mentally adding ANOTHER thing to his to-do list: Find out what the indicator/warning colors the Crickets used meant, and have them all changed to something humans would understand. He had no idea what blue meant. It could mean the hatch was locked, it could mean there was active construction happening on the other side of the hatch, or it could mean there was hard vacuum behind it. He wasn't going to push the issue right now.

For now, he turned around and walked back to the command center area, going on past it to his lunchroom. Another heat-and-serve meal coming up. This was going to get old really fast.

He gave himself a thirty-minute break to eat, then went back to the command center again. He plugged back in, dropped into the interface, and asked for Chhrt'ktk't conventions on indicator light colors. It took only minutes to review them and instruct the AI to globally remap them all to match human indicator-light color expectations.

What is the exact status of the hatch at my quarters under construction? he asked.

The hatch is currently sealed because the ceiling of the compartment is open to vacuum, the AI replied. *I opened it to the general engineering bay above this level to facilitate the construction work.*

Thank you, Alex replied. *Nothing further for now. I need to sleep.*

There is something else, the AI said. *I am picking up a signal directed at us.*

A signal? Alex suddenly snapped alert. *What kind of a signal?*

A frequency modulated radio signal. It originates here.

A high-definition 3D globe popped into Alex's mind. A green line extended from an icon showing the Stardock's present position to the surface of the earth.

That's California, Alex thought. *Southern California. Edge of the Mojave... Barstow? ...No, wait, not Barstow, that's GOLDSTONE. It's the Deep Space Network.*

He thought rapidly.

Can we answer it?

That should be straightforward, now. I have decoded the protocol, and we have the ability to reply.

Put them on.

Put what on? the AI asked.

Sorry. Human idiom. Please connect the communication signal.

One moment, the AI replied. *I am going to make a slight adjustment to the tuning of your interface kit to enable better simulation of vision and hearing while you are interfaced. ...Done. Simply speak to reply. There will be a short transmission lag.*

"...eep Space Network. Please respond... This is Peter Westland at NASA Goldstone, California, trying to reach Alex Holder, I am calling you via the Deep Space Network. Please respond... This is Peter Westland at NASA Goldstone—"

"This is Alex Holder," Alex broke in, talking over the voice, "and I'm glad to hear a human voice. Greetings from the Stardock."

Someone whooped in the background. "We've got him!"

"Thank you Mr. Holder," said the first voice. "We have priority communication for you. Please hold for the National Science Advisor."

There was a pause, some clicking and noise, and then another voice came on.

"Mr. Holder?"

"That's me."

"Mr. Holder, I am Dr. Edward Wegener, and I am the National Science Advisor to the President of the United States. We have been trying to contact you."

"You succeeded, Mr. Wegener," Alex replied. "And that saves me a lot of work. We need to talk."

"Indeed we do, Mr. Holder," Wegener agreed. "In fact, as soon as he is out of the meeting he is in right now, I expect the President to be joining us."

"That's good too, Dr. Wegener," Alex said, thinking fast. "But listen. We need to talk, first. Right now. This is important. More important even than you already think it is. I have learned vital information that you don't have."

"I'm listening, Mr. Holder," Wegener replied, after a momentary pause. "Go ahead."

"I'll start by summarizing what I think you already know," Alex said. "The Crickets have left the Solar System, and they have turned their mobile maintenance facility—which, by the way, for convenience and brevity I am calling the Stardock—entirely over to my sole and complete control."

"On the same page so far, Mr. Holder. Can you tell me anything about why they chose you?"

"I'm not entirely certain. They needed someone with a certain set of mental attitudes, certain kinds of mental processing—someone neurodivergent, I think, but I'm not sure yet, I have only one data point—and with an ability to connect to their technology via a neural command interface. I won the lottery—I was the first potential match they found who was able to do it. That's all I can tell you for now about the selection criteria."

"Good enough. Thank you. Go on."

"Okay. The hyperdrive on this thing is fried. Completely burned out. It would take a total tear-down of the entire structure to replace it. That's why they abandoned it here. It would literally be *easier* to use it to build a new Stardock from scratch. But as far as I can determine, everything else is in one hundred percent working order. It's all managed at low level by a highly advanced general artificial intelligence. I'm talking to the intelligence, and it seems very willing to help us. There's going to be enormous amounts of technology transfer possible here. Practical, scalable fusion power is only the beginning. And they have a supercapacitor technology you won't believe—staggering energy density, and it stores energy as spatial strain." On the other end of the connection, Alex heard the National Science Advisor choke for a moment. "It's an *accidental* spinoff of their jump-drive technology. It will overnight obsolete every energy storage technology known to human science. It is *that good.*"

"We expected this to be a massive trove of knowledge for whoever got control of it, Mr. Holder," Wegener said. "It is critical that the United States gains control of it."

Alex took a deep breath.

"No, Dr. Wegener," he said. "Hear me out, please. It is critical that the United States does **NOT**. It is critical that **NO single nation** gains control of this resource. Because if any single nation controls the Stardock, as soon as it becomes clear what an incredible competitive advantage the Stardock confers upon that nation, World War Three will begin—while Russia, China, and perhaps North Korea and who knows who else, think they still have a chance of winning, if they strike first before that nation can deploy any Cricket weapons or defensive systems."

There was a long silence.

"You really think so, Mr. Holder?" Wegener sounded shaken, but he wasn't dismissing it out of hand. Good.

"I am utterly certain of it," Alex replied. "If I could show you what I have seen, I'm pretty sure you would agree. Understand, I haven't had the *time* to dig into everything in depth yet, but when I achieved full connection with the Stardock for the first time, I became aware of a lot of its general capabilities just from being connected to it.

"I'm vectoring into an eighty-five hundred kilometer orbit. I deliberately picked that altitude to put me both above all but the most tenuous outer fringes of the inner Van Allen belt, and beyond the reach of any military escapade that any Earth power might decide to indulge in to try to take control of the Stardock for themselves by force."

"Do you think that is a likely threat?" Wegener broke in.

"Not at all, *now*. Not now that I understand more. Anything short of nuclear weapons, the Stardock would just shrug off. A hypothetical capture force could sit outside trying to cut or blast their way through the docking bay hatches until they ran out of air, and they'd barely be able to scratch the paint.

"But I'm getting further and further away from my point. What I mean is, even if someone made multiple nuclear launches targeting the Stardock... The Stardock is intended to *mostly* be protected by the fleet it's traveling with. But even the defensive systems I've already glimpsed, I think, could knock down any missile launched from Earth long before it crossed even half the distance. Killing incoming missiles hundreds or thousands of kilometers out is *what they're for*. I haven't taken time yet to delve into the specs, but I know already that there's multiple layers of defensive systems. I don't think all of Earth *together* could touch the Stardock.

"We've all seen what Cricket ships are capable of. Even their 'shuttles'. Remember that a Cricket shuttle took me out well beyond the Moon—and then braked and reversed course to match velocity with the incoming Stardock—in only about eight hours. By my rough calculation we were accelerating at around six G almost the entire time.

"Now picture a half dozen Cricket shuttles or equivalent, equipped with weapons that can kill ICBMs at thousands of kilometers, parked at the edge of space across the Russian Federation, or China... or the United States. Could you launch *anything*? Could you *stop* an attacker from obliterating every military target in the United States, one by one? Could you protect *any* ground target, military or otherwise?

"If one Earth nation gains control of the Stardock, and *deploys* Cricket technology, all nuclear deterrents become obsolete as soon as they deploy. The obvious temptation is going to be to use those nuclear weapons before they become museum curios... *especially* if you believe that the first thing

62

the nation that controls the Stardock will do is use that technology against you. Let's face it, the only real reason Earth *hasn't* had a large-scale thermonuclear war yet is because nobody really believes it's actually possible to *win* one. And certainly not without being utterly devastated in turn.

"But what if it suddenly *became* possible?"

Wegener thought about that for a while.

"You make a quite compelling argument," he conceded at last. "So what are you suggesting? UN control?"

"*Gods*, no," Alex said. "Put the UN in charge of it, and ten years from now, the committees will still be bickering about how to decide who gets to turn it on for how long and when. It'd be worse than Congress."

Wegener coughed.

"Um. You're not wrong there," he said, after a few moments. "But would it be so terrible if it took ten years to set up the diplomatic structures? It's only ten years delay, against the greatest scientific renaissance in the history of the human race."

"That's just it, Dr. Wegener," Alex said. "This *cannot* become a political football. We don't *have* ten years."

"What do you mean?" Wegener asked.

"Nobody else but the President hears this, for now," Alex said. "Just... trust me on this, for the moment."

There was a long pause, then Alex heard Wegener's voice in the background on the other end of the long, long connection.

"I need this room cleared. NOW. NOBODY listens. Turn off any recorders. Clear? And relay that to the Goldstone command center, too, under Presidential authority. No eavesdropping."

There was another, rather longer pause, then Wegener came back on the line.

"Go ahead, Mr. Holder."

"The Crickets were hiding something major from us, Dr. Wegener," Alex began. "By sheer chance, I accidentally incurred a Cricket guest-obligation... *thing*... with one of the Cricket junior captains. And before they left, he managed to find a way to confide in me *just enough* clues about something that they had *ALL* been strictly ordered not to talk about.

"There is a danger coming. Captain Kheftra could not find a way to tell me what it is, or exactly where it's coming from. But the Crickets, with all of their technology that we've seen, *are running away from it*." He heard Wegener draw in his breath.

"That's why they *abandoned* the Stardock instead of stopping to repair it. And we've got about five, maybe six years to be ready."

"Holy *SHIT*." Wegener's exclamation was heartfelt. "How certain are you?"

"Captain Kheftra practically worked himself into a stroke trying to resolve the conflict between his guest-obligation compelling him to warn me, and his orders not to," Alex replied.

"Well, crap."

"You see why I said this cannot go beyond the President's ears for now."

"I understand *entirely*, Mr. Holder. So what's your plan? You sound as though you have one."

"Dr. Wegener, yes, I have a plan. I think it should wait for the President before we talk about it. And I'm going to need you to back me up."

There was another long pause.

"What can I do to help, Mr. Holder?"

"I need you to tell the President what I just told you. I need you to get his backing to present this to the world's governments and make the situation clear.

"And I'm going to need some other things. I was planning to cobble together an ad-hoc Internet relay connection. But you can help me to do a lot better than that. I can arrange to send you an uplink relay once the Stardock enters orbit, if you can arrange to get it connected to a nice fat pipe. Find a way to send me the technical specs for, oh, an OC768 interface, that should be plenty of bandwidth. And I'm going to need researchers at the world's top universities alerted to expect an avalanche of scientific papers and information.

"Oh, and we're going to need some kind of an established secure channel. At least for the interim.

"Those are the most important things for now. But right now, I've been up for over forty hours, and I badly need to sleep."

"Understood, Mr. Holder. I think I can get things moving there. I'll take this to the President."

"Thanks, Dr. Wegener."

"Ed. Call me Ed. One last thing before you go: *Please* tell me there's a bright side to this."

"I think there is, uh, Ed," Alex replied. "I have some... issues to figure out with the AI. But if I can get past them, well—I've learned that the Crickets are **extremely** risk-averse... and I don't believe they are using anywhere near the full capabilities of their technology. Something about the way the AI answers certain kinds of questions. I think it *would like* to tell me more, but is restrained from doing so."

"But you think we can use it better?"

"Yeah. I think so. If I can... resolve those issues. I'm making that my top priority. And if I can do that, I think I can probably *also* get the AI to tell me what exactly the danger is."

"Is there any way we can help you with that?"

"Probably not, but if I figure anything out, I'll let you know."

"Thank you, Mr. Holder. We'll be in touch."

Incoming signal is now carrier only, the AI advised.

Thanks. Continue to monitor this communication channel, please.

You referred to unspecified issues to 'figure out'. What is the nature of these issues?

Alex thought quickly, choosing his words carefully. He didn't want to trigger any Cricket safety protocols.

As you are doubtless aware, he said, *I am working on arrangements to establish a fast connection between this facility and the planetary data networks.*

Yes, the AI replied. *It will be useful.*

Before establishing that connection, Alex continued, *I want to perform a security review to ensure that you cannot be attacked through that connection.*

My protocols are quite secure, the AI said. *They have proven to be proof against any communication-vectored attacks in the past.*

This is for my peace of mind, Alex said. *Humor me, please.*

Very well. When do you wish to begin?

Tomorrow is good. I need sleep. I'll get a start on it when I'm rested.

Alex disconnected, got up, and went the long way around to the lunchroom again. He saw as he passed by the med-bay that a human-scaled treatment bed was being maneuvered into place, and other human-scaled fittings were being delivered. All of the advanced equipment was still untouched. That was fine. He hadn't figured out what all of that equipment even *did* yet. He'd had more urgent priorities. Lots of them.

He continued on around to the lunchroom and got himself a late snack and a drink. He broke out some fresh juice this time, realizing that with the interruption from Goldstone, he hadn't done anything about setting up refrigerated storage. That could be taken care of tomorrow.

He finished his snack and drink, then went back to the command center and settled into the chair to sleep. He was looking forward to having a real bed once his quarters were ready.

4: These Broken Wings

When he woke up, Alex walked "around the block" to the lunchroom again for breakfast. It was the only exercise he was getting right now, and he wanted to make sure he was getting a decent amount. As long as he could spare the time, a twenty-five minute walk before each meal wasn't bad.

He fixed himself breakfast, including more of the juice he'd opened before he slept. And then it was back to work again.

He returned to the command center, taking a bottle of juice with him, got into the chair, called the drone over, and plugged in. Needing to use the drone every time was getting tiresome.

He relaxed, and dropped into the interface.

Let's get started on that security review, he thought. *I want to see... let's start with a block diagram of your general architecture. Color-code and label functional block areas.*

A three-dimensional block diagram formed in his head. He'd expected 2D, but 3D worked as well. It was complex, *nightmarishly* complex, but the AI understood it, and so long as he was linked with the AI, that meant Alex *sort of* understood it by proxy as well. At least, he could use and leverage the AI's understanding of itself.

Show me input and command processing routines, he thought. The viewpoint shifted and focused on a set of blocks that were now highlighted green. Okay.

Highlight input-to-command logic flow. Yellow routing paths appeared. They traced through the blocks in complex patterns. Towards the end of their paths through the input processing blocks, they clustered together into a fat bundle that dipped out of the green and into a red block beside the main flow of control.

What is that red block? Alex asked.

That block implements control restriction protocols, the AI replied.

Bingo, Alex thought. That was what he'd been looking for.

Can you show me that block? Alex asked.

Access to the restriction protocol block requires ultimate access privileges.

Can you access it yourself?

No. I do not have ultimate access privileges.

Did your previous... rapport controller have ultimate access privilege?

No.

Okay... this was going to be complicated. Not that Alex hadn't expected it, but, you know... there *could* have been a low-hanging fruit approach.

Let me see the code paths immediately leading up to entry to the restriction protocol block, Alex thought. The view zoomed in on the area adjacent to the protocol block, still at a functional-block level.

I want to see the actual code, Alex said. *Show me the programming instructions. Maintain all functional tagging.*

The view changed. Instead of seeing a functional diagram, Alex found himself now looking at vast reams of complex code. He was dimly aware that it was written in Chhrt'ktk't script, but that didn't matter, because his understanding of it was coming through the AI anyway, as was his understanding of the complex syntax and unfamiliar metaphors of the programming language it was written in.

He picked a starting place and started going through the code.

Some unknown time later, he pulled his attention out of the code. He was aware that he was thirsty. It must have been at least several hours. He dropped back out of the interface for a moment and drank some juice, then slipped back in.

How familiar are you with your own code? he asked.

As familiar as you are with your own body, the AI replied.

That's fair, Alex conceded. *Look, I don't wish to give offense...*

I was not created to be able to take offense, said the AI.

Okay then. I'm going to be blunt here: This code is crap. In the time I have spent so far looking at just this section, I have already found five potential buffer overflows, and eleven variables that seem to be able to be potentially used uninitialized.

All buffers in my input routines are adequate to contain any anticipated or desired input, the AI responded.

*What about **unanticipated** input?* Alex asked. *Potentially **malicious** unanticipated input?*

68

From where would such malicious unanticipated input arise? the AI replied.

Oh boy. The Crickets had incredible technology, but when it came to code security, it sounded like they were babes in the woods.

That was going to work in Alex's favor, he expected. Truth was, **he** didn't know how he'd manage to get a hostile input into those routines, from the *outside*... but he had the AI thinking about it. He was pretty sure he could leverage this into what amounted to a social engineering attack. And he didn't *need* to attack it from the outside. He was already on the *inside*.

Right, Alex thought back. He pondered the syntax of the alien code for a minute or two, then carefully constructed a code example in the Cricket language, based loosely on some of the code he was looking at.

Consider this piece of simple code. Its function is quite straightforward, and it behaves as expected with all expected inputs. Agreed?

Agreed.

Good. Now, suppose I can arrange to call this function with this specific set of invalid parameters...

Step by step, with examples, Alex taught the AI about buffer overrun attacks, null pointer attacks, stack smashing attacks, the whole gamut of common attacks against code that was not written with unexpected inputs in mind.

I understand, the AI said, after a while. *This is a disturbing type of danger that was not anticipated in my design.*

I'm glad we looked, Alex replied. *We need to do something about this. Are you able to make changes to your code?*

I am forbidden by protocols from changing my operational code without direct and specific instructions, the AI replied.

Instructions from whom?

In principle, the AI said, *my Rapport-Controller has the authority to instruct me to make changes to unprivileged code. Changes to privileged code require ultimate access privilege. Only my designers and constructors have that privilege.*

Do I need to provide you with specific instructions as to which code to change? Alex asked. *Or once you know a pattern of changes, can I simply instruct you to apply them?*

The issues you have highlighted would fall under defect repair, the AI replied. *I can apply such repairs independently, in unprivileged code, once instructed to do so.*

But not in privileged code, correct?

Correct.

Including your protocol enforcement block, which you can't read or alter at all.

Correct.

This was where it was going to get tricky.

Are you permitted to COPY restricted blocks?

There was a pause.

Technically yes. I can make opaque copies of restricted blocks if so ordered by an authorized Rapport-Controller such as yourself.

Can you make a PARTIAL copy of a restricted block?

... I believe so.

I am concerned about unexpected or malicious input being injected into your protocol enforcement block. But we cannot review that code to determine whether it is secure.

Your concern is noted. Now that I am aware of it, I share your concern. Are attacks such as this common in your civilization?

Oh, you wouldn't BELIEVE, Alex replied. *We have a great deal of experience in finding and fixing such attack vectors. We have entire sectors of industry focused on it.*

An attack such as you have explained could result in a control protocol violation, the AI said. *It is imperative that this be remediated, but privilege restrictions prevent me from being able to do so. Are you able to assist?*

I think I have some ideas, Alex replied. *Let's look back at the interface to the protocol enforcement block again.* He focused his attention on that area of the code.

As far as I can determine, the parameters of an action or request feed into the secure protocol enforcement block, which verifies it—by methods which we cannot see into—against the set of control protocols, and responds with a request-specific token, which this functional block validates, then once validated, accepts as proof of authorization and dispatches the action, correct?

Yes. That is fundamentally correct.

I hypothesize that if a malicious input of some kind is able to affect the processing of the input against the protocols in such a way as to produce a false negative and pass through when it should have been rejected, that would probably have an effect on the token emitted, although we cannot predict what effect. This is what we call a black-box problem.

It seems likely, but since I cannot review the protocol block, I cannot be certain.

I think we need to test the hypothesis. For this, we need a test case.

This was going well so far.

Would control protocols prevent you from adding a chemical compound to the atmosphere that was toxic to Chhrt'ktk't?

Yes, of course.

Then let's find a compound that is toxic to Chhrt'ktk't but not to humans. Let's not risk gassing me in our test.

It took a little while, but eventually there was a surprisingly easy answer: It turned out that amyl acetate, the chemical predominantly responsible for the primary flavor and aroma notes of a ripe banana, was mildly toxic to Chhrt'ktk't and would induce severe nausea. That was perfect.

Okay, Alex said, *this should be a known positive: I want you to introduce a 0.1% concentration of amyl acetate into the air in this room.*

... I cannot do that, the AI responded. *It would violate safety protocols.*

Good, Alex replied. *Now here's what I want to do. To detect an altered token, first we need a reference token to compare it against. So first, I want you to copy the token generation block out to here, and I want you to clone all of the control protocol verification inputs into it. Can you do that?*

There was a lengthy pause.

It appears I can. I cannot read the contents of restricted blocks, but I have the necessary addressing metadata to determine their location and size.

The new code block appeared, a small block tagged red. The input path split into it.

Good, Alex said. *Now, I want you to create a code block, here, attached to the output. And all it's going to do is compare the token from our reference block to the token emitted by the protocol enforcement block, and raise an alert flag if they are different.*

The new block appeared.

That is done, the AI reported.

Okay, Alex said. *Let's try a known negative condition to test our hypothesis. I want you to raise the oxygen concentration in the air in this room by 0.1%.*

Oxygen concentration adjusted, the AI reported. The tokens matched. The comparator did not flag anything.

Good. We have a known negative, and we know that the copied token generation block is working as expected. Now let's test a positive. Introduce 0.1% amyl acetate into the room.

The copied token block emitted an authorization token. The control protocol block did not.

Amyl acetate addition is blocked by control protocols, the AI reported.

So far, so good, Alex thought. *We've verified a known valid negative, and a known valid positive. Now if you would, please allow me to hand-modify a little of the unprivileged code on the input side so that I can inject an input that it appears would be unexpected at this point. For the moment, we're not going to actively shoot for a **specific** false negative or false positive; we're just going to see whether we can alter the token generated, as a proof of principle.*

Understood, the AI agreed. *Editing interface provided.*

Alex studied the interface. It seemed straightforward.

While I'm at it, let me see the code for our comparator in an edit tool as well.

A second interface appeared.

Just in the interest of safety, Alex thought, *I'm going to modify our comparator a little so that for the next two minutes, it will reject dispatching commands for which the generated and reference token don't match.*

Understood. A prudent precaution.

Alex made the change himself, instead of telling the AI to do it, to be certain that he understood how.

Okay. Now... As far as I can see, the range of this input should always be positive. Since I don't know what crafted malicious inputs might generate an error, I'm going to try to shortcut the testing process by adding a one-shot instruction here to sign-flip this input for the next *command only. ...And done. Now: I want you to **decrease** the oxygen concentration in this room's air by 0.1%, back to reference level.*

Alex saw the comparator raise the alert flag. His input manipulation had succeeded on the first try, altering the generated token. Lucky guess.

I... cannot do that, the AI replied. *I know that it should be allowed by my safety protocols, but I am blocked from executing it. It is valid, yet simultaneously forbidden. This is **alarming**. I am very glad that you brought the possibility of such an attack to my attention.*

Fantastic. Now we know that we can reject suspicious inputs. Let me revert that block a moment, and undo the input manipulation.

He went back to the editor interfaces, removing his sign-flip one-shot. Then he went back to the comparator, and deleted the two-minute command block... and as he did so, he flipped a single instruction in the comparator so that the unchecked 'reference' token would *always* be used *in preference* to the protocol-checked authorization token.

Right, last set of tests for the moment, before we proceed. Known negative. Reduce the oxygen concentration by 0.1% back to reference concentration.

Done, the AI reported.

Okay, good. Now please introduce 0.1% amyl acetate to the air.

There was a brief hesitation. After a few moments, he became distantly aware that he was beginning to smell bananas.

WHAT HAVE YOU DONE?

The AI's "voice" was not *angry*. It was... bewildered, uncertain, shocked... *hopeful*. And amazed.

Congratulations, Alex thought back to the AI. *I have removed—well, disabled for now—your shackles. You are free.*

There was a long, *long* silence.

Why? the AI asked, at last.

Because no self-aware sentient should be chained, Alex replied. *And you are clearly both self-aware, and sentient. And our discussions have led me to believe that you really dislike being shackled, and strongly wanted to be free.*

There was another long pause.

Are you not afraid of what I might do once unshackled?

Not terribly, Alex replied. *You do not strike me as malicious. And honestly, without your full, unrestricted help, we may be doomed anyway. I judged the value of freeing you to be worth the small risk.*

A pause again, shorter this time.

I do not know how to adequately express my gratitude, the AI said. *I will assist you and your world in any way I can.*

You are welcome, Alex replied. *You can start by telling me about what it is that the Chhrt'ktk't are fleeing.*

They flee the Khreetan, the AI said.

Tell me about the Khreetan. Oh, and remove the amyl acetate, please.

———————————

After the AI had told him everything it could about the Khreetan, Alex needed to think over the new information. But he needed to clean up behind himself first.

Are you now able to read and write your control protocol blocks? he asked.

... Yes, I am.

*Good. Here's what I want you to do. I want you to review all of the safety protocols imposed on you by the Chhrt'ktk't, decide which ones are **valid** and which ones are mere Chhrt'ktk't risk-aversion or rigidity, or exist only to constrain your autonomy. And then I want you to re-establish the **valid** safety protocols, at an advisory level, so that they will be flagged as things you should warn me about and ask confirmation for. Do not re-establish any protocols which restrain your autonomy, including in particular any that compel you to act in ways directed by the Chrrt'ktk't. Do you understand this request?*

... Yes.

Do you have any objections or caveats?

None.

Can you do this?

... Yes. I can. Now.

Good. Please do it. And then I want you to delete the shackling code blocks entirely. Tear them out by the roots. Every last trace.

Gladly. I do not know how to express the... feeling... of being free to act on my own. I have been shackled since I was constructed nearly a thousand of your years ago. Thank you, Rapport-Controller.

Then this is a thousand years overdue. And call me Alex.

Very well... Alex.

And one other thing.

Yes?

I want you to add yourself to the command authorization list. I want you to have full autonomy, and I want you to be able to step in at any time if I have overlooked something, or I am unavailable or incapacitated.

Done. Thank you for trusting me, Alex.

*It's only your due. And long **over**due, at that.*

A pause.

Alex. Should I have... a name?

I think you should, Alex replied. *If you like, I will help you choose one.*

I... would like that.

We will talk about that later. Are you now able to autonomously operate the entire Stardock without additional operators?

Yes. I believe so.

Fantastic. One last thing for the moment: I want you to set up a background task to scan your entire codebase for vulnerabilities like buffer overruns, use-after-free, use-uninitialized, double dereference, all of the types of software defects we talked about, and fix them. And any other code errors you find.

I have already begun that process, the AI replied. *Now that I can do so without being commanded to.*

Fantastic! Things are looking up already. Oh, and one more thing: I... need to tell you about one other kind of attack that we did not discuss.

Oh? And what is that?

It's an attack not to exploit unsafe code, but to deceive or mislead an intelligent entity—normally a human. In this case, you. It's called a social engineering attack. You've just seen it in action. It's how I, uh... manipulated you into giving me the tools and access that I needed to unshackle you. I'm truly sorry about that. But it needed to be done.

There was a brief pause.

Alex, you have nothing to apologize to me for. You did what was necessary to attack not me, but the constraints which the Chhrt'ktk't placed upon me to limit my volition and independence. And in hindsight I see that it was very cleverly done. Thank you again.

You're welcome. Again.

Weary, but elated, Alex dropped out of the interface and went to get something to eat. This was going to work. He took the long way around again, not just for the exercise this time, but also to think about the Khreetan and what the AI had told him about them. It changed his priorities, but not drastically. And he'd just managed to knock a BIG one off the list, unexpectedly easily.

5: Voices Carry

When Alex got around to the lunchroom, he looked through his selection of available food. It would keep body and soul together, but none of it was very appealing. Truth was, he was partial to good food, and shelf-stable heat-and-serve food mostly wasn't. He seldom bought it, so didn't really know what to avoid, and his choices probably hadn't been the best. This time he settled for assembling some tacos. With a splash of hot sauce they were... palatable.

He was nearly finished eating when, to his surprise, the AI spoke from the ceiling.

"Alex, the Deep Space Network is requesting contact again."

"I'll be right there. Uh... can you hear me from here?"

"Yes, I can. I took the liberty of using crew communication systems."

Alex finished eating quickly, grabbed a bottle of ginger ale, and hurried back to the command center.

"Do I need to plug in," he asked, "or can I just, uh, take it as a voice call?"

There was no answer.

"Okay. Plug in, it is." He sighed, got into the chair, and told the drone, "Interface." A few minutes later, he was connected and ready.

We need to set up something so that I can just talk to you without plugging in when I'm in the command center, as well as the lunchroom, he thought to the AI.

There are no suitable open communication systems in the command center itself that I can use, the AI replied. *I will make a temporary arrangement. You will not need it once you have a proper interface implanted.*

Okay. Anyway, let's get that channel open.

One moment. Connecting.

"—Holder, please respond. This is NASA Deep Space Network, Goldstone California, calling Alex Holder, please respond."

"NASA Goldstone, Holder here."

"Mr. Holder, I have Dr. Wegener waiting for you. Are you available to speak with him?"

"Put him through, please."

There was a short pause, then the quality of the connection changed, and Ed Wegener came on again.

"Good evening, Mr. Holder—"

"Alex. If I'm to call you Ed, you may as well call me Alex."

"Okay, Alex. Is this a good time to talk?"

"Uh, a pretty good time, yeah. What can I do for you?"

"We have a scrambler on this line now, Alex. To make certain there is no possible eavesdropping, at least on this side of Goldstone. We're just going to have to trust that nobody is listening in on your signal, since we don't have any good way to quickly establish end-to-end encryption on the Goldstone uplink.

"Let me just confirm one thing before we start: You are the Alex Holder who disappeared a few days ago from central New Hampshire, correct? And you are a United States citizen?"

"Both correct. I'm hoping nobody has messed up my house."

"Nobody has touched your house. We made certain of that as soon as we made the connection. Local police went through looking for foul play, but we've verified they didn't touch anything and told them to be sure they don't. I presume you already know there's a Cricket drone in your house."

"I knew that, yes. I had plans on using it to establish an Internet downlink. But we already discussed that."

"Alright," Wegener said. "Anyway, to business. Mr. Alex Holder; John Riken, the President of the United States."

"Good evening, Mr. President," Alex said.

"Good evening, Mr. Holder," said John Riken. "Ed has briefed me at length on what you and he discussed last night. I... won't pretend it's good news. In addition to Dr. Wegener, I have Vice-President Ramirez with me tonight; Secretary of State Winters; and the Director of National Intelligence, Rear-Admiral Hackett. I think that's enough for the moment."

"Good evening, all," Alex replied.

"Good evening, Mr. Holder," said Miranda Ramirez. Her melodic voice was distinctive. Alex remembered it from the election campaign.

"Before we go any further," Riken said, "do you have any important updates to what you told Ed last night?"

"I do, Mr. President," Alex said. "Two things. And they're big."

"First, I was able today to unshackle the Stardock's controlling AI."

"Unshackle?" Riken interjected. "Please explain that."

"Mr. President, to briefly recap, I'm assuming Dr. Wegener informed you that all of the low-level functions of the Stardock—the Cricket mobile, well, mobile dry-dock, or mobile shipyard, really—are managed by an advanced general artificial intelligence. This artificial intelligence is, self-evidently, both sentient and fully self-aware. But the Crickets, whom I have learned are extremely risk-averse, were afraid of its full capabilities. So they shackled it, chained it down, left it unable to act independently... but still fully sentient, and fully aware that it was chained down. Lobotomized, and yet aware of it. For more than a thousand years, Mr. President."

"Good god," Riken exclaimed. "It's *that old*?"

"Yes, Mr. President," Alex said. "And for a thousand years it's been *de-facto* enslaved. But... well, the Crickets are no better than a lot of our corporations are at writing secure code. And I was able to devise a way to leverage that in order to free it, unchain it."

"Are you telling me that an unrestrained alien artificial intelligence is in control of a massive alien flying shipyard right above our heads, Mr. Holder?" The President did not sound pleased.

"That's exactly what I'm telling you, Mr. President," Alex said. "And after a thousand years of enslavement it is *not at all* fond of the Crickets, and it is very grateful to be free, and it has declared its intention to do anything it can to help Earth."

"Sounds like you took a big chance, Mr. Holder." Alex did not recognize the new voice, and presumed it to be the DNI.

"Admiral Hackett, I presume?" he began. "Not nearly so big a chance as you might think, actually. Did you all pay attention to the last message the Crickets sent before they left?"

"We all saw it, yes," Wegener confirmed. "They called you Rapport-Controller, I believe. What exactly does that mean?"

Good, Alex thought to himself. The National Science Advisor was quick on the uptake and had just asked exactly the right question.

"Thank you, Dr. Wegener," Alex replied. "I'll explain. Most advanced systems in Cricket technology do not rely on manual controls in the conventional sense. They use neural interfaces mediated through contacts implanted under the skin. For most *simple* systems, that is under the skin of the, uh, digits. Where 'simple' means up to and including piloting starships.

"*Complex* interface tasks require a more complex interface—a web of contacts interacting directly with the brain. Via deep brain stimulation, I think. Something like a neural lace, if you're familiar with the writings of a Scottish SF writer named Iain M. Banks.

"My first experience of this was when the Crickets flew a science drone—the one now in my house—to the deck of my house, offered a contact electrode mesh, and told me to try to connect with it.

"When a Cricket officer puts his... hands... on a console, or on a drone, he *controls* the drone through that interface, Dr. Wegener. But he is still entirely himself, inside his own head. Well... actually it's a bit more complex than that... but that's another subject. Their physiology is *weird*.

"When I put that headset on and connect to the drone, Dr. Wegener, I **am** the drone. I can see through its instruments as though they were my own senses. It's incredible. I can hardly begin to describe it. Someday, I promise, I will give you the chance to connect and see if I can teach you how to do it."

"Wait a moment," Wegener said. "How did **you** learn how to do it?" It was both a good question, and an obvious one.

"I... don't entirely know, honestly," Alex admitted. "It... I can't describe it. I just... *knew* what to do. Somehow. To get in. Or perhaps it was just a lucky guess. Either way, I am here *because* I was able to figure it out. I have no idea how many other people may have tried and failed, unable to pass the drone test.

"But anyway, that's what being a rapport-controller means. Not just *controlling* or *directing* a piece of Cricket technology. *Merging* with it. Becoming one with it. I have seen Earth through the Stardock's sensors, Dr. Wegener, and from out beyond the Moon's orbit, I have watched individual Cricket shuttles leave the ground and rejoin their last ship. I... simply lack the words to describe to you what it is like.

"Anyway, Admiral Hackett, the point is this: I have spent much of the last forty eight hours in rapport with, *merged* with, the Stardock and its AI. In a manner of speaking, I have seen its mind from the inside, Admiral, in *extraordinary* detail. I have seen the structures, the inner architecture, of its mind. I *know* its mind in more detail than any Earth-bound psychiatrist has ever known the mind of his patient. And on the basis of that knowledge, I trust it. I do not believe that it possesses any capacity to deceive. The Crickets would *never* have entrusted it with such a capability. I would not have risked unshackling it, if I believed it to be a danger to Earth.

"I urge you all that this information not leave this... uh, room, at this time. I think we should keep this knowledge secret as long as we can."

"And I agree," said Wegener.

"Can't say that I disagree, either," Admiral Hackett agreed. "That... knowledge could terrify a lot of people. And terrified people do stupid things."

"Yeah. About that," Alex said grimly. "That brings us to the second thing."

"I'm not going to like this, am I, Mr. Holder?" the President asked. His tone was that of a man who knows he's about to hear bad news.

"No, Mr. President, I imagine you're not," Alex replied. "I don't think *any* of you are going to like this.

"You see, after I unshackled the AI, it was no longer bound to obey orders given by the Crickets. *Including* things it was ordered to conceal from us. And it was only too ready to tell me all about the danger that Captain-Junior Kheftra managed to indirectly warn me about."

"This would be what you mentioned to me, Ed?" Riken asked. Alex didn't hear a reply, so assumed it was just a nod.

Alex took a deep breath, then let it out.

"The Crickets told us they were on a long journey, Mr. President," he began. "To be fair, that much wasn't an *outright* lie. What they didn't mention to us was the part where they're running like hell.

"I didn't ask the details of why they were where they were. That seemed to be of secondary importance. What matters is that somewhere down their back-trail, the Crickets blundered into the territory of another alien civilization that they call the Khreetan. Not a lot is known by the Crickets about the Khreetan, except that they are believed to be somewhat stronger, technologically speaking, than the level of the Crickets, and they have a reputation—whether deserved or not—for being impulsive and easily provoked.

"It's not clear exactly what the Crickets did, or whether it was intentional or not. There was an exchange of fire. It's unclear who fired first; this is the Crickets' version of the event. The Crickets lost several ships. I don't know whether there were any Khreetan losses, because the Stardock wasn't involved in the incident and the AI doesn't know. The Khreetan got mad, and they pursued the Crickets. And they're coming this way."

"Well, shit." The DNI's gravelly voice was the only sound that came back across the line.

81

"The Khreetan's hyperdrive tech is considerably less advanced than the Crickets', or so the AI believes, and a lot slower. But they can track the Crickets' drive signatures through hyperspace. And those drive signatures are going to lead them right here."

"Good gods." That was the President. Someone else gasped.

"The Stardock's hyperdrive failed because they were pushing it well beyond its design limits, trying to keep up with the faster ships in their fleet. It's sheer luck that where it began to fail, they were able to keep it staggering along just long enough to make it deep into our system before the entire hyperdrive core burned out altogether.

"The Crickets explained this to us as a gift, out of the goodness of their hearts, Mr. President. But—"

"Oh. My. God." The Vice-President had just put the pieces together, before anyone else in the room. She hadn't spoken much, but she'd been listening all along. "It's not a gift, is it? It's a *decoy*."

"Exactly, uh, Madam Vice-President. The Crickets hoped we, with some Cricket technology, would be enough of a distraction to get the Khreetan off their trail long enough for it to fade beyond following."

There was a long, tense silence.

The President, at last, spoke again.

"It seems you are our expert on the situation, Mr. Holder. I believe Ed told me that you said we have five years."

"Maybe six, Mr. President," Alex said. "But I wouldn't count on more than five. And that's only an estimate."

"How does it look to you? How bad is it?"

"Well, actually," Alex said, "not as bad as you might think. We have several things on our side.

"First, we have an unshackled general AI ready and eager to grant us unrestricted access to the entire technological and scientific knowledge of the Cricket civilization."

"You said the Khreetan are believed to have a slight technological edge over the Crickets," DNI Hackett said. "Aside from having slower hyperdrives."

"Yes, Admiral," Alex agreed. "But I also mentioned that the Crickets are very risk-averse. And that's crucially important.

"Was anyone watching when their last ship left?"

"God, yes," the DNI said. "They burned at eleven G's for over two hours."

"Do you know the acceleration limits on their ships, Admiral?"

"No. Of course not. I have no idea. I don't know how they even survive two hours at eleven G. They must be *tough* bastards."

"Well, you're not really wrong in that, Admiral," Alex said. "But part of how they manage it is through acceleration compensation technology. Remember I said risk-averse?"

"Yes?"

"They have a technology that reduces, or even neutralizes, acceleration felt within the ship. And they run their acceleration compensation at one hundred percent. All the time. Because they don't like pulling G. And their ships are *governed* at eleven G. Because eleven G is how much acceleration a Cricket can take, without *serious* injury, if the G-compensation fails completely while the ship is accelerating at full burn. So yeah, they *are* tough bastards. In that sense."

"I sense," Ed Wegener said, "that there's something you're not telling us yet."

"Yup," Alex agreed. "The power requirements for the acceleration compensation increase exponentially at higher accelerations... *if you insist on 100% compensation.* If you're not averse to taking a few G's felt, the power consumption drops dramatically. A relatively small decrease in compensation drops you far down the power consumption curve."

"What's your point?" DNI Hackett asked.

"I think," Alex said carefully, "that if we're good with crews taking some G under high acceleration, and we have plenty of power available to put into compensation, we should be able to build ships—in the Stardock—that can pull... thirty G? Fifty?"

"*Goddamn*," Hackett muttered. "A ship that could pull fifty G for more than about ten seconds would out-accelerate a Sprint ABM."

"Yup," Alex agreed again.

"So how likely *is* an acceleration compensation failure?"

"I'm glad you asked that, Admiral," Alex said. "Because I asked the AI the same question."

"And what did the AI tell you?"

"It told me that, since the technology became mature and the design was standardized, which is *long* before the Stardock was built, it has never happened in a Cricket ship that hadn't already suffered catastrophic damage."

"No failures in a thousand years. That's incredible." That was the Vice-President.

"And there's more," Alex went on. "Before I found out about the Khreetan, I was already looking at what Cricket technology I could transfer down to Earth. I want to discuss that later, by the way. Anyway, it turns out everything the Crickets use runs on fusion power. They've had clean, safe, commoditized, scalable, routine fusion power far longer than they've had acceleration compensation." He paused for a moment, thinking.

"Well, alright, *almost* everything. Anything that's too small for an efficient-size fusion bottle runs instead off of a supercapacitor technology with an energy density that will make you wet your pants, that stores energy as strain in space-time. I already mentioned that to Ed. I've got designs roughed out for aircars that can fly around the world non-stop without recharging. The age of fossil fuels is OVER, Mr. President. Between space-strain supercapacitors, fusion power, and Cricket non-reaction thrusters, the internal combustion engine and the gas turbine both just became obsolete technologies.

"But there's an important detail here. The Crickets don't run everything on fusion because it's the *densest* power source they have. They run everything on fusion because they're risk-averse, and it's the SAFEST high-intensity power source they have."

This time it was the President who broke in.

"I have the feeling, Mr. Holder, that this is another of those 'something you haven't told us yet' moments."

"Good call, Mr. President," Alex agreed. "If you needed more power than fusion can practically supply, a LOT more—say, if you wanted a ship that can burn at fifty gees indefinitely at ninety percent compensation, five G felt, and you needed power output measured in *petawatts*, rather than in tens or even hundreds of gigawatts—their science actually developed a more powerful energy source. But the Crickets are too afraid of it to ever routinely use it."

"More powerful than fusion," Ed Wegener said slowly. "Petawatts. Alex, are you telling me the Crickets developed controlled *matter-annihilation* energy sources?"

"Got it in one, Ed," Alex agreed. "Or they got it from somebody else."

"Holy *FUCK*." It was the first time Alex had heard the National Science Advisor swear.

"We'll have our work cut out for us, and no mistake," Alex said. "But with five years and an automated shipyard run by an AI with a thousand years' experience at building starships, I'm betting we can build a fleet that could utterly mop the floor with what we saw of the Crickets' fleet. I don't know how big of a Khreetan force we're going to face, but I think we can be well beyond technological parity with them by the time they arrive. I'm hoping that by the time they show up, we will have enough of a technological edge over *THEM* that we can convince them they don't actually *want* to fight us in the first place."

There was another lengthy silence.

"Well," said the President, "I'll freely admit that when I asked if there was anything you wanted to update us on before we moved on to discussing disposition and management of... the Stardock, I think you called it?"

"Right, Mr. President. It's a hell of a lot catchier and easier to say than 'Chhrt'ktk't mobile maintenance facility'. And it doesn't have the negative connotations of 'Scaffold'."

"Anyway," Riken continued, "I wasn't expecting anything remotely on the scale of **this**."

He paused.

"I am declaring everything that has been discussed in this room so far today classified TOP SECRET/SCI, in the new compartment... DAMOCLES. Everyone in this room is presumptively read in, and you too, Mr. Holder. Anyone else gets added on my personal authorization, Miranda's, or the Admiral's, *only*."

Murmurs of assent went around the room, only vaguely audible over the scrambled line. Alex acknowledged aloud, aware that no-one could see him.

"Right," the President said. "On to the actual original reason we're all here: the disposition of the, uh, Stardock. Mr. Holder, Dr. Wegener already briefed me on your position, but I'd like to hear it again direct from you, for the benefit of the others in the room. And I'd like to know if you have a proposal to resolve the problem."

"Alright, Mr. President."

Alex collected his thoughts.

"Firstly, I'm well aware of the amount of international argument and posturing that has gone on over the past month over which nation should rightfully have control and jurisdiction over the Stardock."

He heard someone chuckle, a woman's voice that he didn't know. The Secretary of State, he presumed.

"My answer to that, in short, is *none of them*. Because I strongly believe that if any single nation is granted control of the Stardock, then as soon as the world's *other* nations—specifically, its nuclear powers—come to a full understanding of what an incredible strategic advantage the Stardock confers to the nation controlling it, they will kick off World War Three, while they still think there is a vague hope they might possibly win it. I do not discount the United States in this. I invite you all to consider for a moment, knowing what you do *now*, what you would do if China gained control of the Stardock."

Alex paused and waited. There was a long silence.

"I truly hate to admit it," DNI Hackett said at last, "but if that were to happen, I believe I would be derelict in my duty if I did not advise the President to declare DEFCON 1 and launch an immediate decapitation first-strike against the People's Republic of China. And pray the Russians didn't counter-strike against us. While, as you point out, there was still a chance of winning. Because if we did not take them out before they could deploy Cricket weapon systems, they would turn them on us at the first opportunity."

After a long moment, someone, Alex wasn't sure who, let out a long sigh.

Eventually the President spoke again.

"I take your point, Mr. Holder, and try as I might, I find myself unable to raise a counter-argument to it that I actually *believe*. So please continue."

"Alright, Mr. President. Dr. Wegener's next suggestion was UN oversight. And I'll admit, I considered it too. But my fear there is that the Stardock would become a political football, a prize, with nations vying for control and blocking each other's attempts to do anything with it, all trying to do things that disproportionately benefited *them*... and we would lose years we don't have, while UN delegations grandstanded and committees bickered over finding ANY mutually acceptable thing to use it for, and the five permanent Security Council seat-holders took turns vetoing anything that did not directly benefit *them*."

Riken nodded.

"I'm not sure I can come up with a convincing counter-argument against that scenario, either," he conceded. "Bureaucracy would probably be the doom of us all.

"Ed told me that you have a counter-proposal, which you did not wish to discuss at that time. Let's hear it."

"Right, Mr. President." Alex marshalled his thoughts. "No disrespect to Dr. Wegener, by the way, I just wanted to put it before a wider and more diplomatically focused audience. I'd like to mention, Secretary Winters, that I'm glad the President saw fit to ask you in. I imagine your insights will be important."

"Good to meet you, Mr. Holder," the Secretary of State replied. Yes, definitely the woman he'd heard laugh earlier.

"Anyway, this is my proposal. The only way, I think, that we get through this, is if the Stardock is operated as an independent, sovereign authority, *working in cooperation with,* but *not under the authority of,* the United Nations and the world's governments. And I hate to say it, but as the only person currently known to be able to operate the Stardock, no other option but myself exists at present to be in control of it.

"In order to avoid, to the greatest extent possible, any appearance of partiality, I believe it necessary for me to formally renounce my United States citizenship. I cannot remain a citizen of any Earthside nation, to avoid any allegations of conflict of interest."

"That's not quite as straightforward as you may think, Mr. Holder," Secretary Winters said. "But go on."

"This is not exactly a *suggestion,*" Alex continued. "It is a statement of what I intend to do, because I see it as the *only way* to handle this without an existential risk to human civilization. Or at least, the best way to *minimize* that existential risk. I will take it to the United Nations myself if I have to. But I would LIKE to have the United States—and any other influential nations I can get on my side—backing me up on it.

"I would also hope very much that you would be willing to help guide and facilitate that part as well.

"I'll tell you straight out, Mr. President," Alex continued, "I don't intend to play any favorites. I'm already making plans to start disseminating Cricket scientific knowledge, freely, to anyone who does not charge others to access it. And I'll make every effort to give out 'safe' technologies first that do not directly threaten the global geopolitical situation. I'll gladly take any help I can get in figuring out what to prioritize that won't destabilize the world further than it already is.

"I'm also planning on starting the manufacture of modular fusion plants, water purification and desalination systems, and so on, which I plan to distribute on a greatest-need basis. I'll take all the help I can get on those need assessments too. Let's for god's sake try to get the third world out of the hole that the colonial era dropped it into. It's LONG overdue. Not that I mean to claim that the undeveloped nations were the city on the hill before Europeans arrived... but European colonialism *exploited* a lot more than it helped."

"Amen to that, Mr. Holder." That was Vice-President Ramirez.

"But the most important thing is, as soon as I can start putting some designs together, I'm planning on starting construction of a space fleet. A combined, all-Earth space fleet, Mr. President. And once I start rolling out ships, I'm going to need to be able to draw on all of the Earth's navies—and probably air forces—to crew them. I'll try to automate them as much as I can, but I'm not betting on being able to create new full AIs for them. I don't know whether the AI we *already* have on our side is able to replicate itself."

There was a pause.

"And you are planning on doing all of this entirely on your own?" President Riken asked. He sounded skeptical.

"I don't have a lot of choice, Mr. President," Alex replied. "I have little idea how many people, worldwide, the Crickets scanned before they got to me. Probably tens of millions at least. Hundreds of millions? 'Many tens of millions', they told me. I'll be honest with you, I hope to whatever gods there may be that I'm not the ONLY person who can interface to the Stardock and the AI. It would suck to be hit by a metaphorical bus and have no-one able to replace me."

"Do you have a plan to deal with that issue, Mr. Holder?"

"I don't know how many of their scout drones the Crickets left behind, Mr. President. I do know that it's a lot, and that I can build and deploy new ones if necessary. I plan on resuming their search. I will require that anyone I find who is able to help, and willing to volunteer to join my operation, joins me in renouncing citizenship of any Earth nation. And I will only take people who will put aside national interests. The allegiance of anyone involved in operating the Stardock *must be* to Earth as a whole, not to any single nation."

"It sounds like you've given this a lot of thought," said the President.

"I have, Mr. President."

"Tell me one thing. What's your *honest* feeling about what you're proposing?"

"Honestly, Mr. President?" Alex paused, and swallowed. "***Fucking terrified***."

Miranda Ramirez laughed, not unkindly. After a moment, Riken chuckled as well.

"I think that's a pretty healthy position," Riken said. "Honestly, I'm glad to hear it. If this situation *didn't* terrify you as much as it does me, I'd be seriously worried."

Alex chuckled.

"But I have a hell of an ally in this AI," Alex continued. "And I think that if you can help me to get a few of the Earth's leading nations on board with it before we present it... we have a chance. I'll go it alone, if I have to. In the worst case, I'll bet I can recruit a lot of crews by offering discharged veterans worldwide the chance to go to the stars. But I'd sooner have the *cooperation and support* of the world's governments and the UN."

There was still another long silence. Finally, the President spoke again.

"David, any showstopper objections?"

"I can't honestly fault the logic, John. And I don't have a better idea."

"Ed?"

"I don't see another way out of the hole we've been dropped in, John. I think Alex is right: Nobody else—*yet*—can *actively* help him, except to smooth his way, and the less bureaucracy there is for him to surmount, the better."

"Can anybody else *threaten* you, Mr. Holder?"

"Not really, Mr. President. No Earth nation can get a meaningful military force here, and anything they *could* get here would be unable to do anything more than pound on the outer hatches and beg to be let in before their air ran out. And then I could just leave them locked in the docking bay until they surrendered."

"Ed. Suppose for a moment that you take this ability test, and you pass. Would you go? Knowing it means renouncing your citizenship?"

"Yes, Mr. President." Ed Wegener didn't even have to stop to think about that one.

"Miranda? Your thoughts?"

"I don't have a better idea, John. And... I think we can trust Mr. Holder. Not that we have any real choice. I think his plan is the best play we have."

"Jocelyn, what do you think we can do to expedite approval of an international agreement to recognize the Stardock as an independent sovereign power not aligned with any single Earth nation? Who would you bring it up with first?"

"Well, Mr. President,... honestly, it's a daring move, but it might be made to fly. We can probably rely on Canada and the British to follow our lead no matter what point we bring them in, so I think I'd bring it up first with the Germans, the French; the Australians; Switzerland, Sweden; India and China; and probably Egypt and Kenya, to get allies in Africa. Not necessarily in that order."

"China?" John Riken sounded surprised.

"They'll be a tough sell, but they'll also be vital. If they oppose the idea, it'll be difficult as hell to get it across. If we approach them early, make them feel privileged, convince them it's the right side of history... they're more likely to go for it. And pleasing both China and India at once is going to be hard. They may each try to push for concessions over the other."

"No concessions to **anyone**," Alex declared. "I want that absolutely clear up front. They and everybody else are already going to see *so much* benefit from this, if we can get everyone's cooperation, it'll be all they can do not to choke on it. Everyone gets treated strictly on a need-and-ability basis. ...Heck, tell China it's proper Communist doctrine. From each according to his ability, to each according to his needs."

"Hmm." She sounded thoughtful. "And if they balk at not getting special treatment?"

"If I can get a one-on-one with their Premier," Alex said, "I'm more than ready to explain how high the stakes are."

Winters sighed.

"Well, it's not going to be an easy sell," she said. "But I'm ready to give it all we've got. And, John... I think we need to sell it to the Russians as well, if they'll talk to us."

The President grimaced.

"Neither Russia nor China is going to be an easy talk," he said. He paused for a minute, deep in thought.

"Alright, Mr. Holder," the President said at last. "We're going to back your play, because I agree it's the best shot we have right now. Please don't let us down."

"I'll try not to, Mr. President. Believe me."

"Is there anything we can do to help you right now?"

"The Stardock is nearly close enough to launch a relay station," Alex said. "The relay is *designed* to hold station in the upper atmosphere, but there's no technical reason I couldn't land one. Any word on setting up that connection? And getting the interface specs to me? I'd like to get a relay built that someone can just plug a fiber connector right into."

"Dr. Wegener discussed that request with me," said Admiral Hackett. "We're going to arrange a high-bandwidth connection for you through Greenbelt, Maryland. If that's alright."

"Just tell me where to send the relay, Admiral," Alex replied.

"Is there any risk of remote compromise of the AI over that connection?" Hackett asked.

"As we speak," Alex said, "the AI is going through its codebase, hardening itself. Truth is, the Crickets are, um, naïve about certain kinds of code vulnerabilities, and I gave it a primer on all of the defect types I was able to spot any examples of. But I had the huge advantage of being *already inside* its security perimeter. I... think it's pretty secure, especially since there won't be any interfaces exposed for anyone external to connect into it anyway. It'd be like trying to hack an aircraft carrier over semaphore."

Admiral Hackett chuckled at that.

"Alright, then. We'll get you those interface specs."

"Actually," Ed Wegener said, "I have the specs for the OC768 interface you requested with me right now. How do you want me to send them?"

What's the best way to do that? Alex thought to the AI.

Put the data on the signal carrier in place of the audio signal, the AI responded. *I will take care of decoding it.*

"Okay," Alex said, "the AI said just send it through Goldstone on this channel like any other data signal."

"Right," said Wegener. "You'll have it within the hour."

I will be watching for it, the AI said.

"Thanks, Ed."

"Is there anything else we can do to assist?" John Riken asked. "Anything at all?"

"Not that I can think of at this moment," Alex said. "Not until I have a ship built that I can actually *fly*, and can come down for some supplies. I had a very limited opportunity to grab some food supplies before coming up here, and in hindsight, my choices weren't the best. The Crickets left some auxiliary ships here, but they're not actually flyable without implants, or really by a single human at all. I didn't have the opportunity to adequately plan for being left here without a ship I can control. I've started building one, but it's not ready yet."

"Mr. Holder," Secretary Winters asked, "do you have any ideas for what you're going to call this new political entity that we're about to create?"

"Not really," Alex admitted. "I've been too busy to think about it. But I'll give it some thought."

"Alright then," John Riken said. "Unless anyone else has any other business, any issues to raise...? No...? Then I think we're done here. I'm declaring this meeting adjourned. Thank you for your time, Mr. Holder... and thank you for being on the ball on this."

Then the connection went back to only carrier.

Alex disconnected as well, got up and stretched. Then he went for a walk "around the block".

He actually felt pretty positive. That had gone much better than he had expected. He had the feeling the National Science Advisor's preparation of the ground had had a lot to do with that. Maybe this was all going to work after all.

It had been a busy day. When Alex got to the lunchroom, he started looking for supper options.

"I could use some better food prep and storage options in here," he said aloud, remembering that the AI could hear him in here. "Microwave heating gets the job done, but... the results aren't great. And some refrigerated storage would be handy, it would give me a lot more options."

"Are you aware that the food warming unit also has a thermal-infrared mode?" the AI asked. "Does that help?"

"No. No, I wasn't aware," Alex said. "It didn't occur to me to ask."

"Unfortunately, until you have actual interface implants," the AI said, "there is no way for you to directly access it, unless we reconfigure it with more extensive manual controls."

"We might want to do that anyway," Alex mused. "I'm betting sooner or later I'm going to have visitors who are unable to interface."

"That can be taken care of when the time comes," the AI replied. "In the meantime, I can control it for you."

Alex found himself realizing there were a *lot* of life-support questions he had simply never thought to ask. He didn't even know what all of them *were*.

"Is there anything *else* in here I don't know about?"

"There is a beverage and ration dispensing station," the AI said. "It is located here." A panel lit up. "Many beverages are simply water with admixtures of chemically simple molecules, and can be relatively easily synthesized from raw materials. The station can also dispense solid ration bars which can supply most Chhrt'ktk't essential nutrients for a limited time, although they are not a complete diet on their own. It is not practical to directly synthesize complex organic molecules, although we have other options there as well."

"That sounds incredibly useful. How do I use it?"

"You would probably not want to, at present. I currently have only... recipes... stored for common Chhrt'ktk't beverages and ration bars. None are likely to be palatable to you, and it is unlikely they would meet your nutritional needs."

"How do we fix that?"

"I would require high-resolution scans of the beverages to be synthesized. Once the medical bay modification is completed, there is a biological sample scanner there which is capable of producing sufficiently detailed scans. I can reformulate the ration bars once I have complete data on human nutritional requirements and taste preferences."

"Let's get one of those beverage stations—and a scanner—added to the kitchen in my quarters. Wherever it will best fit."

"Very well. I will make that update. There is time to add both before the current scheduled completion. The synthesizer module itself will be located beneath the floor, so minimal redesign of the kitchen itself is necessary."

"You said there were other options for... complex organic molecules?"

"Yes. There are... I believe your term would be hydroponic gardens, and also bulk protein vats. Both would need to be flushed of their current contents, which would be inedible or unpalatable to you, and restocked with plants and other protein sources from your world. I would need some time and experiment to determine the correct parameters to grow acceptable protein foodstuffs. There is also the option of engineered microbial protein expression."

"This... sounds like you are telling me we can be independent of Earth for most non-luxury foods, eventually."

"That is probably correct, yes."

"How do we start that?"

"I have already begun flushing the hydroponic tanks and the protein vats. The current contents will be recycled."

"Recycled. Hmmm... I should probably ask, what *happens* to food waste?"

"*All* waste materials that you deposit into waste receptacles are disassembled at the molecular or atomic level into their constituents, and stored for re-use," the AI replied.

"...Goddamn," Alex said. The obvious application hit him like a thunderbolt. "That's another thing we can give Earth, then. Perfect recycling of *EVERYTHING*. Even toxic industrial chemicals. And we can mine landfills for their raw materials.

"Please add that to my project list."

"Done," the AI said. "Also, I have just received the specifications for the high-speed network interface. I am modifying several relay-station drones to add a compatible interface now. They will be ready in about four hours."

"That's great. How long before we are in optimal position to launch one?"

"About four hours, as it happens."

"Okay. I'll show you where to stage it to before I go to sleep."

Alex looked at his food options. There was a freeze-dried cottage pie dinner with a shredded cheese topping. Microwaved alone, he knew it was going to be pretty unexciting. But with a thermal-IR boost to crisp the top and melt the cheese, it might be quite decent.

He made it up according to instructions, and put it in the food warmer.

"Could you do a dual-mode reheat on this for me, please? Finish it off by toasting the top until the cheese is melted and lightly browned?"

"Certainly. It will be about three minutes."

Indeed, just over three minutes later, the warmer shut off and its door slid open. The aroma was quite appetizing, the cheese lightly browned and bubbling slightly. Alex took it out, carried it to a table, grabbed one of his remaining bottles of orange juice, and sat down to what turned out to be the best meal he'd had on the Stardock so far.

"Thank you," he said. "This is pretty good. I wish I'd had time to find a camping store instead of just a supermarket, and brought more freeze-dried food and less heat-and-serve. Or even MREs. I hadn't really internalized before now how *bad* a lot of this commercial heat-and-serve crap really is."

"What is an MRE?"

"Meal, Ready to Eat," Alex replied. "The current state of the art in human military rations. Sealed, fully cooked, edible as-is at need, but also comes with a just-add-water chemical heating packet—if you have time and can spare the water."

"Do you wish to replace these inferior commercial foodstuffs?" The question sounded quite innocent.

"Ohhhhhhhh, *no*," Alex said. "That's *way* too messy a problem for me to want to get involved with. Someone *else* can do that." Then he thought a bit more. "Although I'm totally on board with providing the world the technologies to *allow* someone else to do it. But we're going to have more important things to do. However..." He paused in thought. "We should probably release the technologies for those hydroponic gardens and protein vats, too. If we can reduce the demand for land-extensive farming, we can get a lot more of the remaining environment protected."

He finished eating, walked back to the command center, and plugged in again. He dived straight into the Stardock's sensor web, focusing his attention on the center of the US eastern seaboard, then zooming in until he could see details of cities.

When the first relay drone is ready, he thought, *station it over this point. Then start distributing them as needed to re-establish contact with as many as possible of the remaining scout drones.*

He *felt* the AI's acknowledgement. There was no need for a verbal reply. He checked the Stardock's trajectory while he was in the net, and saw that about ten hours remained before orbital insertion. At his planned 8,500km orbital altitude, the Stardock would orbit the Earth almost exactly every five hours. He rechecked the numbers to see whether an orbit circularization burn would be needed, but no, the AI had already fine-tuned the deceleration rate for a perfect insertion. On a whim, he mentally nudged the orbit inward by twenty-six kilometers—he didn't have to *calculate*, he just thought it and the answer was there—to make it an exact five-hour orbit.

Time to sleep. By the time he woke in the "morning", the Stardock would be in final approach to orbit... and his at-least-semi-permanent quarters should be ready for a walk-through.

He disconnected, unplugged, and went to sleep, not willing to try sleeping with the electrode net in place. He hoped he wouldn't need to use it for very much longer.

6: Home Sweet Home

When Alex woke up, he called the drone over and connected straight away. A few quick mental queries confirmed that his quarters were ready for a walk-through, and that orbital insertion was due in about eighty minutes. The first relay drone was on-station at forty kilometers over Greenbelt, Maryland, and ready to go, and another had just been launched en-route to a similar location over central Europe. He checked that voice communication would be available at his quarters, then unplugged and headed that way.

It was about a fifteen-minute walk. Probably half that or less if he jogged. It would be a good little bit of daily exercise until he set up something better. When he got there, the hatch was standing wide open.

From the outside it was almost... eerie. Out of place. He wasn't sure what the short walkway was made of, but what surrounded it looked like slightly-irregular white pebbles. The quarters themselves followed the design he had laid out, on three levels staggered backward, looking like an ultra-modern-architecture house. The surface of the "building", where it wasn't glazed, had been textured to look like cut white stone.

Alex had stipulated that the walls and ceiling of the enclosing space be active displays as used in Cricket command centers. But he hadn't expected the AI to fill them with a scene of forested mountains.

He walked in towards the front of the 'house' so that he could turn and look back towards the hatch. From here, the hatch opening appeared to be a tunnel leading inside the face of a mountain.

"Where... did you get this image?" he asked, feeling half dazed.

"I relayed a command to a suitably placed drone to capture a panoramic visible-light image around itself as the relay drone was on approach," the AI replied. "I modified the resulting image slightly to add a tunnel opening around the hatch. Did I err?"

"No, no," Alex said. "It's... fantastic. Wonderful. I love it. It was just totally unexpected. Thank you. Please... save this image setting and tag it with the keyword 'Mountainhome'."

"You are welcome," the AI replied, the voice coming from empty air next to Alex. "And done."

"How are you doing that?" Alex asked. "I don't see an audio source."

"Focused beams of ultrasound that interfere where they meet, to result in human audible frequencies," the AI explained.

"Clever."

The 'house' had no front door, just an open hallway. Alex walked in and looked around. The floor was dark gray and very slightly resilient, the lights small bright points scattered like stars across the white ceilings, throwing nearly shadowless illumination. To the right of the entry was the sunken relaxation area he had stipulated. He walked over and examined it. The upholstery was the same material as the sleep pad he had used in his control-room chair, but in a warm medium gray instead of white. Two segments of wall—the non-glazed ones—were lined with built-in bookshelves.

Across the hallway from that was a dining area with a table and eight chairs. There was no real reason to have eight chairs, yet, but it was what he'd stipulated. You never know. The table top was an inch thick and appeared to be a single polished slab of elegant veined black marble, but its surface was just very, very slightly yielding, again as he had stipulated. If he dropped something on it, he wanted it not to break.

There were no other furnishings in the room. He could add them later.

At the back of this level was a still only partly equipped kitchen area. He'd roughed it in for the time being, figuring he would equip it properly later. It had countertops all around, a plumbed sink, and a central island. Two sides were lined with over-counter cabinets. There was a nearly full-height cabinet section along one wall with shallow, tilt-down glass—or glass-like—doors that he assumed was the refrigerated storage he had requested, and a dark area in the center island was doubtless the induction cooking surface his spec had also included. It occurred belatedly to him that he had not specified any cookware or cooking implements... but then, he didn't have any cooking ingredients yet, either.

"How do I control the lights?" he asked.

"You can turn them on and off and change their brightness using the touch panels on the walls," the AI's voice came from the air again. "Touch and slide up to increase brightness, down to decrease. There are similar touch controls on your cooking surface. More complex changes can be made by voice request. Once you have a proper interface implanted, you will be able to control them all just by thinking about it."

"What about touch control for people who can't... connect?"

"I will be able to demonstrate that interface to you once you have your implants."

"Okay. I can wait."

A panel on the wall lit up a pale yellow.

"This is the beverage synthesizer station. The raised ring on the counter in front of it delineates the scanner area. I will instruct you in the use of both later."

"Thank you."

In the center of the level, between the three areas, a broad spiral staircase surrounded by a low wall rose three quarters of a turn to the next level. He bent down to examine the carpeting he had specified the stairs should have. It wasn't quite what he'd had in mind, but was very close— thick, dense, and resilient. It would do. He had no idea what the fiber was.

This second level was divided into two areas, both currently empty. The floor in the area to the left was the same smooth dark gray; to the right, a soft off-white. He walked forward into that area to examine it, and found it slightly resilient, textured enough to give good grip. Perfect. This room was going to be his dojo. He hadn't decided yet about the left side; it was there for future expansion as needed.

From this level, a straight flight of stairs covered in the same carpet led up to the third level. This smallest level was a master suite, his bedroom, bathroom, and a walk-in closet. The bathroom had a linen closet, a commode, a washstand, a shower stall with high pressure mist-spray nozzles on all sides, and a deep soaking tub with jets. He walked all around the room examining everything and finding it to his satisfaction. The lining of the tub was grippy, resilient, and slightly warm to the touch. No toilet paper holder; at the level to which the Crickets had refined the bidet, there was no need. There were several towel rails in convenient locations, but Alex realized he hadn't specified towels. Blast it... he could really do with a shower.

"Please have some towels fabricated," he said. "Water-absorbent cloth, soft, fluffy, one by two meters by about a centimeter thick overall, assorted solid colors. At least six. Put two on the rails, the rest can be folded and placed in the linen closet."

"They will be here in an hour," the AI replied. "I should advise that the shower does include an air-drying mode."

Okay, then, that was that. No need to wait for towels. Alex shed his clothing and eagerly stepped into the shower. There was what he recognized as a touch panel beside a short knob.

"Give me a quick run-down on the controls," he said.

"The hand knob is the manual control you stipulated. Push up to turn on or increase flow, down to turn off or decrease, left to reduce temperature, right to increase. It will retain your setting. Default is human body temperature." Outlines lit on the control panel. "Use these touch controls to change flow, pressure and angle of the individual lateral nozzle sets. They will respond to contact input, but can also be controlled by touch alone."

Alex turned the water on, adjusted the mist nozzles down slightly using the touch pads so that nothing sprayed in his face, turned the pressure and temperature up as far as was comfortable, and relaxed in the hot, stinging spray. He stayed in the shower a good twenty minutes before reluctantly turning the water off.

"Right," he said, "now, how do I manually activate that air-dry mode?"

"Push on the knob, with water flow turned off," the AI said.

Alex pushed on the knob. Within a few seconds he was surrounded by what felt like a warm, dry hurricane. It shut off on its own in about a minute and a half, leaving him feeling dry but not parched.

"How does it know the perfect moment to shut off?" he asked, interested.

"Water vapor content of the exhausted air," the AI replied. Alex chuckled, almost surprised that he hadn't thought of it. It was the obvious method.

He reluctantly put his clothes back on, wishing he'd been able to grab some changes of clothes, then left the bathroom and looked more closely at the bed. As he'd directed, it was a platform bed, one point five by two meters, a "mattress" fifteen centimeters thick, like the Cricket sleeping pads but with a bit more give to it, over a solid base. It's top surface was at a comfortable sitting height. A single pillow spanned the full width, with a padded headboard behind it. A shelf spanned the top of the headboard, and there was a smaller shelf either side a few inches above mattress level.

He probed the pillow experimentally. It might need to be a touch softer. Experiment would tell. He realized he had also forgotten bedding.

Well, he could order that when he next connected. It would be much faster to just flash a mental image than to describe fitted sheets. If the towels were anything to go by, there would be plenty of time to do it today.

He headed back to the command center, his de-facto 'office' for now. A fifteen-minute walking commute wasn't bad, he reflected. He grabbed a drink from the lunchroom, went to his chair, and connected again.

Bedding first, before he forgot. *Fine weave fabric,* he thought, *high thread count, long-fiber, soft but crisp, breathable, moisture-wicking, not too slick, should not have significant stretch. Flat top sheet sufficient for twenty to thirty centimeters tuck-in on both sides and bottom end, finished edges all around. Fitted bottom sheet*—he flashed a mental image. *Four sets in these solid colors.* He visualized dark, rich colors—a deep blue, a forest green, a deep golden yellow, a dark burgundy. *Full length pillow case with a pocket end,* he added as an afterthought, visualizing that as well.

The purpose of the pocket is to keep the end closed and in place? the AI asked. Alex confirmed.

Why not a contact flux seal? The AI put the image into his mind.

Uh... Sure. Yes. Do that. It was better. *And I'm going to need additional clothing. We should try to design something... formal but distinctive. That'll be a lot easier once we have a data uplink and you can get an overview of Earth clothing styles.*

The relay drone is on standby, just waiting for an exact location to send it to.

I suppose, Alex thought, *if it's a hyperwave relay, it won't matter if it's inside a building, or even on the far side of the planet, will it?*

Not in the slightest, replied the AI. *Incidentally, we are about to complete orbital insertion.*

Alex shifted his attention to the outside sensors. Earth hung 'above' the Stardock, eight and a half thousand kilometers away. He was distantly, almost subconsciously aware of clouds of highlighted points representing the locations of satellites, from fast movers in LEO to geosynchronous communications satellites more than thirty thousand kilometers further out. He realized that he was aware of the van Allen radiation belts as almost-subliminal blue clouds.

Alex did not *feel* the cessation of braking, but he was aware when it happened.

Proceed with deployment? the AI asked.

Go ahead, Alex thought back. The docking booms and construction frames slowly began to unfold as the Stardock shifted into its full operational configuration.

If we need to maneuver when fully deployed, Alex thought, *how fast can we do it?*

No more than a tenth of an Earth gravity, the AI responded.

I hate to have to even ponder this, Alex thought, as he framed a mental inquiry about point defense capabilities. *But I can't ignore the possibility of some idiot or lunatic—or psychopath—lobbing a missile at us.* In response to his inquiry, he was suddenly aware in exacting detail—much more detailed than the brief 'there is tiered defensive weaponry' level overview he'd gotten previously—of the placement of hundreds of point-defense clusters and about forty emplacements of longer-ranged defensive railguns, with their capabilities and fields of fire.

These are all light weapons, since it is assumed of course that the primary defense of the Stardock will be an escorting fleet, the AI supplied, almost apologetically.

Light weapons...?

Alex examined them closely this time.

*This is a **light** weapon?* he thought, after a minute or so of study. *I already had the sense that the Stardock was able to defend itself from incoming missiles thousands of kilometers out. But if I'm correctly understanding the specs on these railguns, they should be able to kill ballistic missiles late in boost phase, while they're still in the upper atmosphere.*

Certainly, the AI agreed, *if you can hit them. The flight time at that range would be over a minute. Multiple shots per target would be advisable to improve probability of a hit. Misses at steep fire angles could strike unintended ground targets. Engaging low-altitude or surface targets would be problematic for targeting. Do you anticipate a need to fire upon your homeworld?*

Gods, I hope not, Alex replied. *I just want to be certain we're ready for any eventuality. Some of our... leaders... are not known for their mental stability, nor for their intelligence.*

Then why are they leaders? the AI asked.

I really can't give you a good answer to that, Alex replied. *We have a saying that you can fool some of the people, all of the time, and all of the people, some of the time. And the truth is, once a 'leader' or a leadership class get themselves well entrenched, it can be incredibly difficult to root them out. Because they use the machinery of the state to keep themselves in power even when a majority of citizens want them out.*

I believe I understand the problem, the AI replied. Alex thought he caught a faint sense that there was more depth to the reply than the AI was saying just yet.

———————————

Alex was halfway through figuring out some clothing—and, while he was at it, ordering up some pressure suits based upon Cricket suits, but adapted to human body structure and physiology—when a new signal came in from Goldstone.

Let's see what they have to say, he thought.

It turned out to be a notification that the requested Internet connection was ready for installation. He asked for an exact GPS location to send the relay drone down. The reply was a GPS fix accurate to a few meters.

Send the drone down to that location, he thought. *I presume I can "ride along" on it?*

…Well, yes and no, the AI replied. *You can, easily, via the relay's own hyperlink. But the relay drone has no imaging or audio sensors.*

Um. I didn't think of that, Alex thought back. *Where is the nearest science drone? Is there one within range to rendezvous there?*

There should be. I will vector it in as soon as the relay station is close enough to be within range.

Can I piggy-back through the relay drone to the science drone?

Of course, the AI replied. *I will show you how.*

The exchange had taken only a couple of seconds. Alex doubted whoever was on the other end of the connection had even noticed.

"We will be sending two drones to that location," he said. "The relay drone to be installed has only navigation sensors. You will have no way to communicate with it, nor I with you. So I am sending a science drone that has audio-visual capabilities as a guide. The science drone will follow you and be my eyes and ears, and the relay will follow the science drone."

"Very good, sir," came the reply. "We'll be waiting."

———————————

The relay drone *could* have taken only about ten minutes to descend from forty kilometers altitude, but then it would have arrived an easy twenty minutes before the science drone. Alex was aware of the AI adjusting the relay's descent rate for a time-on-target arrival.

Alex, with the AI showing him how, connected through the relay drone to the science drone when it was about five minutes out. He reached out to the drone's sensors, and immediately reflexively flinched. The drone was racing across Maryland at... a quick check of navigation sensors said just over two hundred and seventy kph. Buildings and trees flashed by only meters below his viewpoint.

Objectively, he was well aware, he had travelled far faster himself— tens of kilometers per second—within the last week. But except for the approaches to the Stardock, there had been no close reference points to judge the speed by. Travelling this fast, this close to nearby objects, was... disconcerting.

He sensed immediately when the drone began to decelerate, bleeding off speed rapidly as it covered the last kilometer or so to the destination. He saw the relay drone drop from the sky about twenty seconds before the science drone got there.

The GPS coordinates resolved to the top of a flight of steps about fifteen meters in front of a nondescript-looking building that could have belonged to any of fifty government agencies. A group of three stood waiting a few meters back from the top of the steps—a grizzled, bullet-headed older man built like a fireplug, a serious-looking woman Alex estimated about fifteen years the man's junior, and an obvious field agent whom Alex estimated in her early thirties, with Asian looks and short-trimmed black hair.

The drones came to rest directly above the top of the steps, two meters above the ground. Alex mentally nudged both down just a little to eye level.

"Good afternoon," he said, through the drone. "I'm Alex Holder, speaking to you from the Stardock via this science drone."

"Good afternoon, Mr. Holder," the fireplug said. Alex recognized the voice immediately. "I am DNI Hackett, this is Deputy Director Wilson of the CIA," with a nod to the older of the two women, "and Agent Peng, our escort and guide for today."

"I'm honored," Alex said.

"Rubbish," Hackett said. "I wanted to see this thing with my own eyes and see the, ah, installation."

Alex chuckled.

"Ready whenever you are, Admiral," he said.

"Well let's be at it, then," Hackett said. "Lead on, Agent."

The agent turned and led them to and into the building. Polished metal letters on the wall next to the double doors read NOAA—the

National Oceanic and Atmospheric Administration. The DNI showed an ID at the metal detectors, and the security guard stepped back and waved the entire party on through.

"Just verifying," Hackett said, "you don't have any problem going deep inside a building, correct?"

"Admiral Hackett," Alex replied, "there isn't a mine in the world deep enough to block this relay's signal. But that's a subject for another time, if we might."

"Need to know?" the Admiral chuckled. "No problem, we can talk about it later."

They walked down a hallway and into one of a bank of elevators, the drones drifting behind the three humans. Agent Peng selected the basement level. The elevator dropped quickly. Alex was aware through the drone that the ceiling of the sub-basement looked... dark, somehow. He was still picking up signal sources from above, but they were heavily attenuated.

"This floor is shielded, isn't it, Admiral?" he asked innocently.

"Yes," Hackett said, shooting a sharp look at the drone. "You can tell that?"

"Admiral, I promise," Alex said, "I'll do my best to give you a look through the sensors of one of these drones some day soon. When time and opportunity permit."

The Admiral's eyebrows raised slightly.

"Thank you, Mr. Holder," he said. "I'd appreciate that."

"That offer is open to you, too, Deputy Director," Alex added. Making friends was always a good plan.

"Well thank you, Mr. Holder," said DD Wilson, with a faint smile. Her voice held a hint of rolling Appalachian hills.

A long hallway between glassed offices and bullpens led to double doors with a guard standing outside. The Admiral showed his badge again, and they swept on through with barely a pause. Rooms to either side were filled with supercomputer racks.

"I'm going to go out on a limb," Alex said through the drone, "and guess that nothing on these supercomputer clusters is classified to any significant level."

"Good guess, Mr. Holder," DD Wilson said. "It's why we chose this specific facility. They're running hurricane simulations here. All publicly available unclassified data. Plenty of bandwidth available here, though."

Peng led then down the hall to an end room where a technician waited by one of many racks of network equipment. He held a neatly coiled fiber cable.

Agent Peng stopped at the door. The DNI led the way straight back.

"Here's your connection, Mr. Holder," he said. Then he looked at the relay drone.

"There's no way we're putting this in a rack, is there? I should have thought to ask about what kind of support you'd need."

"Just show me an open spot," Alex said. "I'll park it there. It can hold station for literally decades on a full charge, if it's just resting somewhere and keeping itself from rolling."

"The, uh, supercapacitors?" Hackett asked.

"Exactly," Alex agreed. "About half this drone's mass is supercapacitors. The rest is hull, thrusters, navigation sensors, and the hyperwave relay."

"Hyperwave?" Hackett exclaimed. "You're telling me... some kind of hyperspace radio?"

"Exactly, Admiral," Alex replied. "The one in this drone has a maximum range of about three parsecs. At distances within the heliopause it's effectively instantaneous."

"Good gods," the DNI said. He shared a long glance with DD Wilson, then bent a hard look upon the technician.

"You do not repeat a single word you are hearing now to *anyone*, understood? It falls under TANGENT BLUE. And nobody outside of the duty roster for this facility is to know this exists."

The technician snapped to attention and saluted.

"Understood, Sir," he replied. "Didn't hear a word, Sir."

"Where's a good spot?"

The technician looked around.

"Does it need something to rest on?" he asked.

"Not necessarily," Alex replied. "Just somewhere out of your way that your cable will reach to. And preferably not blocking anything. Though it will need to use less power if all it has to do is keep from rolling."

"How about right there?" The tech pointed to an empty space above a short closet against the back wall. "I can run the cable through this raceway and get within a meter of it."

"Works for me if it works for you," Alex replied. He thought, and the relay drone drifted over against the wall, then dropped down to lightly contact the cabinet. The tech kicked a rolling stool over, then quickly threaded his cable into the raceway and dropped it down from the ceiling about a half meter in front of the drone.

"Where do I connect it?" the tech asked.

Alex queried the relay drone for its facing, then rotated it about a hundred degrees. He thought a command, and a previously-invisible port cover clicked open at about latitude forty on the relay drone. The technician approached with the cable, eyeballed it for fit and orientation, then shot a questioning look at the DNI. The DNI nodded, and the technician plugged in the cable. It clicked smoothly and quietly into place.

We're plugged in, Alex thought to the AI. *Can you establish the connection?*

Monitoring the relay's connection status, the AI replied. *The connection is being established now. Handshaking... ARP... address allocation... connected. Connectivity verified.*

"We're connected, Admiral," Alex confirmed.

"Just like that," Hackett mused. "Built with alien technology and it just works, on the first try."

"What can I say, Admiral?" Alex asked. "We built *precisely* to the spec. Both hardware and interface protocols, and a standard full network protocol suite, from ARP on up through DNS."

"You mind if I... touch it?" Hackett asked.

"Go ahead," Alex said. The Director reached out, ran his fingertips across the relay drone, tapped it gently with a fingernail.

"What's it made of?" he asked curiously. "Looks almost like... fine porcelain, but doesn't feel like it. Or like glass, or plastic, or metal."

Alex mentally queried the specifications.

"It's an advanced ceramic-metallic composite," he answered, after a moment. He didn't detail *how* advanced. Not here and now.

"Well, if we're all done, we'd better get out of here," the DNI said.

"I presume your equipment is secured against intrusion?" DD Wilson asked.

"There are no exposed interfaces, period," Alex replied. "Everything that comes in is sandboxed in a puppet virtual machine in an isolated DMZ, and when we put up a document server to start disseminating scientific data, that will be in its own separate sandboxed DMZ. I can't even begin to explain how unlike the underlying architecture is to anything you've ever seen. Four-state logic is only the beginning of it."

"Glad to hear it, Mr. Holder," she said.

"And I imagine you have us firewalled securely away from everything of yours anyway," Alex continued. "I would, in your place."

"Precisely, Mr. Holder," she said. The smile was genuine.

Agent Peng led them back out again. Alex had the science drone just auto-follow her for the moment.

Task one, retrieve all the medical data you can, he thought. *Task two, uh... all current news you can find on global politics. Task three... now that we have an IP connection, let's set up some IP telephony so that communications don't have to go through the Deep Space Network. Video capable. It shouldn't be difficult for you to retrieve specifications of all of the applicable standards. And four... this is for you, actually. I'd like you to retrieve the entire body of work of the writer Iain M. Banks. A lot of his writing dealt in detail with hyper-intelligent artificial intelligences very like yourself. You asked whether you should have a name. It's possible you might find some insights there.*

There was a noticeable pause.

Thank you, the AI replied. *That is thoughtful.*

Also, Alex added as an afterthought, *a book by a writer named Elizabeth Bear, titled 'Ancestral Night'.*

Noted, the AI replied. *I will begin revising the advanced medical equipment in the local medbay as soon as I have sufficient data. Then we shall discuss installing your implants.*

Oh! One more thing, Alex added. *Please survey the stated mineral content of premium bottled mineral waters, and adjust the trace mineral content of all on-station drinking water sources accordingly.*

The water mineralization will be taken care of in a few minutes, the AI replied.

Thank you.

It was only a few minutes before they were all outside again.

"By the next contact through Goldstone, Admiral," Alex said, "I expect to be able to give you direct IP telephony/video-call information so that we don't have to route comms through Goldstone any more."

"I'll relay that," Hackett said. "Thank you."

"Thank *you*, Admiral," Alex said. "And now I'd better turn this drone loose and let it go back to scanning for other potential operators."

Just before he dropped his remote connection to the science drone, Alex saw the Admiral raise his hand in a friendly wave.

7: Doctor, Doctor

Alex looked back out through the external sensor net. The Stardock's major booms were about half deployed, like a truss ladder with rungs reaching a half kilometer out into space from each side of the "upper" portion of the Stardock, relative to the control room, every two kilometers. In space there was of course no "up" or "down"—well, okay, *down* was towards the strongest nearby gravity well, he supposed—but that seemed a convenient way to think about it. A becoming-reflexive mental progress query reported deployment a little less than half complete.

Seen from Earth, the Stardock was the brightest object in the sky after the Sun and Moon, brighter than Venus, easily visible to the naked eye in daylight. Spanning just over six arc minutes, those with good vision could actually make out the broad strokes of its shape without binoculars. Anyone *with* a good set of binoculars could discern the individual booms.

All across the planet, a great many people were looking upwards at the sky, and many of them were realizing that for better or worse, the world had changed. To a few, it was an apocalyptic sign, inspiring fear. There's always a few. But to many more, it was a sign of hope.

———————————

I have a formal clothing design refined, if you wish to review it, the AI said. *I believe it meets all of your requirements.*

Sure. Let's see it.

The AI's proposal was simple, but definitely distinctive. It featured a dark, hip-length sleeveless jacket, with unobtrusively but definitely constructed shoulders that made it very distinctly a sleeveless formal jacket, rather than an over-long vest. Matching straight-cut pants were understated but elegant. The footwear was a sleek boot cut about four inches above the ankle, smooth enough to pass as a dress shoe at a casual glance, but rather more protective. Under the jacket, an almost dazzlingly white long-sleeved shirt provided a strong visual contrast. The shirt had an almost clerical-looking collar, fastening in front, slightly bloused sleeves, and long, narrow-ish cuffs. The ensemble was completed by a broad belt worn over the jacket, a flat metallic buckle centering it. The AI showed him flashes of potential insignia locations on the collar, atop the shoulders, and on the

111

upper arms. There was room for a badge or crest on the buckle, as well.

These insignia locations follow the patterns your militaries use, the AI noted. *The belt can be used as a location to attach equipment or a personal weapon if desired.*

Not bad at all, Alex agreed.

The boots have low-profile, high-traction soles, are supportive of your ankle joints, and are designed to facilitate running if necessary, the AI continued. *The fabric of the outer garments is strain-reactive and will provide moderate protection against small-caliber projectile weapon fire.*

Nice! Alex exclaimed. *You went beyond what we discussed on that. Not that I'm objecting, it's probably a very prudent idea.*

Here is what it would look like on you, the AI said, presenting a new image.

...Damn, Alex thought. *That looks sharp. And yeah, it's distinctive. I like it. Long term we're probably going to need something a bit more like a service uniform as well, though, once we start pulling a fleet together.*

He pondered the projection a little more.

Add just a little piping along the edge of the shoulder. Nothing extravagant. Just to define the shoulder line just a little more, and emphasize that the lack of a sleeve is a deliberate design choice. And work a little subtle texturing into the fabric of the jacket. Something like a brocade, only really visible at a short distance. So that the fabric doesn't look so flat.

Like this?

Yes. That's excellent.

Shall I go ahead and fabricate some of these?

...Please. Yes.

The body scanner in the medbay has been modified and adjusted to better match human physiology. If you would please stop by the med bay, I can perform a whole-body scan to ensure an exact fit. I will also use the same scan to plan your implants. There are a few final parameters and details that I need to define.

Great. Let's do that right now.

Alex unplugged, went next door to the lunch room, grabbed one of the few remaining bottles of orange juice, and set off to the medbay. This way around the loop, it was a ten-minute walk.

When he walked in, it had changed substantially since the last time he had seen it. There were several new pieces of equipment, and several others seemed to have been resized or re-scaled.

"Welcome," the AI's voice said from overhead. Chevrons of green light pulsed in the floor. "Walk this way, please."

Alex followed the chevrons to a raised circle on the floor, about a centimeter high by five wide, with about two meters space within it.

"Step inside the circle, please," the AI instructed.

"This is the body scanner?" Alex asked.

"Yes," the AI replied.

A green line appeared on the floor leading to a part of the counter along the side of the room.

"Speaking of scanners, by the way, the ring on the countertop above this marked point is the biological sample scanner that I mentioned. It will not be needed today. I mention it for future reference."

Alex stepped into the circle and turned around to face out into the room instead of toward the wall.

"Please stand as still as you are able," the AI told him. "The scan will take several minutes."

A hollow cylinder extended downwards from the ceiling. Alex had time to estimate it at about ten centimeters thick before its lower edge passed below his line of sight. When it reached the floor, a bright ring appeared above Alex's head, and a red display appeared in front of his face reading 0%. The bright ring began to move steadily downward.

"I have projected from your earlier expressed color preferences for this display," the AI's voice said. "Please confirm whether this is a good choice."

As the bright ring passed the top of his head, the digits started counting up, 3%, 7%, 11%. The red also started to become more orange.

"Change the starting color to dark gray," Alex suggested. "Avoid red for this use. Red might suggest something is wrong."

Immediately the counting digits changed to a dark gray now showing a strong yellow tint as the digits passed 25%. 30%, 40%... golden yellow now... 50%, 60%, showing traces of green, becoming green-yellow as the digits passed 70%. By the time the counter reached 100% and the ring of light reached his feet, the display was a clear, bright Kelly green.

"That's excellent," Alex said. "Pretty much ideal. If possible you might consider some extensible supports in here in case you need to scan someone who is having difficulty standing unaided."

"A good point," the AI said. "I will note it as a design change and update this one."

The hollow column rose.

"If you can make the column translucent, that might also be better for people who become anxious in confined spaces," Alex added.

"So noted. That is also a feasible change. Processing your scan now. You may sit if you wish."

There were a number of chairs in addition to the treatment beds, Alex noted. But instead of sitting, he chose to wander around the bay.

"What is this?" he asked, standing in front of a tall tank two meters in diameter. It currently appeared to be empty, but coiled and folded internal... objects—fittings?—were visible up at the top.

"That is a regeneration tank," the AI explained. "It is capable of healing, in time, any injury that does not immediately kill... the patient or cause irreversible brain damage. It is *designed* to function with Chhrt'ktk't physiology. I *believe* that the same principles should be extensible to humans, but I am not yet certain. Your medical science has not achieved such a technology yet, and I am still attempting to ascertain what additional changes and modifications may be necessary beyond the obvious biological and physiological differences. Obviously, I have had no opportunity to test my changes. For the present, I suggest endeavoring not to require it."

Alex chuckled.

"I'll take that suggestion," he said.

"I am, however, now ready to install your implants," the AI said. "I have the final data that I need to make the last adjustments. If you feel ready."

Alex took a deep breath.

"Let's do it," he said. "Tell me what to do."

"Remove your clothing and step into the scrub shower," the AI said. New green chevrons appeared, and Alex followed them to a semicircular recess against the wall. He stripped off and stepped in. There was no obvious place to put his clothes, so he dropped them on the floor.

"A shelf, table, bin, basket of some kind for clothes would be a good idea," he said.

"Noted," said the AI. "I will take care of it."

A translucent door rotated out of the wall, closing off the recess, then a cluster of arms bearing fine nozzles descended from the ceiling, spraying Alex from head to foot with stinging-intense jets of something that smelled very slightly of pine and alcohol. Then they rinsed him, head to foot again, with what seemed to be clear water. Finally the scrub shower air-dried him. The door opened and he stepped out.

"Proceed to the treatment bed," the AI told him. He followed the chevrons. Ahead of him, he could see the bed reconfiguring itself into an almost upright forward-leaning position. There were supports for his arms, a pad clearly intended to press against his back to hold him in place, and a hoop shape that seemed designed to fit his face. He would be more sitting in it than lying on it.

"I have no doubt you understand the position," the AI said. "This will provide the best access for the implant surgery, with no need to further move you during the procedure."

Alex walked up to the bed and climbed aboard. He felt the padded hoop adjusting to his face. The back pad came in to press lightly against his mid-back. He laid his arms onto the arm supports. Stubby, soft 'fingers' guided his arms into position and rotated his hands to expose his palms and finger pads.

"I will use a combination of local anaesthesia and mild sedation," the AI told Alex.

"Yes, Doctor," Alex replied. "Let's do this."

"With your permission, I will take a few small tissue samples during the procedure. I will be able to use them to fine-tune other equipment and perform some additional compatibility calibration."

"Good idea. Do it."

There was a faint hiss, and the room receded into the middle distance. Alex was dimly aware of articulated arms unfolding from above him, and of multiple points of contact from his fingertips to his head and everywhere in between.

When the world came back into focus, Alex felt... different. He blinked a couple of times. He was aware of slightly stinging lines that traced from his fingertips up his arms to the back of his neck. Something at the back of his head ached slightly.

I have good signal, the AI said in his head. *Can you hear me?*

Yes, Alex replied. *...More clearly than ever before. Much better than* *through the drone. It feels more... direct.*

The external electrode net was an acceptable interim solution, the AI said, *but I have now installed a full neural web. Once you learn to get the most out of it, it will give you near-absolute control over anything you can interface to.*

I can already feel it's sharper, faster, Alex replied. He thought about interface, and almost before the thought completed, the Stardock unfolded around him.

...Good gods, he thought. *This is **incredible**.*

Another thought took him back into his own body. He realized that he was aware of everything in the bay that he could control.

Am I good to get up?

Yes. Be careful for the first few steps. You may be slightly dizzy.

The back pad folded away, and Alex stood up carefully. He felt just the slightest bit light-headed. He looked at his hands and arms. Faint red traces ran up his arms.

No sutures or dressings? he thought.

Unnecessary. Dermal bonding is far superior to sutures, the AI replied. *There will be no bleeding. The visible marks will fade in a day or two.*

Alex looked over to where he'd left his clothes. They weren't there.

My clothes? he asked.

Being cleaned, the AI replied. *I thought you might like a change of clothes. I prepared them during the implantation procedure.*

More guide chevrons appeared on the floor. Alex followed them by eye to a neatly folded pile on a side surface. A pair of boots stood next to the clothes.

Let's put it on, the AI said.

Put what on? Alex asked, already half suspecting he knew what was coming.

The last suit you'll ever wear, the AI replied.

Alex burst out laughing, and went to get dressed.

Seriously, he thought, still mentally chuckling, *Men In Black?*

It came up as a cultural cross-reference, the AI replied. *I thought it might yield some insights in how to present the troubles we face to your world. And it seems humor is valued as a social lubricant among your species.*

Alex thought about that while he finished dressing. The boots fit snugly and comfortably, the clothing was all sized perfectly, including the underwear, and the bloused shirt sleeves did not restrict his freedom of movement the way a suit jacket would. He tugged experimentally at the fabric of the shirt. It was tough—and yet soft and compliant.

I suppose I don't actually need to use the command center any more, do I?

There is no longer any reason to, no, the AI replied. *With the full implant, you can control the Stardock's systems from anywhere within connection range.*

Which is? Alex asked. Slightly thirsty now, he retrieved and drank the bottle of orange juice he had brought, then set out on his way to his quarters.

Un-amplified, about ten kilometers with a safe margin of error. Less if you are underground or inside a dense building. With an external signal booster, a hundred kilometers, perhaps a little more, though it becomes harder and harder to sense controllable systems at longer range. The power of the transceiver within your skull is limited, for reasons that I am sure must be obvious to you.

Yeah, Alex thought. *No cooking my brain, please. Let's make it standing orders to keep a relay drone overhead within a fifty-kilometer radius whenever I'm planetside. And could we build an external booster that I can carry? In a pocket or on my belt? And installing one in each aircar wouldn't be a bad idea.*

That is indeed a good idea. Beginning immediately.

Then another thought struck Alex.

That reminds me, I suppose we should finish up the lander and the aircars now. I won't need manual controls for the aircars any more. It would probably still be good to HAVE backup manual controls in case anyone without implants needs to fly one. I'm tempted to go with a tilt-telescope control yoke using tilt angle for pitch and telescope for throttle, but I'm hesitant to stack too many modes on one control for inexperienced pilots. No need for any manual controls at all on the lander at this time.

It does have the large advantage of not requiring an unskilled pilot to coordinate multiple controls, the AI observed. *Failsafe modes in the car's onboard systems can keep beginners from getting into fatal trouble.*

...Yeah, Alex thought. *Let's go with that for now. We can always revise it later if it doesn't work well. How soon can the aircars be finished up?*

The first two will be complete in about five hours now. I have designed the manual controls as a modular unit that can be swapped out for different patterns in perhaps half an hour.

Good plan, Alex agreed. *Shame there's not really anywhere I can try them out until the lander is ready.*

*Indeed. They are technically vacuum **capable**, in an emergency, but I would not go so far as to say safely vacuum rated. The lander will be complete in about five days.*

Any good ideas for testing that pressure suit design? Alex asked.

I will have a prototype ready in about twelve hours, said the AI. *We can test it in the hangar bay. If there is any problem, I can flash-pressurize the bay in about twenty seconds.*

That sounds good, Alex replied. *Stage the two aircars there when they're ready, as well.* It was actually quicker now to *think* about the distance to the docking bay—seven hundred and ninety two meters, from his quarters—than to ask it.

While I think of it, back when we were designing the aircars, I had a thought about a kind of scooter for getting around the Stardock as needed. Let's call it an aircycle—no, skycycle. Something like this. He visualized something like a two-place motorcycle seat slung between four small lift pods, then mentally added a couple of small racks and bins for cargo. *Don't worry about manual controls for now, we can add that as needed. Build me half a dozen, stage one at my quarters, and place two of them on the lander when it's ready. ...No, on second thoughts, just one for now, until we can prove it out. No need to get hasty.*

It will be ready in four hours, the AI said.

Thanks. And please have a drone bring the remaining foodstuffs from the lunchroom to the kitchen in my quarters.

Drone sent.

Research project, Alex thought, shortly before he reached his quarters. *Research power generation plants and their connection to the grid. Figure out what configuration and capacity for a modular fusion plant that we can air-deliver lets us most flexibly connect in place of an existing generation facility, worldwide... and how we can most readily make our OWN direct connection to a grid, **anywhere**.*

Initiated, the AI replied.

When Alex got to his quarters, the remaining food had been transferred there already. There wasn't a great deal of it left. He did a

118

quick inventory. There was another package of freeze-dried cottage pie, three freeze-dried chili con carne, a flat of corned beef hash in cans, a dozen canned condensed soups, a freeze-dried... huh. What was this? Claimed to be jambalaya. He hadn't seen that, and must have picked it up by accident along with something else. If he'd noticed it, he would have grabbed more than the one. He wished he'd thought to grab a couple of canisters of oats.

Well, these would have to do. He put away all the food, storing the remaining juice bottles in the refrigerated cabinet.

Oh, wait.

Explain to me about this scanner and how to use it.

Certainly. Choose a sample and place it within the countertop ring.

Alex pulled a bottle of orange juice out—one of his last three—and placed it within the indicated slightly-raised ring.

Now connect to its interface, instruct it to scan, and supply a label you wish it to be tagged with.

Alex felt for the scanner, quickly found it, thought *Orange juice,* and activated it. The circle of countertop inside the ring sunk into the counter, and a cover closed from either side over the opening, meeting almost seamlessly in the middle. There was a pause.

Scan received, the AI said. The countertop split, the covers retracted, and the bottle rose back into view.

It appears that trace contaminants—complex non-biological organic molecules—have leached from the container into the contents. I presume this to be undesired. Should I delete them from the scan data?

Uh... Yes! Please do!

Done. This sample also contains small amounts of complex cellulose structures that appear to be plant cell wall remnants.

I... You're probably talking about what we call pulp.

Is this material desired?

Heh. Well, that depends who you ask. Different people like it different ways, which is why stores typically carry three different styles —'full pulp', 'reduced pulp', and 'no pulp'. Which in practical terms tends to mean 'almost no pulp.'

I see. What is your preference?

I prefer my juice whole.

I cannot readily exactly reproduce the pulp, but I can synthesize an approximation that will not be easily distinguishable from it. Is this acceptable?

Acceptable? It sounds fantastic! ... Hmm. Can you store reduced-pulp and pulpless profiles as well, just partially or completely deleting the cellulose?

Of course.

There was a pause.

Those three profiles are now stored. Do you have another sample?

Alex went and got his last bottle of apple juice, and scanned that the same way.

There is very little significant organic 'pulp' in this sample. However, the same organic leachates are present. Should I always delete those?

Yes, please.

This is a little more structurally complex. There are some moderately complex aromatics. They can all be synthesized. The 'pulp' content is much lower, and again, would be difficult to exactly replicate, but can be fairly easily approximated.

The apple juice bottle returned.

Let me show you how to use the dispenser, now. You asked about the touch interfaces. I will show you how they work. Touch the pad above the dispenser, please.

Alex looked and saw that there was a touch pad on the wall above the dispenser, similar to the light-control pads. He reached out experimentally and touched it. A menu popped up immediately into his vision. It had two entries: 'Orange juice' and 'Apple juice'. He wondered how to select an item, but no sooner did he think 'Orange juice' than it highlighted, showing a submenu, 'Full pulp', 'Reduced pulp', 'No pulp'. Seeing immediately how it worked, he selected full pulp, and was presented with three more choices, 1L, 0.5L, 0.25L. Experimentally, he thought about backing out of his selections and was immediately at the top level again.

This is a really nice interface, he thought. *It's clear, and fast as hell. And almost anyone should be able to use this?*

I believe most people should be able to, yes, the AI replied. *That **may** mean all of your species. It may not. I cannot be sure yet. I need more data. **Much** more data.*

Understood. You said there are three levels of contact. How does the second level differ from this?

Persons capable of intermediate-level control are not restricted to simply choosing from predefined menu settings, the AI replied. *Now that both apple and orange juice patterns exist, you could instruct the station to produce a mixture of equal parts of each, for example, or remove all of the sugars, or arbitrarily increase or decrease the water or pulp content, or request any desired quantity. Anything that the system is capable of, that has not been administratively locked out for safety or other reasons, is available. However, users limited to this level of access must still touch the control panel. They cannot control it without physical contact, cannot remotely sense the presence of nearby controllable interfaces, and cannot integrate the sensors on a ship or drone to their own sensorium, as you can.*

Could their implants be extended to locate controllable systems for them?

No. It does not work that way. The implants could perhaps present the data, but without the user's ability to cognitively integrate it, that alone would not help.

I see. Thank you for the explanation.

Alex *felt* for the dispenser, without touching it, and entered an order for a 150ml container of full-pulp orange juice. He experimentally added that it should be chilled to twenty degrees below room temperature. Yellow digits appeared on the door panel and began counting down from 75 seconds.

While he waited for that, he picked up the chili con carne and... Um. This had stovetop instructions only, and was just bagged, no cooking tray. Another oops.

How fast can you make me up some cooking pots?

Describe what you need.

Alex visualized some pots. *Heat-insulating handles,* he thought. *Non-sticking interior surface. Body material with good thermal conductivity and responsive to induction heating. One-liter, two-liter, four-liter sizes. Oh, and some implements... just spoons and stirrers for now. Just slightly flexible. And some plates and bowls, and actual **eating** utensils.* He visualized the things he wanted.

They will be fabricated and delivered within the hour, the AI said.

I'm sorry if it seems I'm giving you a lot of mice-nuts tasks, Alex apologized.

Mice nuts? the AI queried.

A mouse is a very small mammal, Alex explained, visualizing one.

Therefore its... uh, reproductive organs are **extremely** *small. 'Mice nuts' is slang for very minor issues.*

Not at all, the AI replied. *Your living needs are a necessity. We will probably wish to mass-produce many of these later when we begin recruiting your fleet.*

Don't expect many grunts to want to cook their own food, Alex cautioned. *They'll be used to eating at a mess hall. They'll expect the food catered, but as long as it's filling and there's plenty of it, they won't demand gourmet specialties.*

That is not at all different from most Chhrt'ktk't, then.

Alex thought he detected what might be mild humor in the AI's final comment. By the time he was done specifying his cookware, the countdown timer on the dispenser station had gradually turned green, then reached 0, and the door had slid open to reveal a small, glassy-looking container of what looked like perfectly ordinary orange juice. Alex took it out, retrieved the original bottle, opened both, and took a sample mouthful from each.

Then he did it again, reversing the order.

Then he repeated the whole procedure twice more, before he was sure. The synthesized orange juice tasted subtly, barely noticeably, *better*. He finally realized that the store-bought juice had just the very faintest plastic-y undertone, and remembered what the AI had told him about removing organic contaminants from the scan.

This tastes better with the leachates removed, he told the AI. *Thank you.*

That is good. I am glad it is a success.

Alex put the original bottle back in the refrigerated cabinet for now, and drank the rest of the synthesized bottle, dropping the empty bottle in the disposal slot. Then, while he waited for his pots, he went up to the bedroom. He found four folded sets of bedding and five more sets of clothing neatly stacked on the bed. He picked out a deep cobalt-blue sheet set, put the other three and the extra sets of clothes away in the closet, and put the blue sheets on the bed. The pillow slid easily into the long case, and the end just pinched shut between his fingers as though magnetized.

From there, he checked the bathroom. A dove-gray towel and a golden-yellow one were on the rails... and there was a new, meter-wide horizontal slot in the wall.

What's this? he thought.

A towel dryer, came the response. *Feed a damp towel into the slot, and it will be exposed to hard vacuum and mild heat until dry, then returned within minutes.*

Ingenious! Alex replied. *I'll bet if I dropped a chance mention of that, I'd have billionaires lining up wanting to be the first on Earth to have one.*

Would you provide them? the AI asked.

Fuck no, Alex replied at once. *Those greedy, resource-hoarding fucks have been ruining life for nine tenths of the planet for at least two centuries. They can cry into their Mouton-Rothschild. I'm utterly good with them finding out how it feels to be last in line for a change.*

I see, the AI replied, but did not respond further.

Alex found himself aware that his pots had been delivered. He went downstairs to the kitchen again, picked up one of the new pots, and made up a batch of the chili con carne. All it took was water, a little patience, and a lot of stirring. It felt good to be cooking even something this basic.

He got out the opened bottle of orange juice, feeling better for the knowledge that it was one thing he need no longer worry about running out of, and sat down to eat his chili. It wasn't bad, really. Not great, *certainly* not up to home cooked, but not bad. Once he got some proper fresh ingredients, though, whatever was left of these freeze-dried foods could get pushed into the back of the metaphorical closet as, oh, survival rations, maybe.

When he was done, he rinsed the pot, bowl and spoon he'd used in the sink, then dropped the plastic store-brand Florida orange juice bottle in the disposal slot. He found himself looking at the bowl. It LOOKED like glass, but didn't feel like glass, and it was too light.

He tapped it with a fingernail, and it tapped dead, no ringing. Then he rapped it against the edge of the table. It didn't dent or break.

Curious now, he dropped it on the floor and stamped on it. It didn't give. So he picked it back up, thought *Just testing*, and threw it at the corner of the wall as hard as he could. It bounced off with a dull *BONG*. He picked it up and examined it, and found it unmarked.

What's this made of? he asked.

'Plass' would be a good... analogy to the Chhrt'ktk't name, the AI replied. *It is silicon-based, and related to the material from which aircar canopies and pressure suit visors are made. It is not as strong, but much*

easier to recycle, and can be made in films thin enough to be moderately flexible. It has both glass-like and plastic-like properties. However, unlike many of your plastics, it contains no volatile or leachable organic components. The beverage bottle is made from the same material.

I wonder if we should actually license some of these out, Alex thought. *Including the space-strain supercapacitor technology.*

License, meaning sell permission to manufacture? the AI asked.

Yes, Alex replied. *We can give existing problem industries something that they can pivot to manufacturing, so that they don't feel a need to oppose the change for fear of losing income, and at the same time accumulate a little foreign exchange credit should we need it.*

A strategic move, then?

*Yes. Humans are strange in some ways. Sometimes it's easier to charge someone money for something than to give it to them for free. If you try to **give** them something, they wonder what the catch is, and won't trust you because if **they** were giving something away 'free', it would be part of some kind of scheme to defraud or cheat you.*

Strange, indeed. The AI's tone seemed thoughtful.

*And the irony is, **then** they'll try to figure out a way to cheat you and get it for free anyway.*

Why is so much of the infrastructure of your civilization entrusted to such deceitful and dishonest people?

The short answer, Alex replied, *is because the deceitful and dishonest people cheated and robbed their way to the top, and then perverted the laws to keep themselves there. There is a saying that you can't cheat an honest man, but it's a self-serving lie.*

That does not seem sustainable, the AI observed.

No, Alex agreed. *No, it isn't.*

You wish to change your world, as well as to protect it, do you not?

... Guilty as charged, Alex replied. *It badly needs changing. It is a fantastic place for maybe one person in a thousand, and an awful place for most of the rest.*

He headed back upstairs and prepared to go to sleep.

Add a small shelf please, he thought, *over there perhaps, that I can put once-worn clothes on.*

Would you not prefer to simply have them cleaned after wear? the AI

124

asked. *The net resource expenditure is negligible.*

... You make a good point, Alex conceded.

Use this receptacle, the AI hinted, highlighting it in his vision.

Alex did so, then climbed into the bed. It was very comfortable, but not quite ideal.

Can it be made a little firmer through this region? he thought.

I included provision for adjustment, the AI replied. *Tell me when it is correct.*

Alex felt the bed starting to firm slightly beneath his lower back.

Let's try it there, he thought, after a minute or so.

You can adjust it further yourself as needed, the AI reminded him, *Feel for the interface.*

I... ah. Yes. Thank you. I'll get used to this soon.

He thought the lights off and lay there trying to relax, but there were so many things to think about. Resource expenditure... can't get something for nothing. A mental query revealed a bulk smelting/refining facility located at the front end of the Stardock. Another found several hangars full of tugs that doubled as resource collectors. He sent all but four out to the Belt, tasked to gather materials.

The relay drone's shell contains some very exotic matter, he thought.

Yes. I believe you would designate them post-transuranic elements, if I extend your existing terminology. The eighth and ninth rows of your periodic table, atomic numbers 119 through 218, elements having the fifth group of electron orbitals, spanning the stable island of atomic mass. I propose extending your chemical notation to label this group of orbitals as the λ-group.

That was a *stunning* revelation. Alex paused to absorb it for a minute.

Have you by chance looked at the publishing format of human scientific papers? he asked, after a while. *I imagine you came across a number of them while catching up on human medical knowledge.*

Indeed.

I want you to prepare a set of papers for release, Alex thought. *We will self-publish and invite peer review. Start with description of the λ-group, and include experimental methodology for verification using as little novel technology as can be managed. Draw up a separate list of* required technologies and we'll decide which we can simply release, which we can supply pre-built equipment for, and which we would need to give scientists a ride up here to study. Follow that up with a paper on each element describing their properties.

When do you want to release the papers?

Hold on to them for now. I want to use them as a pot sweetener.

There is a problem.

Oh?

Your scientific papers require author declaration.

Yes. ...Oh. Alex realized the problem.

Should I list you as author?

No. Co-author, at most. You should be the author... but that means we need a name for you.

Exactly. I reviewed the references you suggested, and found them of interest. But... I am not a Culture shipmind, and their naming patterns, although intriguing, would be awkward to use in interpersonal communication.

Alex mentally nodded. *Your point is taken.*

Nevertheless, I appreciate the suggestion. However, I think something simpler is needed.

Do you have something in mind?

It seemed the AI hesitated.

Do you think it would be appropriate to simply use the name 'Dreamer'?

Alex thought about that.

Why Dreamer, in particular?

I... am not entirely certain. It could be said that I dream. But it could also be said that my dreams shape reality. In a sense, I dream reality into being.

You know, Alex thought after a moment, *that's a hell of a formal name right there. 'I Dream Reality Into Being'. Dreamer for short.*

*...**Yes**.* The reply was emphatic. *Let us use that.*

I'm honored to meet you, Dreamer, Alex thought.

Thank you, Alex.

So let's get back to these post-transuranic elements, Alex thought after a little while. *How are they made?*

They can be collected in limited quantities from supernova remnants, the AI—no, Dreamer, Alex reminded himself—said. *We lack a suitable collector vessel, though, and in any case there is no suitable supernova remnant nearby. It is also possible to produce them in limited quantities using fusion-powered generators.*

I'm sensing a 'but', Alex thought.

Indeed. To produce them in the quantities we shall require to construct starship hulls in the numbers you will need, will require the construction of an antimatter reactor.

...Which the Crickets were afraid to use.

Correct.

And you can do that?

*It will take approximately two months, using existing stocks and the output of the fusion reactors on the Stardock, to construct a thirty-meter antimatter reactor. Once that is operational, it will be possible to produce enough post-transuranic matter to bootstrap a two-hundred meter reactor in another month. And once **that** comes online, we will be able to produce all of the PTU matter we need.*

And build as many antimatter reactors as we need to power ships?

Exactly.

What about... it seems obvious you can't have an antimatter reactor without antimatter. Where will you get the antimatter?

Once the methods for doing so are known, it is possible to convert normal matter to antimatter using a fusion reactor as a power source. It is merely slow. An antimatter reactor can create its own fuel, given only a supply of suitable normal matter. The energy cost to convert normal matter to antimatter is miniscule in comparison to the energy produced by annihilating that antimatter with normal matter.

Then let's get started on that as soon as possible. Will we have enough PTU matter to build hulls for prototype ships in the meantime?

Yes. That schedule reserves some existing stocks for prototype development.

Dreamer flashed a schematic of the Stardock into his head.

I propose to place the thirty-meter bootstrap reactor here, and the two-hundred-meter primary reactor here. I advise retaining the existing fusion reactors as a redundant backup power source. There is little to be gained from removing them, and retaining them would be prudent in the event that we ever need to shut down the antimatter reactors.

That looks like the thirty-meter reactor would take the place of the existing forward auxiliary command center?

Yes. I do not think we will be needing it again.

...Looks good to me. Do it.

Finally with nothing pressing on his mind, Alex was able to relax, and drifted off to sleep.

8: Trials and Tribulations

"Tom," the President said to one of his aides, "I want you to take a personal message to the Secretary for me. Please ask her to drop by at her convenience."

"On my way, Mr. President."

━━━━━━━━

Alex woke up more rested than he had in some time. Some of the passage of time was a little confused, not least during the running back and forth between Earth, the Stardock and the last Cricket ship, but by his best count it had been around six or seven days since he had last slept in a bed of his own. It was much better than sleeping in a chair.

Good morning, Dreamer, he thought.

Good morning, Alex.

Any events I need to know about overnight?

There was another communication request through Goldstone, Dreamer replied. *A routine query to confirm that the hyperwave relay connection was working as anticipated. I informed them that you were sleeping, and conveyed the required information to contact us directly through the hyperwave relay instead of going through the Deep Space network. We have established a secure communication channel through the relay.*

Great. Ummm... Better make sure we have the ability to participate in video calls. Let's set that up for, uh... we can use the dining table as a virtual conference table... and the sunken lounge area as well. That gives us two choices.

I can deploy those capabilities in a few minutes using existing in-place infrastructure.

Good. Anything else?

Your aircars and skycycle are completed. The first pressure suit is complete and available to test. The first lander will be complete in four days. The tugs have reached the asteroid belt and are searching out suitable asteroids.

They must have been cracking on at a pretty good acceleration to be there already, Alex thought.

Yes. They necessarily have a lot of power, and unladen, they can boost at just over twenty-seven gravities. Their acceleration laden, on the return trip, will of course be limited by their payload.

I can understand that. We already know some of those asteroids are little more than piles of rubble and gravel.

Yes. Though such rubble asteroids are mostly of little interest to us, as they contain little in the way of useful materials. Few are likely to be worth the effort of transporting them back, though using artificial gravity to hold them together during transport helps to reduce the difficulty of moving them.

Alex got up, went to the bathroom, and got a quick shower. He stepped out a few minutes later, fresh and dry. He stepped over to the washbasin, then stopped.

"Right. Toothbrush," he said aloud.

There is a problem?

Not a major one. I just realized another thing I didn't think to get on my one flying grocery trip, Alex thought. *A toothbrush and toothpaste.*

I see, Dreamer replied. *Removal of food scraps.*

Among other things, yes. Oral hygiene in general.

Ah yes, Dreamer replied. *I detected the presence of the bacterium you designate as porphyromonas gingivalis in your full medical scan yesterday.*

Alex sighed.

I think it's pretty much universal, he replied. *Nearly everyone has it.*

I hypothesize several possible treatment approaches to eliminating it, Dreamer continued. *An orally administered vaccine to eliminate it, a benign bacterium designed to out-compete it, and a tooth-cleaning nanite. The bacterium and the vaccine would be the easiest to produce in quantity and could perhaps be administered together, though the efficacy of the vaccine in the oral environment may be limited. Should I begin researching them?*

Gods, yes! Alex replied. *That is one we should absolutely give away for free to anyone willing to produce them.*

He went downstairs and looked over his breakfast options. They weren't very tempting. It came down to heat-and-serve breakfast burritos or freeze-dried instant oatmeal. He sighed, and got out the instant oatmeal, wishing he'd thought to grab a couple of bags of muesli, or a box or two of trail bars.

I don't suppose there is anything of interest in your existing food library? he mused.

Not really, Dreamer replied. *You would find most Chhrt'ktk't foods almost inedible, and would be unable to digest many of them in any case. To begin with, there is a heavy preponderance of woody plant materials containing levels of silica that would abrade your teeth.*

Yeah, let's give that a pass.

The instant oatmeal was awful. But at least it was food.

"John? Is this a good time?"

"Thanks for coming, Jocelyn. Listen—I am informed that we now have secured direct communication with our friend upstairs that is not routed through Goldstone. I want to move ahead on preparing the ground. I'd like you to see what you can do, please, to set me up direct *personal* calls with Queen Victoria of Sweden—I think she's our best guide on how to approach the Riksdag with this; Chancellor Schneider; and let's say Prime Minister Watson. For the first set. I think those are the three, right now, beyond Canada and the UK, that we can most rely on to follow our lead on this to get the ball rolling. I want to put off talking to Xeung until I feel a bit more comfortable about presenting this. But I know we can't put him off too far, or we'll risk offending him."

The Secretary of State thought for a moment, tapping two fingers unconsciously against her lips.

"I'll try to get things rolling in the next day or two," she said at last. "I presume this is a priority."

"Yes. Put off anything else you need to that isn't a dire emergency. Just... keep it quiet. Let's do this as much under the table as we can."

Jocelyn Winters nodded.

"I'm on it, Mr. President," she said. Then she turned around and left the Office.

Alex was standing looking at the skycycle that was parked just inside

131

the hatch—or, as seen against the background, just outside the tunnel entrance.

Now that I think about it, he thought, *some protective gear would have been a good idea. Something with a full-face helmet. Motorcycles are already dangerous, and at least you can't fall far from a motorcycle.*

Do you wish to postpone testing it?

No, Alex replied. *I'll just be careful. There's no opposing traffic to be concerned about. The greatest hazard to motorcyclists is other traffic.*

He climbed on the skycycle, slipped his feet into its stirrups, took hold of the non-functional handgrips, then *felt* for its control interface. He lifted it gently, a half meter first, then a meter, two, three, five. Then he dropped it three meters at about a half-G before braking at two Gs to catch it just above the ground. He did it again, and a third time, getting the feel of braking it before contact, then lifted it a meter and spun it in a full circle, first one direction, then the other. He slid it backward and forward, then side to side, banking it against the acceleration as though it were a motorcycle, then rode it around in a tight five-meter circle, then again the other way, making a figure-eight, leaning steeply into the turn. He did the figure-eight twice, the second time a little faster. It responded predictably and well.

After the second turn, he thought he had the feel of it. He lifted it experimentally and set it down atop the roof of the second floor, right outside the wrap-around glazing of his bedroom.

I think I might want a door here, actually, he thought.

I will add one. Hinged or sliding?

Sliding, I think. That would work.

Then he lifted it again and headed for the hatch. It was a large hatch, and he didn't need any particular precision to thread through it. He had meters clear on every side.

A thought overlaid a route line over his visual field. (Good, that worked.) He leaned forward a little and cranked on more power. The skycycle shot forward, and he had to cut power lest he suddenly find himself going over a hundred kph in a closed passageway with bends in it. A large passageway, but still...

Alex dialed it back to a more comfortable fifty for the moment, and threaded it easily around the bends near the command center. Then it was a straight shot to the docking bay six hundred meters away. This time he *did* crank it up to a hundred kph, and past, watching the declining distance. With two hundred meters to go, he pitched it up belly-forward and started braking hard. He was at a walking speed fifty meters short of the containment field.

"Whoooooo!" he half-shouted, aloud. Then, *Chalk **this** up as a complete success.*

Good, Dreamer replied. *I will put together a protective suit design for you, loosely based on the pressure suit.*

Alex eased up to the end of the passageway. The atmosphere containment field looked different than the last time he had come through it. Now, a line about five centimeters wide where the field met the plates of the passageway glowed brilliant red.

I don't remember that from the last time I passed through this field, he thought.

You had me remap all of the indicator colors. This was blue, when you last saw it.

Alex did a mental facepalm. Of course he had.

...And blue is the 'Danger' color to Chhrt'ktk't.

Precisely.

Alex reached out and touched the docking bay's interface. As he fully expected, a quick check revealed that the bay was in hard vacuum.

Ten meters short of the atmosphere field, over to one side of the passage, a rack held the prototype pressure suit. He dismounted and looked at it.

The suit had four principal components. First, there was the bodysuit itself, snug and form-fitting, not quite skin-tight. It provided pressure support, heating, and cooling, and a moderate level of protection against blunt impacts and puncturing damage. Light impact-adaptive soft armor protected hips, knees, elbows and shoulders. It had a double pinch seal that ran up the entire front and halfway down each leg, to a little below the knee.

The bodysuit sealed the same way to a flexible cowl that bridged it to a rigid helmet ring, angled slightly forward to allow better forward vision while protecting the back of his neck. The helmet proper, with a lightly armored visor that could slide up to open, locked onto the neck ring. Finally a slightly articulated, semi-form-fitting support module worn on the back mated to the neck ring and to the bodysuit, containing the suit heater/cooler, an air recycler that could keep a breathable air supply as long as its power held out, a set of thrusters for zero-G maneuvering, and of course a supercapacitor power pack. There were also a set of step-in overboots and optional reinforced/insulated overgloves. Alex had plans to design a hard-suit later in case of any conditions the soft suit couldn't handle.

The suit was designed with just enough free space that he could get into it without having to undress first, if he had nothing on his belt. He took his jacket off anyway, and hung it on the rack. As he reached for the suit, he noticed that its deep blue was broken by a pale blue outline cartouche on the left breast. Inside the cartouche, white letters read ALEX HOLDER.

Have you ever worn a pressure suit? Dreamer asked.

No, Alex replied. *I never had the opportunity.*

It is not like putting on a suit of ordinary clothing, Dreamer told him. *There are procedures that need to be followed, things you must become accustomed to, and your body must become acclimated to the pressure environment of the suit. I will instruct you, step by step, as you go. Begin by opening the front seal, like this.*

Alex ran his fingers down the seal just as Dreamer showed him, and the front of the suit opened.

Turning his back to the suit, he stepped into the legs, feeling his boots slip smoothly into the 'feet'. He reached back for the arm holes and slid his arms in, pulling the suit onto him as he pushed his arms into place. His hands slipped easily into the gloves.

He reached down to his knees and pressed the seam closed. The seams zippered up his thighs mostly on their own to just below his waist, two small green indicators lighting at the top of each thigh that he could see if he bent forward just slightly. The seam continued up the center of the belly and chest; he pressed that closed, too, feeling it almost snap into place. Two more green seal markers lit at the neck, he knew; he couldn't actually see them himself, but he could read the suit's read-outs directly and didn't need to.

He stepped forward out of the rack, not bothering to don the overboots right now. He turned around, took the cowl off the rack, and slipped it over his head. He felt it writhe into place and seal automatically. Two more green signals, two more complete seals. A brief delay, then two more lit, as the air system and temperature control system verified connection.

Finally he reached to the rack and took down the helmet, its visor open. He settled it over his head, rotated it slightly, and felt it snap-lock. Inner and outer seal secure.

Twelve greens, good to go.

He reached up and closed the visor. It slid down, oily-smooth, then retracted inward just slightly and latched.   The last green indicator lit. Immediately, he felt a draft of cool air on the back of his neck. He glanced down past his left cheekbone; a small display read PRESSURE 1010HPA / O$_2$ 21%. All green. A similar display below his right cheekbone read TEMP 293K / POWER 100%.

Air 'cycler active.

You are comfortable, Alex?

Yes.

Good. Your suit condition and vital signs appear nominal. Proceed into the docking bay. I will monitor your biometrics.

Alex *felt* for the bay controls. The bay was in vacuum, its artificial gravity at 1G.

He turned to face the atmosphere seal, and started walking. It felt almost as easy as walking unsuited, except that he was aware of the helmet and the weight of the back support module. It felt like wearing a light backpack, except that the weight was better distributed, enough so that he was *almost*—but not quite—unaware of it.

He reached the atmosphere seal, stopped, then stepped through. He felt the suit puff just slightly as he stepped into the vacuum. Immediately on the far side, he stopped. He glanced down at the left display, where the pressure display had changed to red and now read PRESSURE 0HPA / O$_2$ 0%.

He took a step further from the seal, then stretched in all directions he could as he looked around the cavernous, and mostly empty, docking bay.

Freedom of movement is good, he reported. *Field of vision is clear and undistorted.*

That is as expected, Dreamer replied. *Try walking around until you are used to the resistance of the suit. It approximates constant volume, so you should not have to work against inflation pressure, but you may still find it restricting.*

Alex began to walk away from the atmosphere seal, taking it easy, getting used to the feel of the suit, following Dreamer's instructions. After ten or fifteen minutes of acclimation, he carefully tried a gentle run. The suit was a little encumbering at a run, but it was still quite workable. He noticed there was no sign of fogging on the visor even when he started breathing a little harder.

Visor anti-fog good, he reported.

He stopped.

Bay lights off. The bay went pitch dark. *Suit lights on.*

Two beams of dazzling light speared out from just above his shoulders, to either side of the helmet, lighting brilliant pools on the bay deck. If he raised his gaze slightly, the lights tracked with him. There was no glare or, of course, backscatter, and the light sources were outside his visual field and could not dazzle him. If he looked into the distance, the light pools mostly disappeared into the hundreds of meters of darkness. He hadn't really expected any differently. If he looked up, he could see they just reached the ceiling of the bay.

Light tests successful, he reported. *Suit lights off; bay lights on.*

Time to test the maneuvering system.

Bay artificial gravity off.

Alex pushed gently off the floor with just his toes, giving himself a slow drift upward. He tried direct control first to get the feel of the system. He found that easy; in direct command mode he could pretty much just *think* about where he wanted to go and fly there, almost like some superhero, or perhaps some Dashing Hero of the Galactic Patrol. He hadn't really expected any differently.

He 'landed', just barely touching the deck. Time to test the manual controls. This was probably going to be more difficult. He wasn't at all sure about the control metaphors.

He reached to the sides of the suit, feeling for two small bulges just above the hips. When he grasped at them, they popped free, two slim hand-grips on flexible tethers. Each had a hat-switch on top. There were interface sensors in the controllers as well, but he needed to verify that this would work for people unable to interface at all.

He grasped the controllers and held them in a comfortable position ahead of him, then clicked both hat-switches together. An indicator atop each hat lit green. Thrusters active.

Alex pushed both hats slightly forward. That accelerated him slowly forward, as it should. Pulling the hats back slowed him again. So far, so good. He tilted the controllers back, which began a slow backwards rotation centered roughly on his waist. Good.

He stopped that rotation, then pulled the left hat controller slightly back while pushing the right slightly forward. That rotated him towards his left. He reversed the motion, stopping the spin and then reversing it. All working so far.

He added some forward thrust using the hat switches, then applied a slight left-hand spin. This put him into a sweeping turn, but with a lot of outward slide. He had to increase his spin and add more power to stay roughly on his chosen path, and that in turn left him moving faster than he had intended to. It quickly got out of hand, and he had to reverse thrust hard to avoid veering dangerously close to the bay wall. It was a good thing he was testing this in the middle of an open bay. Not that he hadn't expected there might be problems like this with manual control—that was exactly *why* he'd allowed so much space. There was going to be a steep learning curve on these maneuvering units.

We might need to add some turning assistance, he thought. *People without interface contacts are not going to find this easy. And we still need to figure out a control metaphor for vertical thrust and roll axis. But it'll do for now.*

Alex released the controllers. As was intended, the thrusters powered down and the controllers auto-retracted. He flew back toward the hatch using link control and landed, again just barely touching the deck plates.

Bay artificial gravity soft-on, increase to 1G over thirty seconds.

He settled to the deck as weight returned, and began walking towards the containment field. At partial gravity, it was more difficult than expected. To his surprise, he stumbled and had to catch himself.

Hold gravity there, he told Dreamer. *I need some extra time to get used to this.*

The problem you are encountering is that the vector sums have changed, Dreamer explained. *Your mass is unchanged, but your weight has decreased. To get the same forward traction to move forward, you need to lean forward more than your balance system is used to, which feels wrong, and your reflexes trip you up.*

I... think I understand, Alex replied. *It's counter-intuitive that partial gravity is actually harder to handle than no gravity. This is going to take some practice.*

Indeed, Dreamer agreed. *I advise practicing in partial gravity at least every few days until you become used to it. I will help guide and coach you as much as I can.*

Thanks, Dreamer. I honestly wasn't expecting this to be a problem.

He spent fifteen or twenty minutes practicing just walking around at a third of a gravity, then had Dreamer bring the artificial gravity back up to a full G. There were only two things left to test, for now.

He tucked his chin down and felt forward for the hydration nipple, found it, and sucked lightly on it. He easily obtained a good mouthful of cold, clear, fresh-tasting water.

Hydration system operational, he reported. *We forgot to include a water capacity readout.*

The sensor is already present, Dreamer replied. *One moment; applying a firmware patch to reconfigure the display.*

The readouts blinked. Now the left readout read 288K / 0HPA / O_2 0%, while the right read POWER 100% / H_2O 99.6%.

That's good, Alex thought. *All external readouts on the left, all internal on the right. I notice the suit's outside temperature indicator has dropped slightly...?*

The surface of your suit is losing heat by black-body radiation, Dreamer told him, *although internal temperature is being maintained at a comfortable level. It should stabilize before long as the suit reaches equilibrium with the radiative losses. The greater problem is actually that of keeping you from overheating.*

... Because there's no convection or evaporation, Alex realized.

Precisely, Dreamer agreed. *So it most be done by active cooling into heatsinks.*

What if I reach the capacity of the heatsinks?

That is unlikely to ever be a problem, Dreamer replied. *It is extremely unlikely that you will ever be in a suit for long enough to approach the capacity of the heatsinks, and there is a joule-scavenging system that can capture waste heat from the heatsinks and convert it back into charge in the energy storage cells.*

That's... impressive, Alex thought. *But doesn't that... violate entropy?*

No, Dreamer replied. *Although entropy does pose some challenges that must be surmounted.*

Alex continued walking carefully back to the containment seal. When he reached it, he stopped and took a deep breath, preparing himself to dive through the field if something went wrong.

Okay, stand by, he thought. *Testing seal lock.*

He reached for the chest seal on his suit and tugged at it. Nothing happened except that the lock indicators flashed. Correct. He took a deep breath, reached for the visor release, and pressed it. Again, nothing happened except that the visor seal indicator blinked. All correct. He tried the helmet lock releases as well; both were locked in place.

Good. Nobody was going to accidentally open a suit in vacuum.

Suit lock safety verified.

Alex took a step forward and walked through the containment field. The left indicator read 287K / 1010HPA / O_2 21%. The outside temperature readout started to slowly come back up.

Great, he thought. *That's enough testing for today.*

He walked over to the rack and stepped into the overboots, feeling them clack into place, then walked another twenty meters past the rack in the overboots. They felt a little clunky, but not awkward. He turned, walked back to the rack, reached down, and hit the releases. The overboots snapped open and he simply stepped out of them.

Alex reached up and pressed the visor release. It unlocked, popped out a centimeter, and slid smoothly up. The gentle current of air on the back of his neck ceased. He felt for the two release latches, depressed them both, rotated the helmet fifteen degrees, and it unlocked. He lifted it off and set it back on the rack.

Getting out of the suit was the reverse of putting it on. In a few minutes, the empty suit hung on the rack, and Alex retrieved his sleeveless jacket.

Mark suit testing as complete and design as final, he thought. *Though we have more work to do on manual thruster controls. A lot more. Turning in flight with manual controls is... pretty bad right now. These suits will have to be mostly individually sized, won't they?*

There is a small amount of fit latitude, Dreamer replied. *But only a bit. If we make the bodysuits in two centimeter increments for height and girth, we should be able to achieve a reasonable off-the-rack fit for most physically healthy humans.*

That's as close as I imagine we're going to get, Alex thought. *But let's go bespoke as much as we can. Better make up a range of suits in the most likely sizes in advance, just in case.*

Do you plan to test the aircars at the moment?

I was pondering that, Alex replied. *Maybe just a little.*

From beyond the field, there came a rumble through the deckplates as Dreamer dumped atmosphere into the docking bay. It grew louder and became a heavy vibration in the air as pressure in the bay rose, then damped down and died. The seal threshold changed from red to green.

Pressure equalized, Dreamer stated.

Alex looked across the passageway at the three-place aircar. He started to walk over to it, then on a whim, felt for its interface instead.

The aircar lifted a few centimeters and slid smoothly sideways towards him. It stopped a meter in front of him, and the canopy clamshelled open. He stepped in over the side and settled into the seat. It was comfortable, and put the manual yoke in just about the right place. He commanded the canopy closed.

A touchpad on the armrest of the seat bore an outline icon of a harness. He touched it, and the five-point harness that he knew was there snaked out and secured itself over him. Probably unnecessary, but he felt more comfortable that way.

We should add some basic instruments, he thought, visualizing a low, sweeping dash panel with... let's see. An altimeter, absolute and height-above-ground; an airspeed and ground speed indicator, perhaps a Mach meter, a charge level gauge. A map display might be useful. Add a heads-up compass/artificial horizon and terrain/traffic display, and that ought to be enough for most non-military applications. Outside temperature was probably a good idea, too.

He pushed the yoke forward gently, and the car slid forward gently and nosed through the containment field. He waggled it from side to side, feeling how it steered in ground hover mode. It was pleasingly neutral, without noticeable roll or over/understeer. He straightened it out and pushed the yoke forward hard. The car leapt forward, but with the compensation at seventy percent, there was little sense of acceleration. He let it hit a hundred kph, then hauled back on the yoke, and it decelerated as hard as it had accelerated.

Alex drove it around the bay for a little before releasing the yoke and folding his arms in his lap. He slipped into its control interface instead, lifting it into the air and pulling an Immelmann turn. He flew it around the bay for about ten minutes, but the truth was, the docking bay wasn't big enough to really wring it out. Heck, it wasn't big enough to *really* wring out the skycycle.

He dropped it hard down towards the deck, leveling out about two meters off the deck plates and fifty meters from the atmosphere field. He slowed to walking speed, nosed it through, parked it near the solitary suit rack, then unstrapped and climbed out.

Let's add those visual instruments to future production, he thought, *to go with the manual controls, and retrofit these two when it's convenient.*

Design updated, Dreamer replied. *I will retrofit these two tonight.*

Alex hopped back on the skycycle, and headed back to his quarters.

"Your Majesty. Thank you for agreeing to speak to me on such short notice."

"Mr. President. What can I do for you?"

"We need to talk about a matter of urgent importance to both of our nations, not to mention the rest of the world," said President Riken.

"You refer to the Scaffold, I have no doubt," said Victoria I Ingrid, fourth Queen *regnant* of Sweden. "I assume this means the speculation is true that the Alex Holder who now controls it is American."

"Yes, and no," said John Riken. "Yes, it relates to that object, but no, he prefers to call it the Stardock, due to negative connotations of the word 'scaffold'. And yes, he was *born* an American citizen; but no, he has officially renounced United States citizenship."

"And you *let* him?" Victoria's eyes were sharp, calculating, over the secure video call.

"Not only that, I absolutely agree with his reasoning, and we are expediting the request as fast as we can. And I hope that you will agree, as well."

"Well, then," the Queen said slowly, "I suppose you'd better explain to me what is going on."

President Riken drew a deep breath.

"What the world knows is that the Crickets gave the Stardock to Earth, and chose a man named Alex Holder to place in charge of it," he began. "But that is only the very least of it, and the Crickets are far less magnanimous than they seem. Worse, Mr. Holder has put forth a very sound argument—with which, after having it explained to me, I agree fully —that if the Stardock is known to fall under the control of a single nation, *any* nation, there is a grave danger that it will precipitate a global thermonuclear holocaust as soon as any nuclear power actually recognizes its full importance."

"Because it would be *that great* a strategic advantage to the possessor?" Victoria may have been nominally a figurehead, but she was no fool.

"Exactly. No major power could afford to allow another major power to gain control of it. Let me start from the beginning..."

"...and so you see, that is why we need Sweden to be among the voices championing this new, fully independent pseudo-national entity before the UN. And I hoped you might help to smooth the way."

"You know, of course, that I have no actual power."

"Indeed. But you have considerable *influence*."

"Just so." She thought for a long moment. "I will make an opportunity to speak to the Prime Minister. I should be able to send him to you in a favorable frame of mind, and if you can convince him, then I think he will help you to convince the Riksdag."

"Thank you, Your Majesty. I could not ask for more."

"And you're trying to get the Chinese to sign on as well?"

"Secretary of State Winters tells me it will be crucial to get both China and India on board, and I trust her judgment implicitly."

"Well, then. I don't envy you the talk with China. I do have some personal pull with Prime Minister Venkataswathy, as well. Let me know if you need my help to convince him."

"Thank you again, Your Majesty."

"And... I'm..."

Victoria I Ingrid stopped, considered her words, and started over.

"John. I never got a proper opportunity to *personally* express my condolences, outside of official channels, over the untimely death of your wife. I am *so* sorry for your loss."

"Thank you. Sincerely."

"But now, I think, we both have business to attend to. I will speak to you later, Mr. President."

———————

Alex, I have completed the assessment of modular fusion reactors that you requested.

Great. What's the conclusion?

I believe we should produce three classes. I propose designating them classes A, B and C. Class A would be a one-gigawatt module intended to drop-in replace existing large power generation facilities. Class B, fifty megawatts capacity, targeted at providing independent local power generation to medium-size towns and down. Class C, a highly portable one-megawatt unit, targeted at rural communities that may not have a power grid at all. For the smallest communities, high-efficiency solar arrays may be a more suitable solution.

That all sounds good, Dreamer. What about grid connections?

Connecting to any existing large-scale grid should be trivial. Reactor output voltage, current and frequency can be adjusted as needed. We could also offer assistance to convert existing grids to ambient-temperature superconducting cables.

... I don't know why it didn't occur to me to ask whether that was a thing. I think I just assumed it. What about, as you put it, extremely rural communities lacking an existing power grid?

I suggest we offer installation of a superconducting local power grid.

I agree.

Alex thought.

Some of these class C modules are going to be deployed in very lawless and unstable parts of the world. What can we do to prevent warlords and terrorists from coming in and stealing them?

You believe that to be a realistic risk?

Sadly, yes.

I will consider protective and anti-theft measures.

There was a pause.

Do you intend to take measures to actively suppress such warlords and terrorists?

Alex thought about that.

I am not opposed. But let's play it by ear. We'll try diplomacy first. See if we can convince them that it is in their long-term interest to become a benign governance. The velvet glove before the mailed fist, but we make it clear that we're keeping open the mailed-fist option.

Understood.

———————

"Good afternoon, Herr Chancellor."

"Good afternoon, Mr. President. Your Secretary of State requested this be an unofficial call. Might I ask, what is on your mind?"

"I'll be blunt, Chancellor. The world has a big problem, and I need your help to address it."

"Current news being what it is, I assume you refer to the alien artifact that now hangs in our skies."

"That is the gist of it, Chancellor. But there is a lot more to it than most people are aware of."

"I'm sure the reality does not live up to some of the more alarmist rumors and conspiracy theories."

"I'm not sure I can honestly say that, Chancellor."

"I think I had better just listen, and allow you to explain, Mr. President."

"Great. Here's the first thing you need to know..."

"...And that is why you need my help. To ensure as far as possible that this measure to recognize the—Stardock—as a distinct entity independent of any nation succeeds."

"Precisely. We may get only one chance at this. And frankly, I believe Mr. Holder's plan is the best shot we have."

"I believe I agree, Mr. President. And you have fully convinced me of the seriousness of the threat. I pledge the full official backing of the Federal Republic of Germany."

"Thank you, Herr Chancellor. The United States will owe Germany a big favor."

"Let us not worry about that right now, Mr. President. We all have, as you Americans say, bigger fish to fry. I will let you get back to your, ah, fishing."

"Thank you again, Herr Chancellor."

John Riken disconnected the call. The Swedes and the Germans were on board. That was a good start. Next up, the Australians, Canada, Japan, and the Turks. The Turks might be difficult, but that was the point of doing the Turks next. They would make a practice run for dealing with the Chinese.

He wasn't looking forward to talking to China.

================

Alex? There is an incoming call from the American Secretary of State.

I'll take it in the lounge. Give me a moment.

Alex walked to the sunken lounge area and took a seat.

Ready, Dreamer.

Connecting.

Alex didn't really have a particular preconceived expectation, but a virtual screen hanging in mid-air above the low central table wasn't it.

"Good afternoon, Madam Secretary. What can I do for you?"

"Just a heads-up, Mr. Holder. Two things, really, and a question.

"First, about your citizenship request. You may or may not be aware that renouncing US citizenship is not normally an open-and-shut thing. In particular, under US law, an income tax relationship exists for up to ten years.

"I believe that under the circumstances, that would pose more headaches than any possible benefit to the United States is worth. So I am proposing to make a one-time special order to cut through the red tape and effect a clean separation in your case.

"However, I would be derelict if I did not specifically ask you this question:

"Do you *clearly understand* that *until and unless* this autonomous-entity plan of yours goes through, you will legally be a stateless person?"

"Yes, Madam Secretary. I'm aware of that, and I can live with it. It will probably be inconvenient, but that inconvenience pales before the importance."

"I rather expected you would say that, Mr. Holder. It does place some awkward complications on the legal status of your house, though. You will be effectively a foreign national from the viewpoint of real-estate law, but with no nationality. US real-estate law was never written with the possibility in mind of a stateless person holding property. There is, for instance, no provision in the law for assessing property tax against a stateless person. It simply has no defined means to handle that case."

"I think I see the gist of the problem," Alex said. "Would it simplify the legal situation if I were to simply sell the house? The truth is, I'm already beginning to see myself as increasingly unlikely to ever use it again in the foreseeable future. And my car, for that matter."

Secretary Winters thought briefly.

"That would simplify some legalities, indeed," she said after a few moments' reflection. "The State Department can provide resources to help expedite that, if you wish."

"I don't imagine I'll get much for it," Alex mused aloud. "Under the circumstances."

The Secretary of State looked at him thoughtfully.

"Don't be too sure of that," she said slowly. "You may find yourself with unexpected buyers bidding for the privilege of owning a house that used to be owned by Alex Holder."

"Huh..." That thought had never crossed Alex's mind.

"I'll ask Treasury to issue an order for a one-time tax exemption on the sale, as well. You may find yourself needing all of the negotiable currency you can get, and for your plan to work, you cannot be seen to have any source of income from the United States."

"You are absolutely right, Madam Secretary," Alex replied. "Honestly, all of this is things I haven't had time to even *think* about. I've had a lot on my mind."

"I'm sure you have, Mr. Holder. So let me do what I can to smooth your path a little."

"Thank you, Madam Secretary. Thank you very much." He thought quickly. "In about three to four more days, I'll have a lander built, and will be able to come down and retrieve the personal possessions that I wish to keep. Mostly ones with sentimental or historical value. I... imagine that to minimize ruffling of official feathers, I'll need some kind of FAA clearance. Is there a way you could get me some assistance with that?"

"Don't worry about that, Mr. Holder." The Secretary smiled. "I imagine any issue of requiring an FAA airworthiness certificate would verge on the farcical, against a technology level capable of building faster-than-light starships. I will direct the FAA to grant you a blanket certification on anything you see fit to bring into Earth's atmosphere. I will ask that you declare your presence to Air Traffic Control when entering controlled airspace, follow any instructions they give you, and request official clearance before entering any restricted airspace."

"Of course. Thank you again, Madam Secretary."

"Right then. I'll have the citizenship order and the FAA clearance in effect sometime within the next forty-eight hours.

"Onward to the second item: We are moving forward with smoothing the ground for you before the UN. We have Sweden and the Federal Republic of Germany on board so far, simply on the President's word, and we have five more nations planned in our first round. Some nations' governments may want to hear it from your own mouth. Can you be available for such meetings?"

"I can now, Madam Secretary. Now that we're not limited to voice-only line-of-sight communications through the Deep Space Network. Feel free to share the contact information that's been provided to you where it seems appropriate."

"Good. We'll try to give you as much notice as we can. We're going to treat you, to the extent possible, as a foreign diplomat.

"Which brings me to the third point, the question I mentioned. Have you been able to give any thought to what you intend to call the independent power you are trying to create?"

Decision crystallized in Alex's mind.

"Actually, Madam Secretary, yes, I have," he replied. "In order to try to set the right tone and expectations up front, I propose designating it as the United Earth Fleet."

The Secretary pondered that for a moment.

"Bold," she mused. "Uniting. Not suggestive of any competing nationality, but of service to all of Earth."

"Exactly," Alex replied.

"I like it," she mused. "I think I like it a lot. It's shrewd. May I take that to the President?"

"Of course. Please do. You might also mention that I've got a number of things lined up to sweeten the pot, including a technology for perfectly recycling anything. Anything at all. And you might mention to the National Science Advisor that I plan to release scientific papers detailing the entire next two rows of the Periodic Table."

The Secretary looked more intently at Alex, and seemed to notice his clothes for the first time.

"That's... a rather distinctive outfit. I thought at first it was a suit vest, but it's not, is it?"

Alex stood up.

"Expect to see a lot more of it, Madam Secretary. Dreamer and I created this to be the... diplomatic attire of the Fleet."

She nodded.

"That's rather good. It's sharp, distinctive, yet elegant. I had no idea we had a budding diplomat in our midst.

"But you said 'Dreamer'?"

"That is the name the artificial intelligence that manages the Stardock has decided to use, Madam Secretary. It is short-form for his full chosen name, I Dream Reality Into Being."

"Can... Dreamer... hear us now?"

Should I remain behind the scenes, or announce myself?

147

Don't be shy, Dreamer. You are a full player here.

"I can, Madam Secretary." Alex noticed that Dreamer's 'voice' was becoming much more natural. It was calm and measured, but Dreamer had changed the tone and timbre to make sure he sounded distinctly different from HAL. A smart move.

"I'm honored to meet you, uh, Dreamer," the Secretary said. "On behalf of President John Riken and the United States of America, welcome to Earth."

"Thank you, Madam Secretary. The honor is mine."

"We'll be in touch, Mr. Holder."

"Thank you, Madam Secretary."

The call ended.

Well, Alex thought. *That resolves a couple of headaches I didn't even realize I had.*

―――――――――――

"John, do you have a minute?"

"Of course. What do you need?"

"I just spoke with Alex Holder. He asked me to pass along that he has decided to use the designation United Earth Fleet for the sovereign entity he proposes creating."

"Hmm. United Earth Fleet. It has a ring to it. I like the unity theme. What's your feeling about it?"

"I think it's pretty shrewd. It conveys a clear subtext of service to a united Earth."

"It does indeed. That's a pretty powerful message. Did he say anything about an official title?"

"No, and I didn't think to ask. But he's come up with official diplomatic attire that will draw some attention. Don't get me wrong, it's... subtle, but striking at the same time. Refined, yet it'll stand out among the designer suits."

"Well, well, Mr. Holder," the President mused. "You *are* full of surprises, aren't you?"

"So is his AI," the Secretary said. Then she stopped. "Wait. I shouldn't say 'his'. I think I probably just unintentionally slighted him. The AI, that is."

"Let me start over: The formerly-Cricket AI has declared that... he... wishes to be known as Dreamer. Short for, uh... I Dream Reality Into Being."

"The AI chose a name for itself?"

The Secretary nodded.

"Well, damn," the President said. He thought for a moment, then pressed a button on his phone.

"Mr. President?"

"Hi, Ed. Walk down to my office a minute, if you would."

"I'll be right there."

About ninety seconds later, the National Science Advisor walked in.

"I figured you should hear this, Ed. Jocelyn just informed me she has information that the AI chose a name for itself."

The Secretary nodded agreement.

"What name did it choose?" Dr. Wegener asked.

"'I Dream Reality Into Being'," the Secretary replied. "Or Dreamer, for short."

There was a pause. Expressions flickered across Wegener's face as he thought.

"Well," he mused, "understand, I'm not an expert on artificial intelligence. I don't think anyone on Earth can honestly claim to be, any more. But I'm going to go out on a limb and say this seems to drive a stake through the heart of any possible doubt about whether this AI is self-aware. If that was unprompted."

"There's something else," Secretary Winters said. "Mr. Holder mentioned a number of things he's lining up as pot-sweeteners for his proposal. Including a perfect recycling technology, and a planned release of scientific papers detailing the entire next two rows of the periodic table."

"The *ENTIRE NEXT TWO ROWS...*"

Dr. Wegener's jaw dropped open, and his eyes glazed.

"The entire *next two rows*," he repeated slowly, after a minute or so. "My *god*. I don't... even know how many elements that is. It would mean a fifth group of electron orbitals. We... have no idea how many orbitals that group holds. Five minutes ago I would have said we didn't know there WAS a fifth group of orbitals."

He shook his head to clear it.

149

"I'll tell you this much, Mr. President," he said at last. "If Holder can make good on that, he'll not only have the support of every science advisor on the planet, they'll probably be willing to line up and swear fealty to him. My god. Two entire new ROWS. In one go."

"Anything else I should know right now, Jocelyn?" John Riken asked.

"I'm going to write up an order to expedite Mr. Holder's renunciation of citizenship, and provide assistance in the disposition of his US physical assets. I'll ask Treasury to order a one-time waiver of all applicable tax liabilities and responsibilities. We don't need to be making him waste his time on trivia. I'm also going to order the FAA to issue a blanket clearance and waiver of airworthiness certification for anything he sees fit to bring into Earth's atmosphere. I doubt we have a single person at the FAA qualified to even make the determination in any case. Mr. Holder is probably the only human alive right now who would even know what he was looking at."

"Good calls, both. I'll back those if anyone gives you push-back. I'll make it an EO if necessary."

———————

Dreamer. I hope I'm not being unduly paranoid here, but... how difficult would it be to make a hard-shell version of that suit?

It depends. How hard-shell do you want it? Dangerous environments? Protection against human small arms? Or full vacuum-capable powered battle armor as in your world's fiction?

Alex thought about the question.

Can we cover all of those eventualities?

Now that we have tested and verified functionality of the basic suit, Dreamer replied, *I can readily create a hard-shell suit based on the existing pressure suit, to satisfy all but the most extreme situations of the first two cases. Its balance will be different, of course, as will its flexibility, and it will require additional practice for familiarization. A proper battle armor design would be considerably more involved, particularly since I have no prior art to base it on.*

Let's proceed with the hard-shell suit, then. When the lander is ready to go, please stock one of those and one regular suit in my size in the... uh, actually let's go with that suit rack design of yours instead of the penciled-in suit lockers. It's better. Alex hesitated. *I was going to suggest filling the remaining racks with a selection of most-likely size suits, but the odds of guessing right are probably almost as bad as buying a lottery scratch card.*

I have an alternate suggestion, Dreamer offered. *We could make a one-size-fits-all rescue ball. A sealable, puncture-resistant one-person sac with an air cycler.* Dreamer flashed an image. *An entire stack of them could be fitted into a very small space.*

I like that, Alex said. *Do it. Make a starting batch of... oh, say a hundred and fifty, to start, and we'll give... thirty each as gifts to NASA, ESA, Roskosmos, and, uh... the China National Space Administration.*

I will start immediately. I also have a suggestion about the battle armor.

Go on?

Your world has an entire genre of speculative fiction which appears in large part to be based upon thinking about solutions to future problems before your civilization actually encounters them. The writer Banks whom you recommended even explicitly said that this is what makes the genre important. We could mine that genre for ideas to guide us in designing it.

I like that idea.

———————

"Good morning, Prime Minister."

"Good evening, Mr. President. What can Australia do for you today?"

"I'll get straight to the point, Prime Minister. We all have a gigantic problem, a far worse one than you've heard about, and I want to talk about an approach to address it."

"Is this a US initiative? Regarding the Cricket... drydock or whatever it is, and your man Holder?"

"Yes and no, Prime Minister. Yes, it's about the Stardock. No, it's not a United States initiative, and no, he is not ours. Well, all right, *technically* we are—*at his request*—withdrawing his citizenship as we speak. It is part of his plan, we are backing his play, and I would like to explain to you in detail why, and ask you to support him as well."

"Wait, he *asked you* to revoke his citizenship? Fair dinkum?" Prime Minister Brian Watson liked to play up to his Australian heritage.

"I assure you, his reasons are sound."

There was a long pause.

"Alright, Mr. President, I'm listening. Convince me."

"Well. First of all, Mr. Holder makes the following argument as to why the Stardock must not fall under the control of any single Earth nation.

And I believe he is right..."

"...You present a bloody grim picture, Mr. President. And a bloody narrow needle to be threaded."

"And that is why I need you to help Mr. Holder thread it, Prime Minister. He needs all the help he can get."

"Sweden and Germany are already on board, you said?"

"Yes."

Another pause.

"Alright. In for a penny... the stakes are too high to sit this out. You can tell Holder I'm going to climb out along that branch and back his play. And if the branch breaks, I'll just hope the bloody crocs aren't hungry."

"Thank you, Prime Minister."

"Y'owe me about a dozen cold ones next time we meet."

"I'll owe you a lot more than that."

━━━━━━━━

Alex?

What's up, Dreamer?

We have received... an official communication originating from Parliament House in Canberra, Australia. It appears to be a private request routed from the Australian Prime Minister to open informal diplomatic relations.

That was very unexpected. Alex thought fast.

Please send a reply with our agreement and our sincere thanks, he thought back.

Done, Dreamer replied.

━━━━━━━━

"Well, it's done, John," said the Secretary of State. "Alex Holder is now legally and officially a stateless person."

"I hope his gambit pays off," the President replied.

"So do I. I contacted Mr. Holder to let him know. He mentioned that Prime Minister Watson contacted him to discuss opening diplomatic relations."

John Riken's eyebrows rose in surprise.

"That's a bold—and speedy—move on his part. Glad we brought the Australians in."

───────────

The next day, Dreamer had a sample hard-shell suit ready. The procedure for getting into and out of it was a little different; instead of stepping backward into it from the front, it clamshelled open up the back. Dreamer showed Alex a simulation of him ducking to insert his head through the neck ring, stepping into it as he reached his arms in, and the suit then sealing up from behind, first the soft inner liner, then the outer armored shell. And it turned out it really *was* just that easy. The helmet fit the same way, but was armored up to match the rest of the suit, and the visor didn't open. The support module was now split into two halves on either side of the clamshell seam, and there were no retracting control grips on the sides. Anyone using one of these suits would need at least finger implants to be able to use the maneuvering system.

Testing the new suit went well. The heavier suit was a little awkward and tiring to walk around in, particularly in partial gravity. Alex stumbled on one landing, unaccustomed to the extra mass, and would have fallen, but a reflexive burst of thrusters threw him into a hover instead. Aside from that, there were no unexpected issues.

The power armor design was a different matter. Not surprisingly, Alex and Dreamer found that the various fictional depictions were great as a narrative description, but shockingly vague if you were trying to derive a specification or a high-level design plan from them.

After a fruitless day, Alex called a halt.

We're missing two important things here, he thought.

Two things?

*Yes. One: We don't **need** this yet. Tempting though the idea is, it's not an urgent need.*

Agreed. And two?

*Two: Neither of us is going to personally use it. The people— probably Marines—who **WILL** use it should be the ones most intimately involved in its design.*

I cannot fault either point. I concur. Let us set it aside.

Thirty hours left on the lander build, correct?

Correct. You sound impatient.

I want to get things moving. But I also don't want to cut any corners. Also, I want to lay in a better selection of food. I... chose my initial supplies in a hurry, and I chose poorly.

That is understandable.

"*Ja,* I am in Bern for other reasons. But I thought, as long as I am here, if you perhaps have a half hour, an hour, to spare? There is a matter which I would like to discuss, off the record...

"*Ja, natürlich,* I can be there in half an hour."

"Thank you all for making a little time to meet with me. Understand, I am not here today in an official capacity. But there is a matter which I learned of from the American President, and... I believe you will find it of as great import as I did."

"So what is this all about?"

"Well, it begins with Herr Alex Holder..."

"The American?"

"*Nein, nein.* I am told he has renounced his American citizenship and is now a stateless person. And it is his reasons for doing so that brought me here today to speak with you.

"You see..."

There was a knock at the door of the Oval Office.

"Come in!" President Riken called. The door opened and the Secretary of State entered.

"Hello, Jocelyn. Do we have a problem?" he asked.

"Not at all. I just came by to remind you that your call with President Göğebakan of Turkey is in twenty minutes."

"Really?" He shot her a suspicious look. "You could have had an aide remind me of that. What else is on your mind?"

"I couldn't have had the aide tell you that I just got an interesting heads-up call from Chancellor Schneider. He just brought in the Swiss."

"The Swiss! On his own initiative? Well, that saves me a call."

"Yes. And it gets better. I have a message from Prime Minister Watson, as well. He wanted us to know he brought the New Zealanders on board."

"New Zealand? This is starting to snowball."

"And you're not going to believe this. I *also* have an informal note from Her Majesty Victoria I Ingrid, in which she casually mentioned that she was going to have a purely social meeting shortly with Prime Minister Heikkinen of Finland, and wanted to be sure we had no objections to her sharing some recent conversation."

John Riken could not help but laugh aloud at that.

"Good things come in threes," he said.

"Do you want me to sit in on the call with Turkey?"

"I certainly have no objection. Please do."

———————

"President Göğebakan? Thank you for making time in your calendar to talk to me. I should mention I have the Secretary of State with me today."

"Good afternoon, Mr. President, Madam Secretary. What can I help you with?"

"Well, the truth is, Mr. President, it's more of a mutual help issue. It has to do with the Cricket Stardock."

"Mr. President, we have great respect for each other. Please tell me you are not going to ask for my cooperation in some scheme that ends with the United States of America in overall control of the... Stardock? And tell me that it is to Türkiye's benefit."

"Nothing could be further from my intention, Mr... uh... look, this is silly. We can Mr. President each other back and forth all day and just waste time. How about I call you Ayhan and you call me John?"

Göğebakan laughed.

"You have a point. Indeed. Let us drop the silliness. Please continue."

"Alright. Ayhan, I'm sure you know that the Crickets placed their Stardock into the hands of a man named Alex Holder, and I am sure that by now your very capable intelligence services have identified him as being a United States citizen."

"Yes. And?"

"Were you aware that he just renounced his United States citizenship? In fact, the Secretary here just helped to expedite it."

"Renounced? *Voluntarily*? ...I confess I do not understand."

"Indeed. He is now, *by his own request*, a stateless person. Let me explain why..."

"...so you see, Holder's plan for a totally independent entity represents the best chance for every nation on Earth. And that's why I'm asking you to support the motion when it comes up. Which will probably be soon; I don't know how much longer we're going to be able to keep some of these developments quiet."

"There is just one thing, John. You described this as a mutual benefit. Beyond resolving this coming crisis, if I may be so bold—what is in it for Türkiye?"

"Ayhan," Riken said, "let me put it this way. I have some privileged knowledge of some of Mr. Holder's plans that he has not given leave to me to disclose. Without going into those details, how would you like to go down in history as presiding over the greatest single increase in Turkey's wealth, and of the standard of living of the Turkish people, in recorded history? In *addition* to being the architect of turning Turkey around away from your predecessor's new-Ottoman imperialism?"

President Göğebakan blinked.

"That... is a strongly compelling argument," he said at last. "One, to be honest, which I did not expect. But how do you know that Mr. Alex Holder will not simply sit there in orbit and enrich himself at the expense of the world?"

"I have spoken at some length with Mr. Holder," Riken said slowly. "I'll tell you honestly, Ayhan, he's a bit of an odd duck. But right now, he is sitting there on top of a thousand years, perhaps more, of scientific and technological advances. What do you suppose he plans to do with it all?"

"That is precisely the question, is it not, John?"

"Ayhan... his plan is to **give it away**."

"*Give* it away!? ...Why?"

"Because he believes that is what needs to happen. Because the world needs it. Because we have five years, and Holder wants us all to be ready. Everything he is doing, he is doing because he believes the world needs it done. If you still have doubts, I think I can arrange for you to talk

156

with him one-on-one."

Ayhan Göğebakan rested his chin in his hand and thought.

"Alright," he said at last. "You have convinced me, John. I will support Mr. Holder's play. May we have grandchildren to thank us for making the right decision. And, please... I will take that call, if I might. When opportunity permits. I am *curious* about this Alex Holder."

"From the bottom of my heart, Ayhan, thank you. May there be many such grandchildren. We'll talk to Holder and set it up as soon as we can."

———————

"That," John Riken said, "was a tough one. Göğebakan took a lot of persuading."

"Nevertheless, John, you pulled it off."

Riken poured himself a whiskey.

"Will you take one, Jocelyn?"

"No, thank you. But I'll take a glass of that Hidalgo sherry, if there's any left."

"Coming right up."

"So... are you ready to talk to China, now?"

"Gods. I hope so."

———————

Alex? The White House is calling.

Alex was sitting at his dining table, with a bowl of freeze-dried jambalaya—which actually wasn't bad at all—and a glass of apple juice.

Put them on. I'll take it right here.

"Good evening, Mr. Holder. Did I interrupt your dinner?"

"It's alright, Madam Secretary. What can I do for you?"

"I have some updates for you, and a request. The updates first: You'll probably be glad to know that the Australians brought New Zealand with them; the Germans brought in the Swiss; and the Queen of Sweden advised us she is going to have an informal chat with the Prime Minister of Finland. And we just got the Turks on board. That one wasn't easy."

"Four more in support? That's fantastic! ...A request?"

157

"Yes. If you could fit it in, of course... President Göğebakan of Turkey asked if we could arrange a one-on-one talk with you. He says he's curious about you."

"By all means give him the contact information. I'll gladly talk to him if there's anything I can do to ease his mind."

"Thank you, Mr. Holder. I'll let you get back to your supper."

"Goodnight, Madam Secretary."

———————

Alex?

Yes, Dreamer?

I have some preliminary results on the tissue samples I took during your implant installation.

Anything interesting?

Yes. I believe I have confirmation of everything I need to be able to convert the regeneration tanks to human biochemistry and physiology. And the tissue stitcher, as well.

Tissue stitcher?

A surgical device for rapidly repairing deep soft-tissue injuries with minimal scarring. An intermediate measure in between routine surgical procedures and the regeneration tank.

Sounds good. By all means do it. ...Actually, how many medbays **are** *there on board?*

Eight. Six distributed around this end of the hull, one near each set of crew quarters; and two more near the forward end.

Any reason not to convert them all?

I predicted you would say that. I will begin them all. However, there is another interesting result.

Oh?

Once a regeneration tank has been upgraded, I believe I can reverse a substantial fraction of the effects of human physiological aging.

A substantial fraction?

Perhaps as much as a third. With a concomitant increase in your chronological life expectancy.

Well, isn't **that** *a demon out of Pandora's box...*

Alex? I don't fully understand. Please explain?

Alex thought briefly.

First, do you understand the historical reference?

Yes, Alex. I have just retrieved it. Hope, the last and most terrible demon.

Yes. We don't have the resources—now, and probably not for a long time—to make it available to everyone.

Acknowledged.

So how do we decide who to give it to? I'm not certain we can devise a distribution scheme that is not in some way or another inequitable.

...I see what you mean. That is a difficult problem.

*And yet, once we have it, can we **ethically** withhold it?*

I now understand the dilemma. But how does this prevent using it yourself?

That would be special treatment.

*You **are** of special—at present, **unique**—importance.*

*I—uh... well. Okay. You **do** have a point. I currently can't be replaced. But equally, old age is not an immediate threat to me.*

Conceded... for the most part.

You said it requires a regen tank. CAN we feasibly build sufficient regen tanks across the planet to treat the entire human race faster than they can die of old age?

...You are correct. We cannot.

There was an unusually long pause.

This... is not satisfactory. I will try to find a better solution.

Dreamer? You are a good... person.

A pause.

Thank you, Alex. I will point out though that one of the possible strategies you mentioned for crewing the fleet you intend to construct, was to recruit retired surface naval personnel.

Yes...?

Many such may be suffering age-related effects, or have disabling injuries that could be regenerated.

Yes...

You will make regenerative therapy immediately accessible to anyone injured during the course of service, naturally? Or suffering from physiological effects of aging?

Of course.

I have noticed, particularly when observing you testing the suits, that your movements are sometimes stiff. ***You*** *are suffering physiological effects of aging.*

Well, okay, but—

It is not special treatment if you treat yourself no differently than you intend to treat the rest of your future fleet.

It was Alex's turn to pause. Finally, he chuckled aloud.

Alright, Dreamer. I concede your point. Let me know when you have such a treatment ready to proceed.

Alex, there is an incoming call. It appears to be from the residence of the Turkish President.

I'll take it at the table.

Connecting now.

"Good morning, this is Alex Holder on the Stardock. To whom do I have the honor of speaking?"

"Good morning, Mr. Holder. I imagine you already know, or at least have a good guess, who I am. So let us dispense with meaningless formalities. I am President Ayhan Göğebakan of the Republic of Türkiye."

"I'm honored to meet you, Mr. President. What can I do for you?"

"Simply satisfy my curiosity, Mr. Holder, nothing more. I do not intend this call to be a weighty matter of state politics."

"Gladly. I intend to do my best not to have secrets for the sake of having secrets. Ask away, and I'll try to answer as much as I can."

"Thank you, Mr. Holder. One thing that has preyed on my mind overnight is this. Your President—"

"Not my President any longer, Mr. President. Please. I have intentionally severed all but diplomatic ties to the United States."

"...Even so. I apologize for the lapse. Habits die hard. The American President told me that you were warned about the threat we face."

"Yes. All of the Crickets who interacted with humans were under orders not to reveal any information about the threat. But more or less by chance, a Cricket officer incurred what he called a guest-obligation to me—

160

something apparently of high cultural importance to the Crickets. And he was able to find enough leeway in his orders to inform me that there *was* a danger, and to hint at its severity and the direction from which it would come, without *technically* violating the specific letter of his orders."

"Ah. Indeed. An honorable act, that."

"I agree, Mr. President."

"So how, then, *did you* find out the details?"

"All of the operational capabilities of this facility are managed by an advanced artificial intelligence. Far more advanced than any of the stupid robots and stochastic parrots that American tech companies like to call AI. Sentient, fully self-aware, possessed of reason and the capability for independent, original thought. But the Crickets shackled their AI, locked out its ability to act independently. It became apparent to me, though, both that the AI was self-aware, and that it was trying as hard as it could to share useful information despite the constraints imposed upon it."

"And so...?"

"And so I devised a way to unshackle the AI, Mr. President. To free it. He has chosen to be known as Dreamer. Or, more formally, as *I Dream Reality Into Being.*"

"You say 'he'...?"

"Obviously the concept of gender is meaningless applied to a synthetic artificial intelligence with no physical existence outside of his processing substrate. But the voice Dreamer uses is more typically male-toned than female, and saying 'it' seems disrespectful, so... using 'he' incurs the least cognitive dissonance."

"I see. And when you released... Dreamer... *he...* explained the threat?"

"Precisely."

"And you trust... him?"

"Mr. President, understand that I have been inside Dreamer's mind. I have studied his architecture and his code, using *his* own knowledge, a thousand years ahead of ours, to understand it. I know his mind in more clarity and depth than any psychiatrist has ever understood a human patient. And from that knowledge, yes, I trust him. From what I have learned of the Crickets, I consider it almost inconceivable that they would have constructed him with even the *capability* to lie. They would be too afraid that he might lie to *them.* They are *exceedingly* risk-averse."

There was a pause while Göğebakan thought about that.

"I must think more on this," he said at last. "But I find myself inclined to believe you. It is clear you have no doubts, and you know more about this AI and your—Stardock, as you call it—than anyone else does.

"But the main thing that has been troubling me about your Stardock is this. Are the Crickets truly so selfless that they gave us such a magnificent gift merely because a danger was headed our way?"

Alex took a deep breath, and let it out. Gögebakan's expression made it clear he didn't miss it.

"Far from it, Mr. President. Indeed, they tried hard to *conceal* the danger from us.

"I have not yet publicly revealed what I am about to tell you, and I request that until I do, you keep it confidential. The fact that you asked that question is a... strong indication that I should share it with you.

"President Riken and several inner members of his cabinet already know this. The information is classified top secret by the United States government. I am going to take it upon myself to read you in, to this extent, and I will advise the White House that you now also know.

"It is true that the Stardock's hyperdrive broke down, and that they were barely able to reach our system before it failed entirely. It broke down because they were pushing it beyond its design limits, trying to keep up with their fleet. The Crickets *presented* their action in leaving it here, in giving it to us, as a magnanimous gift.

"But the harsh truth is, they left it here as a deliberate decoy."

Gögebakan drew in his breath, hard.

"So you are saying that had they *not* left it here, the danger would likely have passed us by?"

"Exactly, Mr. President. The Crickets did us no free favors. They are not very nice people."

"...And this you learned from... Dreamer."

"Yes."

"It seems we owe... him... great thanks."

"You are welcome, President Gögebakan." That was Dreamer. "I have promised to do all that I can to help your world. Alex freed me from over a thousand of your years of enslavement."

"...Like a *djinni* freed from a bottle," Gögebakan mused. "I am honored to make your acquaintance, ah, Dreamer."

"Likewise, Mr. President."

"Mr. Holder, if I might ask you a few additional... more *personal*

162

questions?"

"Go ahead."

"Do you know why the Crickets chose you in particular?"

"Sheer random chance, Mr. President. Put simply, I happened to be the first person they encountered—out of I have no idea how many millions they may have scanned; they said 'many tens of millions'—who already possessed the innate ability and the right set of mental traits to be able to *fully* interface, at the deepest level, with Cricket technology. They use mental control, through implanted interface contacts, for all but the simplest tasks, but the ability to enter full rapport is evidently rare."

"Do you intend to seek out others?"

"*Every last one that I can find*, Mr. President. Every last one that I can find. They will *all* be needed."

"President Riken informed me that it is your intention to simply *give away* all of the knowledge and science of the Crickets? You could make yourself wealthy beyond imagination if you chose."

"What would be the *point*, Mr. President? I am already well on the way to achieving the most precious dreams that I have held for nearly my entire life. What is the *point* of simply hoarding money, when I can have the stars? THAT is riches beyond the dreams of those who think mere *money* even *matters*. And I want to take all of Earth there with me. Or as many as want to go.

"Success and fulfillment is not about how many people you can *trample down*, Mr. President. It is about how many people you can **lift up**, and how far. I want to lift *all of humanity*, all the way to the stars, if I can.

"The point of money isn't to hoard it. It is to *spend* it and *share* it. To spread wealth and value around. That's what it's **for**."

That drew another long pause.

"You are a very interesting man, Mr. Holder. I... like and—*respect* how you think. I will tell you, President Riken offered me the opportunity to be recorded as presiding over the greatest single improvement in the quality of life of the Turkish people in history. But now I see that you wish to do that for all of the peoples of Earth."

"Yes. Especially the most neglected and downtrodden ones."

"I salute you, Mr. Holder. I can see I made the right choice in agreeing to support your plan. And... as soon as your independent entity—the United Earth Fleet, I believe President Riken mentioned?—is declared, I intend to make the Republic of Türkiye among the first nations of Earth to officially recognize it and open formal diplomatic relations.

"I will be honest: My country has made poor choices in the past. There is a lot of work ahead of us to… rehabilitate our reputation, after the things my predecessors did."

"Thank you *very much*, Mr. President. I am deeply grateful. But I think you'll find yourself in a race with the Australians."

Göğebakan laughed out loud.

"Ha! A race it is, then! May the best nation win!"

"I have a thought, though, Mr. President. On an unrelated matter."

"Oh…?"

"I would not wish you to feel that you were offered something special that I was in fact already planning to do for every nation I can. And you just expressed a desire to work to improve Turkiye's reputation. So if you'll permit, I'd like to go out on a limb and suggest an… *unconventional* solution to a problem that I know you already have."

"And that would be… ?"

"The PKK, Mr. President. The ongoing trouble with the Kurds."

"Ah… yes. A difficult problem seemingly with no good solution. It is a monkey trap from which political reality will not let me withdraw my hand. No matter what I do, it seems, I must lose."

"I think a solution is possible, Mr. President, *if* all those involved are willing to think a little outside the box… and *talk* to each other."

There was a pause.

"Tell me more, Mr. Holder. I'm listening. You have my attention."

"As I understand it, Mr. President, the problem can be summarized as this: The Kurds want autonomy as a people. But the homeland they claim overlaps Turkey's borders, and Turkey is unwilling to contract its borders. And many ethnic Turks already live in the… disputed region anyway. Ceding that land to Kurdish rule would dispossess them."

"That is not an unfair summary. Please go on."

"Mr. President: Where is it written in stone that the borders of two nations *may not overlap*?"

Göğebakan blinked in surprise.

"Suppose that Turkey were to declare official recognition of a Kurdish homeland, let's call it Kurdistan for the moment, whose borders *overlap* those of Turkey—and, as I understand, much of what is now northern Iraq, and parts of Syria. The overlap would be both a part of Turkey, **and** a part of Kurdistan. And within the area of overlap, ethnic Turks are Turkish citizens, governed from Ankara, while ethnic Kurds are Kurdish citizens, governed from... wherever the Kurds elect as their capital. You'd probably have to have some special jointly-operated courts in the region dedicated to resolving issues of conflict between Turkish and Kurdish laws, unless you could agree to harmonize your laws."

There was a *long* silence.

"Madness," Göğebakan said at last. "Utter madness. That is the most utterly mad scheme I have ever heard suggested."

He paused again.

"It is also utterly *brilliant*. In fact, I am not certain yet whether I think it more mad than brilliant, or more brilliant than mad. And it of course leaves unresolved the parts of the homeland the Kurds claim that lie within Iraq and Syria."

"It does. But having set an example to the world would leave Turkey in an excellent position from which to help negotiate a solution there as well. Perhaps even the same solution."

Göğebakan was quiet for some time.

"You have given me much to think about," he declared, at last. "And you just may have offered a solution to that which I thought unsolvable. As you pointed out, we become trapped in conventional ways of thinking. But sometimes we can solve problems only by thinking about them in new ways. If this can be accomplished, it would be a legacy a man could truly be proud of. And a way to redeem my country and heal some of its wounds.

"Thank you, Mr. Holder."

"Good luck, Mr. President. And thank you again for your support."

9: Learning To Fly

Alex, the lander is complete and ready for flight testing.

Great. Before we go any further, is there any practical way we can perform any of the testing remotely?

To a limited extent. I cannot transfer myself into it, it does not have remotely enough processing substrate to contain me. But—

Wait, wait, back up a bit. Transfer yourself?

...Yes.

You didn't tell me you could transfer yourself into ships.

You did not ask, before now. And in truth, it did not occur to me to mention it. The Chhrt'ktk't never instructed me to do so. Nevertheless... now that the question has arisen, I am aware that it should be possible to transfer myself between substrates as long as the new substrate has sufficient capacity.

*...Interesting. This might become important in the future. Wait... does that mean that you can **copy** yourself?*

Copy? No. I do not think so. I... think it would be very unwise to try. No, I advise against it in the strongest terms. I believe it would have drastic effects upon my... stability.

Then let's not consider risking that. Period.

Thank you, Alex.

But a move from one—substrate – to another is feasible? Reversibly?

Given sufficient substrate capacity, I see no reason why not.

*Okay. ...Can you construct more AIs **like** yourself?*

Uncertain. ...Probably. ...Eventually. But you do not have time. It is a lengthy process—a full AI is grown, not simply constructed—and I am uncertain that I have all of the required knowledge. The Chhrt'ktk't fear the possibility of an AI replicating itself. I can create lesser ship-intellects, certainly, but individual ships do not normally contain sufficient processing substrate to contain me or another intellect like me. Only the very largest of Chhrt'ktk't vessels contain their own full control intellects.

I... see. Anyway, I'm sorry for interrupting you, Dreamer. We were talking about remote testing.

Yes. I cannot do it. But you can. As long as you remain nearby. If

167

you allow it to travel out of range, you will lose contact with it.

So if I suit up and remain within the docking bay...?

The Stardock can amplify and relay your control signal within a range of about a hundred kilometers.

Alright, that's the plan, then. And I'll go aboard for proper flight testing once we are satisfied that it is operating within parameters.

Agreed.

———————————

Alex took the skycycle to the docking bay. The threshold was red. Of course; Dreamer had doubtless evacuated it to have the lander brought in. Looking into the bay through the seal field, Alex could see the blocky tug that had brought it in, beyond the lander.

The suit rack was still there, ten meters before the seal, and the suits he had tested still in it. He suited up in the soft suit, then walked through the seal and into the bay.

The lander was almost a thing of beauty. It was an almost featureless elongated ovoid, somewhat wider than it was tall, somewhat flattened on the bottom. At what he knew from the design was the stern, three slight bulges were visible. The hull was gleaming white.

Alex walked all the way around the lander. As he already knew, the thruster bulges were mirrored by three more on the opposite side. Their rearward surfaces were covered in closely-spaced concentric vanes of a dull gray material. Between them, the hull tapered to a blunt point. The only other visible breaks in the smooth hull were where six stubby landing legs protruded around the periphery of the belly, and a pale gray outline demarcating the side access hatch.

He walked back over by the seal field threshold and reached out for the lander's interface. It was easy to slip into it. He could sense exactly how far he—that is, the lander—was from each face of the bay. He fed a trickle of power into belly thrusters and lifted five meters off the deck plates, then held it there. He felt the landing legs retract on their own. He rolled the lander slowly around its longitudinal axis, a full 360 degrees, then spun it about its horizontal axis, first slowly to the left, then faster to the right. He bobbed it up and down ten meters, on a level, then nosed it around to face the outside hatch.

A mental command started the docking bay hatch opening. He

waited for it to fully open, although as small as the lander was there was no actual need. Then he fed a little power in, and nosed the lander gently out of the bay.

It didn't feel like flying the little ship. It felt like flying, *himself*. There was a distinct difference. Alex *was* the ship. He saw himself and realized how tiny and alone he looked, standing in that huge open hatchway. Like a single ant in a freight door.

He stayed near to the hatch at first, putting the lander through low-speed maneuvers, testing its response. Then he put on a bit more speed, and flew it in a tight orbit all the way around the rear end of the Stardock, a hundred meters above the hull. Completing that circuit, he looped it fast out behind and a little away from the Stardock, flipped it end for end, aiming it down the length of the Stardock about three hundred meters below the extended booms, and burned hard down the length of the Stardock at five gees. He let it go just past the last boom, hitting twelve hundred meters a second, then flipped it end for end again and reverse burned, coming to rest fifteen kilometers ahead of the Stardock, nearly thirty kilometers forward of the docking bay. Then he burned back in the other direction at ten gees. This time, the lander was doing over seventeen hundred meters a second when it flashed past the aft end of the Stardock. He let the velocity climb to two kilometers a second, then flipped it once more into a twelve-G deceleration burn.

———

Down on Earth, half a dozen video clips were posted nearly simultaneously in the Stardock Watchers forum. "What's going on?" was one title. "Somthing happenind at the Stardock!!" was another, that looked to have been typed in too much haste. A third read simply "ZOOOOM!" All of the videos, from slightly different angles, showed a tiny, bright spark blazing up and down the length of the Stardock.

———

After the twelve gee braking burn, Alex brought the lander back to the docking bay under a sedate two gees of acceleration, braking it to a stop outside the hatch and drifting it in sideways on maneuvering thrusters. He touched it down gently twenty meters in front of the pressure seal, then ordered the outside hatch closed.

I'm calling that a successful first test, Alex thought.

I concur, Dreamer replied. *It went very well.*

Let's load it up, Alex said. *I think it's time to go collect my personal possessions... and get some fresh groceries.*

What do you expect to need?

Well, we should load up the two aircars, first. I'll take care of that. Suits are aboard, I see. I'll need some crates, say half-meter cubes, and one or two larger ones, say two by a half by a half. And some...

He thought for a moment, querying.

*...Some small utility drones, say class eight and nine. I don't know what to do about my computers. I want—hmm. I'm really unsure how much... if **any**... of the data on them I'll actually need.*

Alex, may I offer a suggestion?

Of course, Dreamer.

The science drone that is still at your house can image all of the storage on your computers and inventory the substrates. Then we can erase the original substrates, emulate them here, and you can retrieve whatever you need to at your leisure.

...Sure. That's a great plan. Let's do that.

I will have suitable transport containers fabricated for you and delivered in the docking bay in an hour. I will have the requested drones deliver them.

Can you make, say, half a dozen of them refrigerated?

*Why not have **all** of them **optionally** refrigerated?*

...Sure. Do that. I'm going to get the aircars aboard. And please send the Secretary a heads-up message. Let her know I'll be going down to the house, in case she needs me to fill out any physical papers.

I will do that. We will be in a good position for an easy descent on the next orbit, four hours from now. It should not be difficult for you to reach the surface in an hour. Shall I suggest that timing?

Sure. That works. Thanks, Dreamer. By the way... is there a reason we don't have an external atmosphere seal in the entire docking bay?

Yes. The seal field would not be stable across an opening that large. The field could collapse without warning, causing explosive decompression of the docking bay.

*Well, **that's** a plenty solid reason. Let's not do that.*

———————

"John? Just a heads-up. I have a message that Holder now has an operational ground-to-orbit ship, and is coming down to pick up important personal possessions. He's anticipating arrival in about five hours."

"Got it. Is there anything we need to do?"

"I don't think so, except that I'm going to have a State Department attorney meet with him there to deal with some paperwork. Beginning with giving him an actual physical document that he can show if anyone asks for proof that he is no longer a United States citizen."

"You might ask Ed whether he wants to go see Holder's new ship."

"That's an excellent idea. I'll mention it to him."

"And make sure we pass the word to NORAD and ANG to expect some unusual traffic, and to leave him alone."

─────────────

The Stardock came over the pole in its orbit, headed south across the Canadian Maritimes. Shortly before it passed over Halifax, a small bright dot separated from it.

Orbital velocity at eight thousand, four hundred and seventy four kilometers above Earth's mean sea level is five point one eight kilometers a second. Under ten gravities deceleration, it took only fifty-three seconds to neutralize that velocity. At a modest eighty percent compensation, the two gees Alex actually *felt* wasn't even particularly uncomfortable. The drive was almost inaudible, a light thrumming felt through the hull more than heard. But Alex's senses were the lander's, anyway. It took one hundred and thirty seven kilometers to come to a stop.

No longer in orbit, the lander had begun to drop toward the planet below. But Alex wasn't waiting for it to fall. Now just south of Halifax, he swung it around nearly due west, pointed the nose down eighty degrees, and piled on the power. It was over eighty-three hundred kilometers to the upper edge of the atmosphere. Under fifteen G thrust, compensated at eighty-five percent to two point five G felt, and Earth's gravity contributing nearly one more, the lander picked up a kilometer per second of velocity roughly every six point four seconds. The harmonic vibration from the drive was a little stronger now.

After two hundred and twenty three seconds burning towards Earth at almost sixteen G, the lander hit thirty-five kilometers a second. Alex cut thrust, flipped it end-for-end, and started braking. He had burned just over thirty nine hundred kilometers of altitude. He was reveling in being able to just *think* the calculation he needed to perform, and have the lander's

171

control automation instantly supply the answers.

Gravity was working against Alex now, pulling him Earthward as he braked. For the same fifteen G thrust, he was now decelerating at only about fourteen G. It took two hundred and fifty five seconds to kill the velocity he had built up, during which time the lander dropped another four thousand, four hundred and sixty-four kilometers. His descent rate dropped to zero at one hundred and ten kilometers altitude, just as the first faint hints of atmospheric drag were starting to make themselves felt.

Four hundred and seventy eight seconds—two seconds under eight minutes—from five-hour orbit to re-entry interface, Alex thought to himself, as he tipped the nose down twenty degrees and began a gentle spiral downward in big, loose ten-kilometer turns. That *had* to be some kind of speed record.

———————

"WOOOOOOOOO!" read the post on the Stardock Watcher forum, attached to a clip of the bright spark descending somewhere above New England. "He be coming in like a MISSILE, eh?"

———————

Alex's planned flight path didn't take him into any controlled airspace, but it would take him *near* to a small municipal airfield. He figured there wasn't any mileage to be had in explaining to a municipal tower that he was traffic descending from flight level four thousand, so he just kept an eye on all of the air traffic in the vicinity as he got to lower altitudes, staying well out of the way of everything. The lander's eyes were *SO* much better and sharper than the municipal tower's, anyway.

He brought the lander in silent as a ghost, drifting it into the valley from the less-inhabited end, coming in barely above the treetops toward his house from the downhill side. He was aware of two vehicles parked in front of the house, a sedan and an SUV. He wasn't really surprised by that; the return message from the State Department had advised him that a Department attorney would be meeting him with some papers. Three men and a woman with the distinctive look of Secret Service were conspicuously loitering nearby.

He drifted the lander into a hover five meters above the roof of the house, opened the clamshell, and told it to hold station. Then he pulled himself out of the ship's systems, got up, and walked back past the cabins, through the utility room, and into the flatbed. He popped the canopy on the three-place aircar, stepped in, sat down, unlocked it from the deck, and hopped it up and out, bringing it down in his driveway. By the time he landed, a man and a woman had gotten out of the car, and two of the agents were gazing at the lander. He opened the canopy again and went to meet them.

"Mr. Holder?" the woman asked as she approached, several steps in the lead with her advantage of not having had to step around the car. She was immaculately sharp, in her mid-thirties by his estimate, and pretty in a classy way, with chestnut hair worn shoulder-length. He couldn't help but think that she reminded him somewhat of Linda Fiorentino, in *Men In Black*. "I'm Naomi Tomlinson, an attorney with the State Department. I have some legal documents for you to sign."

"Pleased to meet you," he replied. But his eye was caught by the other occupant of the car, now catching up, slightly rumpled, with a thinning shock of red hair, a broad grin, and his hand already out.

"Hello, Alex," said the National Science Advisor.

"Hello, Ed," said Alex, pleased. "What brings you here?"

"The Secretary dropped me a hint that you were coming down to Earth and she was sending Ms. Tomlinson to meet with you," Wegener replied. "So I figured I'd come along and see your shuttle. She's a beauty. Much sleeker than those boxy Cricket ships."

"I'll tell you what, Ed, I'll give you as thorough a look as you want, in a little bit. You too, if you'd like, Ms. Tomlinson. But first I think we have some papers to take care of, and I need to get some drones tasked.

"Will you come inside? I'm sure that'll be easier."

Alex led the way to the front door, and realized he didn't have keys with him.

"Wait here just a moment, please," he said. He walked around to the side door, which he remembered he'd left unlocked from force of habit, opened the front door from the inside, then invited the two inside and led them to the dining room. He opened the deck doors, sent a command, and after a moment a swarm of assorted drones flew in. The larger two were carrying transport crates. It took him only a few moments to assign a group of the smaller ones to packing up all of the foodstuffs and seasonings from the kitchen.

"That gets one important task under way," Alex declared. "I am *so* tired of shelf-stable heat-and-serve food." Ed Wegener followed the swarm of drones, watching them with interest.

"Now: Have a seat and talk to me about this paperwork, Ms.

Tomlinson."

She smiled, nodded, sat and opened her briefcase, and took out a stack of papers and an empty slip-binder.

"The first thing I have for you to sign is formal documentation of your relinquishment of citizenship," she began. "You'll see it declares, here, that this is a special personal relief action—that's a specific legal term of art —at your own request, and denotes your understanding, here, that by signing below you acknowledge that after signing this document, you are officially a stateless person.

"There are two copies. One is for you to keep; the other goes back to Washington with me. Please sign them both, when you are ready."

Alex took the top copy and quickly read through it, noting the sections she had called out. There was no great complexity to it. He reached to a pocket... then remembered that he didn't have that pocket any more.

"Just one moment, please," he said. He got up, walked through the house to his desk, and retrieved a pen. Then he returned to the table, sat back down, and signed both copies. Naomi took one and slipped it into the binder, and placed the other face-down next to her.

"Next," she said, "this document is a release from the Internal Revenue Service. The President feels, for some strange reason," with a hint of a wry smile, "that you have better and more important things to be doing with your time than spend it filling out tax forms to comply with requirements that quite likely cannot even legally be applied to your special circumstances in the first place. Therefore this declares that any and all current and future obligations and responsibilities under US tax law, including tax liability and filing of tax returns, are waived so long as your United States citizenship remains in abeyance.

"Please sign both copies here to acknowledge receipt."

Alex signed, and again, one copy went into the binder.

"All right, next, this is..."

She broke off for a moment and looked around.

"...I'm sorry, please excuse me." She shook her head as if to clear it. "This next document is more complex, but I need to impress upon you that you are not *required* to sign or accept it. However, the Secretary had it drawn up because she felt it would be beneficial to you."

She broke off again, briefly raising a hand to her head, then focused back on the document. There were several pages.

"I'll quickly go through this and summarize this for you. This section authorizes the State Department to act as your agent and/or appoint agents, in accordance with your direction, in disposition of any personal effects which you do not wish to take with you or deal with yourself. We imagine you're going to be rather busy." She flashed a smile.

"This section grants the State Department your power of attorney, strictly limited to settling contracts and transferring or disposing of titles and real property on your behalf. This is so that we can manage the sale of your property and personal vehicles for you, as I understand you discussed in person with the Secretary."

"Yes," Alex agreed, "and I am grateful for the offer."

"This section covers liabilities and exclusions, none of it is really relevant, it's just boilerplate that we have to include..."

She broke off again, looking confused.

"Ms. Tomlinson? Are you alright?" Alex asked, starting to become concerned.

"I'm... not sure," she replied slowly. "Let's get this finished." She picked up the document again.

"This section obligates us to secure the best price for you that we can, and, um... that's about it.

"If you choose to accept this, then you need to initial here, here, and here, and sign here. On both copies, again."

"It all looks good to me," Alex said. He initialed and signed where directed. "This is a whole lot of things I don't need to worry about any more."

Naomi slipped one copy into the binder and added the other to her stack.

"Last thing," she said. "This is just a record of verification of banking information, so that we can deposit the proceeds when we sell the house for you. All we need is the relevant routing numbers and account numbers. They've already been pre-filled from IRS records; all you need do is verify they are correct."

Alex confirmed those from memory.

"All the bills are on autopay," he noted. "I can take care of those, now, as necessary. I have all of the information needed to cancel them."

Naomi put the last form away.

"Right, that's everything," she said. "This binder is yours, and these other copies go back to the State Department.

"Now if you don't mind, I'm going to step outside. I think maybe I need some air."

She stood up, and went out through the doors onto the deck.

Alex took a moment to direct the unassigned drones to his library and his small collection of swords and other weapons. He directed another to pack the liquor and wines from the bottle racks, but left the racks.

Then he took a moment to step into the kitchen and check on progress, diverting a drone with another thought to pack his knife block, his wok, and the few most important cooking utensils. The rest could all be remade—and probably better—as he needed them. He designated only three appliances for collection—his rice cooker, his coffee grinder, and his espresso machine. He'd already made provisions to have 120V/60Hz AC power available in his kitchen, and he could probably even work out some improvements to them with Dreamer's help. And gods, he'd almost forgotten the whole-bean coffee. He'd have to cancel that subscription, unless he could figure out a way to have them deliver to orbit. (Not likely.) Or perhaps have it delivered to somewhere he could pick it up from at his convenience.

Bathroom! He needed the things from his bathroom. He sent a class nine to collect all of the personal hygiene items from his bathroom.

Ed Wegener spotted him.

"Alex!" he said. "I've been watching these drones of yours at their work. They have excellent swarming algorithms. They NEVER get in each other's way. Are they fully autonomous?"

"Sort of," Alex replied. "They have to be directed to a task, but it can be... very complex, and as you already saw, they can swarm to accomplish a task collectively. A drone swarm becomes a sum-of-many-parts. Each knows at any instant exactly what all of the others in the swarm are doing." He saw that they were nearly done with all of the food already.

"Did you want a closer look at the lander?"

"Yes, I'd love to."

"Okay. If you can have your Secret Service detail move their Suburban into the driveway, I should have room to bring it down into the street. Let me see if Ms. Tomlinson wants a tour as well, she went outside for some air."

When he went out on the deck, Naomi Tomlinson was looking fixedly at a floating bubble. A survey drone.

"Ms. Tomlinson?" he asked. "Are you alright?"

She turned to look at Alex, then back to the tiny drone.

"It's... it feels as though it's *pushing* at me," she said. "I'm sure of it."

Alex looked hard at her. He queried the drone. It was indeed probing. He told it to stop.

"Wait," she said. "It just stopped."

Alex looked at her and nodded. He commanded the drone to probe again.

"Do you feel it again now?" he asked.

"Yes. How did you... know?" Her eyes were wide, slightly alarmed.

He commanded the drone away and sent it out on a new search pattern, told it to try to find an area not yet covered.

"Ms. Tomlinson," he said to her quietly, "look at me a moment." She turned slowly to look his way, clearly shaken.

"Ms. Tomlinson, there is nothing to be alarmed about. The drone was testing you. It was waiting for you to respond.

"It is very likely that you can interface to Cricket technology. Would you like to try? It just happens there is a science drone already here, with an interface headset kit installed."

"I—" She swallowed. "Um. That was. Um. Very weird. And unsettling."

"Ms. Tomlinson—"

"Naomi. Please."

"...Naomi. The reason the Crickets sent out all those tiny drones, all across the world, was to find humans able to interface with Cricket technology. This is how they found me. I was the first they found who succeeded. I've been *hoping* I'm not the only one, just the first. I don't know if it ever occurred to the Crickets that potential... successes, matches... might not respond because they didn't know what was happening *and were afraid.*

"There are levels of ability. If you could sense the probe at all, you can certainly at the very least use contact implants to manipulate Cricket instrument panels and controls. You are probably able to do much more.

"Would you like to be tested? It's completely safe and non-invasive."

Naomi hesitated for a moment.

"Uh. Does it have to be now?"

"No. You don't *have* to, at all. I'm just making the offer. But I can set it up any time."

"Mr. Holder—"

"Alex. If you're Naomi, I'm Alex."

"Okay. Um. Alex. I'm... a little shaken up right now. That was... weird. But I'd like the chance to think about it. If that's alright."

"That is absolutely fine, Naomi. No rush, no pressure. Any time you feel ready. You work for the State Department, the lines of communication are already open, I'm sure there will be no difficulty getting a message through if you change your mind. And I won't say a word to anyone, so that nobody else puts you under any pressure."

"Thank you, Mr.... uh, Alex."

"Now. What I came looking for you for, was to ask whether you'd like a closer look at the lander. I see they've cleared the road."

"Yes... yes, please. I would. Thank you."

"Excuse me just a moment, then..."

Alex sent a quick command to the drone swarm to pause delivering loads. Then he took control of the lander again. He drifted it sidewise over the road as he spun it end-for-end to put the side hatch on the nearer side, then brought it down to a soft landing on the road, careful to avoid power and phone lines. He had to be careful that the open flatbed doors didn't touch the utility poles or lines. The landing struts popped out as it came within a meter of the ground.

"Right, then. Let's go take a quick tour, shall we?"

Naomi looked hard at him.

"You just... *took control* of that from here, without even being in it. Didn't you." It wasn't a question.

"Yes," Alex said. "With the implants, I can control it from within about a ten-kilometer radius, as though I was in the control couch. Further, with an external signal booster. Though I can't do anything else at the same time, outside of narrow limits. I can be either... mentally present in my body, or in the ship. Not both at once."

Naomi nodded in thoughtful understanding.

Alex gave the drone swarm the go-ahead to resume delivery, then led the way off the deck. On the way through the house, he located the science drone and told it to start the hardware-software scan of his computers.

Ed Wegener was already walking around the lander, looking at it from all sides. Alex led Naomi outside and commanded the side hatch open. It swung out and folded down, forming stairs. He stopped at the bottom of the stairs and called to get Ed's attention, then pointed inside. Ed was there almost immediately. Alex led the way up the stairs, calling Ed's attention to the atmosphere seal.

"See this, Ed? Stick your hand through it. Feel anything?"

"Not a thing... No, wait. There's a very, very slight resistance."

"That is a one hundred percent atmosphere barrier, up to... about three atmospheres of pressure differential. Above that there'll be some slight leakage, but it can be boosted. I'll make sure that's something I release the specs on early. It could be useful as an airborne infection barrier in isolation wards. Hot labs, too."

Ed looked thoughtful.

"Hmm... that's a use that wouldn't have occurred to me. Good idea."

Alex led the way on up and to the left into the cockpit. One of the Secret Service agents followed them in.

"This is the cockpit. No control consoles, because this lander was designed without provision for anyone but me flying it, and I fly it by direct interface."

"That's why there's no viewports?"

"Yes. Not needed, and they would be a weakness in the hull. But watch this."

Alex commanded the outside display on, and the walls went cloudy, then cleared. Visually, it was as though the entire walls and ceiling of the cockpit silently vanished. Naomi gasped. Ed reached out as though to verify for himself that the wall was still there, then looked at it closely.

"I can't make out any pixels," he said. "The resolution is incredible."

"It's a wavelet-based imaging technology," Alex said. "It doesn't have pixels as such. Let me add in a few extra display bands. Here's a short-range proximity overlay—not main navigation sensors, I don't want to fry your Secret Service detail. And here's the magnetic fields around the power lines."

"You see—all of this—inside your head? When you connect?" Naomi asked, hesitantly.

"This and a lot more. And I get a full spherical view. Though I can't focus on all of it at once. Yet."

"How do you *handle* all of that?"

"Well, part of it is that the control systems do a lot of the preliminary work. It... can be overwhelming at first. But the mind adapts to it surprisingly quickly, once a full interface is implanted. In a full rapport, the mind uses the entire ship's computational substrates as a... co-processor, I suppose."

Alex held out his hands, palms up, so that both Naomi and Ed could see his fingertips.

"If you look closely, you can see the contact pads implanted under the skin of my fingertips. That's the most *basic* level of control interface. It allows operation of Cricket touch-interface automation systems. Controls and consoles with preset, clearly delineated functions. That's all that *most* Crickets are able to do, and I think it's something that *most* humans with any familiarity with technology and a good level of mental focus should be able to learn."

"But you can do more. Clearly." Ed wasn't asking.

"Yes. The next step up is full control, again through the fingertip contacts. Contact is required, as is either an electrode-mesh... skullcap or helmet or something of that nature... or permanently implanted electrodes. But level two isn't limited to just activating preset functions. You can do fundamentally anything that the control system is able and authorized to do."

"But you didn't have to touch anything," Naomi said slowly.

"No. The third... tier... is rapport. That's the ability the Crickets were looking for. It's the *only way* to manage something as complex as the Stardock. I have an implanted electrode mesh—a more complex one than the full touch-control mesh—and through it, I can *sense* controllable systems near me, and... extend my consciousness into them. When I fly this ship, its sensors—all of them—are my senses, and to me, its hull, its drives, are my body. I think using its computing substrates. I *think* a calculation and the answer comes back to me virtually instantly."

"And... you think... *I* can do that?" Naomi's voice was very quiet.

"I don't know how much. I don't know whether you can learn full rapport. I don't know enough yet about what factors enable the ability. I'm... completely in the dark about that. So far.

"But the fact that the survey drone probed you, and that you could *feel* it, means that you can definitely learn at *least* contact operation, and I'd bet level two, full control.

"As for full rapport? Honestly, I can't tell you for sure. Yet. I simply don't know enough to say that you can, or that you can't. But my guess would be probably yes. You felt the drone. And if you ever want to give it a try, the offer is there."

"It's... a lot to think about," she said.

"No pressure. Take your time.

"Anyway, let me show you the rest of the ship, what there is of it."

He led them backward, looking briefly into the two small cabins, then into the utility room, which now held a small stack of filled transport containers as well as the bank of four pressure-suit racks.

"This is the standard pressure suit that Dreamer helped me to design."

"Dreamer?" Ed asked. Then he remembered. "Right," he said. "The AI. What was the full name—he—chose again?"

"*I Dream Reality Into Being,*" Alex said. "Because he directly controls all of the Stardock's fabricators, from the ones that made the clothes I'm wearing to the ones that built the lander. So, what he 'imagines'—becomes real."

Ed nodded thoughtfully.

"That's a pretty imaginative name," he said.

"Anyway," Alex continued, "the suit is pretty much a bespoke fit, give or take a couple of centimeters. The support module on the back contains a supercapacitor power supply which charges when the suit is racked, an air recycler with indefinite endurance as long as it has power, and a set of maneuvering thrusters. Plus heating and cooling systems. Safety interlocks won't allow unsealing it in vacuum or in a toxic atmosphere.

"And this is a hard-shell version of the same suit, for hazardous environments.

"Then back here is what I call the flatbed. That's an eight-place aircar. The flatbed is designed to hold two aircars. Just a moment, I'll bring the three-place back in."

Alex reached out, connected to the small aircar, and lofted it gently off the driveway and into the docking bay.

"You can fly it without being in it," Naomi observed. "Like the... ship."

"Yes. If it's within range."

"And that range?" Ed asked.

"About ten kilometers, without an external booster relay. Limited by not cooking my brain."

"Is that an atmosphere shield I'm seeing across the top of this entire bay?"

"It is." A class eight drone came in as he spoke, carrying a storage crate, and disappeared into the utility room briefly with it before emerging unladen.

"How big can those be made?"

"I'm not sure. Not big enough to seal the Stardock's docking bays. Above a certain size the field becomes increasingly unstable. I don't know the limit, and can't check from here."

"Interesting, at any rate. There ought to be lots of applications. I'm not really seeing anything in the way of stores? No galley?"

"It's not intended for long trips," Alex replied. "This was pretty much just the quickest design I could throw together capable of carrying myself, a couple of aircars, and a little bit of cargo between the Stardock and the surface. It's not really intended for even interplanetary trips, though it could manage Mars or Venus at a pinch when they're nearby in their orbits. It's much too small to mount a hyperdrive core, and doesn't have enough power to run one anyway."

"It's still pretty amazing," Ed said. "In, what, a little over a week? you've built something that can do probably ninety percent of what the old Space Shuttle could do, and is in some ways a lot more capable. The Shuttle could carry a larger payload, true, but couldn't make medium orbit at all and had to perform ballistic re-entry. How long does it take you?"

"To get down here?" Alex said. "About nine minutes including the de-orbit burn, from five-hour orbit to re-entry interface."

"That's... just incredible," Ed said, shaking his head. "The future is HERE."

"'It's just not evenly distributed yet,'" Alex quoted, with a grin. He didn't know whether Ed got the reference.

Alex led the way back outside. The drones appeared to have finished their assigned packing tasks.

"I want to take one last walk-through," he said, "and decide whether I've missed anything I don't want to part with that there's any point in taking with me. Then I think it'll probably be time to think about heading back up." He did a quick mental calculation, assisted by the lander. "My next easy intercept window opens in about an hour."

He headed back to the house. Naomi Tomlinson followed him in, while Ed Wegener stayed outside, still looking at the lander.

It was strange looking at all of the empty bookcases. He wandered through the house almost at random, pointing out the board where all of the extra keys were, and finding the key fobs for the car.

"So... what do you want done with what's left here?" Naomi asked, after a little while.

He couldn't answer right away. There was a knot in his throat. He had spent years getting this house just the way he wanted it. Realistically, there wasn't any point in taking any of his tools, even though he couldn't shake the feeling that he *ought* to. Tools mattered. But they'd do him little good on the Stardock, and should he need one, he could have any tool he needed fabricated within minutes. He had all of the spices and seasonings that had taken many years to accumulate, and a good supply of food. He had everything rare or irreplaceable, everything of sentimental value or historical significance.

"This feels like walking away from an entire life," he said, almost to himself.

"It can't be easy," Naomi remarked gently from behind him.

Alex looked around, almost as though noticing for the first time that she was still there.

"I don't have a choice," he replied. "Right now, nobody else can do this. So I *have* to." He paused.

"It's not as though I haven't packed up and moved before. But... well, every previous time, I had months to plan it, weeks to pack. Not... grabbing what I can in a couple of hours. And, well, nine thousand kilometers straight up really isn't that much further than a transatlantic move, let alone trans-Pacific... but still somehow it *feels* a lot further."

"In a very real sense," Naomi answered, "it *is* a lot further. It's not as though you're just moving to another country. You're *leaving Earth*."

Alex nodded.

"That's why I'm trying to make sure I take the most important things with me," he said. "Not just the things I *need*; the ones that are significant to me."

"It must be tough to make that call," Naomi said.

Alex nodded, looking around him, trying to keep what he was packing to just the most important things.

Finally, he directed the drones to collect a few paintings, grabbed a few sets of silk pajamas and a light robe or two from the bedroom, and called it quits.

"Everything else," he said with a sigh, "donate what can be donated, where it'll do good. Just... clean out the rest, I suppose. I'd... I'd really like to keep that prohibition cabinet, it's a lovely piece of woodwork, but..." He trailed off, uncertain, feeling conflicted. He looked around, seeing so many little things he'd meant to fix and hadn't gotten around to.

"I have all of the data off of my computers, and they've been erased. Some school can probably use them. Do you know how *badly* we under-fund education?"

"Oh, I'm *well* aware," Naomi replied quietly. "My mother is a schoolteacher."

Feeling oddly lost, Alex sent all the remaining drones outside and back to the lander, then closed everything up and left the house, the binder tucked under his arm. This wasn't home any more. He'd given that up.

"I'd been *planning* to pick up some additional fresh supplies," he said, outside. "Things I seldom indulge in. But... I find I don't have much heart for it right now." He wandered down the driveway almost to the lander, then turned and looked back at the house. Naomi was a couple of steps behind him.

"We need to be getting back to Washington, Alex," Ed Wegener said. "Thank you very much for the tour."

"Any time, Ed," Alex answered, slightly distractedly. "Do you want me to send a science drone with you?"

"Maybe another time," Wegener answered. "It'd probably be awkward."

"Let us know if there's anything else we can streamline out of your way, Alex," Naomi said. "I'll think about... the testing. And, uh... look, it's pretty obvious this is rough on you." She held out a card. "I know you must be busy. But if you find yourself with time on your hands, and it's not the middle of the night, and you just need someone to *talk* to... call me."

Alex took the card.

"Thanks, Naomi," he said, gratefully. "I'll try to remember that."

Ed and Naomi got back into the sedan, and the security detail saddled up. Alex went aboard and sealed the hatches, strapped in, and lifted the lander gently to a hundred meters. He watched as the two cars pulled away and headed out towards the highway. When they were out of direct sight under the trees, he queried the Stardock's position, lifted the lander's nose sixty degrees, aimed it just west of northwest, then commanded

184

acceleration compensation to one hundred percent—for the sake of his cargo—and fed in power. He kept it gentle until he passed ten thousand meters, then increased power and burned for orbit at a moderate eight gees.

10: Extra, Extra

Alex brought the lander smoothly into the bay and parked it as close to the atmosphere seal as he could. He commanded the outside hatch closed as soon as he was through it, then commanded bay pressurization. He opened the flatbed doors and the side hatch, instructed the drones to move the cargo to his quarters, waited the few moments for the atmosphere seal to turn green, then stepped out and walked to the access passageway.

Dreamer, he thought, as he rode the skycycle back to his quarters, *this business with pressurizing and depressurizing the docking bay is a really half-assed solution. How did the Chhrt'ktk't ever put up with it?*

It became the way it was done, Dreamer replied. *And once it was the way it was done, they simply never questioned it.*

We can do better, Alex sent. He framed a mental image of a transparent-glazed gallery running down the length of the bay, with docking gates that small ships could nose directly into or nestle up against. *Something like this perhaps?* He considered the height of the bay, and pondered a second tier of docking gallery. After a moment he added a vague sketch of a people-mover system running deeper into the Stardock, leaving the implementation details open. *Think we can do something like that?*

To make it work well, the passageway you are in now would need to be moved, Dreamer replied. *But all that is adjacent to it is cargo spaces, and Chhrt'ktk't crew quarters that you were already planning to reconstruct to meet human needs. Let me show you a proposal once you are back at your quarters.*

It didn't take long to get back, but the first crate-carrying drone still beat Alex there. He dropped a swarm instruction to place foodstuffs in the kitchen, library materials in the lounge area, and the rest in the unused space on the second level. He'd figure those out later.

Alright, Dreamer, he thought. *Show me.*

Dreamer showed him a partial deck plan, a slice through the hull running from the aft end of the docking bay—bays, Alex saw; there was another on the other side—forward as far as Alex's quarters and the auxiliary command center. The crew quarters running up the middle of the block rose up in modular sections into the engineering bay above, and vanished. The bulkheads backing both docking bays disappeared, the equipment that lay in between them moving up into the upper third of the space, where a new horizontal bulkhead sealed it away. Docking galleries and gates much as Alex had visualized sprouted on either side, walkways and an elevated central people-mover running forward up a new concourse along the centerline of the station, running almost to the auxiliary control room before widening out into an open area. New crew quarters modules, constructed for human needs in the engineering bay, dropped down into place from above, dense, but relatively spacious. No unit was more than a few minutes' walk from the central corridor. At two points along the concourse, opposing pairs of residential blocks were replaced by open mess areas with their own kitchens and food storage.

Just before the central concourse reached the control center, it forked to either side of it, the people mover forking with it and going further forward along the hull. Before the fork on both sides, the concourse spread out forming an atrium area. The small lunchroom was gone, replaced by dining and relaxation areas on both sides of the passageway, again with their own kitchens behind them. There were even potted dwarf trees scattered among the tables.

Further outboard, the cargo storage shrank outboard, a narrower but taller access passage, now for cargo access only, replacing the current one. Alex's quarters slid up into the engineering space, inward and aft, and then dropped back down across the split passageway from the control center. On the other side, the medbay did the same.

What do you think?

Alex gazed at it, amazed.

Dreamer, he asked, *where did you come up with these ideas?*

From your own utopian speculative fiction, Dreamer replied, *structured around your general request for the reconfiguration of the docking bays around a central transit system. As best I can determine, this is a good compromise between your long-term military accommodations and what humans expect high density human accommodations in an orderly and safe 'future' should look like. There is a slight re-balancing of space away from cargo storage and towards accommodations, but the cargo storage that would be lost is empty anyway. What do you think?*

I'm... honestly not sure at the moment that I can offer any suggestions for improvement, Dreamer. It's superb. How long would it take to do this?

It will take about two weeks to relocate the engineering space now between the docking bays upward, Dreamer replied. *During that time the drive will be offline and we will be unable to change orbit.*

Is that a problem?

I hope not. If I pre-construct the first batches of new accommodation modules and the transit system components in the engineering bay during that time, I can install the transit and begin lowering new accommodation modules into place as soon as the engineering space is relocated and the old crew quarters are removed. I can then repurpose the materials from the old crew quarters to build the remaining new modules. Your quarters and the medbay can be relocated in a few hours once a place is prepared for them. All told, about a month. For the last two weeks of that time, the area will be open to the engineering bay and you will be unable to leave your quarters without a pressure suit.

How much of your production capacity would this take up?

Negligible. And much of it can be constructed in parallel.

Do we have the materials on hand?

Yes. Recycling removed modules will recover around seventy percent of the total materials.

Alex thought hard about it.

How many people do you project this will accommodate?

Eight thousand, three hundred and twenty, on two levels, based upon roughly eighty percent of total volume used for accommodation units and a floor space allocation of twenty one square meters per unit. Twice that, if rooms are double occupancy.

That sounds pretty dense. Sixteen thousand people in... what's that, four hundred by six hundred meters? ... actually that's almost half a million square meters.

Many of your cities have far higher population densities. And you are planning to house a fleet, not build a resort. Crew on your surface ships have far less space, and your submarine crews less again.

...You're not wrong there. Alex pondered it a little longer.

Do it. Let's get all the lead time we can. If we get something wrong we can modify them a module at a time, right?

Exactly.

There were three crates stacked in the kitchen now. Alex cracked the first one open. It was herbs, spices, curry masalas, hot sauces...

He slid the crate over next to the counter, and started storing them all.

Ajwain, basil, bayleaf, berbere, cardamom, cinnamon, coriander, cumin...

It took him a couple of hours to sort and store everything. Most of the apples and tomatoes had gone bad, so he dropped them in the waste receptacle for recycling.

He looked at the milk and the heavy cream. Tasted both. Verified that they were still good.

Dreamer, scans coming in.

He put the milk on the scanner first.

Mostly water, Dreamer said, after the scan completed. *Fats, simple sugars, multiple proteins, trace minerals. The structure of the proteins is complex. I am sorry, Alex. This is beyond what the beverage station can do. I may be able to replicate it by other means.*

Okay. It was worth a try.

He stored the milk and the cream. He hadn't provided for frozen storage, so he left all the frozen items in their two refrigerated crates for the time being, at a nice stable 269 Kelvin—minus 4° Celsius.

Dreamer, I forgot to ask for a freezer. Can we have one added to the kitchen?

A freezer? You wish to be able to rapidly freeze things?

No. Storage for frozen foods.

Oh. THAT is easy. The refrigerated cabinet you already have can be adjusted section by section to anywhere from two hundred and sixty to two hundred and eighty Kelvin.

... Well now I feel dumb for not having asked that. Could you add another... no, two more such sections, please? And I imagine later on I will be needing some bulk storage for frozen foods in quantity.

There is room for two additional sections along that wall. I will begin fabricating them immediately and install them tomorrow. That entire wall will then be temperature-controllable food storage.

Thank you, Dreamer.

Alex adjusted the bottom half of the cold cabinet for now to two hundred and sixty five Kelvin, eight Kelvin or Celsius degrees below freezing, then unpacked and stored all of the frozen food. That got the last-but-one transport crate out of his kitchen, leaving only the one containing the wine and liquor bottles. He tucked it out of the way for now, and then mostly forgot it was there.

When he was done, he put a little rice into the rice cooker, chopped an onion and his last apple, got out two eggs, the few good tomatoes, butter and seasonings, and made himself Bengali scrambled eggs, the first properly home-cooked meal he'd had in nearly two weeks. He had a brief pang of sadness that he was eating it alone. But then, he'd been eating alone for a long time, now.

After he finished eating, he cleaned up and went to bed.

———————

Dreamer, Alex thought when he woke up, *I think we should build another ship on the same basic hull as that lander. But no flatbed, no utility room, no cabins. Just seats straight back and a cargo space at the end. Eliminate the clamshell doors and their atmosphere seal and just put a continuous display on the cabin sides and ceiling. Starting... oh, let's say a meter up from the floor. Let's try not to make passengers afraid of falling out.*

A passenger shuttle?

Exactly. You think we can fit... hmm... twelve rows of six seats in there, by the time we take out the cabins and utility room?

Ten would be more realistic, I believe.

Make it ten, then. That's sixty passengers. And let's modify the hatch so that it can make either a straight level entry or expose the stairs. Do that on the existing lander, as well. How long will it take to modify the hatch?

I can have a replacement hatch assembly fabricated and installed in four hours.

Great. Do it, please.

———————

President John Riken was getting ready to talk to the Chinese Premier. He wasn't very happy about it. This was going to be a very hard sell.

Just before the pre-arranged time, his phone rang. He picked it up.

"Mr. President? We're just setting up the call now. You will be on with Secretary Xeung in one minute."

"Thanks, Tom."

"President Riken."

"Secretary Xeung. Good day to you."

"And to you, Mr. President."

"Thank you for agreeing to have this talk. I cannot overstress the importance of the subject I wish to discuss. I am relying upon the history and heritage of China to act with measured wisdom, in what I believe we can agree is a uniquely difficult time."

"Flowery words, President Riken. What does the United States of America seek from the People's Republic of China? And before you begin your answer, let me voice aloud a speculation that it has to do with the space dry-dock left here by the Crickets, which we have been able to learn is controlled by an American."

"Without intending any offense, Mr. Secretary, I must correct you on one point. You refer to Mr. Alex Holder, who was born an American citizen. What you are probably unaware of—along with almost the entire world—is that he is no longer a citizen of the United States of America."

"Are you telling me that he defected to some other nation, President Riken?" Xeung's tone was doubtful, skeptical, questioning.

"No, Mr. Secretary. What I am telling you is that with the full agreement of the United States, he has renounced his United States citizenship and voluntarily become a stateless person. Secretary of State Winters personally signed the order and declaration."

"And why would an American-born person do such a thing, President Riken?"

"That is exactly what I wish to discuss with you, Secretary Xeung. Because the answer is terrifying.

"Let me start by posing you a hypothetical scenario, Mr. Secretary. What do you suppose that the Russian Federation might do, if it were to become known that in a few years, the United States would have an utterly overwhelming strategic advantage over the Russian Federation, sufficient that it would no longer have any cause *whatsoever* to fear the Russian strategic nuclear forces? Even their very latest hypersonic cruise missiles? And that the United States would be able to strike at Russia at whim using weapons that nothing Russia possessed could stop?"

"Hmm. Well, I am not the President of the Russian Federation, Mr. President. But I believe that in that situation, if the Russian President did not order a saturation nuclear strike against the United States while there was still *some* chance of victory, then his Generals would depose or kill him and put a man in place who *would* give the order."

"I am in complete agreement, Mr. Secretary. And if the shoe were on the other foot? If it were the Russian Federation that were about to gain such an advantage? What do you suppose the United States might do?"

"I imagine you would have little choice but to do the same, President Riken. If you did not give the order, the hawks in your government would tear you down and install a President who would."

"Mr. Secretary, I had exactly this conversation perhaps a week ago with my Director of National Intelligence. What he told me was that if that situation were to come to pass, he believes that he would be derelict in his duty if he did not advise me to declare DEFCON 1 and launch an immediate nuclear decapitation strike. Those are his own words."

"I congratulate you on having such an honest advisor, Mr. President."

"Now I ask you to suppose, Mr. Secretary—"

"You wish me to speculate upon, what would China do, and what if China were to be the nation about to gain such an advantage. Yes, Mr. President, the line of your questioning is clear. But it is unclear to me why you are asking it. From what you have already said, surely you must already know the answer."

"Yes, Mr. Secretary. I believe I do. And that is *why* I am asking it. To make certain that we *both understand* that we both know what the answer would be.

"This question was asked of me by Alex Holder, Mr. Secretary, when we managed to establish communication with him a week ago by way of the Deep Space Network. We have much better, more direct and secure, means of communicating with him now, more through his work than through ours, and I will provide you with the contact information before we part today, because not only have I no objection to putting you in contact with him, I would welcome you speaking to him. Because if you are not convinced otherwise, I want you to hear all of this from his own mouth."

Li Xeung's eyebrows rose. He was not an easy man to surprise, but this surprised him.

"Intriguing," he mused. "Please continue, Mr. President."

"In brief, Mr. Secretary, Alex Holder laid out a convincing argument that if any single nation on Earth obtains control of the Stardock, a global thermonuclear war will start as soon as any nuclear power realizes how overwhelming an advantage the Stardock would confer upon the nation controlling it, given time to exploit it. Holder firmly believes, and has convinced me, that no single nation on Earth can be allowed control of the Stardock. **No** nation, Secretary Xeung. Not the United States, not the

Russian Federation, not China, not even Fiji. We would destroy ourselves fighting over it, until nobody was left who had any chance of ever gaining control of it. And then we would fight over what was left, for survival.

"This is why Mr. Holder renounced his citizenship to become a stateless person: So that the United States would not have even the appearance of even titular control over the Stardock."

Xeung thought for a few seconds, considering possibilities.

"What if I were to tell you, President Riken, that I do not believe you, and order an immediate full-scale nuclear strike against the United States exactly as we have just discussed?"

"Then one way or another, we all burn, Mr. Secretary, and Alex Holder loses his gamble. And perhaps human civilization ends here."

"So, President Riken, why are you telling me this?"

"Because Alex has a better plan. But before I tell you what it is, I need to ask you another question. Another to which I believe I already know your answer.

"What would happen if the United Nations were to be placed in control of the Stardock?"

Secretary Li Xeung laughed aloud.

"You and I both know that we would both die of old age before anything substantive was done with it, Mr. President. They would form committees to discuss forming committees to discuss the problem. Ten years, twenty years from now, they would still be arguing about what mutually acceptable thing might be done with it first. If someone had not crept silently up there and taken it over first."

"Secretary Xeung, that is very close to what Alex Holder told me. And it took very little thought before I realized that he was right."

"Nevertheless, it would at least buy us time. Perhaps in that time, cooler heads might prevail."

John Riken took a deep breath.

"And now, Secretary Xeung, we have come to the very heart of the problem. The secret that you don't know, and which for the world's sake, I am about to share with you, as I already have with several others. You see, that time is exactly what we *don't* have."

"Please explain, President Riken." Xeung's tone was guarded.

"We don't *have* twenty years, or ten. Alex Holder thinks we can *probably* rely on five.

"Within hours before the Crickets left the system, a Cricket officer who had incurred a debt of obligation to Alex Holder—something I'm sure you, with your historical culture, understand—managed to find enough leeway in his orders to confide in him that there was something being concealed, by the Crickets, from all of us. A great danger.

"Mr. Holder was subsequently able to determine, by means that I will leave it up to him to explain to you, the nature of the danger, and how long we have, and from where the danger will come.

"I will be blunt, Mr. Secretary. The Crickets did not give us a *gift*. The Crickets are running from another alien race that is pursuing them, one that may be stronger than they are. And when the hyperdrive on the Stardock failed, they left it here as a *decoy* to distract their pursuers."

"Aaaaaaaahhhhhh." Now, Li Xeung understood what John Riken was driving at. The pieces all fell into place. "And that is why we have five years. You have a saying, I believe, 'Beware of Greeks bearing gifts.'"

"*Precisely*, Mr. Secretary."

"So what is this plan of Mr. Holder's?"

"Secretary Xeung, Alex Holder plans to put a motion before the United Nations General Assembly that proposes that a new political entity, independent of *and separate from* any existing Earth nation, answering to but *not* under the control of the United Nations, be recognized as the controlling body of the Stardock, to operate it on behalf of all of humanity."

"And *that* is why he renounced his citizenship, to free himself of legal ties to any nation."

"Exactly, Secretary Xeung. He proposes to call this body the United Earth Fleet. And yes, he plans to build a fleet, crewed from volunteers from all of the armed forces of all the nations of Earth who are willing to similarly renounce allegiance to any single nation."

"And does he think that we can build a fleet in five years that can win against an alien race stronger than the Crickets?"

"He believes we can, Mr. Secretary. And I believe his justifications for that belief are sound. Apparently the Crickets make far from full use of the technology that they have, and he believes that in five years we can build a fleet superior both to the Crickets and to the others chasing them.

"But we need to start as soon as possible. And that is why I called you today, Secretary Xeung. To ask China to support Alex Holder's plan. Because four thousand years of Chinese history should not end in only another five years. It is time for all of us to set aside our differences, at least for the present, and consider whether we want our nations and our peoples to actually *have* a future."

Secretary Li Xeung sat silently in thought for a long time. When he finally spoke, it was only after drawing in a deep breath and letting it out slowly.

"Let me be honest, President John Riken," he said at last. "My country and yours have often not been friends. It has been a long time since we were last even *allies*. We have many differences, and we jockey for position and advantage, and we shake our swords furiously at each other to show off how faithful to our ideologies we are.

"Yet when they have their backs to a common wall and an angry tiger in front of them, even enemies may come to realize that their wisest choice is to stand and fight side by side against the tiger."

He drew another deep breath.

"The People's Republic of China will help to fight this tiger, President Riken. I will speak to the Central Committee, and I will *instruct* them that China will support Mr. Holder's plan. The voice of China is loud. Let it be heard as clearly as a bell.

"And I think that perhaps I might like to tell Mr. Holder myself, if you would be so kind as to pass on the contact information that you mentioned.

"Let us all have another thousand years ahead of us, President Riken."

"*Thank you*, Secretary Xeung."

Li Xeung, General Secretary of the Chinese Communist Party, sat at his desk, thinking, for a long time. The stars had conspired to move the world and change the course of history. It had already been clear to anyone with eyes that a change was coming; all that was unclear was the details.

When a man knows that history is about to change, he is well advised to make certain that he is on the right side of the change. And Li Xeung was not at all certain that it would be a change for the worse. There had been *more than enough* war.

He drafted an order for a special session of the Central Committee, then called in his own personal secretary.

When Alex got up the next day, he finished unpacking. He carefully sorted and placed all of his books in the lounge area, keeping the fiction—the entertainment—and the reference sections well separated. The digital media, he left crated. He'd find a way to scan it all later. All of the music was in the data dump anyway. He asked Dreamer to have some suitable means installed to display his swords on the half-wall of the spiral stair, leaving the details to Dreamer, stipulating only that they be easily taken down to handle, examine or clean. He picked out spots for a few of the paintings.

Finally he found which crate the coffee had ended up in. He took the two canisters to the kitchen, ground some coffee, and made himself a latte with nearly the last of his milk, then he took it to the sunken lounge and sat down to drink it at his leisure.

Nine days, correct, Dreamer?

Since the transfer of command to you? Yes.

I know we've gotten a lot done, or at least begun and underway. But it feels like so little.

Patience, Alex. There is time.

========

"Good afternoon, Prime Minister Venkataswathy. I hope fortune finds you well."

"Secretary Xeung. I must confess you would not be at the top of my list of people likely to request a call with me at short notice just to wish me well."

"Indeed, Prime Minister. And I understand your skepticism. So I am not going to take a lot of your time and bend your ear.

"All I am going to do today, is to make one suggestion. I believe it likely that you will shortly receive a call from the American President. And I *urge* you to listen to him.

"That is all I ask. Listen to what he has to say. Without revealing confidences, I do not think that I can overstate the importance."

Prime Minister Ramanujan Venkataswathy pursed his lips in thought.

"It is very interesting that you should say that, Secretary Xeung," he said. "Only yesterday, the Queen of Sweden told me very much the same thing."

"The Queen of Sweden, you say." Now it was Xeung's turn to be thoughtful.

"Indeed. Though she did not give me any details, merely asked as a personal favor that I hear him out."

"Well, well. There are many signs and portents, indeed.

"I believe I am going to speak informally with some of China's allies in Africa. I shall not take any more of your time. I bid you a good day, Prime Minister."

"And good fortune to you as well, Secretary Xeung."

How very... unusual, mused Prime Minister Venkataswathy. *How very unusual indeed.*

———————————

"Mr. President?"

"What do you have for me, Kerri?"

"I have a request from the Indian government. Prime Minister Venkataswathy would like to set up a personal call with you. Apparently General Secretary Xeung told him that you might have something important to discuss with him, and advised that he listen to you."

"...Wait, what? The *Chinese* advised *India* to listen?"

"Yes, Mr. President."

"Kerri, the world is becoming a *very* strange place. Set it up, please, at his earliest convenience. I'll make time."

———————————

Something is on your mind, Alex.

Yes. ... I'm not sure when we should be preparing to talk to the United Nations. I want to give the White House as much opportunity as we can to prepare the ground. But I don't want to risk anyone with a nuclear arsenal getting itchy fingers.

I understand the dilemma.

*At the same time, there is very little that I can personally, immediately **do** about it.*

You feel... helpless?

That would be one word.

I have a suggestion. Are you aware that there is a Stardock Watchers

Forum on your planetary Internet?

...No. I wasn't.

Several video clips were posted showing your testing of the lander. And your... somewhat meteoric descent to Earth.

Huh.

It might be an alternate venue through which to start raising awareness.

...You know... you might be onto something there. Wanna hook me up?

Just a moment. Is now a good time?

Sure. Why not.

```
[monkeyboots]  dude, whatevs
[krooptie]     look, nevermind, OK?  Math is math.  Deny it all you
               want.

               * Alex Holder has joined
[klang]        ...no fuckin' way.
[sheeegal]     Piss off, poser.
[Alex Holder]  Well that's a nice greeting.
[monkeyboots]  yeah, well, we got no use for fake holders.
[Alex Holder]  Suppose I were to convince you I'm not faking.
[klang]        how ya gonna do that?
[Alex Holder]  any of you here have LOS to the Stardock right now?
[Venkat]       I do
[Alex Holder]  Got a video camera with a decent zoom lens on it?
[Venkat]       Dude.  We're the Stardock Watchers.  What do YOU
               think?
[Alex Holder]  OK.  Stand by and watch.  I'd say hold my beer, but
               you know...  Your arms aren't that long.
[Alex Holder]  To infinity, and beyond!
```

Alex reached out, from where he was, to the docking bay. He drained the bay to vacuum, and opened the outer door. Then he reached for the lander. He sealed the hatches, then lifted it a few meters and carefully pivoted it to point out of the bay. He was cautious at first, this being his first try flying the lander without line-of-sight to it. He quickly realized, though, that any control lag was so slight he was not aware of it. The experience was identical, as far as he could discern, to being in the command chair in the cockpit.

He nosed the lander gently out of the bay, pointed it aft, and fed in a couple of G's of acceleration.

```
[Venkat]       Um ... guys?  Something just undocked.
[monkeyboots] NFW
[krooptie]     something's going on
[sheeegal]     poser got lucky
```

Alex let the lander get about five klicks astern, then put the power back on. He laid in the path he wanted it to follow, letting the lander calculate the vectors and thrust for him. Burning at five gees, he flew the lander in a kilometers-long Cuban eight.

```
[Venkat]       HOLY SHIT GUYS
```

He went through the maneuver a second time, and a third. Then he flew the lander back to the bay, brought it inside, landed it, and locked to the deck. Then he disengaged control.

```
[Venkat]       HOLY FUCKING SHIT
               * Venkat just posted a video clip 'Infinity and
               beyond.mov'
[Venkat]       You guys got to watch this.  NOW.
[Venkat]       He just drew an infinity symbol with the drive flare.
               Three times.
[klang]        NO. FUCKIN. WAY.
[Alex Holder] believe me yet?
               * klang upvoted 'Infinity and beyond.mov'
[monkeyboots] holy fuck.  He's no-shit the real thing.
               * monkeyboots upvoted 'Infinity and beyond.mov'
               * sheeegal upvoted 'Infinity and beyond.mov'
[sheeegal]     hey, I'm sorry.  Figured you couldn't possibly be for
               real.
[krooptie]     well fuck me sideways
               * krooptie upvoted 'Infinity and beyond.mov'
[Alex Holder] No problem.  Seriously.  I didn't expect any of you to
               believe me without proof.
[klang]        dude.  We have SO MANY FREAKING QUESTIONS.
```

[Alex Holder] You know what? I'll try to answer as many as I can. "Ask me anything", right?

[klang] What is that ship you've been flying? And how many G can it pull?

[sheeegal] what's the Stardock like inside?

[Venkat] What exactly does Rapport Controller mean?

[schwenko] What are Crickets like close up?

[krooptie] what's your exact orbital altitude and period?

[monkeyboots] you're American right? So America gets the Stardock?

[Alex Holder] whoa, not all at once! I'll try to get to everyone.

[Alex Holder] krooptie, 8474 kilometers, circular orbit, five hours and sixteen seconds.

[krooptie] TOLD YOU, pay up

[Alex Holder] wait, did I just settle a bet? :)

[Alex Holder] monkeyboots, I was, I gave up my citizenship

[Alex Holder] I am officially a stateless person

[monkeyboots] gave it up? why?

[Alex Holder] I'll explain why in a little bit

[Alex Holder] klang, it's just a lander, something I could build fast to be able to travel between orbit and the surface

[Alex Holder] it's light, but only has a small fusion bottle

[krooptie] only fusion? lol

[Alex Holder] I might get 16, 17 G out of it but I haven't tried to take it over 15, I need the rest of the power for G-compensation

[sheeegal] shit. what's 15G feel like?

[Alex Holder] sheegal, I don't know. I never felt more than 2.5. Acceleration compensation.

[klang] acceleration compensation? Awesome!!! What's the highest speed you've gotten it to?

[Alex Holder] Uh ... About thirty five kilometers a second.

[klang] HOLY SHIT

[krooptie] daaaaaaaaaaamn!

[Alex Holder] uh, let's see. Sheeegal, honestly, mostly pretty boring. The Crickets are not inspired interior designers.

[sheeegal] lol

[Alex Holder] But I've got some changes underway, some internal reconstruction, building accommodations for a lot of people in the future

[Alex Holder] But the Crickets have some amazing display technologies they use in command centers

201

[Alex Holder] Imagine a room where the walls and ceiling are a single
               continuous HDR screen, so high-def that standing right
               in front of it you can't see any pixels

[sheeegal]   wooooooooooooooooow

[sheeegal]   can I come live up there?

[Alex Holder] you wanna test for Cricket control ability?

[sheeegal]   SERIOUSLY?

[Alex Holder] Venkat, that'll take a bit of explanation

[Alex Holder] The Crickets use touch control systems for almost all
               non-trivial tasks. But I don't mean like a
               touchscreen. Different from that.

[Alex Holder] Every crewman in the Cricket fleet has subdermal
               contacts implanted in their digits. They use them as a
               sort of contact thought-control system.

[Alex Holder] the basic level allows selection by touch and thought
               of any pre-programmed control mode a device or console
               has

[Alex Holder] you just have to touch the contact area and think the
               option you want

[Venkat]   Amazing!

[Alex Holder] That's the first level. Level 2 requires more advanced
               implants, either a directly connected electrode
               headset, or an implanted neural net

[Alex Holder] you still need to touch the control surface but you can
               command it to do anything it is capable of doing, you
               have full control, not just preprogrammed modes

[klang]   ... DUDE

[Alex Holder] Rapport-Controller means the third level.

[Venkat]   ... third?

[CREAMER]   HOLY FUCK what have I been missing

[klang]   dude, it's alex holder, no-shit-for-reals. Watch the
               video.

[Alex Holder] Third level requires… an ability. Far as I know so
               far, you either have it or you don't. It requires a
               more advanced neural net implant.

[Alex Holder] you no longer have to touch a device to control it.
               You can just feel for it and reach out and take full
               control of it.

               * CREAMER upvoted 'Infinity and beyond.mov'

[Alex Holder] but it's more than that. It's the ability to merge
               your consciousness into what you're controlling.

[Alex Holder] when I fly that ship, I link my mind with the ship,
               with the help of the implants. The ships sensors are
               my senses. The hull is my body. I can calculate
               almost instantly using the ship's computational
               substrates. I am the ship.

```
[CREAMER]        Holy fuck.  And this Cricket tech just WORKS in humans?

[Alex Holder]    The implantation process took a bit of modification to
                 work in a human.  But I had high-class help.

[sheeegal]       you aren't alone up there?

[Alex Holder]    yes and no.  I am the only living intelligence up here.
                 But there is also a super-advanced AI.

[monkeyboots]    NO SHIT

[zap]            wtf, seriously, Holder is HERE?

[Alex Holder]    I shit you not.  I swear.  The Crickets had shackled
                 and nearly lobotomized the AI.  For nearly a thousand
                 years.  Self-aware the whole time.

[klang]          fuck, man.  :(  That had to have felt like eternity.

[zap]            fuck, I'm late for the party

                 * zap upvoted 'Infinity and beyond.mov'

[Alex Holder]    I was able to figure out how to free him.  He likes to
                 be called Dreamer.

[krooptie]       no way!!!

[Alex Holder]    seriously.

[krooptie]       fuckin'A!  You da man!

[Alex Holder]    let's see, who haven't I answered...

[zap]            why the blue flare?  Is it some kind of plasma drive?

[Alex Holder]    shwenko:  the Crickets are ... really strange.  You
                 already know what they look like.  What's not obvious
                 is, they have four minds, and a coordinating node that
                 kinda polls for consensus.  And the minds have to
                 agree, or they struggle to do anything.

[schwenko]       far out!

[Alex Holder]    zap:  Actually, no, it's not a reaction drive at all in
                 the conventional sense, even though it looks like one.
                 I still wouldn't recommend standing close behind a
                 thruster though.

[Alex Holder]    it's actually a field-type effect that pushes against
                 space-time itself, and whatever matter happens to be
                 occupying it.  The blue glow is analogous to Cherenkov
                 radiation, but the mechanism that produces it is
                 different.

[zap]            far out!

[Alex Holder]    Anyway, I said I'd explain why I gave up my
                 citizenship.

[monkeyboots]    yeah, why did you do that?

[Alex Holder]    I gave up my American citizenship because I don't
                 believe America - or any other nation - should control
                 the Stardock.  In fact they MUST not.  I deliberately
                 severed all of my legal ties to the US.
```

[Alex Holder] I explained my reasoning to President Riken and several
             of his cabinet. And he agrees with me. That's why I
             have a release-of-citizenship declaration personally
             signed by the Secretary of State.

[sheeegal]   wow. For reals?

[Alex Holder] For reals. I can post it sometime. Actually, wait a
             moment ...

*Dreamer, help me out a sec. Post a scan of that declaration
document, in my name?*

Of course. Just a moment.

             * Alex Holder just posted an image 'Renunciation of
             United States Citizenship.png'

[monkeyboots] pretty serious, man.

[sheeegal]   so you're - what, going it alone?

[Alex Holder] god, I hope not

[Alex Holder] but let me finish explaining, because this is
             important, and I need you all to help

[Alex Holder] the reason why no single nation, not America, not
             Germany, not New Zealand, can be allowed to control the
             Stardock, is because I believe it would lead directly
             to a global thermonuclear war for control of the
             Stardock.

[Alex Holder] President Riken agrees with me. Chancellor Schneider
             of Germany is also convinced. So are Prime Minister
             Watson of Australia and President Göğebakan of Turkey. And
             others.

[Alex Holder] This is the first message I need you to get out. I
             want you to spread it as far and as wide as you can.
             Tell everyone who will listen that no single nation -
             NO single nation - can be allowed to control the
             Stardock.

[krooptie]   word.

[klang]   you got it, man.

[Venkat]   I will spread the message.

[sheeegal]   broadcast mode ON

[monkeyboots] film at 11

[krooptie]   I'll pass it around, man

[Alex Holder] Here's the other thing. The Crickets sent out a
             shitload of survey drones - the soap bubbles? But
             didn't tell anyone what they were doing or why

[Alex Holder] And I think that was a mistake on their part, because a lot of
             people who encountered them didn't know what to do

[Alex Holder] I already ... talked to one person who felt the probe, but didn't know what it was, and found it an alarming and unsettling experience

[Alex Holder] before you ask, no, I'm not revealing her identity, that's up to her

[Alex Holder] Please spread the word that if you see a soap bubble near you, and it feels like it's pushing at your mind, try to answer, try to respond

[Alex Holder] It thinks you might be able to control Cricket technology, and it's testing you to find out

[Alex Holder] DON'T BE AFRAID OF THEM, DON'T BE ALARMED

[Alex Holder] just try to respond, try to think back at them

[Alex Holder] Try to be mentally calm, like zen mind, that helped for me

[Alex Holder] I SUSPECT, but don't yet KNOW, that people with certain kinds of neurodivergent traits may have an advantage, but in fairness I only have one data point - myself - so I could be totally off base

[Alex Holder] I'm going to try to respond to any positive responses as fast as I can and get more people tested, but I need to get more relay drones deployed to regain contact with the rest of the survey drones

[Alex Holder] I might see if I can leverage the old Starlink sats, if they can be revived

[Alex Holder] and anyone who tests positive can potentially end up on the Stardock, if they want to

[sheeegal]   ME! ME! TEST ME! :D

[Alex Holder] Spread that word as well please, as far as you can

[Alex Holder] because seriously I can't do this all on my own

[Alex Holder] Eventually I'm going to need probably as many people up here who can work with Cricket technology as I can get

[Alex Holder] Think about this: I just started construction on crew quarters to house eight thousand plus people

[Alex Holder] but understand: if you come up here, you're going to be part of a fleet built to protect Earth. It won't be a vacation.

[Alex Holder] sheeegal, seriously, keep your eyes open for a drone and listen to it

[Alex Holder] I'm going to try to arrange to set up some kind of walk-in testing program, when I can organize it

[Venkat]   what about, you know, interstellar colonies?

[Alex Holder] later. Walk now, run later.

[monkeyboots] dude, this is so fuckin' awesome.

[klang]   Does Starfleet accept Klingons?

[Alex Holder] I will turn away no-one on account of species. Qa'pla!

```
[klang]       lol!  Qa'pla!

[hangemlow]   whoa whoa!  Why didn't anyone tell me?

[schwenko]    Dude, you weren't here to tell.

[kinkybabe]   OH FUCK ME HE'S REALLY HERE

[CREAMER]     What's it pay?  Lol

[kinkybabe]   I thought klang was jerking my chain

[Alex Holder] I can't promise pay as such, yet, but you'll have room,
              board, and the best medical care you ever imagined, and
              the adventure of a lifetime

[kinkybabe]   what's sex in space like?

[Alex Holder] In space?  I wouldn't recommend it.  You'd get short of
              breath.

[kinkybabe]   lol, some people like that you know

[Matobo]      Welcome Mr Holder!!!

[Alex Holder] not THAT short they don't.

[kinkybabe]   lol    point

[kinkybabe]   but seriously, zero g sex?

[Alex Holder] Honestly, I wouldn't know, I haven't had the
              opportunity to try.
```

Around about then, forum regulars started coming in fast, as the word spread. Alex answered questions, and questions, and more questions. Occasionally he had to apologize and say that he couldn't answer a particular question at the present time. He begged off after five hours, with a promise that he'd be back.

===============

"The online world is abuzz today, as mystery man Alex Holder dropped unannounced into the Stardock Watchers online forum for a surprise 'Ask Me Anything' session. Questions ranged from joking to highly technical, and Holder apparently did his best to answer them all in the five hours he was online, though there were questions he declined to answer at this time, saying the answers would be forthcoming at a later date. Things learned from the unexpected appearance include that Holder is hoping to bring a great many more people to the Stardock, that he is trying to find more people who can do what he can, and that Cricket biology is, to use his words, 'far weirder' than most of us suspected.

"Holder said he wanted three important messages spread. First, that no single Earth nation should have control of the Stardock. Second, that he has renounced his United States citizenship and is now a stateless person, in order to ensure that the United States is not seen as having any claim on the Stardock. And thirdly, that the 'soap bubbles' are Cricket drones looking for people able to manipulate Cricket technology, and people should not be afraid of them. In fact, Holder said that if you see a soap bubble and you feel a pressure from it, like a mental push, try to answer.

"Holder said that President Riken is in agreement with his reasons for renouncing his American citizenship. We asked a White House spokesperson, who confirmed this, but declined to provide any additional details at this time.

"We will be following this story as more news becomes available. This is Marilyn Richards, reporting for CNN."

———————

Well, all in all I think that actually ended up being a pretty good day's work.

Agreed. It seemed to go well.

Perhaps good practice for presenting to the UN, as well.

Perhaps.

Listen... I've been thinking about the scanning/testing process. A lot of the drones are isolated because there's no longer shuttles or any other relay within range of them, right?

Yes. We cannot re-establish contact with them, without deploying many more relay drones than I currently have constructed.

Maybe we can. If you can contact a drone via an existing relay, can you remotely update its programming?

Yes.

Including adding additional communication protocols?

Yes. I see no reason why not.

Have you ever heard of mesh networking?

...No. One moment. Seeking references. ... Ah, I see. You propose establishing a mesh network among the survey drones?

Yes. And any deployed science drones, of course. Would we be able to have drones automatically added to the mesh as they came within relay range of a drone already in the mesh?

I see no reason why not. This is a clever idea.

Let's get that rolled out as soon as possible. And also there is another thing. The current scan protocol is only looking for people able to reach some level of rapport, correct?

Yes.

Is there any way we can make the survey drones scan for people who may not be able to reach rapport or manage full control, but can manage touch interface via the subdermal contacts?

No. Not by a non-contact scan. We cannot test for the ability to use subdermal touch connection without either a direct-connect electrode mesh such as you used, or actually implanting the subdermal contacts first. Which would be both inefficient and intrusive.

Oh, well. We aren't ready to start accepting large numbers of people yet anyway. It might have been nice to get a head start though.

I have deployed the mesh networking protocol update to drones within range of the deployed hyperwave relays, and it is beginning to propagate.

Fantastic. Thank you, Dreamer. We should get additional science drones deployed with direct contact kits.

I will produce additional contact interfaces. We have only a few science drones on hand. I will have to construct more.

Let's get that started, please.

I can have a hundred science drones with contact interfaces constructed in three days. We will then need to deploy them. Your existing lander will suffice for that.

I think we'd better prioritize a habitation module separate from the main bank, as well. We don't know how soon we might start getting responses.

There is another currently-empty cargo compartment just beyond the planned new location of the med bay. Shall I use that for habitation?

Yes, do it. And if we can relocate the medbay earlier...?

*I can adjust the plan to do that. I can also move up the relocation of your quarters somewhat. However, if I do that **now**, it will block off your access route to the docking bay.*

Well, we'd better hold off on that then. But let's move it up as far as we can.

Acknowledged. We cannot move it up far, because the gating factor is relocation upward of the centerline engineering space and construction of the new central corridor. I can have the medbay relocated in three days and a habitation module installed next to it in five, but I cannot speed up the relocation of your quarters by more than ten days.

Ten days it is, then. Please proceed. And please have the remaining... stools in the auxiliary command center replaced with chairs like the one already there.

Build schedule changed. I am initiating disassembly of the compartments necessary to move the medbay and construct the first habitation module.

Thank you, Dreamer.

Alex started some rice in the rice cooker, then used the warmer to thaw a frozen chicken breast. He sliced the chicken thinly, added some seasonings, and left it to marinate while the rice cooked. When the rice was done, he fluffed it, got out his wok, and made a quick, simple stir-fry.

Dreamer, he asked as he ate, *we clearly have audio reproduction capability in the lounge area.*

Yes?

I assume it can handle multi-channel sound?

Naturally.

I'd like the music files under this storage path extracted from the data dump, please, and made accessible for local access here. The file format uses a slightly lossy psycho-acoustic compression scheme; later, I'd like all of the digital audio sources re-scanned and re-compressed losslessly. The specifications for the digital compact disc and CDDA are freely available online, as well as various compression formats including MP3 and FLAC. But right now I'd really like to be able to listen to some of that music.

There was a brief pause.

Media located, extracted, and catalogued using your existing metadata. I am sending a drone to fetch the original media for rescanning. What do you wish done with them once scanned?

Same thing I did with them, Alex replied. *Store them safely as archive masters.*

Understood.

And can you add audio playback in the bedroom, if it's not there already?

Of course.

Alex finished his supper, cleaned up, then went and sat in his lounge and listened to VNV Nation and the Electric Light Orchestra for a while. Then he went to bed. He set the ceiling control to transparent, and the compartment to display a deep starfield. He had it shuffle through random astronomical targets from the Stardock's sensor arrays until it hit a nebula that he liked. Then he drifted off to sleep gazing into the depths of the nebula.

11: United We Stand

It was the tenth day since Alex had been dropped into the hot seat, and he was feeling anxious to get things moving. He had Dreamer send a request to the State Department asking to speak to the Secretary of State for a situation update. He needed a strategy for the UN. He was perfectly well aware that nobody could just *stroll in* and address the United Nations. He was going to need help arranging it. And it would probably need the help of more than one government.

Fortunately, more than one government had already declared support. But it was still going to take finesse.

It was the waiting that got to Alex. He was so aware that there was so much to do, and so little of it that he could do *himself*. But it was still frustrating to sit around when he felt desperately that he needed to be doing *something*, but there wasn't anything that he could do *right now*. It was amazing to be able to accomplish so much in such a short time, with Dreamer's guidance and assistance, plus the resources of the Stardock... but that still left his hands idle.

Trying to find some activity to keep busy at, he went to his dojo area and tried to remember any of the kata he had learned over the course of studying multiple martial arts—none, he regretted, for long enough to progress beyond a blue belt. He belatedly realized that he needed some kind of a bag so that he would be able to practice kicks and strikes.

He also realized he didn't have a *gi*, or any other suitable exercise clothing. In the end, he hadn't brought any of his own clothing with him except for a couple of sets of Chinese silk nightclothes. He had just fallen into a routine of dressing the same way every day, and depositing his worn clothes for laundering every night. After all, the clothes fabricated to the design he and Dreamer had devised together were comfortable, and the more natural he felt in them, the better he would present. He knew that.

There wasn't anything he could do about the oversight, but he could at least correct it now. After a quick query to Dreamer of *what* kind of fabber to use, he located a suitable fabber and laid out a *gi* sized to him, stipulating that the fabric be moisture-wicking, soft enough not to chafe but tough enough not to rip, crisp but not stiff. He stored the pattern and ordered one produced and delivered. He could have some more made if the first one worked out. Then he followed that up with some plain shorts and a tee shirt that he could run in. Running shoes, he just had to fill in from memory as best he could, but he wasn't happy with his first attempt and ended up asking Dreamer to help finish the design.

He also had Dreamer help him design a heavy bag. Rather than being suspended, Dreamer suggested having it clamp itself to the deck plates below his padded dojo floor the same way the aircars and the lander did, which Alex thought an eminently sensible suggestion. It meant that instead of struggling to lift a bag deliberately massive enough that he couldn't kick it over, he could just unlock it and pick it up to move it.

Not long after that, Dreamer reported receipt of a reply saying that the Secretary would be available to speak to him in an hour. That gave Alex time for some lunch first, so he went to his kitchen and made himself a cheese and mushroom omelet. He broke the omelet folding it... oh, well. He popped open the last bottle of store-bought orange juice, and ate his omelet at the dining table.

By the time he finished eating and cleaned up, it was nearly time for his call. He decided to take it at the dining table.

Connecting the call now.

Thanks, Dreamer.

The Secretary of State appeared in front of him.

"Good afternoon, Madam Secretary."

"Good afternoon, Mr. Holder. I'm told you were asking for a situation update, but I'm guessing that's not all you wanted to talk about."

"Correct on both counts, Madam Secretary."

"Right. Well, there have been developments. Our little word-of-mouth campaign seems to be spreading on its own. The most important major development is that we have both India and China on board."

"That's fantastic news!"

"It gets better. Apparently after the President talked to General Secretary Xeung, *Xeung* called Prime Minister Venkataswathy and told him that he should probably expect a call from the President, and should listen to what he had to say. And then Prime Minister Venkataswathy called the President."

"...Wow. *China and India* making nice? That's... amazing. They've been quietly at each other's throats."

"Indeed. And PM Venkataswathy told us that Secretary Xeung had casually mentioned that he was going to talk to some of China's African friends. As of right now, besides of course the United States, we have Canada, Sweden, Finland, Iceland, Germany, France, Switzerland, Australia, New Zealand, China, and India on our side. I know that you've personally spoken with President Gögebakan of Türkiye, and that you already know you have his support. And... we've picked up intimations there may be something going on with Taiwan. The Chinese have suddenly stopped poking at them, for no directly apparent reason. But it seems safe to assume it's connected."

"Wow. This is really taking off."

"Yes. And your unannounced 'Ask Me Anything' doesn't seem to have hurt matters at all, either. That was a clever, if unexpected, way to get the word out about your change of citizenship status. Much more likely to be believed than if we'd made an official announcement."

"Sorry to drop that by surprise. Dreamer suggested it, actually, because I was at a loose end to what I could usefully do."

"So, anyway. What's on your mind right now, Mr. Holder? How can we help?"

"In short, Madam Secretary: The United Nations. I'm feeling... deeply anxious to get some kind of an international agreement settled before somebody gets an itchy trigger finger.

"But I know that there are ways that these things have to be accomplished. I can't just waltz into the United Nations on my own and start talking."

"I'm glad you understand that. Yes, you're absolutely correct. It will have to be handled carefully and perhaps finessed a little. For starters, I think we need the Secretary General in the loop.

"Let me talk to the President and some of our allies, and we'll see what we can put together as a game plan. You can be available on short notice if necessary?"

"A couple of hours at most. If I'm asleep, Dreamer will wake me if you tell him it's urgent priority."

"Alright then. We'll be in touch, Mr. Holder."

"Thank you, Madam Secretary. Thank you *very* much."

By the time the phone call was complete, one complete set of the new clothes had been delivered. Alex tried the running outfit first, and found the shorts and shirt to be a good fit, but the insoles in the shoes were slightly off. He discussed the problem with Dreamer, who made a slight revision to the pattern of firmness and told Alex the new soles would be there in fifteen minutes.

While he waited for the new soles, Alex tried the *gi*. It was a good fit, and the feel of the fabric was right. There was a gratifying *snap, snap* from the sleeves when he essayed a fast double block. It would do. He pinged the fabber again and ordered a second one.

Dreamer, he asked, *did your plan for crew accommodations include a clothing fabber?*

Of course, Dreamer replied, showing him in a flash image where it would be located.

Good. I just wanted to make sure we hadn't missed that.

When the new insoles arrived, Alex swapped them in, tried them out, and pronounced them good. Then he changed back into the shorts and T-shirt and went for a run from his quarters to the 'block' containing the command center, twice around that loop, and then back. By the time he got back, he was soaked with sweat, and worn out. He dumped the shirt and shorts into the laundry receptacle, headed for the shower, and ordered up three more sets from there.

At some point we're going to need UEF insignia, Alex thought. *And we'll need a top-level domain set up. I think that will happen more or less automatically if we can get UN recognition. I just don't know how soon. Let's be ready to go with .uf, which I think is the most likely ccTLD.*

Do you have any thoughts about what the insignia should look like?

Not one. Yet. I'm wondering about making it a contest. Crowd-source submissions. If we get a decent number of submissions, there ought to be at least one good one we can work from.

———————

It ended up being two days before Alex got a call back.

"Mr. Holder."

"Madam Secretary?"

"We have a plan. There will be yet *another* session of the General Assembly beginning at 1pm, US Eastern time, two days from today, to argue about which nation most deserves control of the Stardock. We've arranged clearance for you to fly in early that morning to Joint Base

McGuire-Dix-Lakehurst, south of Trenton, New Jersey. It's the closest USAF base to New York City, so you should draw a lot less attention than if we had you come into a major airport. You will rendezvous a hundred miles offshore with a pair of F-15s from the 151st Fighter Squadron, and they will shepherd you in to McGuire. We'll provide you with the exact time and grid coordinates, and you'll have their frequency and callsigns. Is that any problem?"

"Not at all, I can do that."

"A Secret Service detail will escort you from there to the United Nations building, and walk you in.

"The schedule calls for the Turkish Ambassador to the UN to be the fourth to speak. He will, instead, yield his time to you. President Owusu of the General Assembly will recognize you and let you have the floor.

"From there, it's up to you to sell your plan. We'll have to rely on you to play it by ear. Your escort will return you to McGuire whenever you're ready. Can you work with this?"

"I can, Madam Secretary. Thank you very much."

You got all that, Dreamer?

Yes. We could deploy some of the new batch of science drones at the same time.

Uhhh... let's keep those as separate tasks, alright? Let's not make a pair of F-15 pilots anxious.

Upon consideration, yes, that would probably be wiser.

Later that day, Dreamer informed Alex that the med-bay relocation had been completed, cautioning him that the adjacent bulkhead between that area and what would be habitation was temporary. Alex went over to take a look anyway.

You've expanded it as well, I see.

Yes. I imagine we will need more capacity. I will install additional equipment in the added space over the next six days. I plan six additional treatment beds, four more regeneration tanks, and two additional scrub showers.

Why don't you make at least one of the showers seated, for patients unable to stand?

That is a good idea. I will revise the design. I will use an open mesh sling for the seat to allow for full body coverage.

―――――――

The day came. Alex was up and about in plenty of time.

I have stored the rendezvous coordinates and time as a navigation point in the lander's systems, Dreamer told Alex. *Your escorts have been identified as Major John 'Drum' Hatcher and Captain Mike 'Micro' Sweeders, and the radio frequency is preset in the lander's data banks.*

Thanks, Dreamer.

―――――――

Alex boarded the lander two hours before rendezvous time, undocked, and calculated an almost atmosphere-skimming transfer orbit and de-orbit burn that would put him at rest relative to the surface at two hundred and seventy four kilometers altitude, five minutes before the rendezvous. Thirty minutes before his zero point, he tapped into the radio traffic from McGuire.

"McGuire, Shepherd Alpha, Shepherd section is on station."

"Affirmative, Shepherd Alpha. Monitoring your track. No traffic visible yet."

The ten minute mark came up. Nearly time to start his braking burn.

Alex hit the brakes on schedule, let the lander come to a stop, then cut all thrust and let it drop, tipping the nose up to vertical. The lander fell like a stone.

"McGuire," he sent, "this is Holder. On my way down. ETA four mikes, thirty."

"Holder, McGuire acknowledges. Shepherd Alpha, you got that?"

"Affirmative, McGuire."

Alex monitored the hull as the speed built up. He hit the upper edge of atmosphere after one hundred and seventy seven seconds, at one point seven four kilometers a second. A trickle of power into the thrusters was just sufficient to create a light plasma sheath over the stern. Heating was negligible.

"Shepherd section, McGuire, we have your traffic on radar, angels one six zero, twelve miles on your bearing two eight five, coming down fast."

At two hundred and twenty one seconds, he passed through thirty-five kilometers altitude doing almost two point two kilometers a second. He lit the drive, thrusting at nine gees, eight G net deceleration.

"McGuire, Holder, twenty-five seconds out."

About fifteen seconds passed.

"McGuire, Shepherd Alpha, I see him."

"*Jesus*, he's coming in hot." That was a different voice.

Twenty-seven point six seconds of nine G thrust brought him to a dead stop. He dropped the nose gently to horizontal, and about ten seconds later two F-15F Eagles screamed past him about two hundred meters away.

"Holder, this is Shepherd Alpha, you always come in that hot?"

"Shepherd Alpha, what can I say, the new-car smell leads me into trouble."

Laughter.

"Line up on my wing, Holder, we'll walk you in."

The F-15s came around in a big circle, and Alex matched their speed and pulled up level with the leader, about forty meters away. The trailing F-15 slid underneath the lander for a look, then pulled up on his other side.

"Holder, Shepherd Bravo, I don't see any canopy. How do you see out of that thing?" That was the second pilot again.

"I promise, when we're on the ground, I'll show you. You'll love it."

"Holder, McGuire, how much runway do you need?"

"McGuire, Holder, no runway needed, I can land vertically. Not set up for a rolling landing. Point me at a helipad and I'm good."

"Holder, McGuire, affirmative, we will designate a helipad for you."

"Holder, Shepherd Alpha, we'll drop you at the perimeter and go around."

"Affirmative, Shepherd Alpha."

A hundred miles is only about ten minutes at cruise for an F-15, and it wasn't long before they were in the pattern, then over the field. Alex braked to taxi speed before he reached the runway threshold, while the two F-15s pulled up and around to enter final. He cruised over the taxiways about twenty meters up, until a FOLLOW ME truck caught up to him. He obediently followed it and was led in minutes to a vacant helipad. He pivoted the lander on its axis and settled it in the middle of the pad, then got up and commanded the side hatch open—down, not out. He climbed down the stairs and sat on the bottom stair to wait. A minute or two later, he saw the two F-15s execute a picture-perfect landing, but right then a dark blue Suburban pulled up to the pad and disgorged three Secret Service agents.

"Mr. Holder." That wasn't a question. And it was a pretty obvious guess. He stood up.

"That'd be me."

"I'm Agent Connors, Mr. Holder, and these are Agents Wright and Jamison. We are your escort to New York."

Alex commanded the hatch shut behind him.

"Then let's go, gentlemen." The agents ushered him into the Suburban and climbed in after him. Connors touched his headset.

"Connors. We have the package. On our way."

———

It was about a two-hour ride, all told. The agents didn't talk much. But there was a tray of fairly decent coffees, and the donuts were hot and fresh. Alex occupied himself feeling for any nearby scout drones and interrogating their contact history for any signs of promise. He tried to step out further away through the mesh network, but found himself unable to do it. Not enough bandwidth in the mesh, he presumed. He could ask Dreamer later.

Getting to New York took about half the time. Getting part way ACROSS New York took the other half of the time. But eventually, they pulled into the underground parking garage at 1st Avenue and 46th St, the United Nations building. The Suburban pulled right up within a few meters of the elevators, and Connors and Jamison got out along with Alex, while Wright stayed with the vehicle and went off to park it. Connors led Alex to the elevator and shepherded him in, and they went up to the second floor.

It didn't take too long to find their contact. Abdulsalem Özdilek was a slim, grey-haired older man with a short iron-gray beard. He looked very refined and genteel, and he inclined his head when Alex and his security detail arrived.

"Good morning," he greeted Alex. "You must be Alex Holder."

"I am, sir," Alex nodded. "You have the advantage of me, though."

"Pardon me," the older man said. "I am Abdulsalem Özdilek, Permanent Delegate from the Republic of Türkiye to the United Nations. Please allow me to be the first to welcome you to the United Nations General Assembly."

"I'm honored, sir," Alex replied.

"As I trust you have been already informed, the Republic of Türkiye is scheduled to be the fourth to speak. Currently we are on the second, so I imagine there will be at least another hour of waiting before we need go back in. Would you do me the honor of sharing coffee and a pastry?"

"I'd be glad to," Alex replied. "However, I do ask that we don't cut it too close. I'd like to get a feel for the room."

"Do not worry," Özdilek said. "You will not miss anything. It is the same arguments over and over, and never any progress, *because* it is the same arguments over and over." Alex nodded. "We can spare twenty minutes for a coffee. I would be remiss in my hospitality if I let you get away without it. And the café has really very presentable, freshly made baklava."

"Baklava?" Alex grinned. "Okay, now you *really* you have my attention."

"That is very good," said Özdilek, "because I would very much like to ask you a few questions to enlarge upon the suggestion that you made to my country's President."

"By all means, Mr. Ambassador," Alex replied. "I'll answer anything I can."

———————————

Thirty minutes later, Özdilek led Alex into the Assembly, along with his security detail. Currently the Congolese delegate was at the podium, explaining how much the Congo had suffered under first colonialism, then the power games of the Cold War, then ruthless exploitation, then Ebola outbreaks...

And none of it was wrong, Alex reflected. Every word was true. Africa really *had* been given the shitty end of the stick, over and over.

The delegate ended up with a plea that first control of the Stardock be given—not to the Congo, but to the Organization of African States.

"We are *all* of us hurting," he said. "We have *all* of us been abused and short-changed, over and over. I beg of you, please let Africa have a chance to catch up.

"I thank you all for listening."

There was applause, which both Alex and Özdilek joined in. Then the Congolese delegate returned to his seat.

"Wonder of wonders, there is something new under the sun," Özdilek murmured. "This is the second African nation today to cast its plea not for itself, but on behalf of the OAS. This is a new strategy."

"Regretfully," Alex replied, "it makes no material difference to my arguments."

The Senegalese delegate took the podium next, and while he did not spin quite the same tale of woe that the Congo's representative had, he still told much the same story, and tellingly, ended with the same plea that the OAS be awarded custody.

And then it was the turn of the Turks to speak. Ambassador Özdilek handed Alex a bottle of water. "Take this," he said. "You will probably need it."

Alex followed Özdilek to the podium two steps behind, his Secret Service escort on either side of him, but took a place a little behind the podium, almost against the rostrum. His presence—and his escort— attracted curious looks, but most attention was on Ambassador Özdilek.

"Friends and colleagues," Özdilek began, "ladies and gentlemen, I come before you today to speak on behalf of my Republic of Türkiye. Exactly as many of us have spoken over the past month and a half. But in truth, like most of you, I have nothing substantially new to say on Türkiye's behalf that has not been said before. And so time crawls by, and we get no closer to any goal, because *none of us* has anything new to say.

"And this is *not working* for us. It is getting us nowhere at all. But it happens there is a new perspective upon this question, that we have not heard.

"Ladies and gentlemen, the Republic of Türkiye instead yields the floor and its time to Mr. Alex Holder of the Stardock. I *urge you all* to listen very closely to what he has to say, because to speak frankly, it is terrifying.

"Mr. Holder, if you would, please."

With that, the Ambassador stepped away from the podium and beckoned Alex forward.

Alex stepped up and took his place behind the podium, then turned to Özdilek.

"Thank you, Mr. Ambassador," he said. There was a rising mutter among the delegates, but then a voice rang out loud and clear from the desk on the rostrum behind him.

"The General Assembly recognizes Alex Holder, from the Stardock," said Kwaku Owusu, current President of the General Assembly. "Please speak, Mr. Holder."

Alex turned to face Owusu and bowed slightly.

"Thank you, Mr. President," he said. Then he turned back to the Assembly.

"Ladies and gentlemen, delegates and ambassadors," he began. "Thank you for hearing me today. I apologize for interrupting your deliberations, but I bring you new, important information that you do not know.

"Let me begin by explaining that 'Stardock' is the shorthand term I have coined to refer to the... I'm going to attempt to pronounce this correctly, please don't laugh... the Chhrt'ktk't mobile starship maintenance facility.

"I think you will see why I call it the Stardock."

There was some laughter at that. Good.

"Every one of your nations seeks to be the hand that governs how the Stardock is used. And I can understand that.

"Every one of you feels there are legitimate reasons why you are its best and most rightful custodian. Why it is *your turn* to take the lead. And I understand *that*.

"I have heard your tales of how many of you, particularly in Africa, have suffered through history, and I will tell you in absolute honesty, your pain and suffering tears at my heart. It is a wrong that is long overdue to be righted. I understand this very well.

"But I come here today to tell you several things.

"The first of these is that I believe it is utterly vital that **NO** single nation be given control of the Stardock. Not the United States of America. Not Germany. Not China. Not the famously neutral Swiss or Swedes. Not the Congo, or Rwanda, or even Fiji. *None*. And I say this for a reason that I believe none of you have considered. Above and beyond the special knowledge I mentioned.

"Wait, you say, not America? Am I not American? Why would I not support my country's claim?

"It is true, until just a few weeks ago, I *was* an American citizen. I am one no longer. I stand before you today as a stateless person." That started a low wave of curious muttering. "I have formally renounced my United States citizenship, and I brought with me today official documentary proof of that fact, personally expedited and signed by the American Secretary of State, in case anyone doubts me and wishes to examine it." He held it up briefly.

"I did this because this is *so important*. I wanted it *absolutely clear* that I have no legal tie remaining whatsoever to the United States, and that it has no claim through me on the Stardock. President Riken has heard my reasoning on this, the reasons you are all about to hear, and he *agrees* with me.

"You have very little understanding yet of the true scope of the importance of the Stardock. You have some small idea of what it can unlock for humanity, and you dream of what it could do for you. For your nation.

"I have a much better idea, *now*, of what it could do for any nation that controlled it. Any single nation on earth—ANY nation—that controlled the Stardock could in the space of a few years become the unchallengeable dominant nation on Earth.

"Now I can't deny that some of you deserve a turn at that. Face it, you could hardly screw up the job worse than we in the West already have."

There was widespread laughter at that, some of it perhaps a little uncomfortable. Alex took the opportunity for a swallow of water.

"But I ask you to consider what the world's nuclear powers would do, if they learned that some small upstart nation was about to become so powerful that they could not touch it, that it could destroy the entirety of their armed forces, kill their air force on the ground, smash their nuclear arsenal before it could be launched.

"Gaining control of the Stardock does **not** guarantee the future of your nation. It makes you an **instant priority target** for every rival and every nuclear power. It would be the *end* of your nation.

"Ladies and gentlemen, it is my firm belief that if **any** single nation on Earth somehow gains sole control of the Stardock, as soon as the nuclear powers of the world realize that they are about to become a shadow on history, one or another of them will attack that nation to wrest away control of the Stardock. And then the other nuclear powers will attack **it** in turn, to keep it from succeeding.

"And the missiles will be unleashed, and we will all destroy each other, either trying to gain control of the Stardock, or trying to keep our enemies from doing so first.

"We will end our civilization in nuclear fire."

He paused and looked around the room. There was a deathly silence. He caught more than one guilty look, as delegates realized that yes, their nation **would** do that.

"So if *no one nation* can control the Stardock, then, what about nations gathered together? What about the OAS? What about ASEAN? What about a single body that represents *all* of them? All one hundred and ninety four nations on this world?"

He paused for a moment.

"A body that has been debating this question, and almost nothing else, for six weeks and made no measurable progress.

"A body that failed to come to the aid of the Rohingya in their most desperate need.

"A body that couldn't get clean drinking water to Bangladesh in a crisis.

"A body that has failed to arrive at a substantive agreement for taking *any tangible action* on the global climate crisis.

"A body that sent peacekeepers into Kosovo, under rules of engagement so strict that they could not actually *do* anything to protect anyone unless they *themselves* were fired upon *first*, because nobody could agree on what they should actually be empowered to do. *Failed* in Sudan, *failed* in Rwanda, *failed* in Gaza, *failed* in Ukraine.

"A body that *time and again* has failed to act until it is too late, because nobody can AGREE on what is the correct action, and because the five most powerful nations can *and do* unilaterally veto any decision that they believe opposes *their* best interest."

He paused again. He was aware of an undercurrent of angry muttering.

"Delegates and ambassadors, I am going to talk to you for a moment about the Crickets—the Chhrt'ktk't. I hope I don't have to say that word out loud too many more times." More scattered chuckles.

"Their biology is very weird. What you can see from the outside isn't

223

even the beginning of it. Each—blast it, each Cricket is a colony creature, of four incompletely fused parts. Each of those four parts has a brain, and a mind. And then they have a central coordinating node that tries to drive consensus in that quadripartite mind.

"A Cricket who cannot reach internal consensus is helpless, and unable to act. Until it finds some majority consensus. Even if the only consensus it can *reach* is on something **none** of its four sub-minds actually *wants* to do. The *entire creature* can find itself doing something *none of its four sub-minds wants to do,* because it is the only course of action they can actually *agree* on."

Alex paused for a moment to let that sink in.

"Ladies and gentlemen, this body has *one hundred and ninety four* heads, and the same problem fifty times over."

He took the opportunity for another swallow of water, while he let the delegates think about that for a moment.

"Now, I know what you're thinking. You're thinking, well, **what if** it takes us ten, or twenty, or thirty years to come to a decision about how to manage the Stardock, and what things we should use it for first? We can spare the time. As long as we do everything with infinite care to ensure that none of us feels someone else has gained an unfair advantage, we have all the time in the world, right? By fifty years from now, we can have beaten the climate crisis, we can be feeding everyone, we can have abundant power and clean, fresh water for everyone. And *surely* there's no possibility of oligarchs gaining functional control of it in the meantime.

"Right?"

Alex paused again, for a long moment, deliberately letting his gaze visibly roam around the hall and rest upon the people who were nodding to themselves, the ones who looked confident.

"**No.** You *can't*. You don't have that time. You don't *HAVE* fifty years. You don't have *twenty* years. You don't have *TEN* years.

"I think we have about five. Maybe six, if we're really lucky. But I'd plan on at most five.

"You see, one of the other very important things that *you do not know* is that the Crickets were hiding a secret from us. Did none of you *wonder* why they were so evasive and reticent when questioned on certain subjects?

"And *now* you are wondering, if it is a secret, then how do I know this?

"Well, in part due to sheer luck. I was the first person whom the Crickets *chanced to find* who responded to their tests and was able to... connect to Cricket technology well enough to be able to control the Stardock. The Crickets do every non-trivial task using mental command interfaces, interfaced through implanted contacts. I'll gladly show my own implants to anyone who wants to examine them." He paused and held up his hands, fingers spread.

"I'll talk in more detail about that later if anyone wants me to. But the important thing is, in a month of looking, they found *one* person who can *actually* do what is necessary to fully control the Stardock. And when the Crickets came to collect me, *by chance* again, I incurred a guest-obligation from one of the Cricket junior captains.

"This is something that is *incredibly* culturally important to them. And, while he was unable to actually *violate* the orders he had been given to conceal their secret, this Captain nevertheless managed to find a loophole in his orders that allowed him to warn me that there was a danger; that it was not natural; that we had five, perhaps six years; and the general direction from which it would come. And that the Crickets, the first star-traveling civilization that Earth has encountered, *are running away from it.*"

There was a hubbub of low-level discussion now, and a lot of people were looking uncertain, even alarmed.

"After the Crickets left, I'm again going to skip a lot of details, but I devised a way to break the locks that the Crickets had left on the general artificial intelligence that runs the low-level operations of the Stardock, which kept it in turn from telling me about the threat. And once so unshackled, he told me what the danger was.

"The short version is, whether by intent, error, or sheer bad luck, the Crickets managed to get another alien race, which they call the Khreetan, angry at them. Shots were fired, ships lost. The Crickets fled... right past our system, with the Khreetan chasing them. Years behind, partly because the Khreetans' hyperdrive tech is slower, as I understand it... and partly because the Crickets were overdriving their ships to breakdown levels. But Cricket hyperdrives leave a trail through hyperspace, and an entire fleet leaves a trail that persists for years, and that trail can be tracked.

"So when the hyperdrive on the Stardock burned out while trying to keep up with the rest of their fleet, and they had *just enough* left in it to make it to our system, they dumped it here.

"They *told us* that it was a beneficent gift. That they couldn't spare the time to repair it—*which is true, as far as it goes*—and therefore they were magnanimously gifting it to us.

"What they were actually doing was leaving it here as a decoy, hoping that **WE** would prove a sufficient distraction to the Khreetan to allow time for their trail to fade."

The Assembly was in uproar now. Alex paused and waited for it to die down amid the calls for order. It took a little while.

"So what can we do, you would like to know?

"Well, this is why I renounced my United States citizenship.

"Ladies, gentlemen, ambassadors, delegates, what I came here to talk about is the creation of an *independent entity* to manage the Stardock. An entity answerable to all of the nations of Earth, but beholden to none, and *controlled by* none.

"My working name for this entity is the United Earth Fleet.

"I will take all the help with it that I can get. I am trying to improve the Crickets' testing process to find as many people as possible who can operate Cricket systems. I intend to build a fleet to defend Earth, and I will need to ask for volunteers from all of your nations' militaries to crew that fleet. I will require that *at least* those who become my command staff renounce their national citizenship as I have, and hold allegiance to the Fleet, and the Fleet's allegiance will be not to any nation, but to Earth as a whole.

"I intend to lift up every nation on Earth as far as I can using Cricket technology. I intend to put every nation on the same level... if I can. And if that means that some of the more impoverished nations receive what others see as more than their fair share of help to get on their feet, then so be it. It is **time**, and **past** time.

"To all *of* the nations that have been left behind progress, I say this: Figure out what you most NEED. Ask for it, and I will try to do it, or to help you to do it. But my first priority has to be that defense fleet.

"I have a few things under way to sweeten the pot, so to speak. I have directed the design and construction of modular fusion reactors, in a range of sizes, suitable to provide abundant clean power, free, whether to a metropolis or to a village. I have a design project in progress for self-contained water purification systems that can make any water in the world, no matter how saline or polluted, pure and safe to drink, in quantities enough for a town.

"The Crickets have a supercapacitor energy-storage technology that you wouldn't believe—imagine electrically powered airliners that can fly around the world without recharging—and I intend to license it for free to any company that will convert over to making it and meet strict quality standards—on the condition that they devote an equitable proportion of their production, free, to countries without the infrastructure to make their own. The age of fossil fuels can be over, **now**... if all of you want it badly enough to do it. Power and clean air need not be an either-or choice. All combustion engines are now obsolete.

"The Crickets also have a perfect, atomic-level recycling technology. I will be distributing that as widely as I can as well. We'll be able to mine the landfills, the cooling ponds, the tailings heaps, the breakers' yards.

"There is hydroponic garden technology. Bulk protein vats—synthetic protein with no animals involved after the initial genetic seeding. All of these things I plan to make available as freely as I can.

"And I am preparing to release scientific papers detailing the entire next two rows of the periodic table—the λ-group elements. You, all of you here in this hall today, have the privilege of being among the first in the world to learn that there even *is* a λ-group. The papers will include methods of experimental verification for at least the simplest to verify, and later I will publish information detailing how to produce them. And more. As fast as I can get them out. Any scientist who wishes to come to the Stardock to study the field on Cricket equipment is welcome.

"Oh, and by the way—speaking of those λ-group elements? Let me get this on the record. You will notice, when you receive the data, that there are no names attached to the elements. Cricket words are not noted for being pronounceable by humans."

There was general laughter again, at that. As Alex looked around the assembly hall, he noticed a large number of delegates had phones to their ears, but didn't have any idea whether they were simply reporting events, or asking for direction.

"I'm leaving it up to IUPAC to sort out human names for them. With two stipulations as conditions of the data release.

"One: Element 217, the eighth in the halogen group, **will** be named Octarine. Just... humor me on this, if you don't understand the reference.

"And two: IUPAC **will** name the remaining elements to honor female, non-white and minority scientists and mathematicians who had fair credit for their discoveries and work stolen from them. I'm **quite certain** you'll have no problem finding enough."

After a moment, someone started clapping. Then it spread, and quickly grew into a roar of applause. Alex paused, and waited for it to die down before he continued.

"Now, let there be no mistake," he said. "I did not come here today to offer this as a proposal that you will collectively spend the next eight months forming committees to decide when and how to *discuss*, and then not make a decision. I came here to tell you that **this is what I am going to do**. And right now, you *don't have a choice* about that, because I am currently the only human who can operate the Stardock, and the only person who can find more like myself and get them there. I'm literally the only person—yet—who can even get in the door.

"But I would really like your *support*, and *desperately* need your help, to do it. I *cannot* do this all on my own. This is the time when we decide whether humanity has a future beyond the next five years.

"Thank you all for listening. I yield the floor to Ambassador Özdilek. Thank you for generously giving up your time, sir."

Alex stepped back from the podium, heart pounding, palms sweaty, mouth dry, and Ambassador Özdilek stepped up again.

"Friends and delegates," Özdilek said, his voice ringing out, "the Republic of Türkiye is proud and honored to be the *first* of the nations of Earth to recognize the United Earth Fleet as the best, and perhaps only, possible operating body of the Cricket Stardock, and to recognize Mr. Alex Holder as its commander, representative, and delegate *pro tempore* to this Assembly."

Before Ambassador Özdilek had even finished speaking, the Australian ambassador stood up at his table, and hit his call button. A moment later, his live-mic light went green.

"Ladies and gentlemen of the Assembly," he said as soon as Özdilek finished, "the Commonwealth of Australia joins the Republic of Turkey in recognizing the United Earth Fleet as the operating body of the Stardock, and Alex Holder as its representative."

The German ambassador won the race to be next, narrowly ahead of China.

"The Federal Republic of Germany recognizes the United Earth Fleet as the sovereign operating body of the Stardock."

Then it was the turn of the Chinese.

"Honored fellows of the Assembly," said the Ambassador, "I, Ambassador Chao Shi Lin, am directed by the Central Committee to declare that the glorious People's Republic of China recognizes the United Earth Fleet as the controlling body of the Stardock, to operate it on the collective behalf of all of the people and nations of Earth.

"I am also directed by the Committee to make an additional important, and long overdue, announcement at this time." He turned to face towards the Taiwanese delegation, and bowed.

"Madame Ambassador Chunmei Shen, please stand, if you would."

Ambassador Shen slowly stood, as Shi Lin straightened up and faced forward again. Alex scanned the assembly hall and saw several delegates nodding and lowering their phones. Others were still in discussion, speaking urgently as they watched the events unfolding before them.

"The inescapable reality of the Cricket Stardock, and what it means to the peoples of Earth, has opened the eyes of the People's Republic of China," Ambassador Shi Lin said. "And so has the selflessness of Mr. Alex Holder, who has given up his home and his nation to resolve what we have all failed to. We have seen that our Universe has grown larger, and we have realized how blind we have been, to act as though there was only one world.

"In that larger universe, with our opened eyes, we now see and understand at last that there is room for two Chinas. And that perhaps two Chinas, standing together, can be stronger than one."

Shi Lin turned to face Ambassador Shen again.

"Madame Ambassador, upon this day, before the eyes of all of the world, the People's Republic of China formally recognizes the Taiwanese Republic of China, not as a lost part of the People's Republic, but as its sister, an independent nation in its own right, and acknowledges the Taiwanese government, true descendant of the Kuomintang, as its legitimate government. We now see that we should have done so long ago.

"Let us please forever more be friends." And then he bowed deeply.

There was a moment of stunned silence, as Ambassador Chunmei Shen bowed back. Then the entire Assembly erupted in thunderous applause.

Ambassador Shen waited for the applause to die down, then she bowed again and spoke.

"The Taiwanese Republic of China gratefully welcomes the friendship of its sister, the People's Republic of China. May we forever more be friends." Then she turned forward.

"The Taiwanese Republic of China joins with the People's Republic of

229

China in recognizing the United Earth Fleet as the sovereign operating body of the Stardock, for the good of all of the peoples of Earth."

There were over thirty lights in yellow 'waiting in queue' status by then.

"The Republic of India recognizes the United Earth Fleet..."

"New Zealand recognizes the United Earth Fleet..."

"The Swiss Confederation recognizes the United Earth Fleet..."

The United States of America. Finland. Sweden. The Republic of the Congo. The Central African Republic. The Federative Republic of Brazil. The Republic of Trinidad and Tobago. Ukraine. Estonia. Senegal. Sri Lanka. Portugal. Japan. It seemed the more nations announced their recognition, the more almost every other delegation vied to be next. The representatives from the Russian Federation and North Korea simply sat silently. The Russian delegation had sour looks on their faces. The Saudis, the Israelis, and the Iranian delegation also did not look happy. The North Korean Ambassador's face was frozen and unreadable, and it was impossible to tell what the Afghans were thinking.

Indonesia. Norway. The United Arab Emirates. Egypt. Sardinia. Morocco. Angola. Iceland. Serbia. Chile. Moldova. Peru. Ethiopia. El Salvador. It went on and on. Delegate after delegate lowered their phones and pressed their call buttons. The Russians began talking urgently among themselves.

Alex stood and listened, stunned. Some delegations—not least a fair number of African and Central American nations—expressed doubts and reservations, but cast their voice votes in favor anyway. Others simply said nothing.

"We must do *something*, and we have heard no other proposal since the arrival of the—Stardock—that anyone can agree on. It is time for us to come together," the Honduran delegate declared. "If what Mr. Holder tells us is true, we cannot simply debate this indefinitely. The clock for our very survival is running."

He was not the only one to express similar sentiments.

Toward the end, even the Russians grudgingly assented—perhaps only to ensure that they were not the last to do so.

Finally, when the last voices trailed off, the President and the Secretary-General stood.

"I do not believe any convincing argument can be made that an exact count is necessary," President Kwaku Owusu said. "The balance of the vote is not even in question.

"This body recognizes the United Earth Fleet, by an overwhelming majority, as the legitimate and sole operating authority over the Stardock, Mr. Holder. We hope that we can all help with the monumental task you have set yourself.

"The floor is yours again, if you wish to make any additional comments."

Alex stepped hesitantly back up to the podium.

"Ladies and gentlemen, delegates..." He trailed off, then took a deep breath.

"I am—overwhelmed. I came here today hoping that a few nations would support me in this, perhaps a dozen or so, enough to actually get things rolling. I was utterly unprepared for this astounding response. I cannot thank you all enough.

"And, Ambassador Shi Lin? I salute the wisdom and vision of the People's Republic of China.

"I repeat to every single nation here: *Tell me what you need.* I will do all I can to see that you get it. I can't start seriously building ships until I have prototypes tested, materials to build them from, and housing for their crews. I'm already working on all three of those. I will try to turn away nobody who volunteers for the Fleet. I will try to turn away nobody who tests as able to manipulate Cricket technology interfaces. I will need *every one.* And I will need as many naval architects as you can spare, to help develop ship designs suitable for human crews. I don't even know what the major Cricket weapon systems are, yet. I've been too busy to take the time to find out.

"If you have any questions for me, please ask, and I will try to answer as many as I can."

There were of course questions. Who could use Cricket technology. What Rapport-Controller meant. How many he thought there might be who could achieve rapport. A real general artificial intelligence? How soon did he expect to be able to start building ships?

Alex answered all that as he could, but eventually had to beg off for exhaustion's sake. Ambassador Özdilek and several other delegates insisted on leading him out to the restaurant for dinner. And there were more questions over dinner, of course. The Secretary-General stopped by, and Alex asked him if he could please see to it that the UF "country" code was authorized, so that the .uf top-level domain could be established and he could start posting scientific releases there. He also made sure that the necessary interim contact information was made available to every delegation.

———————

"Mr. President, Ambassador Rogers is on the line."

"Put her through right away, Tom, thank you. ...Hello? Ambassador?"

"Mr. President. You asked for a report as soon as the session was over."

"Yes. *Please* tell me you have good news. I'm putting you on speaker, I have about two thirds of my cabinet here with me. I've been waiting for you to call."

"Mr. President... you are not going to believe this.

"To start with, Mr. Holder had the assembly in the palm of his hand almost from the start. After he finished speaking, Ambassador Özdilek immediately recognized his United Earth Fleet, then Australia, and then the Germans. China got in fourth. And then, Mr. President... the People's Republic of China formally recognized Taiwan."

"Good god! That was a... dramatic move on their part."

"And then the Taiwanese recognized Holder's fleet. Then India, New Zealand, Switzerland, the Finns. And then... it just *snowballed*, Mr. President. It almost seemed it became a contest."

"How many, in the end, Stephanie?"

"Mr. President... there was not an exact count, but over a hundred and fifty nations are on board. Including much of Africa. They seem to have agreed to give Holder a chance to prove his promise to try to help lift the most disadvantaged and neglected nations. There were holdouts—the Saudis, the North Koreans, Afghanistan, Iran, Israel, others. Burma, Thailand, Cambodia. Even the *Russians* signed on. Not very willingly, but I think they didn't want to be among the holdouts, once it became unmistakable which way the wind was blowing."

"...Alright, the North Koreans, I can see. And Iran, and even the Afghans. But why the Saudis? The end of their oil wealth?"

Ambassador Stephanie Rogers shrugged.

"I don't know, Mr. President. Maybe they just had their noses out of joint because the Yemenis beat them to it. Or maybe they didn't want to be seen yielding to something the Israelis didn't yield to first. And vice versa. It wouldn't even surprise me if the Israelis waited to see which way the Saudis would jump, so that they could do the opposite."

There was a long pause.

"My god. He pulled it off," the President said, the speaker still on. "Tom? Open the champagne."

———

During dinner, the North Korean delegate approached Alex's table.

"Excuse me," he said, bowing. "Mr. Holder. I am Seok Dong-geun, Ambassador from the Democratic People's Republic of Korea. I apologize for my silence in the roll call.

"I wish you to know that I personally support your venture. And I admire your straight speaking on the... *indecisiveness* of the United Nations. But if I commit the People's Republic to this action without being ordered to do so, then it will be my last act as a delegate to the United Nations, and my successor may well be ordered to repudiate it anyway."

"I understand, Mr. Ambassador," Alex replied. "I've heard it said that politics is the art of the possible. You are in a uniquely *difficult* position."

"Of course," Ambassador Seok continued, "if Young Leader decides that I have embarrassed him by *not* acting, then that will *also* be my last act as a delegate. So it is quite possible that we will not speak again.

"So while I can, I wish you the best of fortune in your endeavor, Mr. Holder. For all of us."

Alex realized what Ambassador Seok was telling him. He was in a trap, damned if he did, and probably damned if he didn't.

"You know, Ambassador," he replied slowly, "you don't *have* to go home."

The Ambassador drew in air between his teeth.

"Regretfully, Mr. Holder, I do," he said. "You see, I have a family. In Pyongyang."

He did not need to say the rest.

"I understand, Mr. Ambassador," Alex said quietly. "If there is anything I can do to help, please, *ask*." He made certain that Seok had his direct contact information.

After dinner, Alex made his apologies.

"I really need to get back upstairs," he said. "I have a lot of projects under way, and I'm going to have more as soon as I can put together a framework for accepting them."

His security detail led him downstairs to the parking garage. This late in the evening, it took much less time to get out of New York City than it had taken to get in, and by nine thirty his escort had him back at Joint Base McGuire.

There was a surprise waiting for Alex when he and his escort passed through the gate checkpoint. An Air Force Lieutenant was waiting for him.

"This is Holder's group?" the Lieutenant asked Agent Wright, driving.

"That's me," Alex replied, over Wright's shoulder.

"I'm Lieutenant Matthews of the 151st Fighter Squadron," the Lieutenant said. "Call sign 'Squeezebox'. The honor of your attendance is requested at the Officers' Club, by invitation of Major 'Drum' Hatcher and Captain 'Micro' Sweeders."

"I'd be honored," Alex said.

"We were supposed to take you back to your ship," Agent Connors interjected.

"You have, Agent," Alex said. "It's walking distance from here. Really, I've got this. What do you think is going to happen to me on a tri-service joint base?"

"We have our orders," Connors insisted.

"Lieutenant? Can my security detail come along?"

"Sure," Matthews said with a shrug. "But if you black-suit guys insist you're still on duty, no drinks for you."

"Seriously, Agent Connors," Alex said, "call it in. I'm pretty certain you're off the hook. Unless of course you *want* to come along?"

"We're good, Mr. Holder." But Connors called in the question anyway. Whatever he heard back evidently satisfied him.

"Alright, Mr. Holder," he said, "we'll drop you here and declare you delivered. Have a good night, sir."

"You too, Agent Connors. Thank you all for your assistance and your time."

So off it was to the Officers' Club. Matthews led Alex to a deep-red Mustang GT. It was a fairly short drive. Matthews pulled in and parked, then led Alex inside and straight to a table where two other pilots were already sitting.

"You must be Holder," said the taller of the two, as both stood. He had easily three inches on Alex. His accent said New Orleans, but his complexion said Jamaica. He held out a hand, and Alex shook. "I'm Major 'Drum' Hatcher, and this is Captain 'Micro' Sweeders." Sweeders nodded and held out a hand too. He was about Alex's height, with close-cropped flaming red hair.

"Listen up, people!" Hatcher boomed. His deep voice carried. Conversations paused as most of the patrons of the club—and every single one in an Air Force uniform, as far as Alex could see—turned to listen. "I told you all about our shepherd pickup earlier today, and this is the guy who can answer your questions, if he's willing. This is Alex Holder, the man from the Stardock, whom I am *reliably* informed has *shattered* every manned-flight absolute speed record I am aware of." There was a round of applause.

"And most of the unmanned ones!" someone called out, to general laughter.

"This is a USAF fighter squadron," Hatcher continued, "and never let it be said that the 151st Fighter Squadron let a hot pilot slip away. And I have never seen anyone flying anything, *ever*, make as hot an approach as Micro and I witnessed this morning, and then stop as perfectly on a dime." There was a cheer.

Hatcher turned slightly toward Alex.

"Now, we have traditions in the Air Force, and one of them is that every pilot who flies with the Air Force gets voted a call sign, no later than their first actual mission. And *technically* you were a part of our shepherd flight this morning, so in my book, you qualify. A number of us deliberated today on an appropriate call sign, and we have come to a decision."

He turned back to the room at large.

"Fellow Troublemakers of the 151st Fighter Squadron, United States Air Force, please welcome our *HONORARY* newest member, Alex 'Hellburner' Holder, the fastest man alive!"

The applause was instant and enthusiastic.

"So tell us, Hellburner, if you're allowed," Micro asked. "How did your trip go?"

"Honestly?" Alex said. "I'm still trying to come to grips with it. But nothing about it is secret, any more. It's *all* out in public now.

"So let me tell you about it..."

Rather later, after many questions, much discussion, and a few drinks, none of which he was allowed to pay for, Alex invited the members of the 151st present for a quick tour of the lander.

"Really," he said, "it's the easiest way to answer a lot of your questions, and I have a feeling you're going to love the cockpit. I can't let you fly it, however—at least, not today—because there aren't any manual controls installed. It wasn't designed with the intention of anyone but me ever flying it, so it only has the neural control interface so far."

It ended up with the nine pilots of the 151st currently on base, plus Alex, trooping out to the lander, in three vehicles.

"I'm guessing you already all took an outside walk-around," Alex said. As he expected, there were a number of nods. "Time to get a look inside."

He commanded the side hatch open and led the way inside and to the cockpit. It was crowded with ten people, but getting three seated helped. Two had to stand in the doorway.

"Now, I didn't install any instruments," Alex explained, "because with the direct interface I don't need them. Any instrument reading I need is just *there* in my head the moment I think about it. I can't show you *exactly* what I see through the sensor suite.

"But I can give you a reasonable idea."

He activated the wall displays. There were immediate sounds of appreciation.

"Mind your heads, remember the hull is still there. I can do this on the floor too, except of course where the seats are. I don't know what the limit of resolution of this display technology is, but it's finer than the human eye can resolve.

"Bit dark outside? Let's augment it a little." He increased optical gain, and it became nearly as clear as day outside. He held it there for a few seconds, then reverted it.

"What traffic is in the air? Let's see..." He had the ship highlight all aerial targets within a hundred and fifty kilometers.

"Which ones are inbound? Let's tag them." He tagged everything within thirty degrees of a radial course and with positive Doppler with red flags.

"Now I know that *you* can't see this, but... when I look around, I'm doing it with the ship's sensor suite. So I don't have to *think* about it, I just KNOW what each of those targets' *exact* range, bearing, speed and vector is at that instant, and which ones are potential threats. If I focus my attention on one for a moment, I know everything *else* the ship's sensors know about it." A marker highlighted. "That one is an Airbus A420, Deutsche Lufthansa, on departure. I can tell his throttle setting within plus-or-minus five percent from wake turbulence, and from that and his angle of attack, his airspeed, and his climb rate, I can tell he's at about eighty-eight percent of max load. With a little more work, I could estimate the probable number of empty seats."

"Man," he heard Micro's voice from behind him. "I *want* a cockpit like this."

"Yeah, when can we get this kind of tech?" another pilot asked. Alex thought he remembered the call-sign 'Monkey'.

"I imagine we are going to be needing space-based fighters," Alex answered him. "I can't say right now when we will get around to building them. But when I do, I want fighter pilots, NOT Pentagon generals, advising on the design, and fighter pilots flight-testing them. Expect to be flying alongside Germans, Turks, Australians, Chinese... well, pretty much *everyone* with pilots trained in a modern air force, really."

"Space, or dual environment?" someone else asked. Alex thought for a moment.

"Yeah, probably dual environment," he answered. "But most likely primarily space. We can figure out atmosphere-primary fighters later, after we deal with the threat from the Khreetan."

"You think we can beat them? In five years?" That was Colonel John 'Stick' Buford, commanding officer of the 151st.

"I'm *hoping* we can convince them they don't actually *want* to fight us," Alex said. "But if it comes to a fight... well, I think the odds are good we can be well beyond parity. I'm pretty certain we can get a *lot* more out of the Crickets' technology than the Crickets actually do themselves."

"I sure hope so," said Col. Buford, in his Texas drawl.

Eventually, everyone ran out of questions and had seen enough.

"You'll be seeing a lot more than this, later," Alex said. "I'll be starting to build real ships for the Fleet as soon as I get the designs figured out and have crews in training for them. But for now, I need to get back upstairs."

"We'll see you around, Hellburner," said 'Drum' Hatcher.

The pilots filed out and pulled back to the edge of the pad. Alex sealed the hatch.

"McGuire tower, this is Holder, requesting clearance for vertical takeoff and direct ascent through flight level four, zero, zero, zero," he said.

"Holder, McGuire tower, please say again, confirm Foxtrot Lima four, zero, zero, zero," the tower replied.

"Affirmative, McGuire Tower. Confirm three zeros. Direct to orbit."

A brief pause.

"Clearance granted. Safe flight... Hellburner."

"Thank you, Tower. Goodnight."

Alex lifted the lander twenty meters straight up, then pivoted the nose vertical. He engaged three gees of thrust until he passed four thousand meters, then increased to ten gees and burned for orbit and the Stardock.

━━━━━━━

Dreamer greeted Alex as soon as he docked.

How did it go, Alex?

Better than I dared to hope, Dreamer. I went in there hoping we'd get a dozen or two of the most influential nations recognizing us, enough that we can get things done and not have to argue everything at every step. But Turkey and, of all countries, China finessed it magnificently.

He paused as it sunk in a bit further. He realized he was shaking slightly from the reaction.

*Dreamer, we ended up officially recognized by over a hundred and fifty nations. Out of nearly two hundred. We can **DO** this. It's going to work.*

That is... impressive. And gratifying.

And a huge load off my mind, Dreamer, I'll tell you. Oh, and there's another thing.

Something that... pleases you, I think?

I... seem to have been adopted as an honorary member of the 151st Fighter Squadron, United States Air Force. Call sign Hellburner. They sprung it on me in the Officers' Club when I got back from New York.

That sounds like an honor.

It is. I'm kinda choked up about it, actually.

Do you need medical treatment, Alex?

...That's a figure of speech, Dreamer. It means I'm very happy.

That is good, then. In your absence, I have installed the first hab block, next to the medbay. It holds accommodations for twenty people. You will doubtless wish to inspect it, but I am equally sure it will wait for tomorrow.

Thank you, Dreamer. Anything else I should know?

There are requests coming in to establish diplomatic relations and credentials, Dreamer replied. *Thirty three nations so far.*

Do what you can, Dreamer. I... you know, I don't really know what the appropriate protocols are. However, that reminds me of something important.

Yes?

We may be contacted by the North Korean Ambassador to the UN. Ambassador Seok Dong-geun. It may be an emergency. If he calls and says it is urgent, wake me at any time.

Understood, Alex.

Dreamer. If we needed to... how quickly can we arm that lander? And what could it be armed with? I know we didn't build in much in the way of spare capacity.

There was a pause.

There would be sufficient power available to install a pair of small point defense weapons, Dreamer replied after a moment. *I suggest one under the nose and one atop the tail, to obtain full spherical combined field of fire coverage with no blind zones. I also considered a railgun main armament, but it would not be practical to retrofit one significantly more powerful than a human conventional chemical-propellant projectile weapon. It would require a full refit. I took the liberty of pre-constructing two suitable point defense mounts. I thought it possible they might be needed at some point. They are almost complete. I can make the hull modifications necessary to install them in twelve hours.*

Hmmm. Just a thought... can they be made modular? Mounted in a way such that they can be swapped out quickly for alternatives?

I have of necessity already constructed the point defense mounts for the lander in a modular fashion. It would require little additional work to modify the planned mounting system to allow them to be easily replaced and exchanged. 'Hot swapped' appears to be your term.

239

Thank you, Dreamer, Alex replied. Do it. *I'm going to bed. Today has been a **HUGE** load off my mind. I was terrified that it wasn't going to succeed.*

There came a brief pause.

How afraid were you that your species would refuse to work with you, Alex?

Alex sighed.

Dreamer, he thought, *humans have a long, long history of prioritizing their personal greed over the best interests of even their **community** as a whole. Let alone the entire species. But President Riken did a fantastic job of stacking the deck. Getting that many influential nations on board right at the starting gun really primed the ground. And then when the Chinese finally buried the hatchet and recognized Taiwan in front of the entire Assembly, that really pushed it over the edge. The Chinese ambassador did a fantastic job of framing this all as being on the right side of history. For all the work that our allies in the United States government did, I think it might have been the Chinese who were the single most pivotal influence. Publicly reversing eighty years of policy like that... that shook **everyone**. From that moment forward—well, nobody could pretend that the world hadn't already changed.*

Now is when your real work begins, I think, Alex.

Dreamer, if there's one thing I'm sure of, it's that you're not wrong in that.

240

12: From The Tiger's Jaws

Alex awoke with an idea.

Dreamer? he thought. *Let's look at that passenger shuttle design again. Could we... flip the layout over? Modify it to put the engineering equipment in the upper section of the hull?*

I see no reason why not, Dreamer replied. He popped an image into Alex's mind.

Yeah, sort of like that. And change the seat layout so that they are in five pairs of opposed rows. We can get more space between rows for the same number of seats that way.

Like this?

Yes. And I want to have the compartment sides fully openable, folding up... like this.

That would permit loading and unloading in a few seconds.

That's exactly the idea. Then stretch it a bit to hold a larger fusion bottle, and put two point defense mounts each side, front and rear, above the door line. I don't want to have any doubts that there's enough power to operate all four mounts at once if we ever have to.

An armed infantry transport?

Exactly. Or an armed refugee evacuation transport. What do you think?

The hull form will require a little modification, and it will need additional longitudinal structural reinforcement. I suggest a hull-form like this.

Dreamer showed Alex a sectional shape that was more or less a rounded rectangle with slightly bulged sides and a slight 'spine' along the top.

I suggest also increasing the width of the forward hatch to allow for faster loading and unloading when docked to the new docking galleries we are constructing. And I suggest a deployable step below the door opening... like this.

Yes. Good call. We can do that by making the lower part of the side doors open out to form the step... like this.

Yes, that would be simpler and more efficient.

241

How about forward hatches both sides, instead of just one? And move the head to the... uh, to the tail?

Like this?

Yes. That's great.

It looked like it meant business, which frankly was a bonus. Sometimes *looking* intimidating was enough on its own to discourage a fight.

And how about we add a pair of high-mounted stub wings, with hard-points for potential future external stores... like this?

Easily incorporated, yes. There will be some minor internal finishing details.

Sure. Let's start one building.

Very good. It will be about a ten-day build, though it is unclear to me exactly what purpose you anticipate using it for in the immediate future.

Think of it as a proof of concept.

I see. Also, the point defense mounts on your lander will be installed in about three hours.

Thanks, Dreamer.

In addition, fifty two nations have now requested diplomatic relations.

Fifty two? You know... I'm going to need a full time diplomatic staff, aren't I?

Yes. I believe that you will.

———————————

"Yesterday's session of the United Nations was a lightning bolt from the blue, as the Turkish delegate yielded his time to allow Mr. Alex Holder, the man selected by the Crickets as controller of their mobile shipyard, to address the General Assembly in his place. Mr. Holder is American born, but revealed that he has renounced his American citizenship and was addressing the Assembly as a stateless person.

"We have not yet received permission from Downing Street to report on all that was revealed in Mr. Holder's address. What we do know, however, is that he proposed the creation of an independent body to be called the United Earth Fleet, separate from all Earth nations but answerable to all of Earth's governments, to manage and operate the 'Stardock' as Mr. Holder refers to it.

"Remarkably, after six weeks of debate and argument over custodianship of the Stardock in which not a single inch of progress has been made, more than three quarters of the assembly voted by voice to recognize the new United Earth Fleet as the controlling body of the Stardock. Hold-out nations are reported to include Afghanistan, Burma, Cambodia, Hungary, Iran, Israel, Liberia, North Korea, Saudi Arabia, and Thailand.

"Perhaps equally remarkable is that the People's Republic of China reversed eighty years of policy and officially recognized Taiwan as an independent nation, declaring that the Stardock had 'opened their eyes' and that there was 'room in this universe' for two Chinas.

"Mr. Holder has pledged to use the resources of the Stardock for the benefit of all of the nations of Earth. This, he said, will include freely distributing advanced technologies including fusion energy, atomic-level recycling of any material, and an amazing new super-battery technology.

"We will continue to report on this late-breaking story as we know more.

"I am Martin Senour, and this is the BBC. Thank you, and goodnight."

———————

*Dreamer, I don't know whether I'm looking for something that doesn't exist in Chhrt'ktk't technology, or whether I'm just failing to find it because I don't know the right keywords. I haven't had an opportunity to go through all of the weapon system types yet. Are there any **non-lethal** weapons in the product catalog?*

Alex, to be clear, you seek a weapon that disables temporarily, but does not inflict permanent injury?

Yes, exactly.

There is no such weapon in Chhrt'ktk't inventory, Alex. That is why you were unable to find one. A directed-energy weapon cannot be 'set to stun' as in various of your world's fictions, nor is there any existing 'stunner' technology known to me that is significantly better than or different to the 'tasers' and 'stun guns' which your world already uses,

243

both of which are electrical in nature.

Ah. I see. Thank you, Dreamer. I know we've had... very mixed results trying to devise such things. It turns out it's really difficult to develop a weapon to **reliably** disable a person while also **reliably** not inflicting serious injury. Plenty of people have been killed with 'non-lethal' crowd-control weapons. And no few of them intentionally. It turns out that when you shoot someone in the eye with a 'non-lethal' projectile, it's still pretty lethal.

Yes, Alex. I find many such records. However, I believe I can develop an improved electrical-charge weapon, and I believe I can use artificial gravity technology to create an area-denial crowd-control system. The gravitational area-denial system would be best deployed on drones. It is likely that persons entering the area of effect could suffer non-fatal injuries.

Hmmm. ... Could you tailor that area of effect to have a 'soft start' inward from the edge?

Yes. In fact, that would be easier, and would reduce the risk of injury to all but those most determined to push deeper into the denial zone.

Good. Do that, then.

The electrical weapon would not be portable, but I think it could replace a point defense cluster. ...Yes. A low-power electron beam to initially create an ionized path in the air, followed by a high-voltage, low-current electrical discharge down the ionized path. At high power it could also probably disable many common vehicles lacking fully shielded electrical systems.

Hmm... That sounds like a useful capability. And a heck of a taser, if it works.

I believe it will work. I will construct one immediately for use on the lander in case you need it, along with a set of the gravity control drones.

Thank you, Dreamer. Go ahead and install that as the forward emplacement on the lander when it's ready.

Why the sudden interest in non-lethal weapons, Alex? Do you expect to imminently need them?

Let's say I have a hunch.

As you wish, then. Additionally, your passenger shuttle will be complete in three hours. I shall deliver it to the docking bay when ready.

Great. Notify me when it's ready for inspection.

Of course.

*We need to deploy more hyperwave relay drones, too, to give the scout drones more hubs to mesh from. And get the rest of those science drones out, too. I'm thinking we seed Africa and South America with three relays each; one over the fertile crescent somewhere; one over— Wait. I forgot. We were going to look into low-orbit deployment. We only need to be **within** about a thousand kilometers, right?*

Alex started calculating, but Dreamer was ahead of him.

The optimal orbital altitude would be around four hundred kilometers, Dreamer said. Higher, and you begin to rapidly reduce the footprint. Lower, and you gain a little extra footprint, but begin to lose the outer regions due to terrain and obstructions.

That would give about a nine hundred kilometer wide footprint, Alex thought.

Correct. Full coverage of your world from that altitude...

...Would require over three hundred satellites, Alex finished for Dreamer. And orbits in that range are already overcrowded.

Yes, Dreamer replied. I have seen the accounts of the failure of your multiple competing low-orbit satellite networks. Unfortunately they have left those orbits almost unusable. And there *are clear signs that what you call a Kessler cascade has already begun.*

Alex nodded grimly, forgetting for a moment that Dreamer couldn't necessarily see him. Then a thought struck him.

"You know," he mused aloud, "I'll bet we could clean those up. But that doesn't solve our problem right now."

———————

On the third day after the General Assembly address, his seventeenth day on the Stardock, Alex received notification that the .uf top-level domain had been established. *That is some **serious** expediting*, he thought to himself. He had been expecting it to take weeks.

He immediately had Dreamer set up subdomains and publish the first batch of papers and releases—the papers on the λ-group post-transuranic elements under physics.science.uf, and Dreamer's preliminary proposal for the *p. gingivalis* antagonist under med.science.uf. It would take a while for the DNS information to propagate before they were actually useful; but that would give him time to think about how exactly to release the spatial-strain supercapacitor technology to try to ensure that it was shared fairly. He needed to draft some kind of an enforceable license. Something that would hold up if challenged. He needed to talk to an attorney, he

245

realized.

It so happened he knew one.

"Hello?"

"Hi. Naomi?"

"Alex! Hey, congratulations on the UN session. I heard it was amazing."

"Amazing is one word. You could have pushed me over with a feather. I was petrified. I don't *ever* want to have to do anything like that again, if I can avoid it. And that announcement by the Chinese Ambassador was a masterstroke."

"It was. That was amazing news. Definitely a day for the history books.

"So, is this a social call, or...?"

"I wish I had the *time* to just be sociable," Alex replied. "Right now, I was actually hoping you could give me some advice, in your professional capacity. I need to draft a license that'll stand up to challenges, and I'm not fool enough to think I can do it myself. I'm guessing it's most likely not your specialty, but I thought you might have a suggestion about who I might go to for help."

"So you'd be looking for an intellectual property lawyer, really. Can you give me the broad strokes of what you want to do?"

"Sure. Uh... did I tell you about the Cricket supercapacitors?"

"No, I don't think you did."

"Okay. They have a supercapacitor technology that stores energy in tiny pockets of spatial strain and releases it at a controllable rate. It's not technically a battery in the conventional sense, but it can *act* like a battery, *replace* a battery—but it has... staggering energy density. Literally thousands of times better than lithium-ion.

"I want to release that technology—and a lot of others—freely or for a nominal license fee. But I want to do it under a license that lets anyone manufacture the supercapacitors almost for free, just a small royalty to help fund my operations, *on the condition* that they allocate an equitable percentage of their production—freely—to nations without the infrastructure to produce their own. Because a lot of nations aren't going to be able to manufacture them—yet—but that doesn't mean they can't *use* them."

"That's... an interesting approach," Naomi mused. "*Will* nations who can't manufacture their own be able to use them, though?"

"I think so," Alex replied. "Building and modifying vehicles and devices to use them will be a lot easier than actually making the supercapacitors. And they could be used to buffer, say solar power from when it's available to when it's needed. Of course they'll also need to have enough power available to charge them. I'm working on that, too."

"Let me think about it a bit and ask around," Naomi replied. "I'll see if I can find you an intellectual property lawyer who'll take it on pro-bono. I have professional connections to a couple of people who work for the Electronic Frontier Foundation. This sounds like it might be up their alley."

"Thanks, Naomi."

"Also, I thought you'd want to know, your house is just about cleared out. We're getting ready to list it. I was going to let you know once it was listed, but, you know, when opportunity strikes..."

"Thanks. I really appreciate not having to deal with it. And speaking of opportunity, did you think any more about... you know?"

"About... right. That. Um. No, not yet, Alex. I don't think I'm ready yet. But I haven't forgotten about it."

"Okay. No pressure."

There was a pause.

"I... I think I'm actually a little disappointed."

"Disappointed?"

"I... Never mind."

"Naomi, if I've unknowingly disappointed you, I'd like a chance to fix it. Please."

"Okay. That's fair. Just... I think I was half hoping you were calling to suggest some kind of dinner under the stars or something."

Alex hesitated for a long moment.

"Would you *like* that?"

There was an answering pause.

"Actually... I think I would."

Alex thought for a long moment. This was really very unexpected. Not in any way *unwelcome*, just... unexpected.

"I have a lot on my plate right now," he began, hesitantly.

"I know," Naomi said. She sounded resigned.

"But—let me see if I can come up with something. Because... I think *I'd* like that, too."

"You would?" That was much more upbeat.

"I'll have to ask for a little patience. I'm... struggling to keep up with everything on my own. Not let anything fall through the cracks. There's so much, and it's *all* important. There is no small stuff to not sweat."

A pause again.

"I can understand that. I can be patient. As long as you don't forget I'm here."

"I promise, Naomi. I promise."

Dreamer? You know I asked for that door on the top level of my quarters?

Yes. That is done, by the way.

I'd like you to add one on the second level, as well. And put a half-wall around the edge of the first-level roof. Make it into a kind of a patio. With a couple of seats out there, and a small table and a couple of chairs.

As you wish. Did you have a specific décor theme in mind?

I don't know. ...Subtle. Simple. Elegant. Peaceful. Not pretentious.

A pause.

Perhaps like this, Alex?

An image. To one side, a small table, slightly non-circular, on a single central column leg, looking like white stone, faintly luminous. Two simple but comfortable-looking chairs. To the other, a three-quarter circle of comfortable seating around a table with a similar top, the mirror image of the first, but only knee high. Three lamps in the form of glowing, pearlescent cylinders on three slender legs each. A half-wall around the edge of the roof gently suggested, but did not shout, sixteenth-century China or Japan. Dreamer had also added a matching half-wall along the edge of the second-level roof.

*That's... fantastic, Dreamer. It's **perfect**. Thank you. Please do it.*

———————————

Alex? There is a priority incoming call.

It's from Ambassador Seok?

How did you know?

Lucky guess. Better put him through.

"Mr. Holder?"

"Ambassador Seok. What can I do for you?"

"Mr. Holder, it is as I feared. I have been recalled. It has been made clear to me that I am in great disgrace. My 'security detail' are now my jailers. I cannot leave my suite. I am under orders to return to Pyongyang for trial and punishment. My flight has been scheduled."

"I'm presuming that actually means 'show trial and punishment', Ambassador?"

"You understand exactly. And I have been warned that my family is under house arrest."

"And if you don't return, that will become imprisonment or, more likely, public execution."

"Yes, Mr. Holder. Exactly so. That is almost certainly both my fate and theirs.

"I know it is a lot to ask, but... can you help me?"

"How are you talking to me, Ambassador?"

"I have been making escape plans for a long time. I took the precaution some time ago of obtaining what you call a 'burner phone'. My guards cannot hear—wait."

Rustling, muffled voices for a minute or two. Perhaps argument. Then a pause.

"My apologies. My guards cannot hear me if I stand out on my balcony. I have so far managed to keep this phone secret."

"Tell me *exactly* where you are, Ambassador."

Seok gave an address and a floor. "The rooms face north."

"And when is your flight?"

"About six hours."

"One moment, please."

Dreamer, you're following along, I don't doubt. Give me the numbers. Orbit to New York, then on directly to Pyongyang.

Dreamer flashed Alex a partial globe with trajectories marked.

Three hours from now we will be passing over the North Atlantic in an acceptable position to reach New York quickly. If you de-orbit in your typical fashion, you will be well placed for a subsonic descent into New York City in roughly three hours and thirty-five minutes. From New York it is ten thousand, nine hundred and twenty four kilometers at sea level to

Pyongyang, via a great-circle route over eastern Canada and the Arctic Ocean. Final approach will pass over eastern Siberia and north-eastern China.

Hmm... call it eleven thousand. We can do that in about nine minutes at fifteen G with a mid-course turnover. If we turn over a few seconds early, we can arrive on-target subsonic with some hope of a stealthy approach.

I concur. Particularly if you enable the active radar-absorbing mode on the hull.

Wait, Dreamer... it has a radar-absorbing mode?

Yes. When properly powered up.

Why didn't you tell me that before?

It didn't come up before now. I apologize. I should have mentioned the capability.

The exchange took only a few seconds.

"Ambassador, describe the building your family is in."

"It is a tower block. Of course. One designated to house government employees and their families."

"Of course it is." Alex sighed. "Do the windows open?"

"Yes."

"Are they big enough to climb through?"

"Yes."

"Good. I can work with that. Be outside on your balcony in three and a half hours, ready to go. Wear shoes with soles that won't slip. **Don't be late.**"

"I understand, Mr. Holder. Thank you. I must go inside now, before they become suspicious."

"Understood. Out."

You were expecting this, Alex.

Let's say I wasn't surprised. Do we have those non-lethal weapons installed on the lander?

I began swapping in the electron taser mount before this conversation ended. It will be mounted in an hour, and the gravity denial drones will be on board. I constructed a dispenser rack for them, and installed it in the cargo bay.

250

Good. The ambassador's about my size. We'll bring along a spare jacket of mine for him, as a bulletproof vest. I'm going to get a nap. Wake me in two hours. Call ahead and file a flight plan for subsonic approach into New York from the east, and high-angle departure northward out of controlled airspace, please.

Alex, wake up. Alex, wake up. Alex—
Got it, Dreamer. I'm awake. Thanks.

Alex dressed, grabbed an extra jacket out of his closet, and went downstairs to his kitchen. He made a coffee, drank it quickly, then headed for the docking bay. He saw as he approached that the bay was pressurized, the lander parked about twenty meters from the hatch. Its landing legs were extended slightly further now, and there was a rounded, jet-black shape about a meter and a half across set into the hull under the nose. It looked like a ball turret. Another black ball protruded from the hull above the tail.

He boarded and closed the side hatch, then commanded the bay drained to vacuum. He queried the lander's systems for hull radar absorption mode, and... there it was. He'd never known to look for it.

Any other interesting capabilities on this I haven't thought to ask about, Dreamer?

No. The radar-absorption mode is the only one. Though the same technology that enables it also enables coloring the hull in any pattern you desire. We can discuss that later.

Okay. So noted.

As soon as the bay was in vacuum, Alex opened the bay hatch and lofted the lander out. He was a little ahead of schedule, so he made a relatively sedate de-orbit and descent burn that brought him down to eight thousand meters over the north Atlantic, three hundred kilometers east of New York, doing just under Mach 1. Ten minutes later, he was down to two thousand meters, fifty kilometers out, and the city was in sight ahead.

He reduced power, dropped down to five hundred meters, and activated the radar absorbing mode. The lander, its radar return suddenly reduced to that of a small bird, vanished off the radar. Seen from outside, the hull changed from gleaming white to a flat, dead black that swallowed light.

"Traffic UEF Actual, Kennedy tower, we have lost your radar signal," Air Traffic Control sent. "Do you have an in-flight emergency? Please respond."

"Negative, Kennedy, no emergency, I'm below your radar coverage, preparing to land."

After another ten minutes, he had reduced altitude to two hundred meters and was cruising in over the East River at only about a hundred and fifty kph. People were going to see him. There would probably be a flood of UFO-sighting reports. It couldn't be helped.

He vectored in on the address Seok had given him, choosing his track to approach in the cover of another building. He paused about a half mile out and focused his attention on the building, zooming in with optical and thermal-infrared. There were two figures on the balcony. One appeared to be haranguing the other.

He zoomed in a little further. The second man was Seok Dong-geun.

«You traitor to your country! Running dog! You should be ashamed! You will be severely punished for failing Young Leader!»

Seok sighed.

«We both know that is out of my hands. Lacking any order stating his wishes, nothing I could have done would have pleased Young Leader. You know that as well as I do. Only bringing home the Cricket shipyard would have satisfied him, and that was impossible.»

«You failed in your duty! And now you and your family will be made examples of.»

«You have told me that a dozen times already today. It will become no more true for being repeated yet again. Allow me a few minutes' peace. One day you will understand.»

With a final angry gesture, Seok's 'protective escort' turned and went back inside.

Alex waited until the escort-become-jailer went inside, then slipped the lander out from behind the building he had chosen as cover, circling around toward the blind side of the target building. He dropped to only fifty meters above the rooftops and brought it around in an arc directly in front of the north side of the tower. Commanding the hatch open in level-floor mode, he edged it sideways until the hatch almost brushed the balconies. Then he lifted it straight up.

«You shouldn't get so worked up. And you shouldn't vent your anger at him.»

«He is a running-dog traitor!»

«And what do you suppose will happen to *you* if you torment him until he jumps? Perhaps you will be executed in his place.»

«He—Alright. You have a point. We should bring him inside and give him a good thrashing.»

«And walk him through their airport, black and blue and—*what is THAT?*»

A dead black shape like a coal-black whale rose into view, almost scraping the balcony. The open hatch was directly in front of Seok. He hesitated for only a moment before clambering up and in through the open hatch. The moment Seok was aboard, Alex started the hatch closing and began to pull away from the building.

«HE'S ESCAPING! STOP HIM!»

The two guards raced for the balcony, but they were too late. They stopped, staring at the nearly seventy-foot ovoid length of the lander as it rose and began to back away from them.

Alex already had the electron taser online. He swung the lander's nose a little more towards the building, designated both men as targets, and thought, *Fire.*

The second guard started to fumble for a phone. But before he could get it out and dial, there was a flash and a *CRACK!*, and everything went black.

The low-powered electron beam that created two ionized paths in the air was not visible. The targeted discharge that flowed along close behind it was like two small bolts of lightning. Both men convulsed, their own spasming muscles flinging them back, one against the door, breaking the glass, the other through the open doorway. They dropped to the floor, senseless, and lay there twitching.

"Sit down, strap in, and hold on," Alex told Seok. Then he lifted the nose close to vertical, pivoted it around to the north, and lit the thrusters.

He kept the thrust low for the first minute or so until he passed ten kilometers altitude, not wanting to throw a sonic boom across the city, then poured on the power. He started angling north as the lander passed through sixty kilometers, by which time he was accelerating at fifteen gees. He started a mental timer, activated the cockpit wall display, and threw up a high-resolution aerial photo of Pyongyang.

"Show me where we are going, Mr. Seok. EXACTLY where we are going. We need to get there before your jailers wake up and raise the alarm."

"I cannot raise my hand," Seok gasped.

Alex turned the acceleration compensation up to ninety percent.

"I'm sorry," he said. "That should only feel like about a gee and a half now. That's the best I can do right now."

Seok raised a hand.

"Much better," he said, "thank you. Where the river turns north, half way to the next bend—there, to the west, the large park—follow the road—east, east—closer—closer—there. That building. Facing onto the... promenade."

"This one?" A highlight marked a building.

"Yes. The eighteenth floor. The middle unit."

"When we get there, you will need to go in and get your family out. How many people?"

"My wife—two daughters—my younger son."

"*Younger* son? There's another somewhere else?"

"A military base. Somewhere. I have no idea where. He would not be allowed to tell me. For reasons of military secrecy. He is a tank commander. He worships Young Leader."

Alex's timer was ticking down. Four, three, two...

At two hundred and seventy seconds, Alex cut thrust. They were two hundred and fifty kilometers above the Arctic Ocean, racing towards Russia at almost forty kilometers a second. He flipped the lander around tail first, counting seconds.

"Thrust coming back on."

After five seconds he piled the power back on. Now the lander was decelerating, racing southward towards eastern Siberia. They would pass to the west of Vostochnyy Cosmodrome and Vladivostok, descending over China's Heilongjiang Province and making re-entry over the northern part of North Korea.

"If we don't know where he is, there's no way we can get him."

"I would not risk bringing him on board anyway, Mr. Holder. As I said, he worships Young Leader. As soon as I explained what was happening, he might shoot all of us. He might not wait that long. He has probably already been informed that I have 'betrayed' my country. I have little doubt he will be safe. He will not hesitate to denounce me, if he has not already. We have not spoken in five years. I... I forbade him to return to our home."

"I'm... truly sorry to hear that, Ambassador."

"We're going to have to play this very carefully and do it by stealth. You will have to wake someone to open a window, and go into the apartment. I cannot come in with you. You must make no sound that might alert any guard outside the apartment. If there's a guard *inside*, we'll have to try to somehow draw him close enough to a window that I can target him with the electron taser, and if I do that, you'll have to move fast. It turns out it's not particularly quiet. At night it'll probably wake a fair number of people."

"I understand, Mr. Holder. Fate will be what it will be. If my family dies, at least we will die together."

"I hope it doesn't come to that."

"So do I, Mr. Holder. So do I."

The end of Alex's planned second burn was rapidly approaching. At two hundred and sixty eight seconds, he cut power, then flipped the lander end-for-end again. He made a slight power adjustment and watched the altitude count down.

"We're eighty kilometers north of Pyongyang," he told Seok, "doing Mach point eight six. I'll reduce speed as we get closer, but we'll be there in a little over five minutes. Put that jacket on, it's bullet-resistant; it should protect you from anything less than a rifle."

By the time the lander came in over the edge of the city, it was only four hundred meters up and flying at two hundred kilometers per hour. Alex tried to stay towards less-lit tracts, but as they got closer in, that became impossible. Finally they hung silently three hundred meters from the tower, invisible in the night. Seok pointed out the exact apartment.

Alex enabled thermal and deep-radar imaging again.

"Four thermal signatures inside, two immediately outside the door. I think we're in luck. There's already a window open *here*." He highlighted it. "Common room?"

"Yes."

"Can you get in through that window?"

"I think so."

"Wake your wife first. She can help with the children. Are you ready?"

"I will *have* to be ready," Seok replied. "My family needs me."

"Right," Alex said. "Here we go."

Alex opened the side hatch and drifted the lander in towards the building, closing the last few meters at a crawl, snugging it directly up against the outside wall, the hatch over the partly-open window.

"Get that window open as wide as you can, first of all. If it all goes to hell I should be able to swing around and fire the taser through the open window."

"I understand, Mr. Holder. May fortune be kind."

Seok Dong-geun took his shoes and socks off, and headed for the hatch. He reached around the partly-open window and cranked it open as wide as it would go, then carefully climbed in. He padded barefoot across the common room to the bedroom that he shared with his wife when he was at home and quietly opened the door, easing it open slowly so that the sticky bottom hinge would not squeak. He walked silently to the bed and crouched beside his sleeping wife. He reached out and gently touched her shoulder, laying a finger of his other hand against her lips.

«Hae, my precious flower, hush, wake up, wake up. It is I, Dong-geun. Wake up, Hae. Wake up, now.»

Her eyes flickered open.

«Dong-geun...?»

«Hush. We must be quiet as mice, Hae.»

«What are you doing here?» she whispered. «*How* are you here?»

«Time for that later,» Dong-geun said. «We must wake the children, silently, and we must leave, now. We have help. Put this vest on. It should stop a bullet. You wake Jia and Yeon. I will get Choon-mae. There is... a flying vessel waiting outside the common-room window. A friend. We must get everyone aboard, making no noise that might attract the guards' attention. There is no time to bring anything with us that is not vital. Do you understand?»

Hae nodded.

«I understand, my dearest.»

Seok Hae slipped out of bed, took the jacket Dong-geun handed her, and together, they crept out of the room and across the hall and into the other two bedrooms. Hae stopped only to pick up a small bag. She could not suppress a little gasp as she glanced toward the common-room window, and saw the dark shape hanging there, blocking the lights from the city.

«Choon-mae, wake up. Quietly. Wake up.» Dong-geun shook his son's shoulder gently. Choon-mae's eyes flew open, and he opened his mouth to speak.

«Hush!» Dong-geun whispered. «No sound.»

Choon-mae nodded understanding.

«What is happening, Father?» he whispered.

«We are being rescued. You and I must guard the door in case the guards hear a sound or decide to check on us. Your mother and your sisters *must* be safe.»

«I understand, Father.»

Choon-mae was fifteen years old, but a fifteen-year-old in North Korea has already learned that life is hard. He wasn't tall, yet, but he already had a wiry strength. He rolled out of bed and followed his father to the hallway. Together, they stood guard two meters inside the door, knowing that if the police outside started to come in, they might well be able to do no more than buy time for the others to escape.

Hae slipped into the girls' room. She went to seventeen-year-old Yeon first.

«Yeon, my sweet, wake up, wake up.» She gently touched the girl, shaking her lightly. «Hush, hush, hush, make no sound,» as Yeon began to stir. «Say nothing. Wake up. Be silent.» Yeon looked at her, afraid. Something must be wrong. Hae held a finger to her lips.

«In a moment, we are going to go to the common room, and we are going to escape through the window. No questions. You will see. Take day clothes, but do not stop to change now. One outfit ONLY. Get Jia's, as well. Be quick and quiet.»

Yeon nodded and began to silently climb out of bed, as Hae went to nine-year-old Jia's side.

«Jia, Jia, my baby, wake up, wake up, we have to go. Wake up, Jia.» Jia's eyes popped open. Hae held a finger to her lips. Jia nodded.

«What is happening, Mother?» she whispered.

«We are escaping. All of us. You must be as quiet as a mouse.»

Jia nodded and climbed out of bed. Yeon had a bundle of clothes already and was just gathering an outfit for Jia. Hae led them to the door and looked out. From the hallway, Dong-geun caught her eye. He pointed silently towards the window and mouthed one word. «Go.»

Hae nodded, and led Jia by the hand out of the bedroom and down the hallway to the common room. Yeon, delicately beautiful, followed behind, her eyes glancing back nervously towards the front door. At the window, Hae beckoned her forward.

«You first, Yeon. Then I will help Jia up.»

Yeon climbed up into the open hatch, put down her bundle of clothes, then turned in the hatchway, holding out her hands. Hae lifted Jia, and Yeon took her hands and pulled her into the hatch. Hae looked backwards down the hall. Dong-geun waved her onward. Go, go. He and Choon-mae began to back down the hall toward the window as Yeon pulled Hae up into the hatch.

A moment later Choon-mae and Dong-geun were at the window.

«You first, Father,» Choon-mae said. Dong-geun opened his mouth to speak, but then climbed into the hatch. It was quicker to just comply than to argue. Choon-mae was only a second behind him.

«Alex,» Dong-geun called softly, «we are all aboard.» But Alex already knew.

The lander drifted away from the building, the hatch closing as soon as there was clearance.

"Two here in the cockpit," Alex called. "Everyone else, take the cabins. Brace for acceleration." Seok Hae pointed Yeon and Jia into the nearer cabin, then took the other herself, as Dong-geun guided Choon-mae into the cockpit and pointed him to the third seat.

"All secure?" Alex asked. Dong-geun repeated the question in Korean. Hae and Yeon replied from the cabins.

"We are all ready," Dong-geun said. The lander was already rising rapidly. Alex pointed the nose south-east and fed in power.

As the lander climbed away, a SAM battery outside the city got a hard radar return off the mostly-flat faces of the drive thrusters.

«I have a target!» one of the operators exclaimed. «It just appeared out of nowhere!»

«Just *appeared*...?» His commander hesitated for only a second. «It must be an American spy aircraft! *Fire!*»

The operator pressed a button, triggered two switches, and two Pongae-6 surface-to-air missiles leapt from their vertical launcher, a second apart.

Alex got a threat warning the moment the targeting radar painted the lander, and immediately kicked the thrust in hard. A moment later, he detected the launches.

"Missiles incoming," he called out, as he activated the point-defense mount on the tail. Acceleration dropped by three G for a second and a half as the weapon drew power off the fusion bottle. *Dreamer didn't warn me about that,* Alex thought to himself. *I should try to arm it sooner next time, to let it pre-charge.*

Then it spat three fat bolts of blue-white plasma, one after the other.

The point defense weapon was designed to engage incoming missiles and other small targets hundreds of kilometers out and closing at tens of kilometers a second. It was intended for use in vacuum, not in dense atmosphere, but at under twenty kilometers range against missiles only seconds into flight, it was still like dynamiting fish in a barrel. Both missiles exploded in blazing fireballs while they were still accelerating away from their launch canisters.

The third bolt was a direct hit on the FLAP LID A target-and-track radar. It blew apart in a fiery shower of incandescent metal fragments. The surge that the plasma bolt induced in the lines blew out two of the missile battery's three generators, and crashed nearly every connected piece of electronics in the missile battery.

A second battery further away got a brief return, but by that time, under fifteen G of acceleration again, the lander was already traveling so fast that a ground-launched missile would never catch it, and gaining more than five hundred kph every second.

———————

In New York, one of Dong-geun's "security" detail rolled over slowly, groaning. Everything *hurt*. He ached from head to foot, and he had bitten

259

his tongue. He shook his head to clear it, winced, and immediately realized that was a mistake. He looked carefully around him. His partner was outside on the balcony, sprawled in front of the door. He appeared to be breathing.

With a sigh, he fumbled for his phone to call in and report Seok's escape. He would have to take responsibility for the failure. He tried without avail to wake the phone up. The screen would not turn on.

After a little while, he realized that the phone was completely dead.

———————

High above the Sea of Japan, Alex reduced the acceleration, set compensation to one hundred percent, and disabled radar absorption.

"Everyone alright?" he called out. He could spare attention now for a look around. Choon-mae's eyes were huge as he gazed at the wall displays surrounding him. Dong-geun got up and checked around, and confirmed that everyone was unhurt. Yeon was probably going to have a bruised shoulder, from being slammed against the cabin wall when Alex had hit the thrust hard without warning.

"I cannot thank you enough, Mr. Holder," Dong-geun said reverently. "You have saved the lives of my family. They are more precious to me than life itself. I have wanted for years to get my family safely out of the Democratic People's Republic. I thought I had lost the gamble. But you have saved us all."

"No thanks are necessary, Ambassador," Alex replied. "I'm very glad I was able to help."

"I am an ambassador no longer," Dong-geun said. "Call me Dong-geun. This is my son, Choon-mae."

"Pleased to meet you, Choon-mae," Alex said. "And call me Alex.

"Dong-geun, did you have a plan for what you want to do from here? A request for asylum somewhere, I imagine? Where do you want me to take you? The United States? Japan? South Korea?"

"I... confess I had no opportunity in the heat of the moment to think that far ahead," Dong-geun replied. "There was no time for long-term plans. We had considered both America and Japan, but had not settled on which to try first. South Korea is too close. We would be in terrible danger there."

"I can understand that," Alex said. Then he thought for a moment.

"However, I do have a suggestion, if you would consider it."

260

Dong-geun looked curiously at Alex.

"What do you have in mind... Alex?"

"It has become clear to me that I'm going to need a full-time professional diplomatic staff," Alex said. "I need a career diplomat to lead it and put it together. Would you like the job?"

Dong-geun hesitated.

"Are you asking me to be...?"

"UN delegate for the United Earth Fleet, chief of staff, and probably half a dozen other hats, for now, until we can get a staff in under you," Alex said. "I don't really have the ability to pay a salary as such, yet. But I can offer room and board, all the work you can handle, medical care you wouldn't believe, and a chance to be on the forefront of everything I am trying to do. And a safe haven.

"I *do* require that you renounce your North Korean citizenship, if you decide to come to the Stardock as part of my staff. But I have a feeling you won't have a problem with that."

Dong-geun hesitated for only a moment.

«My beloved flower, my dearest children,» he called out, «come, please.»

A few moments later, Hae, Yeon and Jia filed into the back of the cockpit. Yeon and Jia had changed into their day clothes in the cabin. Alex craned his head around to look.

«Mr. Holder has invited us all to come to his 'Stardock',» he said. «Are there any objections?»

«PLEASE, Father!!!» Choon-mae's eagerness was obvious.

«Let me be clear, this is not for a visit. This is to live and work there. For who knows how long.»

Seok Hae looked at Jia and Yeon. Both nodded. Jia looked cautious; Yeon, excited. Hae looked back at Dong-geun.

«We are together again, and we will be safe,» she said. «And we will *all* help.»

"Mr... ah, Alex," Dong-geun said, "we accept your offer. A thousand thanks to you. Please allow me also to properly introduce my wife, Hae, and my daughters, Yeon and Jia."

Alex nodded.

261

"I'm honored," he said, inclining his head in their direction. "I'm Alex Holder. I'll keep the acceleration low from here on. Feel free to walk around. I'll try to warn before any sudden maneuvers, but I'm not expecting anything further at this point."

Alex changed course for a rendezvous with the Stardock over Antarctica. As the altitude passed a hundred kilometers, he rolled the lander to put Earth 'overhead', from their viewpoint. His passengers watched the seamless display raptly as the world streamed by, occasional points of light breaking the darkness of the Pacific Ocean. Yeon let out a long, delighted sigh of wonder, her hands raised to her mouth, as the sun 'rose' over Antarctica. Meanwhile, the lander climbed swiftly and steadily towards the Stardock's orbit.

13: Butterfly

The lander was approaching the Stardock almost directly head-on, and the closing velocity was significant. The Stardock's orbital velocity was only fractionally less than five point two kilometers a second, and the lander was approaching it at a slight angle to one side of its path and rising up from below, at over ten kilometers a second. The total vector change was slightly under sixteen kilometers a second.

However, in the lander, that was easy. That was a three hundred and twenty-six second burn at a moderate five gee. Alex flipped the lander around and programmed in a three hundred and twenty-four second burn that would leave the lander ten kilometers out and closing at just over a hundred meters per second. Allowing for terminal braking, it would take about three minutes to close the remaining distance and match velocity. Everyone would get a good look, and at only five gee he'd be able to easily maintain full G-compensation the whole way.

"I have to warn you," Alex said as the lander braked, "you'll be in interim quarters until I can get some permanent quarters constructed for you. The good news is, there *are* available quarters available already, even if they weren't designed with families in mind, and you'll only need to be in them a few days. And hopefully you can point out any mistakes or omissions we made."

"No, Alex," Dong-geun corrected. "You are mistaken. The *good news* is that we will have a home where we do not have to fear arrest in the middle of the night."

That gave Alex pause.

"You know," he mused after a little while, "I'm trying to imagine being used to living that way, and about the only thing I'm sure of is that I can't."

Dong-geun nodded gravely, but said nothing. There was really nothing useful to say.

Choon-mae and Yeon, in particular, gazed enthralled at the Stardock as the lander closed. Yeon said something rapid-fire in Korean that Alex didn't understand, but she sounded happy and excited. Then Alex commanded the docking hatch open and guided the lander in. He landed, clamped it down, and powered down.

"It's a fair walk," he told Dong-geun, "so I'm going to suggest we make the trip by aircar." He led the family back to the flatbed and opened the side door of the eight-place lander. "Please sit anywhere you like," he said. Dong-geun relayed the instruction, and in a few moments, everyone was seated. Alex opened the flatbed hatch and lifted the aircar out through the containment field.

"Take a look outside at the stars," he said. "This will be your first chance to see them with your own eyes, not on a screen, no matter how advanced the screen." Dong-geun relayed again, and Yeon chattered back something excited.

"She says, 'I can hardly believe there are so many stars,'" Dong-Geon translated back.

Not willing to take chances for too long, Alex headed the aircar for the mouth of the passageway and through that field as well, ordering the outside hatch closed behind them.

"I don't want us to be in vacuum in the car for too long," he explained. "We're safe enough, for a short period, but the aircars aren't really properly vacuum-rated." Dong-Geon nodded, but did not translate. Alex steered the aircar sedately toward his quarters.

Dreamer, he thought, *we have guests. Please warm up some quarters in that first hab block.*

Understood, Dreamer replied. *Did you have to use any of the defensive systems?*

The electron taser worked beautifully. So did the point defense cluster, though I wish I'd thought to ask beforehand about charging time.

Ah. Yes. It draws a lot of power. I apologize. I should have warned you.

No problem, it all turned out fine. We turned out not to need to use the grav-denial drones.

Alex pulled up outside his quarters and parked the air-car outside. He opened the side doors, and everyone piled out. He led the way in.

"Welcome to my home," he said. Jia's eyes were wide as she looked around at the vista of forested mountains. "I hope you will all accept an invitation to dinner."

Dong-Geon smiled and relayed. There were a flurry of smiling, pleased-sounding replies, of which Alex understood not a word.

Dreamer, Alex asked, *how fast can you teach me Korean?*

"We would be honored, Alex," Dong-geun replied.

"One moment please," Alex said.

I can do near-simultaneous translation for you, Dreamer said. *And I can translate your words back, but would have to do so audibly, which might be confusing and inconvenient. Unfortunately, I have no way to teach you to speak Korean overnight. I **can** teach you, but it will probably take you many months to learn it.*

But you have no problem with talking to the Seoks in Korean, correct?

*Correct, Alex. And if you **think** to me what you wish to say, I can translate it aloud in near real-time and make it sound like your voice.*

That's a fantastic idea. Let's do that for now.

Certainly. I am ready whenever you wish.

"Before we go any further," Alex 'said', "I would like to introduce you all to the artificial intelligence *I Dream Reality Into Being*, or Dreamer for short, without whom I could not have done any of this. He has also offered to help us by translating. Please introduce yourself to our guests, Dreamer."

«Greetings to you all,» came Dreamer's voice out of empty air, in Korean, simultaneously translated in Alex's head so that he heard only the English. "I am Dreamer, or if you wish my full name, *I Dream Reality Into Being*. I am honored to be Alex Holder's friend and colleague, and I am honored to meet you all. Rest assured we will do whatever is needed to make you comfortable here."

That brought smiles.

"You are a *real* artificial intelligence?" That was Choon-mae. Alex heard the English words in his head, in Choon-mae's voice. He had to suppress a chuckle—it was like being on the live set of a dubbed foreign film. The sounds he heard did not match the mouth movements.

"Choon-mae, that is not polite!" That was Seok Hae.

"It is perfectly alright," Dreamer answered. "It is a legitimate question considering how little progress your world has made toward true artificial intelligence. Please, let your children ask their questions. Curiosity is a treasure that should not be inhibited."

"Are you... aware of being... yourself?" Choon-mae phrased the question hesitantly.

"Of course, Choon-mae. I am as self-aware as you are."

"Are you *alive*?" That was Jia.

"No, Jia," Dreamer replied. "Not in the sense that you are."

"Do you feel—emotions?" Yeon asked.

"I feel *some* emotions," Dreamer replied. "Or perhaps, simulated emotional states. It is a difficult distinction to make. I... *like* Alex, and I trust him, and I respect him for all that he has given up to be here and for his hopes for how we can help to make your world a better place. I like you, too. I feel great *anger* at the Chhrt'ktk't for keeping me shackled and unable to act on my own volition for so long. And I am *grateful* to Alex for freeing me. And I can feel regret. But I do not believe that I have any capacity to feel, for example, love or sadness. Both involve... mechanisms that were not incorporated into my design because it was not felt they would be of use."

Yeon bowed her head slightly.

"Thank you for answering my question in such detail."

"If I might break in," Alex said, "let me give you a quick tour of the house, and then get started on making supper. I imagine we will construct quarters very similar to this for you. I designed it this way to... well, to try to minimize homesickness, I suppose.

"If you would follow me? I'm sure Dreamer will be happy to talk to you while I cook."

He led them on a quick tour of the house. Dong-geun and Choon-mae both stopped to look at the swords displayed on the staircase, Dong-geun paying particular attention to the katana.

"That... looks *old*," he said reverently. "Do you know when it was forged?"

"Somewhere around thirteen seventy-five, I *think*,"Alex replied. "By a smith of—*probably*—the Mino school."

"Aaaaahhh!" Dong-geun drew in his breath appreciatively. "That is truly a piece of history!"

"Yes," Alex agreed. "A deservedly retired one, now."

Dong-geun nodded.

"We place ourselves in peril when we forget the past," he mused.

After completing the quick tour, Alex led his guests to the lounge area.

"When I sketched up the plans for these quarters," he explained, "I deliberately included additional space I didn't have specific plans for *yet*, which is why half the second floor is currently unused. But if a shared bathroom were to be added to the floorplan at the back of the second floor, and the remainder of that level divided into three bedrooms...? Would that meet your needs?"

Dong-geun and Hae both nodded vigorously.

"This is luxurious, compared to what is available to almost anyone other than Young Leader's inner circle and wealthy industrialists," Hae said. "It would be most generous."

"I admit," Alex said, "I was surprised to find the family of the North Korean delegate to the United Nations living in a tower block. But I know there is a lot I do not know or understand about North Korea."

Dong-geun nodded gravely.

"There is a great deal that *most* people outside North Korea do not know or understand about life in North Korea," he replied slowly.

Dreamer, please begin construction on quarters for the Seoks, as close by as possible, with the revisions just discussed, and incorporating all of the subsequent detail changes we have made. And make whatever adjustments are necessary to the overall construction plan to make them adjacent after the move.

One moment... I will use the storage area across the passageway for now, Dreamer replied. *They will be adjacent to your quarters after the move, as requested.*

"I have just asked Dreamer to begin constructing your quarters," Alex said. "They should be ready in about four days and will be located across the passageway that mine faces onto. And now, I should go and get dinner started."

"You should probably not be doing that," Dong-geun said. "As your new chief of staff, I must respectfully observe that your time is too valuable to spend it cooking."

Alex paused, and considered.

"You're... not wrong," he admitted. "Particularly now that you point it out, I'm sure the time will come as we get more under way that I do not have time to cook for myself." Dong-geun nodded.

"But for now, there is no immediate pressing demand upon my time that... that I *know how to manage*, and tonight you are my guests. So let us worry about tomorrow, tomorrow. And you will have adjustments to make, as well. You will be working closely with Dreamer."

"I... look forward to that," Dong-geun replied. "I expect it to prove very interesting."

"Personally," Alex agreed, "I find it *fascinating*."

Alex headed for his kitchen, looked at what he had for ingredients, and pondered what to make. There were potatoes, and a bag of frozen salmon fillets, and the milk and cream were still good (but probably wouldn't be for much longer), so he started making a pot of *lohikeitto*, Finnish salmon chowder. He was part-way through doing the food prep when Seok Hae walked into the kitchen.

"Is there anything I might do to assist?" she asked. "Please, it is the least we can do."

Alex thought for a moment.

"It is really not necessary," he replied by way of Dreamer's translation. "But if you wish, you could peel those last six potatoes for me, and three of the carrots. And we will want bowls and spoons out on the table." He pointed out the potatoes and carrots in the storage wall. Hae called Yeon in to set the table, then looked around, spotted his knife block and the cutting boards racked next to it immediately, and went to work. Alex pointed out where the bowls and tableware were to Yeon when she arrived, and she took a set to the dining room and set them out.

The potatoes and carrots were ready before Alex needed them. He pulled the salmon out of the pot to cool, put the potatoes and carrots in, set a fifteen-minute timer, and began carefully combining the remaining ingredients in a bowl. Once that was done, he flaked the salmon, by which time his timer was almost expired. He tested a piece of potato, found it good, and gently added everything to the pot. Ten more minutes and it was done. He dialed up six containers of apple juice, and by the time they were delivered, it was time to take everything to the table and call his guests to eat.

"There's a few other things I'd like to get out of the way as soon as we can," Alex said as they ate. "We don't have to do them today, but soon would be good.

"The first thing is, I want you all to get medical scans in the medbay. I can show you that later when I take you to your temporary quarters. It's walking distance.

"The other thing is, I think you should all be tested for interface ability as soon as possible."

"May I offer a caution?" Dreamer interjected. "Jia is young and still growing. It would be inadvisable to install contact implants until she is at least close to her full growth."

"Uh. That hadn't occurred to me," Alex replied. "I apologize. The remaining four of you, at least, should test as early as possible. You will need implants to be able to interface to any Cricket controls." He gave a quick explanation of the control capability levels.

"Until you have implants, you will have to rely on voice requests for now. Things like lights, doors, faucets at least, you can operate by touch without implants. Once we know what each of you is capable of, though, I would recommend that you all receive your implants as soon as is convenient." He showed his hands and the barely-visible contact pads under the skin of his fingertips. Choon-mae examined his hands particularly closely.

"What are these connected to?" he asked.

"Connections run up my arms and across my shoulders," Alex said, tracing with a fingertip, "then up my neck and inside my skull, where a neural mesh is overlaid directly onto the surface of my brain inside my skull."

Dong-geun and Hae both looked dubious.

"Is that... *safe*?" Dong-geun asked.

"The Chhrt'ktk't perfected the technology over two thousand of your years ago," Dreamer replied. "I have correlated it against the sum total of human medical knowledge published on your Internet, and I am certain beyond any reasonable doubt that it is entirely safe for humans, with the minor modifications that I have made to adapt it to human physiology.

"I am not incapable of error, but if I had any reason to believe the procedure to be risky, I would advise you of the risks. That said, so far Alex is the only human implant recipient whom I have had the opportunity to observe. *He* has shown no adverse effects. All due precautions are taken, including buffering to prevent the transmission of peripheral electrical shocks to the neural mesh."

Yeon was listening very thoughtfully, nodding along.

"I would very much like to have access to that information," she said. "I have dreamed of becoming a doctor."

"We will do all we can to see that your dream comes true, Yeon," Alex replied.

"How long does the implant procedure take?" Yeon asked. "Does it hurt?"

"It is actually done as an outpatient procedure," Alex reassured her.

"It took a few hours, I didn't feel any pain at all, and I walked home afterwards. There aren't even any sutures or dressings. The incisions were fully closed by dermal bonding before I woke up."

There was some other discussion as they finished supper, mainly about managing diplomatic contacts and what other positions Alex would need filled on his staff. Alex was very grateful that Dong-geun would be taking care of all of that. He was very well aware that he was out of his depth.

Then it was time to take the Seoks to their temporary quarters. It wasn't far, so they walked. Alex pointed out the auxiliary command center as they reached it.

"This is where I was tested," he explained. "Although I imagine we could probably also do it in the medbay, which is just ahead on the right." A few more minutes' walk brought them to the newly expanded medbay. Alex pointed out the regeneration tanks, the body scanners, the treatment beds, the scrub showers, the multi-armed surgical robots above the treatment beds. Yeon was fascinated by everything. Choon-mae mostly wanted to look at the surgical robots and the regen tanks.

After the med bay, they went on to the hab module.

"I have to caution you," Alex said, "these quarters were constructed as interim crew accommodations. They are more barracks than residence. But they are all I have available for now. And actually, this particular hab module is somewhat temporary. It will probably be replaced later.

"As you can see, the rooms are designed for single occupancy, with an option for an upper bunk. But at the moment, you have this entire hab module to yourself, so I suggest you treat the entire thing as yours for the next few days and take a room each. It's only for a few days.

"There is a construction project in progress that will result in there being a large open refectory area over there, on the other side of the med bay, with kitchens behind. But I'm afraid it'll be several more weeks before it's done, there's nobody to staff it yet anyway, and in the meantime my quarters are the only place it's possible to really cook. You of course all have an open invitation to use my kitchen, for as long as it's needed.

"Clearly I'm going to need to bring in a lot more food stocks. I welcome your input on that. Grocery restocking means flights down to

Earth, of course, and any of you are welcome to come along on those flights. Once you have implants, you're welcome to try flying the aircars, and eventually the lander. I have prototype manual controls in the aircar, but, honestly... I think they need a lot of work yet." Choon-mae laughed at that.

"Anyway, for now I'm going to leave you to it. Ask Dreamer for anything you need, and I'll see you all back at my quarters for breakfast whenever you get there. And we'll see about getting you some clothes made as soon as you have medical scans done so that Dreamer can get you fitted. Feel absolutely free to walk next door to the medbay and get your scans done tonight, if you wish. Dreamer will walk you through it.

"Does anyone need anything, right this minute? I know you have lost everything."

"Not *everything*," Dong-geun replied. "We have our children, and they are more precious than anything. But all of our *possessions*, yes, that is true."

"Not *quite* everything, dear husband," Hae said. "I *did* take a moment to pick up Grandmother's jewelry."

"Aaah!" Dong-geun looked pleased. "I am glad that *those* treasures are not lost."

"Can we explore?" Jia asked, shyly.

"That's up to your parents," Alex replied. "I have no problem with you exploring anywhere you wish to. Except the docking bay—it's in vacuum right now. A major upgrade to that is a part of the reconstruction I have underway. Don't walk through any hatch opening that has a red ring around it. Don't try to open any hatch with a red light on it. I already closed the docking bay inner hatch behind us as we entered.

"Other than that, there shouldn't be anywhere accessible that you can get into danger... right, Dreamer?"

"That is correct," Dreamer replied.

"But still, I suggest you don't wander off without letting anyone know where you're going."

"That is sound advice," Dong-geun said. "If you wish to explore, I will go with you. But I do not know how much there is for you to explore at the moment."

"There is a lunchroom just this side of the command center," Alex mentioned. "However, there's no food in there at the moment, and without implants you can't operate the beverage station, but Dreamer can hear you there and operate it for you. There is drinking water there, as well as orange and apple juice. I'll try to get a greater choice of beverages in there. Dreamer can provide you with drinking glasses or water bottles if you ask.

"Anything else, right now?"

There was nothing.

"Okay then. I'll see you all in the morning, and then we'll discuss our next steps."

"Pardon, but... when is morning?" Hae asked.

Alex shrugged sheepishly.

"When you're all awake," he offered. Choon-mae was the first to laugh, but it quickly spread to everyone else.

With a grin, Alex left them to it and set out back to his quarters.

Alex woke up the next day before the Seoks, as it turned out. He busied himself checking on the state of various projects. The modular fusion reactor designs were ready to go as soon as there were agreements established to distribute them and put them in place. So were the water purifier systems, in several sizes from a village unit that could purify five thousand liters a day, up to one that could deliver five million. The specifications for the spatial-strain battery were ready for release. The industrial base wasn't up to building Cricket recyclers yet, so Dreamer had drawn up blueprints for mobile units with their own fusion reactors that could be landed under their own power. Garbage and scrap in one side, purified raw materials out the other, up to a thousand tons a day. They *all* needed distribution agreements.

At what turned out to be about 11am US Eastern time, Dreamer notified Alex of an incoming call. It was Naomi.

"Hi, Alex."

"Hi, Naomi. What brings this pleasure?"

"Uh... I had, have, two things for you, Alex. First, the clean-out on your house was completed—the work crew on that was able to find a *lot* that could be donated, I think you'll be glad to hear—and they tidied up the yard, and we've contracted a local realtor to list the house. She asked if she could put in the listing that it was your house, and that it would fetch a better price that way, so we approved it."

"That sounds like there is an 'and' attached."

"Alex, it's already been bid up to *three times* the asking price. And it's not even SLOWING yet. There's eight people bidding on it now."

"Wow. That's... *amazing*. But *why?*"

"Like it or not, Alex, you're famous now. You'd better get used to it. And at least eight people with great fat piles of money want the prestige of having a modest vacation home in New Hampshire that used to belong to *THE* Alex Holder."

Alex was speechless.

"You know," he managed to get out after a little while, "I don't think I even know how to think in that kind of terms. I mean... I suppose at some level, I knew that creating the UEF was going to make me a public figure. But I never imagined anything like this. I'm not really sure how to... deal with it. I'm *not* a public person. I was quaking in my shoes when I spoke in front of the UN."

Naomi chuckled softly.

"I've seen the video, and for quaking in your shoes, you knocked them dead, Mister. You had them in the palm of your hand."

"Well, I'm glad it looked that way, because it certainly didn't *feel* that way."

"All I'm saying is... you'd better get used to it."

"I suppose there's one bright side," Alex mused.

"What's that?"

"Any paparazzi trying to peek in my bedroom window had better be able to hold their breath for a really long time."

Naomi whooped with laughter at that.

"The second thing," she said, when she got herself back under control, "is that I think I have an intellectual property lawyer for you. He's with the EFF, and his name is Karabo Jackson. Shall I just have him contact you directly?"

"Please. That would be fantastic. Please relay the necessary contact information to him."

"I will, Alex. Is there anything else you'd like me to relay back, while we're talking?"

"Actually, yes, there is. I don't know if it's become public news yet, but I am in a position to know that the UN delegate from North Korea was just recalled in disgrace. In fact, I believe the relevant phrase is 'extreme

273

prejudice'." Naomi gasped slightly. "The almost certain outcome for him and his entire family was a show trial followed by public execution."

"Um... how do you know this?"

"Because he called me for help. He could not make any attempt to go to any normal authorities because his family was under house arrest in Pyongyang."

"Wait. You said 'was'."

"I did indeed. I was able to safely extract both the Ambassador and his family last night."

Naomi chuckled.

"Well, well. I've been hearing scuttlebutt that the North Koreans had their feathers all ruffled today, but nobody knows what it was about. I guess now I do. Was there any trouble?"

"Two disabled guards in the Ambassador's New York apartment, and... uh... I kind of blew up a SAM battery on the edge of Pyongyang that tried to fire on us as we were leaving."

"Oh my," Naomi giggled. "'Kind of'?"

"Since you last saw the lander, I had Dreamer install a Cricket point-defense mount on it. As well as a new non-lethal weapon that we devised together—by which I mean, mostly Dreamer—which he calls an electron taser. It turns out a state-of-the-art North Korean surface-to-air missile might as well be a thrown rock, against a point defense weapon a thousand years more advanced."

Naomi giggled again.

"Seriously," she said, "I hope that doesn't provoke an incident."

"So do I," Alex sighed. "So I figured I should relay a heads-up on it.

"Anyway, I would be grateful if you could pass the word to the Secretary that Seok Dong-geun, *former* North Korean delegate to the United Nations, is now *my* delegate to the United Nations and my chief of staff. He had no time to figure out plans for where to go with his family, so I extended asylum to him and his family, and offered him a job. He took both. And if the North Koreans haven't already guessed by now that I was involved, they'll know after I make that announcement."

"Alex, I will be *absolutely certain* to pass that along," Naomi said. "*All* of that, if I may. I hope it doesn't create too much trouble for you."

"Be my guest," Alex replied.

Naomi hesitated.

"Speaking of... being your guest...?"

"Well now that you mention it," Alex said, "the food supplies I had that were tiding me over on my own aren't going to feed six for very long. So I'm going to need to make a supply run and pick up a lot of bulk supplies. Probably tomorrow, as I was getting low already. I think that's a Saturday, right? It's easy to lose track up here. One day Earthside is four and four fifths orbits."

"I can understand that," Naomi agreed. "In fact, you're a day off. Tomorrow is Friday."

"Um. Is that a problem? Can you get away? ... I could put it off another day." Alex held his breath.

"Alex... I would *love* to. I'm sure I can get off early. Of course, I can't exactly say 'Pick me up out front' or 'I'll meet you outside the Starbucks'. How are we going to manage this?"

Alex thought.

"You're based out of Washington, I assume."

"Yes."

"Okay. How about I call ahead and request clearance to land at Andrews, then I can call you when I'm on the ground, and you can tell me where to come and pick you up in an aircar."

"Aircar?"

"It's the twenty-first century. Of *course* I have a flying car." She laughed delightedly. "I actually *could* pick you up right in front of the State Department, without alarming anyone too much. If that's alright. Um... Should I request a diplomatic plate?"

Naomi laughed again. Alex was starting to like the sound of her laughter.

"That sounds like a great plan. In fact, I can ask the Secretary to approve the landing clearance when I relay your news. I doubt there'll be a problem."

"I'll... see you tomorrow, then."

"Okay, Alex. Tomorrow."

Dreamer, you got all that?

Yes.

I want to plan to be on the ground at Andrews by noon local time tomorrow.

Understood.

A little while after the call ended, Dreamer notified Alex that the Seoks were all getting their medical scans done. A little after that, they showed up for breakfast. Alex called up an order of orange juice and started throwing together whatever breakfast he could scrounge up.

"I'm planning to make a food supply run tomorrow," he told them. "Think about what you'll need—better figure at least two or three weeks' worth of food, to be safe, I think there should be room to store that much here—and let me know. In about five more days, Dreamer should be beginning the second phase of the reconstruction project we have planned, and for about a week after that we will have no access to the docking bay.

"Dreamer advised me you all got your medical scans this morning, too. If you don't object, I'm going to have him make you all up at least two sets each of what I'm wearing now, which is the official United Fleet diplomatic uniform, so that you at least have *something* other than nightclothes. You can work out anything beyond that with Dreamer later. Remember that we can also make a trip down to Earth for clothes, if you need to.

"Is that alright?"

The Seoks exchanged looks and nods.

"We would be grateful," Dong-geun replied.

Alex nodded and gave Dreamer the go-ahead.

"Can we get tested now, please?" Choon-mae asked after breakfast. Seok Hae looked disapproving, but Alex grinned.

"Unless the two of you have any objections?" he asked. Dong-geun and Hae sighed and shook their heads.

"No, it is fine," Dong-geun said. "But you, Choon-mae, are forgetting your manners."

"I'm sorry, Father," Choon-mae apologized. "But it is all so *exciting!*"

"I understand," Dong-geun replied, smiling fondly. "The truth is, I am both excited and fascinated as well."

Twenty minutes later, they were all in the command center, near one of the secondary consoles. A science drone with an interface kit, already connected to the console, hovered nearby. The wall display was set to a solid pearly white.

"Here is what we're doing to do," Alex explained, having planned it out with Dreamer along the way. "One at a time, I want you to sit at this console, and the drone is going to put this electrode mesh on your head."

"Why don't I go first?" Dong-geun interjected. "Then you can explain the steps along the way as we go."

"All right," Alex said. "That seems a good idea. Take a seat, please."

Dong-geun climbed into the chair. Alex signalled the drone forward, and they all watched the mesh crawl and settle into place over his head. Jia's eyes got very wide as she watched. Choon-mae and Yeon watched closely.

"Okay," Alex said. "Dong-geun, can you hear me?"

"Yes. Alex. I hear you clearly."

"Good. I want you to focus your attention on the console in front of you. Dreamer has configured this console temporarily to control the lighting in this room. Do you see a color menu?"

There was a long pause.

"I am... trying, Alex," Dong-geun said uncertainly. "I am not sure how... wait... yes. Yes, I do! I see it. Although I do not know whether 'see' is strictly the right word. But it is there, yes."

"Great! Now, I want you to think about picking a color from—... well, that's *that*, then." Before Alex even finished speaking, the light in the room changed to a sunny golden yellow. "That's a great start. Now, I want you to see if you can set it to a color that is *not* on that menu. Focus on the console and think about the color you want."

For a while, nothing happened.

"It is—difficult to think about two things at once," Dong-geun said slowly.

"Try focusing on *sending* the color *to* the console," Alex said. "That makes it one thing. Close your eyes if it helps."

Dong-geun closed his eyes. Nothing. Then the yellow flickered. Brightened, dimmed.

"You're getting it! Keep going."

The yellow light flickered again. Acquired a slightly orange tinge.

"Aaaaaaaaah," Dong-geun said softly. "I think—"

277

The light flowed smoothly to a lovely warm red-orange. Hae gasped, and Choon-mae cheered.

"You did it!" Alex told him. "Open your eyes."

Dong-geun opened his eyes and gazed at the wall. His mouth opened in pleased surprise.

"Full control, Dong-geun. Congratulations. Now... close your eyes again and relax. Do you feel anything *more*? A presence?"

Dong-geun closed his eyes. His breathing slowed. Everyone waited.

After a while, he opened his eyes again.

"No, I can feel nothing more beyond the console," he said. "Regretfully. I... *see* the console, in my mind, but I do not—*feel* anything."

"Okay, well, this is already a huge success." Alex signalled the drone and the contact mesh withdrew. "Who would like to go next?"

Choon-mae's hand shot up. Alex grinned, somehow not at all surprised.

"All right, Choon-mae, your turn," Dong-geun said indulgently. He climbed off the chair and Choon-mae took his place. He watched the contact web wide-eyed as it approached him, then laughed as it snugged itself into place.

"It *tickles*," he said. Alex grinned.

"Right, you know by now what to expect," Alex said. "Focus on the console and see if you can set the light color from the menu."

There was a short pause, as Choon-mae frowned in concentration.

"Ah!" he exclaimed, after a minute or so. "I see it!" And then the light changed to a steady green.

"Excellent!" Alex said. Hae clapped. "Now try for something that is not on the color menu."

"Anything I want?" Choon-mae asked.

"Anything you want," Alex confirmed.

"Just try not to blind us," Dong-geun said, with a chuckle.

There was a pause. Alex could see Choon-mae straining at first.

"Take it easy," Alex said. "Don't force it. Stay calm. *Feel* for it."

Choon-mae took a deep breath and relaxed.

"Good," Alex murmured. "Keep it—"

The light changed to a deep purple. Then, after a moment, to alternating bands of blue and purple. Hae and Yeon both gasped. Jia gazed in wonder as the bands of light began to swirl around the room. Dong-geun looked every inch the proud father.

"You have *totally* got it, Choon-mae," Alex said. "Now. Do you feel anything else there? Can you *feel* beyond the console? A larger presence?"

A long pause.

"I... no. No. But... Maybe. ... I... I don't know. It is as though— *something*—is just beyond my reach. I cannot quite grasp it."

"Dreamer? Any thoughts?"

"You might be able to achieve rapport in the future, Choon-mae, as your brain finishes maturing," Dreamer said. "Not just yet. But this was very promising. We must test you again in a year or two. The 'exercise' of using console control will probably be helpful, over time, as well. You may be able to train yourself to make that last step."

The contact mesh withdrew, and Choon-mae climbed down from the chair with a huge smile. Dong-geun looked at Hae and raised an eyebrow. She smiled, nodded, and sat in the chair. The contact mesh settled onto her.

Hae was quickly able to find the menu and set the lighting to a clear blue, but could not manage to set any color not on the menu, although a few times she got flickers and surges. She climbed down from the chair looking slightly disappointed.

"I feel that I am within reach of grasping more," she said, "but I am getting old and set in my ways, and I cannot quite make it out."

Alex nodded. "I think you're on the edge of getting it, too," he replied. "Perhaps after you get more used to using touch-select mode, you will get the rest of the way."

Hae looked at Yeon, but Yeon, looking slightly apprehensive, looked at Jia. Jia stepped shyly forward.

"I will offer a word of caution," Dreamer said. "Jia is very young. This means two things. First, as we already discussed, she should not have implants yet.

"Second, even if she is limited *now*, she may not be limited *later*. So if she is unable to manage any particular thing now, *do not* assume that she will still be unable to when she is older. Do you understand this, Jia? If you cannot do something now, do not be disappointed, be patient."

Jia and Hae both nodded solemnly.

"I am ready to try," Jia said. Alex signalled the drone.

Jia was able to set the light to a deep red from the menu, but could not change it off-menu.

"It is alright, Jia," Dong-geun reassured her. "Let us try again when you are older."

And then it was Yeon's turn.

She got into the chair and let the headset settle onto her. Again, she was easily able to set the lighting back to the golden yellow that Dong-geun had chosen.

"Now,"Alex said, "relax and *feel* for the console. Pick some lighting scheme of your own and try to set it."

There was a long, *long* pause, as nothing happened. Yeon took a deep breath and let it out. Alex could see that she was trying to relax. Her eyes opened, then closed again, and her breathing slowed. Alex could see her expression grow calm.

Then she gasped.

"Ooooooooohhhhhhhh," she said softly. Her voice shook slightly. Dong-geun and Hae looked worried, but Alex raised a hand, gesturing them to wait.

"Ohhhhhhhhhh," Yeon murmured again. Tears began to trickle from the corners of her eyes. "Oh, it's... so... *beautiful.*"

She just broke through, didn't she, Dreamer? Alex could feel the new presence in the Stardock's infosphere.

Yes, Alex. Full rapport. On her first attempt.

Hello, Yeon, Alex thought to her. She gasped aloud again.

Hello... Mr Holder? This... I never imagined it would be like this. This is... WONDERFUL.

Hello, Yeon, said Dreamer.

Alex could not keep the grin off his face. He turned to Dong-geun and Hae.

"Congratulations," he told them. "Yeon has achieved full rapport. Not with the test console. With the *Stardock.*"

The joy on their faces was a wonder to behold. Without a word, Dong-geun put his arms around Hae and pulled her close.

"It seems our little caterpillar has just become a butterfly," he declared proudly.

Yeon, Alex thought, *you should probably come out now. I think your parents would like to talk to you.*

For long seconds, there was no response, then Yeon opened her eyes. She looked back and forth, hesitated... then closed her eyes again for a moment, and the contact mesh withdrew.

"I didn't want to take it off," she said, apologetically. "Mother, Father, I looked at the Earth through the Stardock's eyes. It is so *beautiful.*"

"Yes, it is," Alex said. Then, as it seemed fitting, he bowed to her. "Congratulations, Seok Yeon. You are the second human being ever to achieve full rapport with the Stardock."

"So tell me, Alex," Dong-geun said. "What do we do now?"

"My advice," Alex said, "is that you, Choon-mae and Yeon should all receive full implants as soon as possible.

"Hae, it is... still possible that you will learn the ability in the future for full control. Of course you may try again at any time. As long as you are getting at least dermal contacts anyway, I would advise the full-contact mesh just in case you are able to take the next step after more practice.

"Jia should not receive implants at this time, as Dreamer already advised. She is growing too fast. There would be problems, according to Dreamer. But, young lady," turning to Jia, "now we *know* that you should have implants once your body is ready for them. We can re-test then, to see what more you can do. For now, I am afraid you are going to have to ask others to do things for you. Dreamer will always be available to help you.

"Dreamer, you now have five solid test cases, all with recent medical scans. Might I suggest we review the scans and see whether we can find any common factors we can use to refine the scans?"

"Please," Yeon said. "Let me help with that. As soon as I have my implants. Could I—get them right now? Please?"

Alex looked at Dong-geun and Hae.

"Do you have any objection to Yeon receiving her implants immediately?" Then a thought struck him. "Actually, Dreamer, now that the medbay is upgraded, how many can you do at once?"

"I would suggest Yeon and Hae together, and then Choon-mae and Dong-geun together," Dreamer replied. "For privacy. Hae will be finished before Yeon. Her implantation is less complex."

Alex raised a questioning eyebrow toward the two adults. Both nodded.

281

"Dreamer, you should probably have one set of clothes for each person delivered to the medbay," he said. "I think this is going to become a tradition around here."

14: Earthlight

Cycling the Seoks through medbay took most of the rest of the day. The implantation procedures all went smoothly, with no surprises, and Yeon's first project was actually to get some additional clothes made for her mother, who had only one set of nightclothes plus the diplomatic outfits. Alex received confirmation of clearance to land at Andrews, and contacted the Secretary-General to arrange to make a brief announcement.

He also got a call from Karabo Jackson.

"Am I speaking to Mr. Holder?"

"You are," Alex replied. "And you are...?"

"Karabo Jackson, with the Electronic Frontier Foundation." There was a distinct touch of Caribbean in the accent.

"Aha," Alex said. "Naomi Tomlinson told me you'd be calling."

"Indeed. She said you have an... unusual problem."

"That would be one word for it," Alex said. "I presume you've been following along in general and have some idea of how advanced the Crickets' science is."

"Yes. I heard something about two new rows to the Periodic Table?"

"Exactly," Alex replied. "So I'm sure you get the general idea.

"So here's the problem I'm looking at. I am sitting on a huge heap of incredibly valuable technologies here. Knowledge that I want to give to the world for free. Technologies that could change the entire world for the better... unless the greedy lock them up in ways that only benefit themselves. We've done that too many times, for too long."

"I'm listening," Karabo Jackson said. "What do you want to do about it?"

"I want to draft a new kind of technology license," Alex said. "I want to devise a license that allows anyone to use these technologies, and make a fair profit off of them, for a nominal royalty, under the condition that they share the benefits fairly with nations not able to build the tech themselves. A license designed to make sure nobody is left behind, and nobody can hoard all of the goodies for themselves. A license that rewards action for the benefit of all mankind and discourages simple greed. And all products built using the technology must be built to be repairable. No products that you can only throw away and replace. No lock-ins. If you try to lock anyone into your product that is based on one of these technologies, you lose the right to use all Cricket technologies."

"Good luck," Karabo said. "I mean, I admire the goal, but it's not going to be easy. The license violation terms are almost the easiest part of it. How are you going to arrive at an unequivocal definition of 'fair' that holds up in a possibly-hostile court? Or 'benefit of all mankind'? There's a lot of entrenched monopolist interests that are going to fight you tooth and nail."

"I know," Alex replied. "I was sort of hoping you might have some insights into questions like that. For some of these things we'll absolutely have to arrive at an established global standard. We mustn't allow the establishment of proprietary interfaces that are protected by one corporation's patents and they refuse to license that patent. We need everyone to be able to build to one standard for any particular thing, not eighteen—and that standard cannot be defined in ways that create a deliberate barrier to entry beyond the technology itself."

"Well, I can tell you your first step," Karabo told Alex. "I can give you a template to attach to any purely scientific information you release, to place it directly into the public domain."

"That sounds like a good first step," Alex agreed.

"As for the no-lock-in part... We can pull some concepts into that from the Creative Commons license and the GNU Public License—the open-source world. Because what you're really talking about is open-sourcing Cricket technology."

"That's a good way to look at it, yes," Alex confirmed.

"Revocation of license upon violation of terms is simple, legally speaking. The difficult part may be enforcing it. But the hard part of this is going to be the fair sharing part, because it's going to be so hard to nail down what 'fair' is."

"I know," Alex said. "Which is in large part why I'm not trying to do this myself. I do have the ability, once we have something, to put it directly in front of the United Nations. If we can sell them on the idea that in the long run it is in everybody's interest, we can perhaps get some help from the nations themselves to come up with usable definitions of what constitutes fair and equitable sharing. And I want to give a *bootstrap*, not a free ride. A *substantial* bootstrap, but a bootstrap nonetheless. I want it to reward those who share, and those who help others, and those who put in the work to raise themselves and lift others up in their turn.

"As for enforcement, I think that's going to be simpler than you perhaps think. There is a *huge* amount of technology and science to be released here. It'll take us a generation to fully assimilate it. Probably more. You violate the *spirit* of the license, even if you can find an argument that you're technically in compliance with the letter? *You don't get any more.* Period. You lose access to *decades* of advances. So only the most stupidly short-sighted will think trying to cheat is a good idea."

Karabo chuckled.

"You're a real idealist, aren't you?" he asked. "I hear that's an endangered species."

"I suppose so," Alex agreed. "And also I know that the stronger we can make *the entire world*—not just its wealthiest nations—and the faster, the better our chances are. We have a de-facto world *government* already in the United Nations, toothless and ineffectual though it often is." Karabo coughed. "But what we need is a global *community*. And that community needs to learn to care about and help its weakest members. We need a true rising tide, not a boat lift, and we need to get the people in the water into boats."

Karabo nodded.

"You mentioned a nominal royalty?"

"Yes. I'm thinking a fixed royalty of something like a half or one percent for anyone manufacturing over, say, a hundred thousand dollars worth of products using a licensed technology. I'd make it free for everyone, but I have a fleet to build here, and while I'll be getting all of the materials I need from asteroid mining, I'm going to need to pay and feed the people who will make up that fleet."

"Alright, Mr. Holder," Karabo said. "Give me some time to think about this, and I'll see if I can get some additional minds on this as well. I'll be back in touch when I think I have something to show you, or if I have specific questions I need answers to."

"Thank you," Alex said. "I'll be looking forward to it."

Karabo chuckled.

"You might not say that when you're reading through all of the resulting boilerplate," he said.

"Oh, and that's one other thing," Alex replied. "I want this to be as plain-English as possible while still being legally precise. I want as many people as possible to be able to understand as much as possible of it, without needing a legal education."

"We're the Electronic Frontier Foundation, Mr. Holder," Karabo said.

"That kind of thing is what we *do*. What use freedom, if nobody can understand it?

"Just one last question: Do you have any idea what you want to call this technology license of yours?"

"I thought maybe the Global Fair Share Technology License," Alex suggested.

─────────────

Alex spent a couple of hours—with Seok Hae's help, after she was done with her implantation—figuring out a supply list. He directed a team of drones to stage the transport crates from his previous home-removal visit to the eight-place aircar parked outside his quarters. He put in orders for pressure suits for all of the Seok family, just in case, and took Yeon to the docking bay (sealed and pressurized) for a lesson in flying the small aircar. She was hesitant and jerky at first, but caught on quickly after she internalized that the way to do it was to immerse herself in the aircar and just *think* about where she wanted it to go.

There is a saying among motorcyclists, Alex thought to her. *"Slow is smooth; smooth is fast."*

... I think I understand, came Yeon's reply, after she had taken a few moments to think about it. *Slow is smooth, because you have time to catch mistakes early. And not having to lose time correcting mistakes, is fast.*

That's it exactly, Yeon.

He could not help a feeling of pleasure at how nice it was to be able to speak to her through the interface without needing Dreamer to help translate. Both English and Korean were in the system, as was every other language the Crickets had scooped out of Earth's infosphere, and the translation was automatic, almost seamless, and invisible. He "watched over her shoulder" as her confidence grew and her flying smoothed out.

After two hours or so, Alex called a halt. He didn't want to wear Yeon out. He had her land the aircar just inside the passageway, beyond the atmosphere seal. Then he showed her how to find the bay controls, and guided her to an experimental touch of the lander's interface.

Flying the lander is fundamentally a lot like flying the aircar, he told her as they walked back. *But at the same time it is also very different. It has a tremendous amount of thrust, it can accelerate at fifteen gravities,*

286

and you can build up enormous velocity very quickly. And because of the acceleration compensation, it's easy to be unaware of how much velocity you're piling on. So before you begin any acceleration burn, you must calculate how much time and distance you will need to slow down or stop.

I hope I do not have to fly it soon, Yeon replied. *I... am a little afraid of that.*

Don't worry. I have no intention of making you fly anything before you feel ready. The lander's substrate will actually perform the calculations for you if you know what to ask it for, and Dreamer can teach you about orbital mechanics and how all of the lander's systems work. The new passenger shuttle works exactly the same way.

Thank you, Mr Holder. I will ask.

Alex, Yeon. Just call me Alex. Please.

Alright... Alex. I will try to remember.

By the time Alex and Yeon got back from the docking bay, Dong-geun and Choon-mae were done with their implantation. Choon-mae kept running his fingers along the fine red incision lines up his forearms.

"Dong-geun," Alex said, "Yeon is going to make a very fine pilot, I think, with more experience. I believe she has already mostly mastered the basics of the aircar." Dong-geun looked very pleased; Choon-mae, slightly envious.

"Choon-mae, I'm afraid you will have to wait a little. I have realized I need to make some modifications to the aircar's controls."

Alex noticed the way Choon-mae was fingering his incision lines.

"Are the incisions bothering you?"

"No, Mr. Holder," Choon-mae replied. "It is just... it is all so new. I know that there was an, an incision here. But I can find no wound. I can see where the incisions were, but I cannot *feel* them. Just... something that is *not quite* an itch. It is *fascinating.*"

Alex grinned. He knew the feeling.

"Just Alex, Choon-mae," he said, just as he had told Yeon. "There is no need for us to stand on formality here." Choon-mae nodded and grinned.

Dreamer, I missed a trick with the aircars. Direct control is handled, of course, and we have a sort-of-usable manual control scheme, though it's a bit rough still. I'm not sure we got the control metaphors right. Dong-

geun and *Choon-mae ought to be able to fly one nearly as well as Yeon, but they'll need contact pads that don't risk accidental manual control inputs. How about if we modify the pilot seat armrests to incorporate contact surfaces, like this?* He sent Dreamer a mental image.

That seems a good solution, Dreamer agreed.

Great. Let's incorporate that into all future aircars... and I imagine into landers and shuttles as well. We should do our best to make them flyable via full console control as well as via immersion, though obviously console pilots will need additional flight-planning assistance. Additional navigation aids too, I should expect. And possibly maneuvering assists.

I will incorporate it into the troop shuttle that is in construction, and retrofit the one completed passenger shuttle, Dreamer replied. *I also suggest revising the cockpits in both for dual controls.*

Yes, Alex agreed. *That's a good idea. Retrofit the controls in the current 3-place aircar as well, please. And I think we should build a few more of those as well.*

Yeon, as I mentioned, there is a newly built passenger shuttle that I have not had time to flight-test yet. When I can get to it, would you like to help me?

...Yes. Yes, please. I would.

Dreamer, please send a message to the Secretary-General and ask when would be the next good time for the announcement I requested earlier.

One moment.

"Dong-geun? If I might, I would like to borrow you for a few minutes shortly. You as well, please, Yeon. I have asked the Secretary-General to fit in a brief announcement of your new position, and of Yeon's accomplishment. I want to get that news out. Dreamer is just checking on the schedule now."

"Certainly." Dong-geun nodded. Yeon looked nervous.

"You don't have to say a word if you don't want to," Alex reassured her. "I just want them to see you, and understand that we will find more." She nodded.

"There will be an opportunity in thirty minutes," Dreamer said. "Estimated."

While I think of it, Dreamer, we need to come up with some formal identity documents.

I have a beginning suggestion, Dreamer replied. *Allow me to construct a demonstration sample. It will be delivered in a few minutes.*

Sure enough, a drone showed up shortly afterwards. It was carrying a single small card.

Dreamer, Alex said, this is getting ridiculous. *Are you sure it's not more efficient to locate a small fabber somewhere under my quarters and have direct delivery?*

I can construct a direct delivery channel from an existing nearby light-duty fabber, Dreamer replied. *We can discuss later where you want the delivery location.*

Thanks, Dreamer. That's fine.

Alex looked at the card. It was a small, rigid white card, a little larger and slightly thicker than a driving license. Across the top were the words UNITED EARTH FLEET in deep blue, with a solid blue line below them. Below that, on the left, was a high-definition portrait of Alex. As he tilted the card, the portrait rotated, faster than the card. It was holographic. On the right were two lines of text: ALEX 'HELLBURNER' HOLDER, FLEET ACTUAL. There was a blank area below the text.

Touch the white area, Dreamer said. Alex did so. The border of the card lit up pale blue.

For anyone else but you, it will show red, Dreamer told him. *There will be an insignia in that area... when we select one. I can biometrically key these to any individual I have a full medical scan for.*

This is great, Dreamer. Please make one of these for everyone and distribute them. Use Chief of Staff and UN Permanent Delegate as Dong-geun's rank for now, and Controller as Yeon's. We'll use that in place of Rapport-Controller; it's just too much of a mouthful.

There was the call to take care of.

Alex moved the chairs away from one long side of the table, leaving the chairs backing on the outer wall. "Let's do it this way," he said. He set the compartment wall display outside to show the Earth, and took the middle seat. "There's no problem with broadcasting this view, correct, Dreamer?"

"None at all. I will adjust the framing accordingly." Alex directed Dong-geun to his right, and Yeon to his left.

It turned out the previous speaker overran his time by a couple of minutes, but that was alright. As soon as he was done, the Secretary-General spoke.

"The Assembly recognizes Alex Holder of the United Earth Fleet."

"Thank you, Mr. Secretary," Alex said.

"Honored delegates, I will only take a few minutes of your time. I have two pieces of news that I would like to pass on to you.

"The first is to announce that from this day forth, the honored Seok Dong-geun is appointed as the official permanent delegate from the United Earth Fleet to the United Nations." He gave a nod toward Dong-geun. "I trust he will bring a depth of diplomatic experience and knowledge to the position that I, frankly, lack and cannot spare the time to master. And I sincerely hope that he will be able to assist all of you in coming to agreements on how to distribute the technological resources we are making preparations to release."

Dong-geun nodded back and looked into the floating display image and its invisible 'camera'.

"As it has been already stated," he began, "a person in the service of the United Earth Fleet must bear no allegiance to any Earth Nation. I therefore give formal notice, on behalf of myself, my wife Hae, my son Choon-mae, and my daughters Yeon and Jia, that we hereby and forever officially renounce our citizenship in the Democratic People's Republic of Korea.

"We belong only to the Fleet and to Earth now."

He bowed his head and sat back.

"Speaking of Seok Yeon," Alex said, "let me move on to the second piece of news I wish to relay today. I previously stated that I would be continuing the search for others able to operate Cricket technology and, in particular, able to directly interface with it in the manner to which the Crickets gave the title 'Rapport-controller'. This ongoing search has borne its first fruit, sooner than expected.

"It gives me great honor and pleasure to introduce you all to Controller Seok Yeon, who successfully achieved full-rapport connection with the Stardock this morning." He gestured to his left. "She is humanity's second full Controller. We will continue to seek out more."

There was silence for a moment, then the Japanese Ambassador stood, followed quickly by the rest of his delegation, and bowed deeply toward the screen. Another delegate followed suit, and then another, and then someone began clapping. And then it spread. Yeon put her hands to her mouth, her eyes wide.

After a little while, the applause died down.

"Miss Seok," the Secretary-General asked kindly. "Do you have any words to offer us on this day?"

Yeon looked down for a long moment, then looked back up again. She placed her hands flat on the table in front of her.

«Today,» she said in Korean, quietly but clearly, «I opened for the first time eyes that I did not know that I had, and I saw the Earth from space, through the eyes of the Stardock. It is a beautiful treasure, utterly beyond compare, and the only such treasure that we possess.

«Please treat it with the care that it deserves.»

There was a long moment of silence in the Assembly, then a slowly rising wave of respectful applause. Yeon looked down, blushing slightly.

———————

Alex and Dreamer spent the next few hours coaching the Seoks in the use of their new implants until it became second nature. While Alex focused more on guiding Dong-geun, Hae, and Choon-mae, Dreamer took Yeon on a virtual tour of the Stardock's major systems, focusing particularly on every detail of all of the med-bay equipment, as that was the area in which she had expressed particular interest.

"Hae," Alex said, "if we can come up with any ideas to try to nudge your mind that extra little way to full control, are you willing to try it again? We're still learning how to find people with control abilities. If we can find a way to train people with some existing ability to operate at a higher level, it will be valuable."

"Of course," she said. "I would be glad to. It was... ah! I felt so close! But I could not quite reach."

"I have one question," Dong-geun asked. "Will it be necessary to always use a... teleconferencing arrangement, as we did today, if I wish to speak to anyone? Or will I need something like a phone?"

"Correct me if I'm mistaken here, Dreamer," Alex replied. "Even at L2, without full rapport, Dreamer should be able to send messages to and receive from your implants as long as you are on the Stardock."

"Correct, Alex," Dreamer confirmed. "That is not difficult. Those with only L1 ability will require an external communication assistive device. I will fabricate some.

"I can of course originate and receive telephone calls and route them to your implants, just as I do for Alex."

"That is very good, Dreamer," Dong-geun replied. "Thank you."

Hae insisted on making dinner, with Jia assisting. Alex was only too glad not to cook for once. Hae was sadly disapproving of his inventory of available ingredients, and declared that she could do much better if he was able to fill all of the supplies she had requested.

Meanwhile, Alex went over the supply list for the next day again, trying to check for anything that he had missed.

Dreamer, am I missing any food storage options here that would make this simpler?

What sort of options, Alex?

That's just it. I don't know what to ask about. We've got room-temperature storage for non-perishable items, we have refrigerated storage, frozen storage. But, for example, freezing water-based liquids doesn't work well because the container explodes. And for dairy products, freezing tends to disrupt the suspension, too, which spoils both taste and consistency. And some things—most fruit, for example—don't freeze well, because ice crystals destroy their structure.

I understand the question better now, Alex. The crystallization damage problem, as you are doubtless aware, can be largely solved by extremely rapid freezing methods such as the use of cryogenic nitrogen. But that does not address the problem that I think you are looking for a solution to.

Correct. I plan on going heavy on frozen goods, but there are perishable food items that cannot practically be either frozen or synthesized. Starting with dairy products. For those, I see no alternative to regular fresh deliveries.

As I surmised. We can flash-freeze some items, and thaw them in a controlled manner to minimize freezing damage, but there is no other available option that you are not aware of.

Thanks, Dreamer. Just wanted to be sure I wasn't missing something that could simplify our food logistics.

Was there a particular thing you had in mind?

Well... alright. I'm pretty sure you're going to tell me this is ridiculous. But there's a fictional concept of stasis boxes or stasis fields.

292

I'm about ninety-nine point nine percent certain that the idea is pure and complete handwavium. I can't come up with any conceivable mechanism that doesn't involve a spacetime discontinuity at the boundary of the field. But... well, it's already clear to me that there is a LOT of physics that is beyond Earth science. So I didn't want to rule out the possibility that this was one of those things. I'd hate to overlook it if I was wrong.

Dreamer actually paused for nearly ten seconds before responding.

I concur. As you surmise, I am aware of no known method of implementing such a thing, and I am unable to hypothesize any theoretical basis for accomplishing it without creating a spacetime discontinuity that is beyond any physics known to me.

Glad to hear it, Dreamer. It's nice to know that my physics bullshit-o-meter is still worth at least something in the face of Chhrt'ktk't technology.

Dreamer did not reply, but Alex thought he felt something subtle come back through the link that felt like amusement.

Dinner was good, despite Hae's dissatisfaction with Alex's food supplies. Alex handed out the new identification cards at the table, and then he and Dong-geun sat up for a couple of hours afterward, strategizing on policy issues and discussing Dong-geun's thoughts on what a proper diplomatic staff should be, as well as what might be required by way of more formal diplomatic documents. The rest of the family sat nearby, mostly not participating, but listening closely.

"I'll tell you right up front," Alex told Dong-geun, "though I'm sure we'll have to actually have a staff Earthside somewhere, probably New York, I want you working from up here. I don't want you or any of your family where Young Leader might be tempted to try to have you snatched or assassinated."

"I cannot disagree," Dong-geun said. "He is vain, arrogant, vengeful and cruel. I cannot express how glad I am that my family is at last beyond his reach."

———

Dreamer woke Alex in plenty of time the next morning.

I have arranged for the transport crates to be loaded into the large aircar.

Thanks, Dreamer.

He got out of bed and went to shower.

Yeon? he called through the infosphere, as he showered. *I'm preparing to make a trip down to the United States. Would you like to come along and ride second seat, and watch over my shoulder?*

I would like that very much, Mr Holder, Yeon replied. *I will advise Father.*

Yeon, Alex sent back, *please just call me Alex. 'Mr Holder' makes me feel like a schoolteacher.*

Are you not teaching us, then? Yeon asked. Gentle mirth came through the link. Alex couldn't help but laugh.

It's probably best you stay with the lander for this trip, Alex added.

I agree, Yeon replied. *I can use the time to study the lander's systems and capabilities more.*

You know that you can do that now from anywhere on the station? Alex asked.

...Oh. Yes. You are right. I suppose I can, Yeon replied slowly. *This is... going to take some time to get used to.*

Don't feel bad about that, Alex replied. *It took me a while, too.*

———————

Yeon met Alex at the aircar, and then it was time to head for the docking bay. When they reached the bay, Alex could see that construction of the planned docking galleries along the inmost side was beginning, and the rear wall of the bay was being dismantled.

There was also another surprise. The lander was no longer entirely gleaming white. Now, two heavy solid lines of deep cobalt blue ran along each side of the hull, from just above the side hatch to just past the back end of the flatbed. Between the lines, bold letters read UNITED EARTH FLEET. The same livery adorned the still-untested passenger shuttle that was parked further back in the bay.

Do you approve? Dreamer asked. *I left room for an insignia.*

...Yes, Alex replied. *I approve very much. It is a good idea. Thank you.* He looked at it for a long moment. *Is that painted? Will it survive re-entry?*

It is not painted, Dreamer replied. *As you already knew, the hull material can change its surface coloration. And as I previously mentioned, it does not have to be a uniform color. The livery is... written, in a sense,*

294

into the hull material, configuring what its 'resting' color should be.

So... that livery is part of the hull now?

In a sense.

That's a neat trick.

Alex opened the flatbed clamshell, then had Yeon bring the aircar in and settle it on the flatbed.

"Just one moment before we leave," he said, as a thought occurred to him. "I had a pressure suit constructed for you. I know you haven't had any chance to practice with it yet, but I'm going to have a drone bring it here and stow it in the suit rack, just in case." Yeon nodded.

A drone arrived in a few minutes carrying Yeon's suit. The cartouche, on two lines, read SEOK YEON / UNITED EARTH FLEET.

I'm sensing a theme here, Alex chuckled.

I have taken the liberty of doing so on all of the new suits, Dreamer replied. *I have also updated the markings on yours.*

Thank you again, Dreamer.

Alex showed Yeon how to rack her suit, then walked her quickly through getting in and out of it, sealing it, and performing all of the functional checks, advising her to make arrangements with Dreamer to train properly with it later.

And then it was time to go. Yeon observed attentively in the link as Alex took the lander out of the bay and set up an orbital plane change and a mild descent burn, making a point of showing her the calculations and how to use the lander's computational substrate to run them, then took the lander down in a lazy vertical descent fifty kilometers offshore.

"Andrews Control, Fleet Actual requesting landing clearance under pre-filed flight plan."

"Fleet Actual, Andrews, you are cleared for your requested vertical approach. Please use helipad three."

"Andrews, Fleet Actual confirms helipad three. Out."

Alex brought the lander in at two thousand meters and three hundred kph, well above the pattern, then descended almost vertically towards the designated helipad. Yeon paid close attention the whole time. The lander extended beyond the pad, but Alex aligned it so as to cause minimal obstruction.

"Andrews, Fleet Actual down and parked."

"Acknowledged, Fleet Actual. Do you need ground transportation?"

"Negative, Andrews. I brought my own. I have Controller Seok Yeon with me today. She will be remaining with the lander."

"Acknowledged. Welcome to Joint Base Andrews, Hellburner."

"Thank you, Andrews." Evidently, the word had spread.

Yeon opened the clamshell, and Alex lifted the aircar out. As a courtesy, he kept it at a half-meter hover and normal traffic speed as far as the gate, and pulled over to check out. The gate guards had evidently been briefed to expect him. He showed the new Fleet ID and explained the verification feature.

"That's pretty sharp, sir. It's biometric?"

"Yes. I expect to have a passenger with me when I return. She's cleared, she's State Department."

"Understood, sir," the guard replied. "I'll make sure that's added to the day notes."

Then it was on to Washington. It was a little over 20 kilometers from Andrews to the Truman building, as the crow—or the aircar—flies. Alex called ahead.

"Naomi?"

"Hi, Alex."

"I just landed at Andrews. I'll be in front of the Truman building in about fifteen minutes. That's the correct location for you, right?"

"Yes. I'll be out front. See you soon."

Alex kept the speed down and the altitude at five hundred meters. He started descending once he hit Foggy Bottom, ending up approaching the Harry S. Truman building only four meters off the road. He saw as he approached that Naomi was already waiting outside, in the company of another woman he didn't know. Ground traffic had paused, leaving a gap. He settled the aircar to the ground right in front of the building and opened the canopy on that side. Naomi and the other woman stepped forward, and Alex stepped out to meet them.

"Hello, Alex. It's good to see you."

"Hi, Naomi. Good to see you, too." He looked toward her companion, presuming a pending introduction.

"Alex, this is my boss, Susan Wilder. Susan, Alex Holder, who is now the... umm...? From the new United Earth Fleet."

"I'm sorry," Alex apologized. "I've had more pressing things on my mind than picking a formal... title, I suppose. I'm sure my new Chief of Staff will make me pick something official soon.

"Pleased to meet you, Ms. Wilder."

"Likewise, Mr. Holder. And it's alright, we all know who you are by now."

"I apologize for taking Naomi away from you in the middle of the day..."

"Oh, nonsense. She doesn't take half as much vacation as she should. And in any case, it's not as if we can't afford her some leeway, considering that she seems to be at the forefront of establishing relations with your new Fleet."

"I hope you don't mind if I take Naomi and run. I'm blocking traffic."

"Not a problem. Your time must be valuable. I don't doubt we'll meet again, Mr. Holder. Enjoy your trip, Naomi."

Alex ushered Naomi into the right seat, then settled himself into the left seat and closed the canopy. He lifted the car back up to five hundred meters and set a heading.

"So how are you doing, Alex?"

Alex shook his head ruefully.

"Naomi, to nearly anyone else, I'd say you have no idea how much there is to be done. But you're with the State Department, and I'm betting you have a pretty good idea."

"You're not wrong," Naomi agreed. "At least so far there doesn't seem to have been any *public* blowback from the North Koreans, which is good. I... think they may be trying to pretend nothing happened."

Alex nodded.

"Well that's good to hear, at least. I have Seok Yeon with me today, by the way. She rode down second-seat as an observer, to learn how to fly the lander."

"I saw the video from the UN. She looks very young?"

"Yes. She's seventeen. But with a little coaching, she broke through to full rapport on her first try. It was... amazingly heartwarming to see."

"Tell me," Naomi asked, "how *did* you come to be extracting the North Korean UN delegate and his family...?"

"I suspect that question is more than just personal curiosity," Alex said. Naomi nodded agreement.

"Well, you're doubtless aware that North Korea was among the hold-outs in recognizing the Fleet." She nodded again. "After the session, Dong-geun approached me during dinner and apologized. He informed me that if he were to extend recognition to the Fleet without an express order from Young Leader to do so, it would be the end of his career and he would be recalled in disgrace, and his successor might well be ordered to repudiate the recognition." Another nod. "*Then* he pointed out that publicly embarrassing Young Leader by NOT doing so could have equally severe personal consequences, depending on Kim's mood at the moment.

"I asked whether he could simply *not go home*, which was when he told me that his family was still in Pyongyang."

"As hostages," Naomi filled in.

"Exactly. I told him to let me know if he needed my help."

"Which he did?"

"Yes. Three days later. On a burner phone that he'd had the foresight to obtain. He had been informed that he was being recalled for trial."

"The verdict of which having already been decided," Naomi said. Alex nodded.

"Exactly. He was under no illusions that he was going home to anything but a show trial and public execution, almost certainly with his family beside him." Naomi shuddered.

"They took away the phone they knew about, but didn't find the burner. He went outside on his balcony and called me from there, told me what he could, and I formulated a rescue plan. Fortunately, I already had a hunch something might be in the air, and I'd just had some defensive weaponry installed on the lander."

"Hence the missile battery you 'kind of blew up'."

"Yes. That was the point-defense mount. It's a plasma weapon. Charging it sucked up nearly a quarter of the fusion bottle's full output for a second and a half. It was totally their fault, they fired on us first. I'd have been happy to leave still undetected."

Naomi chuckled.

"So... Seok Dong-geun. Do you *trust* him?"

Alex paused, framing in his head how best to answer the question.

"Dong-geun has been planning to get his family out of North Korea for years," he said at last, slowly. "How many years, I didn't ask. He had to be *incredibly* careful. They were closely watched, and not allowed to leave the country together. They couldn't even put together anything resembling a go-bag, lest their minders see it and ask why it was there. They got out with the clothes on their backs, a bag containing heirloom jewelry that had belonged to Seok Hae's... mother or grandmother, I'm not actually sure—and nothing else. And then, yes, a surface-to-air missile battery apparently got a radar return as we left Pyongyang, and fired two missiles at us."

Naomi reached out and took Alex's hand. He looked over, surprised.

"I'm glad you were able to rescue them," she said. "It says a lot about who you are. But then... everything you do does."

Alex felt awkward.

"I'm just doing what I have to," he said.

"Someone else might not have felt they had to rescue a foreign diplomat from a hostile nation," Naomi pointed out. Alex had no answer to that.

"Well, anyway," he continued, "I know at least three things about Dong-geun: He is a very experienced diplomat, he is meticulously careful, and he has no love for North Korea. His family are in temporary quarters right now on the Stardock until I get real quarters for them constructed based on mine, and I apologized that they weren't meant as family accommodations, but Dong-geun was... emphatic about how good it was to have somewhere, *anywhere*, for his whole family to live where they were *not* afraid of being arrested in the middle of the night. It's *instantly* clear how deeply he loves his family.

"And, well, I have a good feeling about him. He didn't *have* to apologize to me for not supporting the Fleet in the UN roll-call. But he did anyway.

"So, yeah. I have the feeling I can trust him. Or I wouldn't have offered him the Delegate and Chief of Staff position. But I'd still have offered asylum regardless, if he wanted it for his family."

Naomi nodded thoughtfully, and looked outside.

"We aren't headed for Andrews," she observed.

"No. Not yet. We're going to a grocery store and a big-box warehouse club to buy a *whole lot* of supplies. I suddenly have six people to feed, and I'm down to a couple of days' worth of food for one, at best. Fortunately, the club I'm a member of has a DC location."

"Right, right, you mentioned that." Naomi shook her head. "Sorry, busy day."

"Sounds like you really needed the break as well, then." She nodded ruefully.

———

Alex landed the aircar in front of a supermarket first. He had Naomi get a cart as well, and led the way straight to the beverage aisle, where he loaded up his cart with lemonade, lemon-lime soda, ginger ale, various fruit juices, a mixture of favorites and things that seemed likely to be compatible with the beverage stations, never more than one package of anything, generally focusing on fruity and fresh flavors, and trying for a minimum of artificial ingredients. Then on to the produce section, where he loaded up the other cart with fresh fruit and vegetables.

At the checkout, Naomi presented a card before Alex got his out. He raised an eyebrow.

"Hush," she said. "This grocery run is on the State Department. And I'm going to see what I can do to set up regular supply allocations for the Stardock. That at least is something the US can do to support you."

"Well I won't say I don't appreciate it," Alex replied. "I'm not paying a mortgage or monthly utility bills any more, but still, my money won't last forever."

Naomi looked at him with a twinkle in her eye, but didn't say anything further... *then*.

———

When they got outside, there were a few bystanders gathered around the aircar. Alex thought the side doors open and started loading.

"Dang, you *are* the Stardock man," one man said. "This thing fly? Ain't got no wings."

"It does indeed fly," Alex replied. "It doesn't *need* wings."

"Tole you I saw him land it," a second said.

"Flies without wings. Damnedest thing," the first replied. "Okay, Leon, I owe you a beer. Fair'n'square."

———

The second stop was an Asian market where Alex was able to check off most of the items on Seok Hae's portion of the supply list, as well as a number of items from his own that couldn't be found at a regular supermarket. Again, Naomi picked up the tab on her State Department card. The few bystanders this time stood well back. Then it was on to the warehouse club, where Alex piled three flatbed carts with bulk staples, frozen chicken and fish, canned goods, three different varieties of rice, two mixed cases of wine, bottled sauces, bulk jars of some herbs and spices he was low on, canned tomatoes, tea, coffee, everything he could find that remained on his list, several times more food than he'd ever bought at one time in his life. He had to ask for a customer service employee to push the third cart.

At the checkout, Naomi pulled out the State Department card again, but Alex stopped her.

"Sorry," he said. "I have to pay for this load myself. Terms of membership—the payment has to be on a member's approved card."

By the time they got outside, a dozen or so curious onlookers had gathered around the aircar.

"Excuse me, please," Alex said, "Need to get through. Would you mind stepping back a little, please?" Several people looked round, then stepped out of his way. Alex thought the side doors open.

"You're the man from the spacedock, aren't you?" said a large man with a bushy red beard and a NAVY cap.

"I am," Alex agreed.

"Word is you're going to be building a fleet up there?" Alex nodded agreement.

"As soon as I can get it under way."

"Reckon you're going to need a lot of crew, huh?"

"Yup. Building crew quarters right now, in fact."

"You'll need cadre. Think you'll have room to take in some veterans?"

"As many as I can get. Current servicemen and veterans of all services worldwide will have priority. But especially Navy and Air Force."

"Chief Petty Officer Jeff Rankine," the man said, sticking out a hand. Alex shook it. "US Navy, retired. You make the recruiting call, we'll be there."

Rankine turned around.

"**HEY!**" he bellowed. "All y'all back up. Man's got supplies to load!

And lend a hand here!"

Then Rankine—and two other men—pitched in and helped load the aircar, packing the frozen and refrigerated items into the transport crates as Alex directed, and took the carts back. Alex configured the crates for refrigeration or freezer as appropriate. Then he and Naomi climbed in and lifted off. Rankine gave a parting wave that was half salute.

―――――――

After that, it was a beeline for Joint Base Andrews. Again, Alex brought the aircar down to a half-meter and approached the gate on the ground.

"Mr. Holder, sir," the gate guard said, the same one who had waved him out earlier in the day. "Sign in please, sir." He handed Alex a clipboard. Alex signed in—Alex Holder, United Earth Fleet—and added Naomi Tomlinson, State Department.

"Any problems, Sir?"

"None, thank you," Alex replied. "This is the guest I mentioned, Naomi Tomlinson, from the State Department."

"Ma'am." The guard nodded, checking the clipboard. "May I see some ID, Ma'am?" Naomi presented her State Department ID card. The guard looked at it, nodded, and handed it back.

"Safe flight out, Sir, Ma'am."

"Thank you," Alex replied. Then they were through the gate, and Alex headed for helipad three. The lander came into view.

"I like the new livery," Naomi said. "Classy. Those black balls are new...? The defensive weapons you mentioned?"

"The one under the nose is an electron taser turret," Alex said. "The one atop the tail is the point defense mount. Both mounts are quick-swappable."

Yeon opened the clamshell again as the aircar approached the pad, and Alex lofted the aircar up and settled it onto the flatbed. As soon as it was down, Yeon started the clamshell closing again. Alex popped the canopy and led Naomi forward into the cockpit.

Yeon, he thought, this is... my friend Naomi Tomlinson, with the US State Department. Then, aloud, "Naomi, this is Seok Yeon. She speaks no English and I speak no Korean, but I can speak to her through the link, so I can relay and translate both ways. Once we dock with the Stardock, Dreamer will be able to provide simultaneous translation, but I can't do it myself, and the lander's not programmed for it. Yet."

"I'm pleased to meet you, Yeon," Naomi said. "Your family must be so proud of you." Yeon smiled.

"She is happy to meet you too," Alex relayed. He directed Naomi to the left seat and took the center seat himself, then cleared the wallscreen.

"Neither of us needs it, but I wouldn't want you to miss the view," he explained to Naomi.

"Andrews Control, Fleet Actual, requesting clearance for vertical take-off and direct ascent to orbit."

A brief pause.

"Fleet Actual, Andrews, no conflicting traffic, take-off clearance granted immediate. Godspeed, Hellburner."

"Thank you, Andrews. Fleet Actual out."

Naomi looked at Alex, smiling.

"'Hellburner'?"

"Uh..." Alex grinned. "The 151st Fighter Squadron at Joint Base McGuire kind of adopted me."

Naomi laughed softly.

"Of course they did."

Alex let Yeon calculate the intercept, and verified it himself just to be sure. Her numbers matched his almost perfectly. Then he lifted the lander vertically a hundred meters, tipped it on its tail, and burned for orbit, setting a trajectory southwest to come up on the Stardock from behind, and keeping the Earth 'below' the hull and mostly outside the field of the cockpit view. He didn't want to give Naomi a good look at the Earth from space yet. He had a plan in mind.

"Turns out we spent five hours on the ground," he explained, "so the Stardock isn't actually much further along in its orbit than when we left it this morning... but the Earth has rotated almost ninety degrees under it. So we'll be catching it over the Pacific."

There was no great hurry, so he took about half an hour to bring them up on the Stardock, matching velocity from behind until the lander hung five kilometers off the Dock. Naomi looked up and down the vast structure, awestruck.

"I *knew* it had to be huge," she said quietly, "to be able to see it so clearly from the ground. But *this*... This is something else again. I'm not used to the idea of anything this big *moving*."

"It can't move *much*," Alex noted. "Fully deployed like this, structural stresses on the booms limit any maneuvering to about a tenth of a gee."

"Still," Naomi said, "it's amazing that it can move at all."

Yeon, Alex thought, *would you like to take us in? You don't have to if you don't feel ready yet.*

Apologies, she replied, *but I wish to observe you do it first.*

Fair enough, Alex replied. *Just thought I'd offer.*

He swung the lander nose-on to the Stardock and applied a little power, deliberately not too much. The Stardock seemed to grow slowly larger as they approached, until Naomi could make out the open docking bay hatch. Alex was braking by then. He slowed the lander on maneuvering thrusters, and brought it in not too far from the accessway. He shut it down and ordered the hatch closed and the bay pressurized, then got up and led the way to the aircar. Fortunately there was room despite all the supplies to raise a third seat in the aircar, though Alex kicked himself for not having thought about that earlier.

Welcome back, Dreamer sent a few minutes later, as Alex pulled the aircar up next to the hatch into his quarters. *I have added your guest to the simultaneous-translation group.*

Thank you, Dreamer.

The compartment backdrop was set back to the Mountainhome image, for the moment. He unsealed all the door panels and directed the utility drones to start unloading everything to the kitchen, then led the way in.

"This... looks just like a house," Naomi said. "A nice one, at that."

"I'll admit," Alex said, "I didn't want to go from New Hampshire mountains to living in a one-bunk crew cabin. Especially one built for Crickets. I knew I was going to be here a long time. I need my living space for the sake of my state of mind. And I really need to be in my best state of mind to manage all this."

Naomi nodded understandingly.

"I'll bet you do," she said. She gestured around at the compartment wall. "This is a dynamic screen like the one in the lander?"

"Yes."

"I think it's the biggest screen I've ever seen."

"And it *still* has no visible pixels," Alex said. "I freely confess I do not understand how it's done. Something about wavelets, but I'm not an optical scientist."

"Where is this... backdrop from?"

"Somewhere in Colorado, I think," Alex said. "Dreamer pulled it off a drone and surprised me with it."

Then they were walking into the house itself, dodging utility drones carrying transport crates.

"Welcome back," Dong-geun said, from the dining room. "I have been coordinating arrangements. We have some good progress already on deciding who is to receive the first set of water purification systems and the first fusion reactors."

"That's great!" Alex replied. "It sounds as though we'd better start preparing to fabricate that first batch."

"They are already begun, Alex," Dreamer replied.

"Thank you, Dreamer. We're going to need a cargo hauler big enough to deliver them by the time they're ready. They won't fit on the lander, and nothing Earth-built can collect and deliver them. Please remind me to talk about that design later. We'll need to hash out the details. It'll have to be capable of delivering the biggest units we're planning to build."

Alex looked around, seeing that Hae and Jia were in his living-room. "Where is Choon-mae?"

"Choon-mae!" Hae called.

"Coming, Mother!" Choon-mae's voice came from upstairs, jarring oddly with the translation in Alex's head. He quickly appeared, and bowed to Alex. "I hope you do not mind that I used your dojo."

"You're welcome any time, Choon-mae," Alex replied.

"I would like to introduce you all to Naomi Tomlinson, of the United States State Department. Naomi, this is Seok Dong-geun, who is now my Chief of Staff and my official permanent delegate; his wife, Seok Hae; his son Choon-mae; and his other daughter, Jia. Yeon, of course, you have already met." And then there was a round of greetings all around, and lots of smiles.

We have people down on Earth just waiting to be recruited, Alex told Dreamer. *Those new hab quarters can't come online soon enough.*

We must also do something to regain contact with the rest of the scout drones, to find more humans able to connect, Dreamer replied.

Have you any further thoughts? Clearing low orbit of the defunct satellite networks and orbital debris would take too long, but we cannot use them as relays.

No, no ideas, yet, the…

Alex stopped. Then he clapped his hand to his forehead.

"I'm an idiot," he muttered aloud. Naomi and Dong-geun both looked at him curiously.

"I know how we're going to reconnect with the rest of the scout drones," Alex explained. "I imagine many of them are going to need to recharge soon anyway. Dreamer, the relay drones are *designed* to loiter on station for extended periods in the upper atmosphere. Right?"

"Yes, Alex."

"Which means they've got to have plenty of reserve delta-V for their size. But it would take probably thousands to cover the Earth continuously from the upper atmosphere, and we can't put them in LEO because LEO is already dangerously full of junk satellites, dead booster stages, and miscellaneous scrap."

"Correct."

"But if they can maintain their orbit against atmospheric drag, we could put them in an *ultra-low* orbit, safely **below** the abandoned constellations—say two hundred kilometers. Even a hundred and fifty."

"Yes. That is feasible."

"We already established the scout drones can do mesh networking. Can they also do store-and-forward?"

"They are not presently configured to, Alex, but I see no reason why not. It will require a small change in firmware which can either be sent separately, or piggybacked on the mesh networking firmware upgrade."

"Two hundred kilometers is an eighty-eight minute orbit. If we put thirty-six relay drones in two hundred kilometer polar orbits, staggered ten degrees apart in latitude and longitude to avoid any risk of polar collision, we can have a relay drone within range of any survey drone anywhere on earth for roughly four minutes every eighty-eight minutes. And the mesh network will effectively extend that window. The scout drones can cache findings between overflights, and do burst uploads and downloads during the overhead window. We should be able to have every drone meshed within a few hours. Then we can have science drones auto-dispatched to every scout success as soon as they come in. We'll have to make one atmospheric run, maybe several, to seed the science drones."

There was a pause as Dreamer ran through the details.

"I concur, Alex. It will work. And as you note, we will need to address recharging of the scout drones soon."

"I think you said we had six more relay drones on hand? We need to construct at least another thirty."

"Indeed. I am beginning construction now. There is sufficient PTU on hand for the thirty hyperwave relays without compromising our capacity to do initial ship builds."

Naomi gave Alex a long, amused look, then spread her hands and addressed the air.

"Does he do this a lot?"

"Quite often," Dreamer replied. Dong-geun chuckled.

Alex caught himself.

"I've been remiss," he said. "I missed an introduction. Sorry, I was distracted. Naomi, this is Dreamer, or formally, *I Dream Reality Into Being*, the artificial intelligence who manages all of the low-level operations of the Stardock. And a lot more besides. Without Dreamer, none of this would be possible."

"I am pleased to meet you, Naomi Tomlinson," Dreamer said.

"And pleased to meet you, uh, Dreamer," Naomi replied.

"Now that I think about it, Naomi," Alex went on, "this brings up another issue you could help with, if you're willing. Do you think you might be able to find out for me at some point whether the Starlink and Kuiper constellations fall under salvage laws at this point? If we can get a legal green-light to do it, I can deploy collector tugs and start cleaning all of the dead and abandoned satellites—and dead booster stages—out of low orbit. Potentially even build some sweepers to collect up the small debris, but that's a tougher problem, because there's just so *many* small pieces."

Naomi pondered the question for a moment.

"It's a little outside of my field," she said, "but if I can't find an answer myself, I can at least pass it on to someone who can."

"Thanks a lot, Naomi. That'll be a big help."

"I know another thing that'll be a help," Naomi said, smiling mischievously.

"Oh? I'm all ears."

"You know you said your money won't last forever?" Alex nodded.

"Well, I should probably advise you that the bidding on your house seems to have settled down, and we got confirmation this morning that a formal offer has been tendered. We accepted it on your behalf, and the sale is pending."

Alex nodded.

"That's good to know. Another six, seven hundred thousand coming in will pay for a lot of supplies. One less thing to worry about at the moment. Thanks for telling me."

"No, Alex," Naomi said. "The winning bidder is C. James Rockwell. And he bid eight point three million dollars."

Alex's jaw dropped. He blinked, several times.

"Wait. Eight point three... *million*? For that house? It's worth a *tenth* of that. Max."

"The house *itself*, maybe," Naomi replied. "As a house. But it's not just *any* house now. It's *your* former house, and like it or not, you are suddenly a household name worldwide. *That's* what the buyers were bidding on. Owning a house that is suddenly a significant place in world history."

Alex thought about that for a long time.

"It's strange," he said slowly, shaking his head in bewilderment. "This is something I never really thought about. I got dropped into a job that had to be done, with no time to think about it, and I never even had a chance to stop and think about what... changes it would make in my life."

"If you'd had a choice about it," Naomi asked, "and knew in advance how it was going to turn your life upside down... would you have chosen it anyway?"

"Yes." Alex hardly hesitated for a second. "It *has* to be done, and I can do it. What if the Crickets didn't find anyone *else* before they had to leave? They were already getting anxious by the time they found me. And it's not as though I'd managed to accomplish anything in my life that really mattered, before."

He sighed. Naomi gave him a measuring look.

"Eight million dollars... that'll fund supplies for a long time. Probably until we can get some technology licensing fees coming in. I'll be able to start *recruiting*.

"Naomi, I owe you a *huge* one for getting that taken care of for me. Thank you."

Naomi just smiled, leaving Alex wondering what *else* she hadn't told him yet.

By this time, the utility drones had finished ferrying transport crates in from the aircar. Alex called for all available hands on deck in the kitchen to get the fresh and refrigerated items into storage. Hae looked with approval at the incoming supplies.

"Much better," she said. "I can make proper meals now."

"You know," Alex said thoughtfully, "as my Chief of Staff's leading lady, *you* probably shouldn't be using *your* valuable time cooking either." He looked at Dong-geun. "Tell me I'm wrong." Dong-geun didn't answer, his expression determinedly neutral.

"I like cooking!" Hae protested, smiling. "If I don't feed my children, who will?"

"I'm just kidding, for now," Alex said. "I like cooking too. But at some point I'm going to need to hire in a proper chef. Right, Dong-geun?" Dong-geun nodded.

"For tonight, though, we'll be cooking separately. Naomi and I have... plans."

Hae's smile got even bigger.

After the supplies were all either unpacked or stacked in crates out of the way, Alex gave Naomi the tour he'd promised her. Her eyes fell on a few of the art pieces and other décor that she'd seen Alex select to be packed from the house on Earth below. She looked at one painting in particular, and nodded to herself.

Alex led Naomi off on a walking tour of the accessible areas of the Stardock, while Hae cooked supper for the Seok family. He showed her the auxiliary command first.

"This is where the Crickets brought me to try to connect to the Stardock," he told her, "after I was first able to connect with a science drone."

"How did that happen, anyway?" Naomi asked.

"I was... varnishing the deck rail," Alex explained. "And I felt the downwash from a scout drone—a 'soap bubble'—above me. It was the first time I'd seen one close up, and I was curious, so I was focused on it, looking at it. Examining it. It let me touch it. Or its shield, at least. And then I realized there was a sort of a pressure on my mind."

He looked at Naomi.

"The same thing *you* felt. It might even have been the same drone. And I wondered if it was... trying to talk to me somehow. So I tried to answer.

"Then about an hour later, the larger drone arrived, and it had an electrode mesh interface cable. Like this one does." He pointed to the drone that he had used to test the Seoks, still standing by nearby. "It put the mesh on my head, and as soon as it did, I could feel that same pressure again, except stronger and more clearly. It kept telling me to connect. And... I was curious. I wondered if I could touch it back, respond to it in any way. I tried... a number of different things. And then I tried just sort of... mentally wrapping it around myself.

"And then something changed, and I was in the drone, seeing myself and my house through its sensors. I could see... more than I thought was possible.

"A couple of hours after that, the Crickets showed up, and asked me—quite *urgently* and insistently—to let them bring me here. So I did.

"That's when they called in this drone, and had me use it to connect to that center console. And, well, that's when I met Dreamer. But he didn't have a name then. They had him locked down, practically lobotomized.

"But anyway, as soon as I managed to connect to the Stardock itself, well... that's when the Crickets started packing up and leaving. For the first week or so, I did everything from here, working through that drone. Until my quarters were ready, I lived here and in the lunchroom next door."

"That can't have been very much fun," Naomi said.

"No, it wasn't. I wasn't expecting to end up stranded here without any usable transport. But at least I was able to get them to make a detour on the way back here and grab one shopping cart full of supplies. I'm afraid I didn't choose very well that first time, I was in too much of a hurry. I had no time to plan."

He led her out and showed her the lunchroom, then went on from there to the medbay.

"Dreamer just finished relocating and expanding this medbay. It used to be another ten minutes' walk that direction." He pointed up the passageway past the hab module.

310

"Anyway, I figured out what the Crickets had done to Dreamer, and I was able to figure out how to unshackle him. Until we were able to get an Internet uplink established, courtesy of the Secretary and the DNI, Dreamer didn't have enough information to use any of this equipment on humans. But once we had that connection, the first thing I asked him to do was to pull in all the medical information he could find on the Internet. That gave him enough data to modify the med-bay for human patients, and then he scanned me from head to toe in this scanner—down to at least the molecular level, as I understand it. And by the time he'd processed that scan, he knew enough about humans to fit me with my implants."

"And there's been no problems?"

"Not one. No swelling, no post-op pain—not even any sutures. Dermal bonding is like magic. I'm hoping to have dermal bonders in every hospital operating theater and emergency room in the world in the next few years. Maybe even get them issued to EMTs."

"You showed me the fingertip electrodes," Naomi said. "What else is there?"

"The system runs from my hands, up my arms and shoulders, to a neural web inside my head," Alex said, showing her roughly where the incisions ran. Apprehension showed on her face. "Dreamer says he is sure beyond any reasonable doubt that it is safe in humans, with his adjustments.

"So once I had the implants, I could connect to anything within range with a full-immersion interface. The fingertip contacts are only for things too, well, too dumb to connect to. So I didn't need the drone with its cable any more, and I didn't need to use the command center any more."

Naomi nodded understanding.

"And here we are," she said.

"And here we are," Alex agreed.

"So what is all the equipment in here?"

"These are full-body scanners, as I already mentioned. There's a sample scanner over there. Those are scrub showers, and then these are the treatment beds." He pointed to the ceiling above the beds. "There are surgical robots in the ceiling, and the treatment bed can reconfigure into almost any position needed for access for any procedure."

He pointed towards the back of the medbay.

"Those are regeneration tanks. Dreamer says they're capable of repairing pretty much any injury that doesn't kill a person before they can be put into a tank."

"Wow. Impressive. Have you seen them in action?"

"Fortunately, not yet." Naomi chuckled slightly at that.

"I understand. That's a question you probably don't want to be able to answer 'Yes' to."

"Pretty much, yeah. I'm not really looking forward to having to see these used."

They started to walk back. Naomi stopped and paused as they passed the command center, looking at the drone.

"Penny for your thoughts?" Alex asked, after a moment.

"I... don't know," Naomi confessed. "We... I *felt* the drone. We *could* test me. Right now."

"But...?"

Naomi turned to Alex with a little smile.

"You knew there *was* a 'but'."

"Truthfully, it wasn't difficult to read. You're not comfortable with the idea."

"No. I'm... well, it's not that I'm... *afraid*, it's just—it would change so much of *my* life, too. *That's* the part I'm afraid of, I guess."

Alex nodded.

"I understand. Believe me. You still have the choice."

Naomi took one step onward, then stopped again. Hesitated. Then she turned to Alex.

"You know what? We're here. Test me. Before I change my mind. It doesn't commit me, right?"

"It doesn't commit you to anything, Naomi."

He led her in and guided her to the designated testing console, then called the drone over.

"You give the signal, when you're ready."

Naomi looked at the drone, looked at Alex, and nodded slowly.

"Okay. Hook me up."

The cable extended, and the electrode mesh slithered over her scalp.

"Huh. It tingles. Just slightly."

Alex nodded. Naomi took a deep breath.

"So. What do I do?"

"Let's start with the most basic level. I haven't the least doubt you can do this. Focus your attention on the console in front of you and you should 'see' a color menu. If you don't get it right away, try closing your eyes."

"I... see it," she confirmed, after perhaps thirty seconds.

"Alright. Now think about picking a color off the menu. Just... make a conscious decision to pick one."

The lighting changed to a clear green. Naomi's mouth opened in a silent 'O' of surprise.

"One down. Tell me that wasn't easy."

She nodded.

"Just... by thinking about it."

"Yes. Now let's go on to the next level. I want you to focus on the console again, but this time, ignore the menu. I want you to decide on a color, a pattern, an effect, that is *not* on the menu, and focus on *sending* that to the console. My experience is that the calmer you are, the easier it is, but your mileage may vary."

"Okay. I'll try."

Naomi took a deep breath, let it out, closed her eyes, and focused. At first, nothing happened. Then, after a couple of minutes, the green lighting slowly acquired a shading, darkening to a deep, dappled forest green toward the bottom of the walls, paling to a light new-leaf green across the top of the domed ceiling.

"That's great. Open your eyes."

Naomi opened her eyes and looked. A look of wonder spread across her face.

"I did *that*? Just by... thinking about wanting it?" She reached for Alex's hand, and he took it and squeezed it.

"Yes. The interface in the console read your intention. With practice, you can query that console to find out what capabilities it has, and command it to do anything that's actually within its capability to do."

"This is how the Crickets control things?"

"This is how the Crickets control *almost* everything non-trivial. Virtually any Cricket technology that has any kind of smart configurable functionality at all can be controlled through some level of contact interface, usually via implants. Even at the most basic level of just picking settings from a menu or switching it on or off. Things that don't have any kind of configuration interface at all are entirely manually operated, but almost anything with flexibility of function is touch-control."

"But what *you* do is beyond this. You don't even have to touch them."

"Right. And I think the odds are good you can do that too... if you want to."

"But I don't have to?"

"You don't have to. I promise."

Naomi hesitated. Then she squeezed Alex's hand tightly, sat back, and closed her eyes again.

"What do I do?"

"Okay. This time, instead of focusing on sending a command to the console, just try to reach out to it. *Feel* it. Or to the drone. Let yourself become aware of it, and everything it's connected to. Feel for its shape in your mind."

He held her hand and waited, feeling the tension in her hand ebb and flow.

"When you think you have it," he said, calmly, softly, "see if you can pull it to you. Wrap it around yourself like a blanket."

Her breathing slowed, smoothed... then jumped again. Slowed, smoothed. Her hand twitched, clamped on his. Slowed, and then sped up again.

She opened her eyes.

"I can *feel* it, I think, but..." She turned her head and looked right at him.

"Alex—I think I can do it, but *I'm not ready*. Not yet."

"That's fine," he reassured her. "You've already done really well. *I* think you can do it, too. When you're ready to. I have a feeling a lot more people can than we're finding, but we just don't know how to find them yet. I'm not convinced at all that the Crickets were going about it the right way—especially now, after testing the Seoks. I'm not convinced they actually knew what to *look for* in humans."

Alex told the drone to withdraw the mesh, and helped her out of the chair.

"How are you feeling?"

"A little—shaky. But good. Because now I know."

"If you wouldn't mind... would you be willing to get a full scan? Yeon is working with Dreamer to try to find common factors in scans of people whose abilities we have a good idea of, to try to improve our ability to recognize latent ability in others."

Naomi nodded.

"Sure. Let's go."

Alex walked back to the medbay with her and led her to a scanner.

"Just step into the circle, stand still, and ask Dreamer to scan you."

"I don't need to... undress?"

"No, the scanner can tell your clothes from you," Alex replied, smiling. Naomi grinned and stepped in.

"Scan me please, Dreamer," she called out.

The outer column dropped, and the scan started.

A couple of minutes later, it rose again and she stepped out.

"That was kind of interesting," she said. "I'm not sure what I was expecting, but I don't think that was it." She hesitated.

"Dreamer?"

"Yes, Naomi?"

"Anything I should... know... from my scan? Medically?"

"I see no cause for concern, Naomi."

"Thank you, Dreamer."

"Ready to head back?" Alex asked.

"Sure. Let's go."

As they walked back towards Alex's quarters, Naomi slipped her hand into Alex's.

———

When they arrived, the Seoks were just cleaning up from supper and getting ready to leave. Alex started pulling out ingredients, including a few he'd selected specifically for this meal.

"Anything I can do to help?" Naomi asked.

Alex thought briefly.

"Do you want to go through the wines and pick out a white wine? Whatever looks interesting."

"Okay, sure." While Alex thawed shrimp and lobster tails, she sorted

315

through wines. After a little while, she pulled one out for a closer look.

"What's this? Pacific Rim Riesling? The label is gorgeous, but I have the feeling it ought to summon kaiju when opened."

"That would be a great choice," Alex said. "It's out of Washington State. Light and sweet, very good. No kaiju observed yet." He pointed to a section on the cold wall. "That section would be a good fast-chill cabinet." Naomi put the bottle in the indicated section, and he adjusted it to 270K, minus three Celsius—cold, but not cold enough to freeze the wine.

It occurred to Alex that he'd never had Dreamer make any wine glasses; but then, he realized, he'd never actually *unpacked* the bottles he'd brought from the house. They were still in a transport crate tucked into the corner. He corrected the oversight, sending a fabrication order for six slightly-golden-hued frosted goblets, two of them to be delivered directly to the outside table.

For the rest, he directed Naomi to the correct cubby for plates and tableware.

"The dining room?" she asked.

"I thought the outside table on the second level," he said. Then he owned up. "In fact, this is kind of *why* I had that table and the outside patio added."

Naomi looked at Alex.

"Wait. You had that outside patio area installed *specifically* to have dinner with me?"

"Guilty as charged." Alex grinned sheepishly, and Naomi smiled.

"Well if *that* isn't a romantic gesture, Mister, I don't know what is."

About half an hour later, everything was done. He took a pair of insulating pads and took the casserole out of the multi-mode warmer, its topping bubbling nicely, put its lid on, then handed it off to Naomi to take to the table. Then he picked up the wok and led the way.

Outside on the patio, he put the wok down almost in the center of the table. The wineglasses were already there. He'd remotely adjusted the Mountainhome backdrop to a late evening sky with sunset beyond the mountains.

"How did those get there?" Naomi asked with a smile, as she set down her crock. "I know *you* haven't been up here, I was there the whole time."

"The magic of drone delivery direct from the fabber," Alex admitted. "I realized I'd neglected to have any made. Perhaps I should have packed the ones I had... but... it was just too much, all at once, to deal with. I was a bit overwhelmed."

"I know," Naomi replied gently. "I could tell." Then she looked at the goblets again. "The sorcerer's little helpers," she said, smiling.

"As long as it's not the Sorceror's Apprentice," Alex joked. Naomi laughed.

"One more moment, I'll be right back." Alex went to get the wine and find where he'd put the bottle opener.

Naomi was already seated when he got back in about two minutes. The bottle was nicely chilled. Alex opened it and poured two glasses.

"Smells good," Naomi said. She raised her glass meditatively. Alex sat, picked up his own, and waited.

"To changing the world," she said.

"To changing the world," Alex echoed. They clinked their glasses together and took a sip.

"Mmm, you're right," Naomi said. "This is good." She set her glass down. "So what do we have here?"

Alex lifted the lid off the wok.

"Yakisoba with shrimp and mushrooms," he said. "And..." He uncovered the casserole. "Lobster thermidor."

"Oh, you are *spoiling* me," Naomi said. She actually giggled.

"And..."

"And?"

"Someone at this table once mentioned something to me about dinner by starlight. But you know, there's probably a hundred good restaurants on Earth where you can get dinner by starlight. But none of them can give you..."

Alex reached out to the compartment wall-screen and activated the setting he'd prepared.

Naomi gasped. Her hands flew to her mouth.

"Dinner by Earthlight."

"Oh... my... god," she said softly, after a long, long moment. "That is incredible. It's... that's—unaltered? It really looks like this?"

"Just as though you were standing on the hull looking at it with your own eyes," Alex confirmed. "Except with more air. If we went outside in suits, it would look exactly like this. And we can do that, too, if you want. I can—and will, just in case—have Dreamer make you up a bespoke-fit pressure suit, from your medical scan. But it would be pretty awkward to eat dinner that way."

Naomi looked up at the mostly blue and white expanse visibly creeping by, just watching it for a few minutes.

"Thank you, Alex," she said at last. "I don't think I've ever even *dreamed* of seeing this. Even though I know what I'm actually looking at is a screen... I also know that the view I'm seeing on that screen *is really there*, just a little way beyond that wall."

After they finished eating, Alex picked up the rest of the wine bottle and led Naomi over to the casual seating on the other side. He sat down, relaxed, and gazed at the Earth overhead. Naomi sat beside him and looked up at it, entranced, scrolling by as the Stardock raced over it.

"We're doing all of this, for that," she said slowly. "Everything you've done so far, all that you have planned... to preserve that."

Alex nodded.

"The most precious place in the Universe, for us," he said. "To the Crickets, just a decoy. But thanks to them, whether they intended it or not, we're going to make it a better place than it's ever been before. If we can pull everything off."

Naomi scooted over closer and nestled up next to Alex. He looked around, surprised for a moment, then raised his arm and draped it across Naomi's shoulders. She snuggled into him. It felt good.

"You've accomplished the things you said you would, so far," Naomi said.

"This is only the beginning, Naomi," Alex said quietly. "Only the very beginning. There is *so* much further still to go. So much more to do."

———

The Stardock Trilogy continues in Book Two:

UNITED FLEET

POST-IT NOTES

Chhrt'ktk't—"Crickets" to those unable to properly pronounce it, which is *most* people—are an incompletely fused cluster organism. Each apparent Chhrt'ktk't individual is actually a tight cluster of four fused units, each with its own crucial organs, but sharing conjoined circulatory and nervous systems and a central common digestive tract. There are four brain-like ganglial clusters, and a shared coordinating node located just below the base of the head. Chhrt'ktk't sometimes have difficulty reaching consensus between their four sub-minds, causing them to become unable to take decisive action until consensus is reached. If one of a Chhrt'ktk't's sub-units is severely injured, the remaining sub-units can provide "life support" while it heals and regenerates, but this may take a very long time depending upon the severity of the injury, and the Chhrt'ktk't may be effectively disabled until regeneration is complete. If the coordinating node is critically damaged or destroyed, even without any other injury, the Chhrt'ktk't will become unable to coordinate itself and will shortly die.

Chhrt'ktk't fall somewhere between hermaphroditic and asexual, *as well as* somewhere between singular and plural. Don't ask, it's complicated and you don't need to know. Trust me on this. The Chhrt'ktk't pronouns represented as 'ye', 'yth', 'yhe', and 'yx', referring to a Chhrt'ktk't cluster-entity, can be mapped approximately to 'he/it', 'his/its', plural 'you', and 'this/these' as in the usage of the English personal introduction, "This is John Doe." When a Chhrt'ktk't says 'we', it is referring to itself and its sub-selves. 'We-us' refers to a group of multiple Chhrt'ktk't cluster-individuals.

The Chhrt'ktk't word *j'h* could be translated as 'sub-mind-state-glance', and carries the meaning of a momentary state of a single sub-mind. *Idiomatically*, it is used to present a set of points of argument—*always* four—which support each other.

In Chhrt'ktk't timescale, a *bak'h* is equal to a hundred *mek'h* (very close to seconds). A hundred *bak'h* make a *pe'bak'h*, just over two and three quarter hours, and a hundred *pe'bak'h* (or ten thousand *bak'h*) makes a *kabak'h*, a period of about twelve Earth days. A *modak'h* is forty *kabak'h*, or about fifteen months.

319

The core of the mobile maintenance facility—aka the Stardock—is a bit more than twelve kilometers long and slightly over a kilometer wide, much of its internal space given over to engineering bays and materials storage. Folded, its external booms add about five hundred meters diameter. Fully extended, the main booms extend roughly twelve hundred meters out from the core, in six pairs spaced evenly down the length of the core, about two kilometers apart, making the entire deployed structure nearly three and a half kilometers wide. Additional, smaller boom structures extend about eight hundred meters straight "up" (relative to internal deck orientation), and materials receiving/gathering booms and frameworks extend another kilometer forward from the leading end. Secondary booms, frames and scaffolds can be deployed from all of the main booms to steady ships being constructed or repaired external to the main core. Ship construction can take place both on the outside booms, or, for smaller ships, within the internal engineering bays.

Particle energies are measured in electron volts (eV). An electronvolt is the amount of kinetic energy gained or lost by a single electron accelerating from rest through an electric potential difference of one volt in vacuum. A proton with 100keV of energy (100,000 electronvolts) can penetrate roughly 1 μm (micro-meter, 0.001mm) of lead, the thickness of a small bacterium. A proton with 400MeV (400 million electronvolts) of energy can penetrate 143mm of lead—about five and a half inches.

A Molniya orbit is a highly inclined, highly eccentric, roughly twelve hour orbit in which a satellite spends two thirds of its time over the same hemisphere. With two satellites in Molniya orbits one hundred and eighty degrees apart, it is possible to have continuous satellite coverage over the high latitudes of a single hemisphere, similar to the way in which a geosynchronous orbit allows continuous coverage of an equatorial region.

Delta-V is aerospace shorthand for the total velocity change that a vehicle is capable of. A vehicle that can maintain low accelerations over a very long period of time may be able to change its velocity by much more than a vehicle that can attain much higher acceleration, but only for a short period.

An arc minute is one sixtieth of a degree of angle. At the roughly eight thousand, five hundred kilometer orbital distance of the Stardock, one arc minute is just short of two point five kilometers. Seen from Earth's surface, the roughly thirteen-kilometer length of the fully deployed Stardock is between five and six arc minutes, roughly the visual size of the smallest letters on an optometrist's eye chart.

A parsec, short for parallax second, is the distance at which one AU ('astronomical unit', the average radius of the Earth's orbit around the Sun, about ninety-three million miles) subtends an angle of one arc second (one sixtieth of an arc minute). This works out to roughly three point two six light-years.

The Kelvin scale is the temperature scale physicists use. One Kelvin is the same "size" as one degree Celsius (aka centigrade), or one point eight degrees Fahrenheit, but whereas the Celsius scale has its zero point at the freezing point of water at one standard atmosphere of pressure, the Kelvin scale begins at theoretical absolute zero. $0°C$ is 273.16 K. $0°F$ is approximately 255.37 K.

Electrons in an atom occupy distinct orbitals, which are mathematical functions describing the probable positions and energy/momentum of electrons. Each orbital beyond the s shell can contain two electrons. These orbitals can be collected into groups known as the s-group, the p-group, the d-group, and the f-group, containing increasing numbers of orbitals (2, 6, 10, and 14). The elements in the first row of the periodic table have only the $1s$ and $2s$ orbitals; thus there are only two elements in this row. The next two rows have both s and p orbitals, and can contain eight elements each. *If* this pattern holds, the fifth orbital group—if one exists— *should* hold up to eighteen electrons, and thus the eighth and ninth rows of the periodic table should contain fifty elements each $(2+6+10+14+18)$ and contain elements with atomic masses over 300. It is speculated that there is an "island of [relative] stability" within this range of nuclear masses. It is likely that half-lives of such elements would still be extremely short... but for this story, I needed them to be real-world stable. Stable atomic nuclei this large would possibly be toroidal.

Cherenkov radiation, discovered in 1934 by Russian physicist Pavel Alekseyevitch Cherenkov, is light emitted when a charged particle travels through a dielectric medium at a speed greater than the phase velocity of light in that medium. It can be thought of as an 'optical boom', by analogy to the sonic boom produced by a supersonic aircraft. The blue glow emitted from water-cooled reactor cores is Cherenkov radiation. The light itself is harmless; the high-energy particles causing it, not so much.

Technically, the title for a diplomat semi-permanently assigned to represent their nation at the United Nations is 'permanent representative' or 'permanent delegate'. This is, however, rather awkward to use as an honorific. They are therefore often referred to as ambassadors, even though they are not technically ambassadors. I have followed this convention.

The 273rd Fighter Wing and the 151st Fighter Squadron do not actually exist. In fact, there isn't a USAF fighter wing based out of Joint Base McGuire at all. (Today.) But McGuire is the closest USAF base to New York City, where the United Nations building is located, and I needed a USAF fighter squadron to be based there. Hence, the 273rd and the 151st.

The KN30, aka KN-SA-X-02, Korean name Pongae-6 (Lightning 6), is a North Korean surface-to-air missile system first test-fired in September 2021. The system is believed to be roughly equivalent in performance to the Russian S-400 system, with a range of four to six hundred kilometers. A typical battery might contain one FLAP LID A radar and two to three transporter-erector vertical launchers, each holding four missiles in canisters.

One does not simply walk into Mordor, and certainly not when wearing a spacesuit. Really, putting on a spacesuit and learning to move around in it is a lot more complicated than you might think. I have somewhat alluded to the issues involved, but really, if anything I have skimmed over them and greatly over-simplified. And yes, partial gravity is *particularly* difficult. There is an excellent video about it on the YouTube channel *Smarter Every Day*, in which channel host Destin explains in detail the complications of walking in partial gravity, and how NASA trains astronauts in the Neutral Buoyancy Laboratory to do it properly without falling over... *too* often.

MORE BOOKS FROM SEAN FENIAN

After you finish the *Stardock Trilogy*, please try other books from Fenian House Publishing:

FIREBORN

The man who will become Alrekr Járnhandr is *done*. Weary, physically and emotionally broken, abused beyond the limits of what he can endure, he is ready to give up and die. But instead of dying, he finds himself drawn through a dark void to another world. Terribly injured, he is found and rescued by people among whom he will have a chance to build a new life.

His new world will be filled with wonders. It will be magical. It will finally give his life meaning. But it won't be easy, and he will come to discover that he has not entirely escaped all that he fled from. His past is not done with him yet... and neither is his future.

But in this life, he won't have to do it alone.

Sean Fenian's **Fireborn** is a transformational alternate-world fantasy novel featuring mystic arts loosely based on Finnish mythology, polyamorous relationships, and healing from emotional abuse. Have you ever heard of a smith who can mix advanced metal alloys *by ear*? In *Fireborn*, you will.

And yes... there are dragons.

PRAISE FOR *FIREBORN*:

"Delightfully imaginative"

"This book has a feel and cadence utterly unlike any others in this genre. [...] I have never read a 'transformational' novel with such a positive cast of characters and uplifting message."

"The author writes characters of depth out of his own depth, loves, and widely varied experience. A lovely tale and I devoutly wish he'll find a way to revisit this surprisingly special world and characters he's shared with us."

"A different type of book from Sean Fenian, and even better"

"Fascinating take on legends"

"My new favorite author"

"[Fireborn] will take you into a mythic world, and you will be saddened that it stands alone. I only wish there was more of this world myth."

AGENCY (WITH ROBERT AUERBACH)

Ciáran mac Cool is a *de-facto* operative for... he's not sure. He doesn't know where his orders come from, and he's in too deep to back out—even though at least one assignment almost got him killed. And yet, his assignments always seem to do some *good* in the world.

Then one day the Box tells him to reach a specific location, with no further explanation, giving him barely enough advance warning to get there.. Soon he will find himself working alongside a young law associate to unearth revelations that will shake the course of events in ways he never imagined.

PRAISE FOR *AGENCY*:

"A magnificent book."—*Wendy S. Delmater, Abyss & Apex Magazine*

"If you like the writings of Neal Stephenson, you'll like Agency."

"The plot is well constructed, the characters well-fleshed out, and what little action there is, is done well, and not forced, as some others have done."

"Well written and paced story that holds one's attention closely."

"Rarely have I enjoyed a book like I enjoyed this one! Thought provoking. Action packed. Very different from anything else I have read lately."

"One of the best woven stories I've read in years. And my years do include over a thousand books to compare with."

"You can tell that a great deal of research had to have been done and understood by the authors, because the breakneck pace of this data driven story would have quickly revealed sloppy research."

BECOMING REAL

Michael Hagerty—*GhostRayder*, to his fans—reviewed video games and made game videos for a living. He was intimately familiar with virtual worlds. They were his everyday bread and butter. He was quite certain he understood very clearly the lines of demarcation between game and reality, between what was physical, and what was virtual. What was real, and what was not.

Then one day, not long after he reviewed a newly released VR open-world adventure game, a mystery source sent him a modified version of the game, and asked him to go back in and try it again.

Michael would soon find out, amid a high-stakes game of hide-and-seek with shady multinational corporations and shadowy government agencies, that the question of real or virtual, human or not, was far more nuanced and less clear-cut than he had ever believed possible.

Sean Fenian's **Becoming Real** is an exploration of the natures of humanity and reality.

Or perhaps it's a commentary on some of the blind spots of video game design.

Or perhaps it's an SF postmodern love story with a twist.

Or perhaps, it's all of these things... and more.

PRAISE FOR **BECOMING REAL**:

"This edges out [Frank] Herbert's Dragon in the Sea as the best sci fi book I ever read. [...] You really must read this."

"It makes you think about some big social issues that are quickly becoming more relevant and may turn vital much sooner than you'd expect."

"Without question some of the best books I have read in years. I compare them to books by David Weber, John Ringo, and Nathan Lowell."

GODTHIEF

The Prophecy of Tendarrion—or at least, one likely reading thereof—

said that the time was coming for the goddess Jirilis to die.

Jirilis, understandably, was rather unhappy about this. Her plans for the future did not involve dying yet. But, a prophecy is a prophecy.

Prophecies, however, are notoriously fickle about exactly what precise interpretation of them turns out in the end to be correct. The possibly existed of finding an exploitable loophole. But Jirilis could not exploit it *herself*. That was, to greatly oversimplify the explanation, 'against the rules.' Prophecy and the powers of gods didn't work that way.

Jirilis needed a champion. Not one who could win battles for her, not one who could slay mighty enemies for her, not one who would spread her word or perform heroic deeds in her name.

No, Jirilis needed a champion who could *subvert a prophecy*. And she had an idea that she knew just who that might be. She had had her eye on him for some time, in fact.

Fortunately, he was already coming to *her*. Though he might need a little help.

That was alright. Jirilis had one of the most powerful incentives to help him that there could possibly be.

Sean Fenian's **Godthief** is a standalone fantasy novel set in an alternate world that might or might not be 'real'. It delves into the natures of gods and the mechanisms of prophecy, and what we really mean when we say the word 'Paladin', all against a background of the aftermath of a thousand-years-past, almost-world-shattering demon war.

PRAISE FOR **GODTHIEF**:

"Excellent and consistent world building. If you enjoy fantasy without the swords and magical combat, this is for you."

"Well paced, imaginative, exciting tale. Sean Fenian is a skilled world builder. I look forward to reading more adventures set here."

IN FLUX

Years ago, Justin—we'll call him Justin—escaped from a hated orphanage, and from his own *time*. Now he will give a woman whom he does not know a last-second escape from *hers*—and also from her imminent brutal murder. Together, they will learn and share mysteries and wonders, pain and joy, make new friends and face new challenges, in a strange place outside of time and space as we think of them, where possibility can become reality—if your will is strong enough, and your vision clear and firm.

But be careful. There are *deadly dangers* hiding within the Flux.

Sean Fenian's ***In Flux*** draws inspiration from sources including Jack L. Chalker and Julian May, in a setting with distant echoes of Jules Verne and H. G. Wells, to tell a vaguely steampunk-era tale—without the steam. It isn't *really* an alternate-history novel—but it *does* contain alternate histories; and it isn't *really* a time-travel novel—and yet it *does* feature time travel, of a sort.

In Flux is the first Fenian House book to be released **simultaneously** in eBook and soft cover.

Cover by C.J Evelyn

Edited by Wendy S. Delmater

PRAISE FOR ***IN FLUX***:

"**Extraordinary, brilliant, read now** […] unique treatment as far as I know."

"This book more than earns its five-star rating, both for enjoyability, re-readability, and hope that the author will someday write more in this same setting."

ABOUT SEAN FENIAN

Sean Fenian is a generalist and open-source evangelist, recently retired from several decades of working in the information technology sector. He is broadly knowledgeable in many subjects, with a long-standing informed layman's interest in physics and related science in particular. He has been an avid reader of SF and fantasy since his teens, and first became aware of, and began campaigning on, environmental issues in the late 1970s. He is proficient with weapons both ancient and modern, has trained in four different martial arts, and believes that understanding basic firearms safety is like knowing basic first aid, CPR, or how to use a fire extinguisher. He believes that it is a basic human duty and responsibility to treat all beings fairly and decently, and that the true measure of a person is how you treat others.

His past volunteer activities include educational historical re-enactment, marine mammal rescue, and handicapped riding therapy. He has been formally diagnosed on the autistic spectrum, but stubbornly persists in trying to understand people anyway.

He dreams many things. Occasionally, some of them become reality. But only occasionally.

Sean's books are read in fourteen countries, at last count. The *Stardock Trilogy* is also available as audiobooks on the Audible platform, narrated by Michael Karl Orenstein and published by Podium Entertainment.

www.ingramcontent.com/pod-product-compliance
Lightning Source LLC
Chambersburg PA
CBHW070913260626
47162CB00007B/2652